MECHANIZE
MY HANDS
TO WAR

MECHANIZE MY HANDS TO WAR

ERIN K. WAGNER

DAW BOOKS
New York

Jacket design by Faceout Studio, Tim Green

Book design by Fine Design

DAW Book Collectors No. 1973

DAW Books
An imprint of Astra Publishing House
dawbooks.com
DAW Books and its logo are registered trademarks of Astra Publishing House

Printed in the United States of America

Library of Congress Cataloging-in-Publication Data

Names: Wagner, Erin K., author.
Title: Mechanize my hands to war / Erin K. Wagner.
Description: First edition. | New York : DAW Books, 2024. |
Series: DAW Book Collectors ; no. 1973
Identifiers: LCCN 2024041551 (print) | LCCN 2024041552 (ebook) |
ISBN 9780756419349 (hardcover) | ISBN 9780756419356 (ebook)
Subjects: LCGFT: Science fiction. | Novels.
Classification: LCC PS3623.A35626 M43 2024 (print) | LCC PS3623.A35626 (ebook) |
DDC 813/.6--dc23/eng/20240906
LC record available at https://lccn.loc.gov/2024041551
LC ebook record available at https://lccn.loc.gov/2024041552

First edition: December 2024
10 9 8 7 6 5 4 3 2 1

To my niblings, who should wait to read this until they're a bit older.

Ashes in the roses. Ashes in the roses.
The feds ring round. We all fall down.

PRELUDE

The weeds were high, almost as high as his chest, and they scratched the boy's arms. Burrs stuck to his clothing and caught on his legs. He was tired, so tired that he could not think about how much or he would stop right where he was. He would drop to his knees and he would let the weeds fold over him and hide the sky. But the soldiers might still be following him, so he could not risk stopping.

And so he did not think. He just listened to the breath rasping in his throat and felt the sweat tickling down his temple.

It had been his birthday last week, but no one had celebrated it. He was eleven now. His boots were a little too small, but he hadn't told anyone yet. He had debated taking one of the rifles with him, but he didn't want to shoot anyone and he wasn't entirely sure the guards wouldn't shoot him if he threatened them. There were no empty threats in his experience, so why would they think any different?

His pockets were empty except for a granola bar and the wad of bills he had swiped from Eli's dresser.

And he was tired.

He was not sure what time it was. The sky was growing purple on the horizon behind him and his shadow stretched out long in front. He was so focused on the ground and his next step that he did not see the woman at first. She stood so very still. As if she had grown where planted.

The boy came up short, swallowing a scream. He held his hands up in front of him in one of the defensive postures they had taught him. His only hope, if she was here to hurt him, would be to surprise her, knock her off balance. Otherwise, she had the advantage of height and weight.

She was facing him and she did not move, but she watched him closely. The boy was not sure she blinked as he studied her. She wore combat gear, camo pants tucked into high boots and a black t-shirt. She wore no armor, but her arms gleamed white and silver in the setting sunlight. She held an M4 carbine tucked close under her arm. There was something preternaturally still and unmoving about her face. A shiver ran up the boy's spine.

"Whitaker's?"

It took him a moment to recognize Eli's last name. He always insisted the kids call him by his first.

"Not anymore."

And he could feel his chest crumpling, his lungs heaving. He gasped for breath and began to cry.

"It's all right. You're safe." The words sounded practiced, but her voice was comforting nonetheless. She slung her carbine onto her back and set a hand on his shoulder. "I will take you someplace safe."

"How do I know—" And he couldn't get the rest of the sentence out, couldn't voice the sheer terror that Eli had planted in his head about androids. The other kids parroted him, talked about their parents being replaced with metal scarecrows. A girl his own age, Lia, said her dad was dead because of them. But sometimes she didn't sound so sure.

"I am AS 542." She dropped her hand. "Sephone," she added. "US government."

The panic was there, in the back of the boy's head, the names that

Eli used for the AS. But he couldn't run anymore. And what had he been running toward, anyways?

"Help me," he said. His legs collapsed under him, and he fell. He did not hear her move, but she bent down and lifted him. The movement was easy and smooth as if it were no effort to her at all. Her arms were hard and unyielding around him, strangely transparent against his darker skin.

"I will take you back now," she said.

He managed to nod and then he relaxed in her arms, unable to stay alert, unable to resist any longer. He was tired. And he told himself it was alright to cry. It was alright now.

The gun clacked gently at her back. Now that he was so close, he could hear the slight whir, the whisper of her joints moving. As his eyelids grew heavy, blinking, he tried to recall if his mother had ever held him like this.

He could not remember, and fell asleep.

ADRIAN

The air conditioning was not working in the train car. It had been a long day and would be a longer night. Adrian collapsed onto one of the many free seats with a sigh, crossed her legs, and pulled her bag close to her stomach. There was nothing much of importance in the bag tonight, no classified documents, not even her tablet. Now it was just a waiting game, and all she hoped for was that the corner bodega would still be open so she could grab food before falling into bed, perhaps to sleep, perhaps to wait anxiously for the call.

She glanced at her watch, set to military time. It blinked at her, reminding her of unread mail. 22:14. It was even later than she'd thought. She shifted in her seat. Her right leg, a biomechatronic prosthesis below the knee, generated a small amount of heat, usually unnoticeable, but uncomfortable now in the stuffy car. She scanned the other passengers, who were doing their best to ignore their neighbors, studying their tablets and phones. The train rattled and screeched around a corner in the tunnel.

She read half of a newspaper article through one man's transparent tablet, trying to hold off sleep as she deciphered the story in reverse. The woman beside her, who still looked neat and put together in a tailored suit, noticed her effort, laughed a little, then turned back to her own device.

The train jolted to a stop. Adrian rocked slightly in her seat. The doors hissed open and closed at one of the Metro stops. A pregnant woman got on and sidestepped down the aisle, picking over the feet of those sitting down. She held her hands protectively over her stomach, a large bag swinging at her shoulder. Adrian leaned back to avoid getting hit in the face.

"Here." A thin young man stood up and made room for her near the door. "Take my seat." Adrian couldn't tell if he was impatient or charitable.

He grabbed onto an overhead handrail to steady himself as the woman took his place. She nodded her thanks but didn't say anything. Her lips and face tightened, and Adrian recognized the look. It was not a good look. It was one she'd seen before battle. One she saw now before a particularly bad briefing. The man diagonal from her, a few seats down from the pregnant woman, grunted and muttered something under his breath. She glanced at him and then followed his gaze to the man who had given up his seat. As he had reached for the handrail, the man's shirt had come untucked, leaving a small strip of his back exposed to the other passengers in the car. There, the skin was almost bright pink, like that of a white plastic baby doll. It did not match the tan of his face or hands. She recognized the color, the hallmark of Haven Corp's androids, whose skin *naturalized* with exposure. Androids for the private market, undoubtedly with the language skills and neural network to match.

She ducked her head and tried to ignore the scene playing out in front of her, pulling out her phone. It was barely the size of her hand, certainly thinner, and she could see her fingers through the screen until it shifted in opacity, registering the pattern of her iris. It had taken her a while to readjust to commercial cell phones after comms in the field. She skimmed the headlines, scrolling past celebrity gossip, lingering briefly on reports from the White House. The man's muttering had grown louder.

Out of the corner of her eye, she saw the android shift his footing. He was tense, his stance and posture ready to strike. If she had to guess, there were no active protocols limiting an act of self-defense. Her heart began to beat a little bit faster. She was no longer sleepy and, without conscious intent, her muscles tightened. A tiny gear buzzed, almost below hearing, at her ankle. There was a wireless taser in her bag and her hand hovered over the outline of it. It had a charge that could kill a man if applied to the right point.

"Why don't you just keep on moving?" The man finally raised his voice so the whole car could hear. The pregnant woman winced and looked down at her nails. The businesswoman looked at him, side-eyed, and moved to a seat on the other side of Adrian, further away.

The android did not move. He stood so still that Adrian could hardly discern his mimetic breathing.

"Did you hear me, rubber?"

It was an insult that had never made full sense to Adrian, given how much more familiar she was with the hard plastics and metal of military-grade androids, of automated soldiers. But she supposed there was some crude connection to be drawn, some allusion to cast-off condoms. Her niece had used the slur once, casually, over dinner, tearing bread as she did so. Adrian had looked at her sister and her husband, but they had said nothing and so she hadn't either.

A muscle—or something approximating it—jumped in the android's cheek. He turned his head to meet the man's eyes. "I'm not trying to cause trouble."

"You are trouble," the man growled.

Adrian uncrossed her legs. The man's face was pale in an unhealthy way, the skin of a heavy drinker, though he did not smell of alcohol right now. But his fingers twitched once—twice—on his knee. She was glad she was still dressed for the field from earlier, with combat boots and pants that wouldn't restrict her movement.

The android did not flinch. "I just gave the woman my seat. I don't think that's a crime." He tightened his grip on the rail. Adrian thought she probably imagined the unnatural creasing of the skin at his knuckles, because he seemed human, standing there, down to the pain and anger in the tightness of his mouth.

"Leave him alone," she said, begrudgingly, tired.

The man looked at her, a sort of disbelief blooming in his eyes. She steadied herself for the rage that would follow, dipping her hand into her bag. He followed the movement of her arm, studied her clothes.

"What—you have a gun in there? You going to take me out for defending what I believe?"

The words echoed humanist propaganda, but were nothing so extreme as the rhetoric of the Civil Union Militia she had been studying for the last three or four years.

"I don't care what you believe." She shifted so she could face him directly, feet planted on the ground, bending forward slightly at the waist. "But I want to get home and I want to sleep and I don't want to be forced to fight my way out of whatever brawl you start."

The businesswoman snorted under her breath. The lights in the car flickered and the train rushed through a short tunnel and came jerkily to a halt at the next station. Adrian glanced up and saw that it was hers, but she didn't move.

"Bitch." The man finally broke eye contact with her. He staggered to his feet and shoved past the android, who barely budged as he passed by. The businesswoman followed, as did many of the other passengers. Adrian let out a short breath as the doors closed and the train picked up speed again.

"You missed your stop," the android said. He moved to sit across from her now that the car was nearly empty. He rested his messenger bag in his lap and set his hands atop that. She could discern more of the telltale signs now—the slight hint of circuitry under the nails, the lack of folds or bags around the eyes, the rigidity of the hair.

"Excuse me?" And she kept her hand on the taser in the bag.

"You ride this train a lot. I notice things." She realized he was probably speaking more literally than most humans. And that his tone should not be automatically read as threatening.

"Don't worry about me." She tried to smile.

"I'm not." His voice was oddly soft and even. "I don't care what you do." His words were an echo of her own. She shifted, uncomfortable. She wondered if she had expected him to be grateful for her interference.

Though she had seen what androids could do—even with all of the proper training, even with safeguards in place. This one was no AS, but he had probably never needed her help.

"Sorry," she said, an instinctive apology.

He just nodded and gazed out the window past her head as if he had already forgotten her and the man with his threats, even the pregnant woman who still breathed heavily at the front of the car. Adrian tried to do the same. She studied the lights and bold-colored posters that flashed by and were gone before she could read them. And she sighed a little as she realized she would have to ride the train to the end of the line and back to her stop at this time of night.

She was not scared. Fear, at least fear of death or physical harm, had long ago been burned out of her. But she could feel the tension building in her shoulders and neck. She practiced some of the stress-relief exercises her physical therapist had taught her when she was trying to regain full range of motion in her leg. She rolled her shoulders and then dropped her chin to her chest and slowly raised it. The android watched her, his eyes flicking between her and the window. She looked at her own reflection behind him and wondered what he saw.

She cleared her throat and pulled out her phone again. Emails were piling up in her inbox but she ignored that. Anything she needed to know tonight would not come via email. Instead, she pulled up the menu for the Thai place near her walk-up. She was hungry now and interested in more than a pre-made sandwich from the bodega. In the time it took her to place an order, the train passed another station and finally pulled into the last stop of the line. There were no passengers waiting to get on and the platform was empty. The lights blinked. The android stood up and swung the bag over his shoulder. She smiled in case he glanced at her. He did not.

"Have a good one," she said, not quite sure why. Perhaps angry that he ignored her.

The door slid shut on his back. She watched him walk down the platform, his pace deliberate and his stance perfectly straight. She was surprised she had overlooked him when she first got on the train.

She was alone now. The pregnant woman had also gotten off at the last stop. The car lurched, then sat still. She sighed, more loudly now, and sank down further into her seat. The train lurched again and began to speed up, back toward her stop.

Her phone rang. She looked down at it in surprise. The noise was loud in the silence of the car. Her thumb hovered over the screen. The number was blocked.

"Hello?" There was no immediate answer. She glanced at her screen to see if the call was active. "Hello?"

And the hairs on her neck stood up just before he answered. As if she could feel him breathing by her ear. As if she knew it would be him before he spoke. Maybe it was something in the confidence of that pause. He knew she would not hang up without hearing what he had to say. She hoped her voice wouldn't betray her.

"How are you doing, Adrian?" Eli's voice was rougher than she expected, as if he was getting over a cold. Or perhaps it was just the years since they had last talked. "You seem good. Judging by the press conference this afternoon. *Still at large*, I think your words were."

She couldn't tell what he knew, not from that alone, so she didn't answer right away. She waited, collected herself. If she was lucky, and if they needed it, her surveillance team would be able to pinpoint where he was calling from later. But it certainly wouldn't dispel the rumors around her childhood, about her connection with the militia leader.

"What do you want, Eli?" she asked finally.

1.2:   **SEPTEMBER 2060**
_____

A s of 0845 today, Eli Whitaker is still at large."
    Adrian glanced out over the small crowd of reporters and the semi-intelligent drones sent from the bigger media outlets. They had promised her, when she agreed to serve as acting director, that the position would be temporary. Yet she had stood up here and made this admission, as if going to confession, every week for at least four months. The reporters did not even make a note of the fact anymore. The drones blinked red, recording.

"But I am working closely with our field office in the Appalachian Region, with the Louisville Field Division, to do regular sweeps and to act on any intel we receive. Raids over the last two months have disrupted cells of the insurgent Civil Union Militia in Ohio, Kentucky, and West Virginia. We are making progress."

She paused and glanced down at her notes. Security guards shifted at the exits and her assistant Peter, at the back of the room, was mouthing the next words in the notes they had prepared together. She breathed out.

"As we have stated before, we estimate that the Civil Union has between fifty thousand and seventy-five thousand official members." She would not call them soldiers. "There are certainly pockets of community support that we do not include in these numbers. And the children that have been pressed into the militia."

The reporters, almost simultaneously, straightened. The room was warm. The AC shut off for a half hour every two as part of its conservation cycle, and the humidity was building up in the room.

"Two months ago, I had the sad duty to report to you the death of one of these children during a raid on a compound in Kentucky."

The drones clicked and buzzed. She tried to ignore them and the memories of the Russo-Iran front they conjured up. She shifted her weight onto her left leg and reminded herself that it was not real, the whistling sound of the missile on the horizon that would decimate her bivouac.

"In that raid, we took into custody eighteen children, ages ranging between seven and sixteen. Most of these children did not have homes to which we could return them. No guardians. They are severely traumatized and need to be deprogrammed. It has not been easy to determine how best to reintegrate them into general society."

The video of the raid replayed in her head, overlapping with her own combat history, a tympanic symphony of gunshots. She gripped the podium and tried to keep her face neutral, professional. She skimmed the notes to find her place, hoping the hesitation was not noticeable.

"I am announcing today a new task force within the Bureau of Alcohol, Tobacco, and Firearms, one developed in coordination with the Department of Health and Human Services. This task force, the Active

Operation Foster Corps, will include field agents who have seen the compounds and know the conditions from which these children come. These agents have been handpicked for their extensive training not only in all aspects of search and seizure, investigation, containment, and combat but also for their education and backgrounds in psychology, sociology, and social work. They will be critical in aiding Social Services at the state level to place these children with foster parents who are trained and equipped to deal with their very unique needs." She paused. "It is important that we start developing some nonviolent solutions to our problems."

She looked up. "I'll take some questions."

There was a second or two of silence as the reporters finished jotting down her announcement or reread their notes or consulted with their bosses. Styluses clicked against tablets, and there was a whisper here and there. She could imagine Eli watching her now, his beard and mustache gray and stained with tobacco, his skin sallow, as she tried to stand very still, tried to show no impatience. She tried to remind herself that they hadn't lost yet. They would find him. They would. She set her jaw as if they were facing each other in person, not in her imagination.

"NCBS here," a reporter announced himself and broke the quiet.

She nodded to him. "Yes. Wyatt." She had made it a point to learn the journalists' names after her first press conference.

He smiled, glancing up and then back at his notes, as if apologizing for his question. "I appreciate your concern for the children here, your reasoning in establishing the task force. But can you tell us what action has been taken in regards to the automated soldier, the android with call sign Ora, who shot and killed the child in that raid two months ago?"

She looked quickly at Peter. They had prepared for this question, they'd answered it more than once, but it had felt easier rehearsing the answer in the stillness of her office.

"As I've said before, the AS has been withdrawn from the field for observation and tests. Nothing has changed there." She avoided using the android's call sign. Polling showed that the names generated a poor response from much of the public when AS were the topic of conversation.

Wyatt followed up on his question. "Do you anticipate it returning to the field?"

She cleared her throat. "We will not return any technology, AS or otherwise, if we find that they are a continuing threat."

Wyatt raised a finger as if to press her further. She continued. "I think it is important, though, that we do not lose sight of the threat of the Civil Union. They are the ones militarizing these children and placing them in harm's way. Our priority, in any raid, is always to extricate these innocents first and foremost."

"Director." Sherri from CWE, a venue transitioning from tabloid to legitimate outlet. "We have a source that draws a connection, a personal one, between yourself and Eli Whitaker. Can you speak to that?"

Adrian's fingers twitched on the podium. This, she was not prepared for. How had they dug that up? Peter, at the back of the room, immediately began searching on his tablet. He would send anything he could find to her own.

She tried to smile. "Could you clarify what kind of connection you're talking about?" It was probably a mistake to ask that, to allow her to say more. It left her at a tactical disadvantage. The journalist's face showed that she knew that.

"Sure. My source says that you dated Mr. Whitaker's son, a Trey Caudill."

"His foster son. In high school."

"But you did date him?"

"Yes."

"And Trey Caudill is now the special agent in charge of the Louisville field office, is that correct?"

She was tired of answering these questions. She had gone through a battery of them when they vetted her for acting director, a position she had never wanted or asked for. And hard as it was for even herself to believe, Trey's promotion to the Louisville office after her departure had happened without her knowledge. She would have been happy, then, to have never talked to him again.

"Where Trey and I grew up, there weren't a lot of options after high school." She felt her stance relax, the slightest twang of her Appalachian accent creep into her speech. The reporters looked a little bemused, surprised at the direction of her answer. "I went into the military. He got his college degree and then became an agent for the ATF. It was only much later that I decided I wanted to move closer to home and opted for a career change. I joined the ATF to try and make things better *here*."

A forensic accountant had sifted through her financial records. She had agreed to an interview with lie-detecting technology.

"So your answer is *yes*?" Sherri was obstinate and blunt.

"It is. An equal and opposite reaction. I don't think it's too surprising that two kids who knew Eli Whitaker should run in the opposite direction."

"But, Director, don't you think—"

"And I will let you know"—she spoke loudly—"you can't ask any harder questions than the ATF already has. I know firsthand the damage that Eli Whitaker can do. I can assure you, in my role as acting director, that there is no one who will approach this task with more diligence and dedication than myself."

Peter had worked his way around the room and he reached out now to take her tablet and notes, signaling that the press conference was at a close. There was a hubbub of noise as a few reporters tried to get in another question.

"Thank you all for your service and your support." She nodded and waved, while Peter added, "I'm afraid we're out of time for today. We'll see you next week."

The security detail converged on her as she reached the door of the room and she exited into the hallway in a small knot of people.

"Peter." She glanced around to find him. He was typing up notes as he walked. She waited for him to look up and meet her eyes. "Peter, that was a shit show."

"We knew, I guess, that the connection would come out sooner or later."

"We should have controlled that story, been the ones to release it."

He shrugged. "Maybe. But put on the spot, you managed to seem pretty genuine. We might have lucked out."

"I am genuine."

His mouth crooked up in a smile. "We know the terrifying nature of your sincerity all too well."

She grunted and quickened her pace. She wanted to be back in the quiet and shadow of her office. Sweat prickled at the back of her neck.

"Do you think we can scrounge up any coffee, Peter? Real coffee?"

He shrugged. "We can try." He didn't sound hopeful. She couldn't remember the last time she'd had any. Reports of crop failures in South America didn't make it seem too likely in the immediate future either.

"At least find me some lunch." She tried to keep the growing irritation, the flood of anger and doubt, she felt post-briefing out of her voice.

"Sure. Yep." That meant the most she could hope for was a hot dog from one of the corner stands. It seemed like the world never ran out of hot dogs while vegetables shriveled on the vine.

Late morning sunlight glowed on the tiled floor of the hallway, but it was cool in her office. The windows were opaque, and she didn't brighten them immediately. Her security detail peeled away. They weren't truly concerned for her safety anyway. Assassinations weren't the Civil Union's style. Their style was to entrench themselves on private property, in front of factories, like some over-armed union. To sweep the factories and destroy any androids or robots they found working there. Occasionally, a human worker got caught in the crossfire.

She'd seen pictures of the bodies piled outside the factories, metal and plastic limbs strewn at odd angles and Whitaker's symbol graffitied on the wall behind. When the corporations had called in state support, then she'd seen other bodies as well, human ones, tossed around the manicured courtyards and parking lots. Children posing with automatic rifles by the corpses of soldiers.

And yet—Adrian slammed her open palm onto her desk, used the smarting pain to distract herself and break the chain of images in her head. She knew, she knew why these images were haunting her now. In this moment. After the journalist had called into question her connection with Whitaker. As if any part of her, even the bone in her little finger, supported that man.

"Director?" Peter's voice was tentative. "Awfully dark in here." He searched for the switch on the wall. The windows brightened by gradual degrees until she could see the lawn and the willow trees, yellower than they should be for the time of year.

"I found some tea. Matcha."

He placed the cup on her desk. She sat down in her chair and leaned back. The tea smelled earthy, as close to coffee as she could hope for.

"Peter, what do you think of android labor?"

Peter stood very still in the doorway. He glanced at the window and back to the desk, to the tea and the steam rising from it. In the distance, she could hear the honks and screech of midday traffic.

"I'm not asking whether you support the militia, Peter." He breathed out almost audibly. "Trust me."

He finally met her eyes. "My mom is part of an anti-android union." She sometimes forgot how young he was. "I grew up thinking robots would take away our jobs. Not sure that wasn't true."

She nodded, acknowledging his statement, not agreeing or disagreeing with it.

"Trey Caudill has requested a meeting, ma'am."

She looked at him and laughed, almost amused. "Not this week, I think. Push him off as long as you can."

Peter tapped out a short note on his watch. "You don't have to meet with him at all."

"I wish that were true."

1.3: SEPTEMBER 2060 & OCTOBER 2028

W e should have listened to your mom." Trey waited in the door for her to look up. Peter retreated into the outer office after having shown him in.

She tried to smile. "And what did she say?" She couldn't remember much that had been coherent in conversations with her mother.

He waited until she gestured to the chair across from her desk. Then, he came in. He walked with an anxiety, almost a vibration, in his step, as if he were uncomfortable in the quiet of her office. His white skin looked even paler than usual. She dimmed the windows just a little so that the sun was not so bright.

"She said there's no such thing as freedom."

Adrian sighed and nodded. "It sounds like something she would say. Just the freedom to destroy yourself." She didn't bother hiding the bitterness in her voice from Trey. She wondered what he remembered of the staleness of her house, the smoke that hung in the kitchen, the peeling linoleum under the sink. "When did she say that to you, anyways?"

"I saw her right after my high school graduation. I came by the house, hoping to see you. But you'd already gone. She said you'd gone into the military, seeking some sort of freedom, and that there was none to be found."

Adrian laughed, humorless. "If only she knew why I'd really gone."

"I think she did." His voice was quiet.

The clock ticked on her wall in the silence that fell. It was old-fashioned, but she liked the noise. It grounded her. She took a sip of the tea that Peter had brought her earlier that morning. It was lukewarm now.

"Do you want anything?" she asked him. A convention held over from better times. Unless he asked for water, there wouldn't be much to offer him. He shook his head anyway.

"It always surprises me, how well you talk, how well you handle yourself in those press briefings." He glanced around her office, taking in the expensive wood, metal, marble décor.

"Should I take that as a compliment?"

It was his turn to laugh, though there was something real there, actual amusement mixed with embarrassment. "Sorry. I hear it now. You've done well for yourself, Adrian. That's all I meant. I couldn't deal with all of those reporters."

"You've had your fair share in the last two months."

He swallowed, nodded, ducked his head.

She kept her eyes fixed on his face. "Anyway." She cleared her throat. "It's no thanks to my connections. You must have heard their questions then. It's been those ones, over and over again, all week."

"I don't know what to say. I wish neither of us had known Eli." The first name alone, connoting familiarity and intimacy, made her flesh crawl.

"Why'd you ask for this meeting, Trey?" She couldn't dwell in that past for long. She'd played the protector for too long. She was tired. She was scared for her own career.

Trey sighed. He held his arms on his knees, interlaced his fingers, hunched over.

"Active Operation Foster Corps," he said, finally. "I like the idea of it."

"Well, it was necessary. Too many kids sitting in government custody. With no idea what homes to send them to."

He smiled, a little sadly. "I don't know that everyone in your position would have thought of it, though." There was some of the teenaged boy in him still, the boy who had sat quiet at his own kitchen table and hers, the boy who had never felt truly at home since he was put in the foster system himself. There was a time, more than thirty years ago now, when she'd found that awkward moodiness attractive.

Then she reminded herself—and it made her a little sick each time she had to think of it, as frequent as that was—that Trey was an experienced agent, that a kid had been killed under his watch, on his raid. He wasn't an innocent. Neither was she.

"How are you holding up?" They both knew what she was referencing. "Last time we talked, you weren't so good."

She felt bad saying it, understatement as it was, trivializing as it could be.

He glanced up. "One way to describe it."

"Have you talked with the therapist?"

He nodded. "Mandated, wasn't it?"

"What did he say?"

"He said I could go back into the field." His face flushed red. "If you can believe that bullshit."

She didn't answer right away and watched him. He opened his mouth to say something else, then thought better of it. She did the same. Finally, he coughed and broke the silence.

"I still stand by what I said then."

Adrian tried to remember if it had really been an argument. Trey had been distraught. She had been defensive.

"We've removed Ora from the field," she said. "The lab techs are

running a whole panel of diagnostics. They're working on a new training module for the other AS."

"There are limits to how much you can train a metal box." His voice
was hard now. "I'm here, Adrian, because I can't do it anymore. Let me
work on the Foster Corps. Remove me from field operations."

"Trey." She ground her back teeth, tightened her jaw. She already
regretted the words and she hadn't even spoken them yet. "I can't reas-
sign you. Not yet."

"Why not?"

"You're one of my best." Trite, maybe, but not untrue.

"I don't think that's true."

She shifted in her seat. "You know Eli." Her throat was tight. She
wondered if she would be able to forgive herself for this later.

He flung up his hands in an exaggerated gesture, searching frantically for a response. "You heard the reporters. That makes me a liability."

"Trey." She bit the inside of her lip and steadied herself. "I'm sorry—"

"You're not sorry." He pushed his chair back, stood up. He stared
out the window, caught in a sort of desperate stillness. There was almost a child's petulance in his voice, if not for the deadly seriousness
of the conversation.

"You can't ask me to appoint a new field director in the middle of
an operation like this. We've got Whitaker on the run."

"Do we?" He looked back at her, his eyes large and dark. His hair
was uncombed, or too quickly combed before leaving his hotel room.

When pressed to it, she could not say for sure. It was something she
had become used to telling herself. Otherwise, it was hard to sit home
at night with a tumbler of whiskey and try to pretend everything was
alright.

"Each compound we take down, each house, gives him less to work
with. He'll run out of resources sooner or later. Let's say sooner."

"Are you going to ask me to keep working with the AS?"

"They'll do what we train them to do, Trey."

"See, we've had this conversation before—two minutes ago, two months ago."

Adrian straightened in her seat, tapped at her tablet to see if any pressing messages had come through during the meeting. She could feel Trey's eyes on her, watching her.

"I could quit," he said. Maybe it was a bid for attention. Maybe not. She raised her eyes, clicking off her tablet as she did so.

She stood up and came around the desk. He looked at her leg as he always did, as if he could never quite get used to it. She didn't put her hand on his shoulder, but she came close enough that she could.

"Trey, I know it's a terrible thing we're doing here. I know it's hard. That it might seem impossibly hard. I just need you to give me a bit more time. You know Whitaker better than most. You know what he's capable of."

He dropped his head and picked at the back of the chair near him. Whitaker had never beat him, not with his hand or a belt, she knew that much. He'd never touched him inappropriately. But something had happened in that house, something that had almost crushed Trey. Something she'd dreamed of saving him from when she was only a kid herself.

"I will let you go into the Foster Corps after that. I will." She knew the tone of voice she was using, remembered the cajoling register of it. It was for a different time, a different relationship. But he grasped onto that.

"Just a little while, Adrian. Not much more."

"No. Not much."

He sighed, his whole body shifting with the depth of it. She wasn't sure if he believed her, but he was choosing to do so for the moment. She wanted to believe herself.

"It won't happen again," he whispered.

She stared at him, waited for clarification. Finally, the pallor of his face, the red streak across his forehead turned her in the right direction.

She hoped for the same. But she wasn't sure any longer if it was possible. She cleared her throat.

"That's another reason you should be there." She tried to convince herself that she was genuine when she said that, that she wasn't using Trey's trauma against him. *I don't want to be the one who has to make those terrible decisions, those life and death decisions,* she'd told a friend in her squadron when she'd been promoted to her first commission. *Too late,* her friend had responded.

"Capturing Eli," she continued, "is the only way to help those children. The only way to save them."

He almost laughed, but it was voiceless, strangled in his throat. "If we don't kill them in the process. If a robot doesn't shoot them."

"Helios took in that girl without harming her, a girl with a gun who was shooting at you all."

Trey licked his lips as if trying to compose himself. He straightened. "You don't have to go over the arguments again. You tell me how high to jump, to work with AS, I say how high, how low."

Her throat was tight, from anger, from grief. "No real comeback to that, is there? Glad you recognize the chain of command." Her voice was brittle.

He looked at her, his eyes red-rimmed, as if he might apologize. But he didn't say anything.

"I wouldn't argue with anyone else like this, Trey. I wouldn't let them speak to me like this."

He nodded, but still didn't answer. It was as if he had run out of words.

"You might go and talk with Helios. You might feel better." There it was again, her attempt to fix what was broken.

"No. I can't. Not yet." He walked to the door, rested his hand on the knob. "If you're assigning AS to my office, send me new ones."

"You can have your pick," she said slowly.

"Lucky me." He opened the door. "I'll see you, Director."

She didn't move or say goodbye as the door closed, a quiet click. She placed her hand over her mouth. Her fingers trembled.

"Keep your head down. Eye to that sight. It's easy to think you're following with the gun when you're just following with your eyes." Eli pushed her head down toward the rifle, not roughly but firmly, unrelenting. She blinked and squirmed, the leaves crunching beneath her. "And stay quiet." There was a harder edge to that, more of a warning. Adrian tried not to look away, as much as her instincts wanted to keep watch on him as well as the squirrel.

Trey grunted from his position behind the blind. She wanted to glare at him too. He had already bagged one squirrel. Sheer luck. He'd admitted as much to her, in a whisper, once they'd changed locations.

The morning was getting late, though, and game harder to find. The woods were falling to sleep, the trees almost drowsy in the listlessness of the wind. She felt too warm and sweaty in her camo. She shifted one hand free, quickly, to shove her collar down. Eli heard her move, she knew. But he didn't say anything.

The brush rustled against the trunk of the tree in her line of sight. The squirrel scampered up, its tail bottle-brush and puffed up behind. She tried to follow it, quick as it was. She kept her finger poised on the trigger and did not lose sight of it. One pause, one moment in which the animal stopped still and glanced about—almost at her—and she squeezed the trigger. The jolt of the gun in her armpit was familiar and did not jostle her much. But she realized she had closed her eyes a mere second before shooting. She opened them slowly, breathed in deeply, and tried to quiet the sudden uptick of anxiety. She waited to hear Eli's approval or disapproval.

"Go get it."

She had been lying so long in the same position that her body was stiff when she moved. She grunted and shoved herself to her knees and then to her feet. She set the safety on her rifle, then tucked it under her arm. The leaves rustled around her waders, dry and brown in the late October sunlight.

She'd blinked and the kill wasn't clean. The squirrel still twitched at the trunk of the tree. Its eyes were wide open, black and unblinking, and its mouth quivered. She winced, biting the inside of her cheek, and pulled out her knife. She slit the animal's throat and then cleaned the blade on a small patch of grass. She tucked the squirrel into her bag and wove her way back through the brush to Eli. Trey had abandoned his blind and joined him.

"First rule?" Eli cocked his head and looped his thumbs through his belt. There was something almost fatherly in the stance. Something almost threatening. She was not sure if they were one and the same.

"Keep your eye on it."

He didn't respond, but let her answer hang in the air. Then he nodded sharply and turned away. He started picking up the gear they had shed as they settled into their positions. He tossed the bag with ammo to Trey.

"Not much chance to shoot at anything today. We'll head to the firing range and practice there."

"I'm tired," she said. And there was still the nagging uneasiness from when she had stared at the squirrel's desperate spasms. She would never say that aloud. Perhaps not even to Trey, later, when they lay curled together.

"You're seventeen and in the prime of your life," Eli answered. "You have no right to be tired yet."

"Didn't know it was a right." She said the words too quickly, right off the tongue. And it was too late to take them back.

He let his arms fall, weighted down on each side by the rifles in their cases and the folded-up stools and blind. She glanced at Trey, a panicked nerve twitching at the corner of her eye. She could feel it there, tickling tickling tickling.

"Say that again." It wasn't a challenge or an angry retort. He said it calmly, as an order.

She swallowed. Her stomach was queasy, but there was a heat there too, a building rage.

"You're not my father," she said. "And you don't get to tell me what to say. But if you want to hear it again, I said I'm tired." She wished she had the courage to go even further. To stand up to him like a character on TV. *Tired of your bullshit. Tired of what you're doing to Trey.*

Trey stared at his feet, his fists clenched tight in the pockets of his camo vest.

Eli moved quickly. He dropped the gear and stepped up to her. He hit her, open-handed, across the cheek so that her neck snapped to the left. She tasted blood before she felt it, welling up under her tongue. Tears, pure shock, sprung into her eyes.

Then he spoke, quiet, his breath hot on her face. It smelled like mint. He chewed leaves of it after meals.

"No one asked to be your father, girl. And I'm certainly not him. But no one wanted to be your father either. Whatever stranger knocked up your mom, he didn't stick around for long. And if you don't want the food I put in front of you and the training I give you, then you grow up and you leave. Leave him"—and his voice dropped even lower, but he thrust one finger at Trey—"and all you do when you don't think I'm looking. Because I don't have the time or the inclination to have someone visiting my kid, eating under my roof, who don't respect the head of it."

It was there, in those few words, all the lectures on hard work and responsibility and not taking things for granted, the bitter blessing before every meal she'd eaten with Trey. It almost made her grateful for her own mother's skittish silence and flavorless meals.

There was no such thing as not answering Eli. He held her eyes, and she couldn't look at Trey. She couldn't look anywhere but at him. His eyes were gray and green, his skin tanned in the way of someone who spends his time working outside.

"You coming or going, girl?"

1.4:   MAY 2058 & SEPTEMBER 2061

"You don't have to go in." Felix watched her as she tightened the vest and checked her weapon.

"I want to. Might be my last operation before they stick me behind a desk."

"You make it sound like you're getting demoted instead of the other way round."

She smiled. She would miss Felix once they moved her to the DC office. He was a good agent who'd managed to keep hold of a sense of humor, something she was sure she was losing.

"Besides, I want eyes on this. There's something not right, something missing in the reports."

"You think someone left something off?"

"More that I think there's something no one is seeing."

Felix glanced to the back door of the van, waiting for their signal to go in. "I'm just saying we're going to get spoiled if the division director keeps coming out on raids with us."

She didn't answer. She ran over the map of the property in her head, two double-wides in the clearing, a shed in the brush, an old treehouse at the edge of the woods. They suspected the guns were in the shed, enough for a small militia, none of them registered. It was the purchase of explosives, however, that had moved the operation from observation to raid.

"Don't you worry," she finally said. "I've heard the new guy is a hard-ass." Felix grimaced. She dropped her hand to her knee and checked the tension in the artificial joint.

She replayed the video footage of the woman in the hardware store, a skeleton of a woman but with swollen ankles and extra weight around the middle. Her hair had been cut close to her head, ragged and un-kempt. She'd treated the supplies she was purchasing with confidence, unafraid, unhesitating.

"You sure they didn't hear us coming?" The agent at the wheel walkied the scouts.

There was a second's pause before the reply came through. "We're in position. No sign that they know we're coming."

Adrian tapped the driver on the shoulder. "When she says *they*, how many are we talking?"

"You read the report, right?" Felix asked behind her. She waved a hand at him to shut him up. The driver relayed her question.

"Three outside. No one near the shed. I'm counting . . ." The agent on the other side was whispering, counting under her breath. "I'm counting at least five bodies, if not more, in the trailers."

Adrian glanced at Felix. "That's more than we accounted for." She fixed her own comms in her ear.

"How could we have gotten that wrong?"

"Maybe they have friends over," the driver pitched in. And Adrian remembered why humor had lost its sheen for her.

An agent swung the door of the van open. "We're a go."

Felix jumped down first, falling into a crouching run as soon as his feet hit the ground. Adrian followed. The sunlight was startling at first.

The van was pulled up on the graveled side of an old rural highway. The agents descended into the ditch by the road and then waded into the overgrown field beyond. The line of woods looked shallow against the horizon, a small break between two fields.

The high grass left burrs and prickles on their jumpsuits and armor. Beneath them, the ground was soft from a rain the night before. And there was a heat trapped in the field, weltering up damp from below and oppressing them from above.

The scouts were silent on the comms, waiting.

"Secure the shed," she reminded the team of their priorities. "And make sure they don't make use of that armory."

The rest of the walk was silence, the grass brushing against their legs. In the woods, once they reached them, it felt comparatively cool, shadowed. It was not far from here to the trailers. She readjusted her grip on her gun and crouched lower. The rest of the team followed her example as they wove between the trees. Sticks and twigs cracked under their feet. That was unavoidable with this number of people, but there was the cringe of shame and judgment as she recalled her old lessons in hunting.

When she came into eyeline of the scouts, she stopped and squatted against a tree, peering toward the trailers. The scouts motioned to her where the three outside were, two women and a man smoking between the trailers by a dug-out firepit. She heard their voices, high, thin, and largely indecipherable. One of them laughed, then coughed. The man threw his cigarette butt into the pit and then looked up as if he had heard something.

"Chris!"

When he yelled, the door to the near trailer slammed open. Adrian scanned right and left and saw that her agents were in position, flanking the clearing. She signaled for them to move in.

Like a held breath released, the clearing burst into noise. The smokers started screaming, obscenities and shouts for help. The man at the trailer door looked stunned, his eyes widening. He was wearing an odd number of layers, an open plaid shirt and a robe with hood over his t-shirt. Behind him, there were a number of people. She could not get a clear count.

"Step down. Up against the wall." She shouted her orders and he followed them, no resistance, still in shock. Other agents swarmed around her. One twisted the man's arms behind his back and cuffed him. Three others moved around to apprehend the man and women by the firepit.

There was another noise above the shouting, above the coughs and gasps of shock. Her first instinct was to glance at the shed, but agents had peeled off there as well to secure the door and make sure no one was inside. When she finally recognized the sound, she stopped cold in her tracks. It was a child's wail, high and trembling, and others crying with it.

"Felix," she reached out on the comms, to anyone who would answer, but to Felix especially, Felix who kept every detail of a mission in his almost photographic memory. "Were there supposed to be children?" She realized, after she'd spoken, how fast, how breathless the words were.

Immediately, even before he answered, she felt overwhelmed by a sense of failure. This—the gap in knowledge—was her fault.

"No report of, no sightings of children in any of the flyovers."

"Ask him." She gestured to the agents guarding the man against the wall. "Ask him." She could ask him herself, but she was breathless. She did not move from her position facing the door, but she could not bring herself to aim the gun inside.

"How many children?"

The man squirmed, trying to turn his face in Adrian's direction.

"Well, ma'am, personally, I've only got one kid to my name." The shock had worn off and there was a surly arrogance in his tone.

"How many children are inside?" she repeated the question. The rest of the property had grown quiet. There didn't seem to be any danger of other unaccounted-for adults rushing the shed. She could hear shuffling and whispers from inside the trailer, muffled crying.

"You can't expect me to 'count for children that ain't my own?" One of the agents pressed the man closer against the flimsy corrugated metal of the wall.

"Fuck it." She engaged the safety on her gun. "Any drug paraphernalia?" she asked the agents who were exiting the second trailer.

They shook their heads.

She went up to the door of the trailer and looked in. "Boss, don't be reckless," Felix hissed in her ear.

"We're not going to hurt you," she said into the darkness as her eyes adjusted.

A small figure bounced up and hurled themself at her ankles. She sidestepped and the child collided with a couch.

"We're not going to hurt you," she repeated. Her heart was beating fast, her blood thumping in her neck. She fumbled for a light switch. A fluorescent light cracked and flickered on above her. It cast a sallow light over a crowded group of six children in the kitchenette. She glanced at the one who had rushed her, a boy who could be no older than eight.

None of them were carrying guns, but a young girl—maybe twelve—held a knife in her hand. It was not a kitchen knife, but a hunting knife with a serrated blade.

"Drop the weapon. Drop any weapons that you have." One child dropped a pocket knife on the ground.

The girl set her jaw. Her hair was brown and curly and dirty, half up in a ponytail. "We've been taught better than that," she said. Her voice was rough. "We don't need to listen to feds." She spit the last word like a curse.

"Your parents listened. They're outside in handcuffs."

She tilted her head as if trying to listen for someone outside. "My dad's dead. My mom's in jail."

"You're a foster kid." She said it half to herself, and there was that old ache at her chest.

"I'm myself. I came here on my own." The girl's cheeks flushed pink.

Adrian wondered, briefly, a flashing second, whether it was possible that children were stronger than adults.

"We're here to help. Drop the knife."

"The government don't help nobody."

"I'm not the government. I'm Adrian. And I'm here to help. You don't need to live like this."

The girl faltered. She dropped her chin and looked at the knife she was gripping. Felix showed up in the door behind her.

"Who wants a candy bar?" He pitched his voice loud and boisterous. But none of the kids responded to his offer. The twelve-year-old was the oldest among them, and they huddled close to her.

"We don't want anything from you." But her voice was softer now, less sure. And her eyes looked a little watery.

"And we're not going to take anything from you."

The girl met Adrian's eyes with something like an accusation. And Adrian understood that. They would be taking something from that girl—a home, however bad and messed up it was.

Finally, through clenched teeth, she said, "Doesn't look like we're going to be able to stop you." She reached above the heads of the younger kids around her and placed the knife on the countertop.

Felix audibly released his breath. "Come on," he said. "This way."

The tone was still cheerful, modulated for children. Some of them now scurried forward, a look almost like excitement on their faces, including the boy on the sofa. Three of them lingered, walking more slowly, including the oldest girl.

When the other two had finally left the trailer, the girl stopped next to Adrian. "We were supposed to kill you," she said, voice unnervingly steady and soft. Then she went out the door.

Adrian clutched her stomach. She tried to steady herself before facing the other agents. The girl had unnerved her more with that one line than any combat she'd been in. Adrian didn't understand the fear, or the intensity of it, which only frightened her more. She supported herself with a hand on the wall.

"Director, you might want to see this." The crackle of the comms in her ear jolted her out of her haze. She shook her head and stepped out of the trailer.

"What?"

One of her agents waved a hand at her. She was standing near the shed. Another agent was taking pictures of the wall.

"What did you find?" She was distracted as she headed over, studying the surly faces of the men and women handcuffed and sitting in an outward-facing circle on the lawn. An agent stood guard over them. She signaled him to keep a close watch. Stockpiling weapons was one thing, a dangerous thing, the makings of a militia. Those children, militarized and primed to attack, that was another thing. It felt cultish and it made her skin crawl.

The wall of the shed didn't help.

"Thought you might want to see it. It looked familiar." The agent traced the lines of the design in the air with her finger as if trying to jog her memory.

Spray-painted on the corrugated steel was a large image of a flag torn in two, grasped in clenched fists. Adrian stepped forward and rubbed at the edge of it with her thumb, but the paint was dry. The wall was hot from the sun.

"We have seen it before. Flyers in the town a mile back." Her voice dropped at the end and her throat closed up a bit.

It was not something she had spent thought on at the time driving through, the flapping weather-stained pages stapled to telephone poles, but the images came together in retrospect. As did a memory of Eli Whitaker, tearing a flag into strips and feeding it into the wood-burning stove. It was just a flash, his face, his hands in the firelight. She hadn't cared much about the flag at the time, but the slow steady way in which he'd done it, the tirade of words, had unnerved her.

The agent was talking to her, speculating on the connection, but Adrian didn't follow her, couldn't really hear her. Her face felt numb, and her chest. It was the feeling one gets when trapped and unable to move in a nightmare.

She only let it last a second. She couldn't afford more. But it crawled there, under her skin, for the ride back, the trucks filled with children.

"What do you want, Eli?" The train lurched and rumbled, screeching around a corner. The lights flickered off and the darkness lasted for a full minute.

His laughter was soft, controlled. "I've never needed anything from you, Adrian."

"I didn't say *need*." She bit off each word, brittle. She glanced around the car as if hoping to see there was another passenger she had not noticed before. But the car was empty and its walls painted beige and the torn-up red cushions of the seats were far from comforting. She stood up, grabbing onto the handrail above, and leaned toward the doors as if she could force the train to go faster.

"What I want," he said—and it was buried there, the nights and nights of lectures differentiating need from want, villainizing desire— but he stopped short.

"Say what you called to say."

"I think you know what I'm doing is right. You know that our world is out of control."

She knew it was a mistake to stay on the phone with him. There was a chance she might tip him off to the impending raid. There was a chance she would lose her temper. And then it wouldn't matter if they traced the call, nothing to find in the morning if all went to hell tonight.

"We will catch you, Eli." There was no winning a conversation with Eli. She knew that in her gut, but she hoped nonetheless that he heard the threat in her voice.

The train alerted her to the fact that they were nearing her stop. She swayed with the rhythm of the track. Her bag bounced at her shoulder, her taser tucked away. She remembered again the stiff back of the android exiting the train.

"You took him from me." The words didn't register with her right away. Eli's voice was almost raw, something approaching anger at the edge of his words. She blinked and adjusted her grip on the rail. *I don't care what you do.* Is that what the android had said?

"He left you."

Because he hadn't come with her. In the early morning. When the fog was still heavy on the ground and the first birds were calling in the dawn. She had sat at the end of the driveway in her mother's two-door, idling. She could remember still, sharper than any memory of early-morning hunts, the smell of the gas, the warmth of the car heater in the cold hour before sunrise. She could remember how desperately she wanted to grab his hand and how much she worried he would not come, that he would not be able to come.

"And now he's coming back." The voice hesitated a tick, the voice she knew so well. "Isn't he?"

There were tears at the back of her eyes and she did not know why. She was angry and her face was hot, but the tears were there, a sadness greater than she could explain underneath the anger and the heat.

You don't get to pretend, is what she wanted to say, *you don't get to pretend that you care who comes after you. That you care about him.* But she couldn't say it. It wasn't true. She knew that Eli cared about Trey. In some twisted part of him that thought discipline—and only discipline—equated to love.

"Make your peace, Eli. In whatever way you can."

She gasped, the tears welling up in a rush, and hung up.

The train stopped and the doors opened. The name of her stop blinked in digital letters over her head. She stumbled onto the platform, wiping at her eyes, rubbing the palms of her hands into her cheeks. The electronic joint in her knee paused for less than a second, just enough to throw off her gait, and she stopped to collect herself. The doors of the train slid closed and, with a rush of warm stale air, it took off down the tunnel. She forced herself to breathe.

The tears were gone. A small auto-cleaner whirred on the platform across the tracks. Shops and businesses might be shuttering at an unprecedented pace above, but the subway was cleaner than it had ever been.

The station was almost empty when she exited above. And no one had seen her cry as she left the train. Cry like a teenager when her boyfriend tapped on the window of the car and she leaned across to open it for him. When she could finally breathe. When she hadn't yet heard what he had to say.

ERNST & SHAY

JULY 2058

Shay was tired, so tired that she could barely force herself to raise her head and look at her husband when he entered the hospital room. She lifted a few fingers, her hand still resting on the bed, to greet him.

"I brought you some fake coffee from the vending machine," he said, his voice just above a whisper.

"Thanks." She watched him set the cup down on the bedside table. The smell of it made her want to throw up.

"The nurses said you were tired."

She nodded.

"They also said that you could be released tomorrow. But they recommended we get some help at home. An android aide to help administer the immunotherapy. To help around the house."

"I can take care of myself." She was surprised at how defiant she sounded, at the energy in her own voice.

"Honey." He rested a hand on top of hers, but he did so gingerly. "There's no need to turn down help. The insurance will cover the cost. Most of it."

"Who cares about the cost?" She was aware of the bitterness there, almost wished she could tamp it down.

"I wasn't saying that." He frowned a little and then pulled a chair close up to the bed. She picked at the small knots of lint that dotted the blanket.

"It's going to take time," he said softly.

She didn't answer, picked furiously at the lint.

"I'm sorry. I didn't mean to upset you."

"Everything's not your fault, Ernst." Even that, even that sounded accusatory.

In the awkward silence that followed, a service bot wheeled into the room, a tray balanced on what served it for a head. A small paper cup of pills rested on the tray, and a plastic cup of water. Ernst reached for the pills, turned her hand, and poured the pills into her palm. Then he gave her the cup of water. She swallowed the pills and knocked back the water. Probably just antibiotics. They wouldn't start the cancer treatment until she had recovered from the miscarriage. The service bot retreated, its wheels squeaking and in need of oil.

"Nurse can't be bothered to come in herself," Shay grumbled.

"I don't think—" He stopped mid-sentence and sank back into silence.

The windows in her room faced west, and the setting sunlight was red and bloody on the floor. She began to cry, quietly at first, trembling. Ernst scooted closer, and he took both her hands in his. He rested his head on her legs, and she stared at the small bald spot on the back of his head, at the light freckled scalp.

"What would you have named him?" she said. Her voice wasn't steady and she could barely hear it herself, but Ernst knew what she had asked.

"Whatever name you wanted, Shay. Whatever name." He looked up at her, and she saw the bags under his eyes, the lines of pain around his mouth. But she could barely feel anything for him. Not past her own pain, swelling around her heart and crowding her lungs.

"I thought Cary," she said. And perhaps there had been some sleeping meds among the pills as well, because her words slurred. She felt Ernst squeeze her hand, and then it was darkness, edging into nothingness.

"Easy, easy." Ernst held one of her hands and braced her back as she stepped out of bed and into the wheelchair.

"I can show you how the controls work." The nurse bent close to the tiny screen on the arm of the chair. Shay shifted away instinctively.

"It's all right," Ernst interrupted as the screen began to load, a cascade of black and white pixels settling into images of buttons to control direction and speed. "I'll push her. Besides, can't be too much harder to figure out than the new combine models." Shay could hear, in the way he spoke, that he was smiling at the nurse, attempting to lighten the mood. "Thank you," he said. "Thank you for all you've done for us."

Shay couldn't think of anything the nurse had done.

"Where was it we needed to stop before we could leave?" she asked, cutting off the nurse before she could express more sympathy.

"Take care of yourself," the nurse said, pressing Shay's hand at the same time as Ernst bent over her shoulder and whispered, ever patient, "We need to stop by the robotics wing. We'll find a home health aide that you like."

"Just another metal contraption," she answered. But she could not convince Ernst to give up the idea. She kicked her foot violently against the footrest.

The nurse left them, her white, rubber-soled shoes squeaking down the sanitized hall.

"Wait, we've forgotten a bag," Shay said as Ernst pushed her toward the door. The nagging reminder, the words, came before she could process them. The bag was there, half-shoved under the bed, striped in green and beige. "No, never mind," she stumbled on. But Ernst, a second behind her, had already stopped and was looking for it. "Never mind," she repeated sharply.

Ernst pushed her in silence to the elevators. They watched the numbers climb on the LCD screen.

"Do you remember what floor the robotics department is on?" he asked as they entered the elevator, the wheels jostling over the lip of the floor.

"No." But he seemed to know after all, because he pushed a button.

"I don't need an aide," she tried once again as the door slipped shut. There was the whir and hum of the elevator's motors.

"Maybe not," he said. "But it will put my mind at ease."

She could not think of an answer to that, at least no answer that wasn't *I don't give a fuck what you think.* And she realized that answer was not quite true, so she kept her mouth shut. She bit the inside of her cheek, and there were ridges of skin, raw and bloody, where she had been biting her cheek for the past three days.

The elevator opened onto a hallway where the lights were almost blue in color, aggressively fluorescent. There was a neat placard on the wall, pointing out the direction of the Robotics Division and the R&D Department. The placard bore the signature of a wealthy patron.

"This way." Ernst began to walk more quickly and the chair, with Shay in it, raced ahead of him.

They passed doors with frosted glass, opaque enough that Shay could only make out the silhouettes of the people behind them. If they were people, and not androids.

"Mr. and Mrs. Ohleg," a voice, high and cheery, with a slight Russian accent, greeted them before they could see the person who spoke. He came out from a sliding door ahead of them. "The nurse called to say you were on your way. I'm Dr. Pnuchin."

"You're an engineer," Shay said.

"Nope." Pnuchin smiled. He was short, round around the waist, hair too long, brushing his shoulders. "PhD in Communications. I'm the liaison between R&D and the patients. Occasionally, I dabble in AI language. I help train the androids."

"Well, I'm leaving. I've checked out. I'm no longer a patient." And she forced herself to smile, broadly.

"And that's why you're here," Pnuchin said, unfazed. "Please, come in."

The door slid open again and he led them forward.

"We're here to pick out an aide," Ernst said, businesslike, checking off the list. "We're preapproved with our insurance. Everything should be set."

It seemed like he was going to say something more, but he fell abruptly silent as they entered the room. Shay was shocked as well. She clutched the arms of her chair.

"You've come to the right place," Pnuchin said. He waved his arms wide. The room was almost empty, a large holographic screen thrown up on the right-side wall with their medical information. Shay barely noticed that, however, in the face of the three silent figures who sat at the table directly in front of them. They looked human to her, but they sat so preternaturally still that she could only assume them to be the android aides. She shivered. She craned her neck to look at Ernst. He swallowed, then smiled at her.

"As you know," Pnuchin said, "androids are the more cost-efficient way to provide twenty-four-hour home healthcare. Insurances prefer them in cases like yours."

Shay had seen androids before—on TV mostly, but occasionally in person, as drivers and aides to people in town. On the farm, though, it was just her and her husband, some migrant workers in the fall and spring. And unmoving as these androids were, they did not feel akin to humans, waving on the street, lifting bags of groceries. They seemed like what they were—machines, waiting for orders. She felt almost sick to her stomach.

"Ernst," she whispered, nearly frantic. "No, I don't think this is a good idea."

Pnuchin smiled, pretending not to hear.

"Let's just wait and see," Ernst answered, but his voice was strained. He stepped up to stand beside her. It was comforting to see him there, moving in infinitesimal ways even when he stood still.

"Doctor, could you explain"—he struggled for the right words—"how all of this works?"

"Certainly! That's my job." Pnuchin moved over to the table where the androids sat. Walking behind the three figures, he briefly touched their necks. All three androids, the two females and the one male, had short hair, cropped close to the head. For a moment, nothing happened.

"There are privacy policies you'll have to sign off on. We do collect a limited amount of data, for example, of the android's activities in your home—for your own protection and so that we can continue to improve on the networks. Other than that, since you've been pre-authorized on your insurance, you'll be responsible for a small co-pay. It's just a matter of picking the model you feel most comfortable with, and then we'll get started." Pnuchin stood back from the table.

With a jerk and an almost inaudible whine, the three androids lifted their heads simultaneously. Ernst flinched. Shay breathed in through her nostrils. The androids lifted their arms, blinked their eyes, almost synchronized in their motions. Then they grew still again. Now, though, there was a sentience about their stillness. One of the females had a flush in her cheeks. Their chests seemed to lift and fall ever so slightly, imitating breath. Shay looked at Pnuchin.

"You expect me to take one of these home?"

"Mrs. Ohleg —"

"It's not Mrs. Ohleg. We don't have the same last name."

"Ah. You didn't say before." Pnuchin paused, his arm uplifted awkwardly. He drew the arm down, folded his hands together. "I'm simply here to help you. We're not forcing you to accept an aide. Your doctor recommended it, but you can certainly leave if you want."

"Honey," Ernst took on the tone of voice, the tone that indicated that he was calm and that she was not. "I know it's weird, but let's give this a chance. At least talk to them." And then he glanced up at Pnuchin. "I mean, can we talk to them?"

An android answered instead. One of the females, dressed in pastel colors, a shirt of light blue and yellow pants, pushed herself up from the table. She stood. She was sturdy, short, with a determined set to her features now that she was animate.

"Ask us anything you like." The voice was comforting, encouraging, non-pressuring.

"You're a machine?" Shay said, half-asking, half-stating.

"We are not programmed to think of ourselves in that way." The android dipped her head. "My name is Sarah. I am a caretaker."

"I don't need a caretaker," Shay answered. "I need a registered nurse."

The android smiled slightly, and she nodded her head. "I am sorry if I misled you. I am fully trained and licensed."

Pnuchin started to speak. He held out a tablet. There was a document on the screen, a list of certifications or titles.

"They license androids?" Shay looked at Ernst in disbelief.

"They're qualified to do anything a human nurse might do. In many ways, more qualified." Pnuchin gestured with the tablet again, trying to catch Shay's eye.

The android moved around the table. She put a hand on Pnuchin's arm as if to interrupt him. He glanced at her quickly, a twitch of his eyebrows betraying momentary aggravation.

"I promise you, Shay." She came near Shay, but not within distance of touch. "I can do as much or as little as you like. When you don't want me, it will be like I am not even there."

"Just collecting data," Shay whispered, looking at her, but speaking primarily to Ernst.

"I'm sorry," Ernst said to the android. Shay twisted to look at him. She regretted the movement. She was still sore. Ernst looked away and refused to meet her eyes.

"I transmit data, yes." The android looked at Pnuchin, then back to Shay. "But I am merely a transmitter. I do not interpret. I do not analyze. That happens here, in R&D." She came a step closer. Now, if she reached out, she might be able to lay her hand on Shay's. Shay wondered what it would feel like. "When I am in your house, you are my sole concern."

"No." Shay's voice rose in pitch. "No, Ernst. I don't want this." She tapped on the chair's touchpad, looking for the controls to maneuver the chair.

"Okay, okay," Ernst tried to quiet her. He pulled her chair back toward the door. "I'm sorry, Dr. Pnuchin. We didn't mean to waste your time. It's been . . ." He was searching for the right words, and Shay focused intently to hear what he would say next. "It's been a rough few days."

"No—of course. Don't worry about it. It's not for everybody. I'm sure if you reached out to your insurance, they would approve a regular aide, though I don't know for how many hours."

Pnuchin walked up behind the android, behind Sarah, and he reached his hand up toward her neck. Shay glanced at the android's face, dark like she'd lived in sun her whole life. She had gone very still.

Shay could not even catch her eyes blinking. But the flush had returned to her cheeks. There were wrinkles at the corner of her mouth, almost as if she was setting her teeth in preparation for something unpleasant. Shay felt her breathing tighten. Her face was warm.

"Wait," she said softly. She repeated it louder. "Wait."

Pnuchin lowered his hand, shook his lab coat down to his wrist. "Yes?"

Ernst bent over her left shoulder. "Shay?"

"I don't feel like arguing with the insurance." Her throat was dry. "If you're insisting I have an aide, we might as well take her."

Ernst sighed heavily, out of relief or confusion.

"Great." Pnuchin clapped his hands. "Let's just fill out the paperwork."

As Ernst moved into the small adjoining office to complete the necessary forms, Shay looked at the android and tried to see if she was happy or sad to hear the news. She just looked down at her hands.

"Sarah." She spoke the name slowly, testing it out. The android raised her head. She smiled brightly, each tooth white and straight.

"It's all right," she answered, as if she understood some question that Shay was afraid to ask. "You will feel better."

There was a flash of anger, hot as sulfur. "Fuck you." She had wanted to say the words, to someone, to anyone, for days.

Sarah did not flinch away or shift uncomfortably. Her eyes grew sad, though Shay was not sure how.

Then, feeling as if she owed the android some further answer, Shay added, "I don't think I will." Shay saw the truth of it as she said it, understood the fear of all that time stretched out in front of her, the fear of looking in Ernst's face every day and seeing an accusation there. Maybe not every day, but one day, unexpectedly after a fight. She felt it like a gut punch now.

"What does it feel like?" Sarah's question was simple. It seemed to come from ignorance rather than care. But no one else had asked, not even Ernst. They had assumed.

She blinked and tried to find the right words. "Like I never want to see another human being as long as I live."

2.2:   SEPTEMBER 2058

They're sending someone out tomorrow to test the soil."

Ernst set his phone down on the dining room table. Plates and silverware were laid out for dinner. Sarah was chopping up the last of the tomatoes from the store for a salad. There had been a tiny placard hanging over that part of the produce section, explaining predicted shortages for many of the fruits and vegetables. Shay had still taken two, green around the stem, with the neighbor staring at her the whole time.

She unwrapped the bread from its cellophane. "What will that turn up?"

Ernst shrugged his shoulders. "If I knew, I wouldn't need to get it tested."

"From the county?"

He looked at her, one eyebrow raised in question.

"Someone from the county is coming to do the test? Not one of Greenex's reps?"

"Yeah." He fiddled with the glass of water at his place setting. "Is this from the tap?"

"Yeah. I can throw it out if you want. There's bottled." Ernst nodded. But it was Sarah who took the glass and emptied it, grabbing a cold bottle from the fridge. Shay moved slowly. Today, the pain was sharp, stabbing into her abdomen.

"I saw a bird near the porch," Sarah said. As happened often, Shay and Ernst looked at her, struggling for context. Her face didn't give them any hint.

"What type of bird?" Shay asked.

"A dead one."

The words fell heavy in the room. Ernst cleared his throat as if trying to come up with an appropriate response. Shay thought the air felt warm and stale. So as to do something, she hobbled to the oven and checked the chicken.

"You feeling alright, Shay?" Ernst leaned on the counter, fiddling with the top of the bottle. He just couldn't let his hands rest, be still. He'd hollowed out over the past three months, ever since they'd left the hospital. She ignored his question.

"Did you hear Sarah?" she countered. "Another one. How many did you find yesterday?"

"Maybe one of the neighbors put out poison." He looked down, refused to meet her eyes.

"There hasn't been a coyote around in ages. Why would they? Would be more danger for the local dogs than anything else."

Ernst shrugged. He also refused to look at Sarah, and it sat there, unspoken between them. The neighbors had had an odd way of welcoming them home, with Sarah pushing the wheelchair.

"Well, screw them," Shay said. Sarah looked at her, a question on her face. Shay waved her off. "Dinner is coming out now, so better sit down."

She couldn't lift the pan out of the oven, so she stepped aside and Sarah came near, unobtrusively as she did, and helped her. The steam condensed on her cheek ever so briefly and then it was gone, like frost on a windowpane in the sun.

"The vegetables too," Shay said, her way of contributing, though it was doubtful Sarah would forget.

From the table, sitting down, Ernst said quietly, "I called about the crop insurance today."

"And?" She was afraid to round the island and join him.

Sarah went anyway, carrying both trays of food. She had forgotten to use pot holders, though usually she did to ease the discomfort of those watching. *It's just a different type of organ,* she had explained once when Shay had wondered about her skin. You could, after all, stab an android like her, one from the medical labs, and there would be blood and some simulation of pain. She had not thought of doing so for months. Sarah had become so indispensable.

"Well, they're not sure. They're the ones who put me onto the soil test."

"Not sure?" She supported herself with one hand on the wall and left the kitchen. Sarah had already pulled out her chair. *So gallant,* Ernst had teased. Once. "Not sure they can pay what they owe us? We paid into it enough over the years. Did you talk to Simon? Or just the assistant?"

"Give me a little bit of credit. I talked to Simon."

She felt it, the little pang of regret. She tried to bite her tongue, but her temper was so fragile now, easily lost. She held out a spoonful of carrots and he accepted them on his plate.

"Can you get the salad dressing, Sarah?" She tried to smile. The android nodded and returned to the kitchen. When she had gone, lingering in the kitchen because she had learned Shay's cues by now, Shay rested the serving spoon on the table and looked at Ernst. She was quiet and waited for him to speak. He didn't. He began to saw at his chicken.

"Ernst." She tried to remember what it was like to say that name when she had been in love. She loved him now, she knew that, but she no longer had the patience to be in love. Some days it was all she could think about, the loves she had lost. "Tell me what he said."

"He doesn't know if it will qualify under natural causes." He held his knife in his hand, expectantly, requesting permission to return to his food.

"Plants. And they died. It's the most natural thing in the world."

"There are new reports coming out. About the fumigant we used."

"The pesticide?"

He nodded. He laid the knife down and dropped his forehead into his hands. There was something like the tension of tears in the tight slope of his shoulders. She shoved herself up from her chair and went to him. She rested one hand at the nape of his neck and gently rubbed it. His shoulders shuddered.

"Ernst," she said. And this time it was not a request, but a consolation. She nestled her chin into his hair. "It will be alright."

"No." He pushed back his chair, almost violently. She stumbled back a step. "Damn it, Shay. We fucked ourselves out of everything."

"Well, what are they saying? I thought it was a new formula, something safer. It was supposed to make the plants hardier."

"That's what they always say. At first." A laugh trembled at the corner of his mouth, frightening to watch.

"But the EPA—"

"It doesn't matter, Shay." He said each word slowly, a long pause between each. "It's in the groundwater now. And in the soil. Hell, probably in the air, too. With a longer half-life and less discrimination in what it kills."

The tears were standing in his eyes, the corners of his lids red. He looked at her and there was something else he wanted to say, something she didn't want to hear. She swallowed and, with effort, forced herself to keep her hands at her side, not to wrap them around where she felt the echo of an older pain.

"So that's what Simon said? All of that?"

"Might as well have." And he suddenly slumped, pulling the chair back to the table, wrapping an arm around her waist, and staring at his plate. She wanted to shift herself and break free, but she felt frozen there, trapped by his arm.

"Honey," she said, trying to find her way back to the names they used to call each other.

"We've lost it all," he said, under his breath, perhaps to himself. "Your cancer, our—"

She cut him off. "It might still qualify. Maybe the insurance money will still come through."

He lifted his head and his eyes were dark and wet in his pale face. He read something in her face of what she couldn't say and it quieted him. "And the year after that? And the year after that? The soil is ruined. I don't see how we can even afford to move."

"Wait for the test," she whispered back, fighting against the gorge rising in her throat.

"Sure, yeah." And he released her. She used the table as a support and returned to her own chair. He lifted his fork and speared the chicken. And he began to eat as if nothing had happened.

Shay rubbed her left hand with her right, trying to soothe the tremors in her fingers. Sarah cleared her throat and came back into the room, two bottles of dressing in her hand. A fly tapped against the light fixture above.

"I wasn't sure which type you wanted." She set them both on the table, then looked from one to the other of them. "Can I help you with anything else?"

"We're alright, Sarah." Shay tried to smile. "You can come in and sit with us if you'd like."

Sarah tilted her head, her understated way of saying *no* or disagreeing. "I'll start the dishes."

Shay bit her lip, fighting something, tears or screaming.

———

"Hey, Simon, didn't know you would be out, too." Ernst shook his hand as cheerfully as he could, trying to forget his tone in their last conversation. Shay had given him a lecture as she lay in bed, the early light creeping between the blinds and resting on the dark skin of her cheek, warning him not to assume the worst until the worst was confirmed. There was something perversely comforting in the conversation after months of quiet.

A woman stood quietly behind Simon, her dark hair caught back under a scarf. She wore a short lab coat, and the pockets of it were stuffed full of folded papers. She carried a large bag under one arm that clanked slightly as she moved.

"Ernst Ohleg." Ernst reached out a hand to her, but she had none free to return the gesture. She smiled and nodded, but he found himself questioning every move she made. Had she already condemned the soil as no good?

"Sadi," she said. Her voice was deep, raspy.

"The fields are out back." He waved his hand expansively. "Obviously."

Sadi humored him and laughed. Simon shook his head and hung back to walk with Ernst as she forged ahead. She walked with heavy, deliberate steps, like someone almost too comfortable with the ground.

"Why are you here?" Ernst asked the question explicitly now.

Simon shrugged his shoulders, but there was an answer waiting.

"Be straight with me, Simon. I'm not in a mood for dancing."

The insurance agent had thick eyebrows and he used them to good effect. "We've known each other a long time, Ernst. And I have to say, upfront. I have a bad feeling about this."

Ernst's initial instinct was to quibble about the definition of *up-front.*

"What do you mean by that? Be upfront if you're going to be upfront."

"We were out at the Jansens' farm last week. I think she knew just by the feel of the soil itself." The last observation was spoken almost in awe. Ernst looked skeptically after Sadi.

"Jansens are only a bit down the road from us."

Simon nodded, waiting for Ernst to piece it together, refusing to say it himself.

"You're saying the Jansens' soil was bad. How bad?"

Simon shrugged sadly as if delivering condolences. For that matter, he was. Break out the black suit and tie. "Half-life of this new stuff is off the charts. And it leaches away everything."

"Recovery time?"

They had reached the backyard, a gentle slope down to the fields with plateaued flower and vegetable gardens that Shay used to tend. Sarah was out there now, tying together empty stalks from the plants that were done producing. Simon almost waved to her, mistaking her for Shay. He lowered his hand sheepishly when he realized his mistake, but she did not look their way or respond.

Maybe half of the fields, patchy and balding, were covered with corn and soybeans. But the bare soil stood out, paler than it should be. He could see the dry clods from here. It wasn't the rich dark earth he remembered watching his father till up as a kid, when the thump and buzz of the plow and tractor whirred in his ears even after he had climbed into bed, the noise drilling deep into his subconscious, establishing the way the world should sound.

"I don't think they have sense memories," Ernst said absently, out of rhythm with the present conversation and half-stuck in the past where the soil was healthy.

"Huh?" Simon also looked preoccupied. He was watching Sadi progress through the fields. Every half-acre she would pause, kneel in the troughs of the field, open her toolbox, remove her drill, obtain a plug of dirt, capsule and label it, then stand again to continue down the field. "Sense memories?"

"Nothing." What he meant had been grounded in some undergrad memories of Proust and madeleines. "I was just thinking about Sarah, about androids in general."

"I have to admit, Ernst, I was surprised when I heard you were bringing that one home with you."

Something angry and sad shifted like acid in Ernst's gut. He cleared his throat. "What did you say the recovery time would be?"

Simon stared at him a second. Then he realized what Ernst was actually asking. "The soil? There are only guesses now. New formula, new problems, no solutions worked out yet."

"It would be nice if they figured out the answers alongside the problems."

Simon tried to laugh and failed. The air was heavy around them, the humidity of early fall in Ohio.

"I guess if I'm just being honest, Ernst, it might be five to ten years, best estimate, until this soil is producing normally again."

"What are you basing that on?"

Simon shrugged. "Can only be so bad, right?"

Ernst felt a little light-headed. "Not sure how you define bad, Simon. Especially when what you're going to tell me next is that you're off the hook and that my insurance won't cover this."

"Unless you're God, applying pesticide ain't an act of God." Simon stiffened, crossed his arms, and looked straight ahead.

"Screw you too, Simon."

Sadi glanced back, a figure in miniature with white coat and a box full of instruments. A stereotype of a scientist at that distance. She waved when she noticed them watching her.

"Not that I'm in the mood for giving advice." Simon's voice

tightened. "But you might also consider moving Shay off this property, what with her illness and all."

"Maybe I could if the insurance money came through."

Simon didn't answer, but he turned around and headed back to his car, which was the second best thing that could have happened.

"Not much worse can happen now," he whispered to himself, as he followed Sadi's progress. And he tried to believe it.

2.3: FEBRUARY 2059

Ernst coughed and the sound was sharp, like a pistol shot, in the cold air. He could see his breath and he could feel the hairs in his nose freezing. He looked down at the bird at his feet and nudged it with the toe of his boot. Then he sighed and rubbed at his forehead and nose. He tugged back on his gloves and bent his fingers, open and closed, open and closed, to limber them up.

The loose board on the porch creaked when Shay came out behind him. He did not turn to look at her, but he could imagine the way she stood, just beyond the door but still holding it open as if afraid to commit to stepping outside. She would hold her cardigan close around her with her free hand, its gray and purple wool faded from years of wear.

"Is he here yet?"

"Soon." Ernst didn't know how he felt about the pronoun, probably wouldn't know until he saw the android step out of Burt's truck.

"You sure we can afford this?" The question, asked in that tone that set the hairs of his neck on edge, was an old one, asked night and night again.

"Nope. But we gotta spend some now in the hopes of making money back in the future. This growing season or next." And it was an old answer, recited now and worn down at the edges. The words came almost too easily. He was starting to believe them himself. He refused to let her see any more doubt, not after the day that Simon had called up with Sadi's results. She'd been in bed for three days after that. She'd only talked to Sarah. "Besides, federal policy is going to mandate it sooner or later anyways, with the new decontamination and safety protocols."

"Sarah wants to run into town to grab a few things. Do you need anything?"

He turned. "Are you going with her?" He was struck by how gaunt she looked, by how much the February sunlight washed out her skin.

"I don't think so. Not today. She—we—only need a few things."

"Don't worry about me." He tried to say it without resentment, without implications. He looked back down the driveway. A truck was turning in by the mailbox, tires spinning up the gravel. Shay coughed. She let the door finally slip closed behind her. He heard it click shut. She stepped down and stood behind him.

"You're going to catch a cold," he said, watching the truck. The sun bounced off the front window so he couldn't see either driver or passenger.

"I'm fine." Her voice was short, maybe a bit angry. He didn't check her face. "What is his name again?"

"Burt calls him John." And he slipped into using the pronoun himself. Pretty soon, he would be reading the same android rights screeds that Shay had started citing.

"But is that his name or a John Doe situation?"

The conversation was cut short by the slam of the car doors. Burt smiled at them and waved. "Hi there, Ohlegs!"

Ernst waited for Shay to scold or flinch, but she was gazing too intently at the passenger-side door.

"Burt. How's it going?"

Burt shrugged, shifting his ball cap off and on, smoothing the bill. "Day by day, neighbor. Day by day."

"I assume you brought John with you," he said, half-joking. He couldn't keep the note of hesitancy from creeping in at the back.

"He's here. He's just shy." Burt talked about the android as one might a small child. There was a moment when Ernst made the mental comparison, a moment where his brain shut off and restarted.

"So you don't need anything?" Sarah opened the door into the middle of the conversation, bags under her arm and a paper list folded in her fingers.

Shay shook her head as if breaking from a daze. "No, Sarah. Thank you."

"I have the keys, then. I'll take the jeep."

Shay nodded. Ernst glanced at her and noted again how sickly his wife looked, especially next to Sarah's obvious health.

As if triggered by Sarah's appearance, the truck door opened and a man stepped out. There was a fleeting instance in which Ernst could almost put his finger on exactly what made the man not a man, something rough about the face or distant about the eyes. But the sensation passed quickly. He had a farmer's tan untouched by months of winter.

"John?" Ernst took a step forward and held out his hand, mindful still of polite convention. John did not smile, but he took Ernst's hand. His grip was firm and unhesitating. Ernst could feel the lines and calluses of heavy labor. He was surprised artificial skin could replicate that, but then, the skin felt real enough too.

"I brought the contract with me." Burt reached back into the truck. As he rummaged for the paperwork, Ernst looked at Shay. Sarah had paused on the steps, watching the interaction intently.

"We don't need a notary or anything?" Ernst found himself reluctant to see the paperwork. He glanced at John, who stood silently by him.

"Not a car," Burt said quickly. He sounded almost irritated now, as if he wanted to be done with the transaction. "I think a signature is good enough. You'll just sign below my name. It's pretty typical to pass these leases around anyways. Who can afford to keep one on full time?" He finally appeared with a crumpled sheet in his hand, his face red, and he snapped his mouth shut quickly as he noted. "They have their own records, black boxes. So this is pretty much just a formality. Financial stuff is taken care of by the dealership once GPS and chip are synced up here. I've given them the heads up."

Ernst caught himself, forced himself not to shudder. After such a long time with Sarah, it was hard to hear Burt's casual description of the AI's less human qualities. He was growing soft, too used to the simulated expressions and personalities. And the transactions for Sarah had been shrouded in medical legalese.

"I called them this morning." Burt held out the contract to him, an old ballpoint pen under his thumb.

"And it's all set up?"

"I think that's what I've been saying." The tightness of Burt's voice was less disguised now. Burt crossed his arms and stared at the paper and pen in Ernst's hand as if forcing him to sign by sheer willpower.

The android moved slowly, tilting his head back toward the sky. He shifted his hat as if he was worried about keeping the sun out of his eyes.

"See? Syncing." Burt jabbed a finger toward the android.

Ernst nodded tightly, forcibly disillusioned of the fancy that the worker was watching for birds or feeling the wind on his face. There were hardly any birds to see, anyway. He squinted at the paper, scanning the lines of the contract and searching out where he should sign. The contract was fairly standard, if wrinkled and stained with dirty fingerprints. There was, in fact, another signature above Burt's. It had been a while since John had been turned back to the shop or received maintenance.

Beside him, the android dipped his head and his gaze settled on the porch. Ernst followed it, glancing protectively first at Shay. Then he realized that John was staring at Sarah. Sarah stood so still that the hair moving about her face looked unnatural. The keys swung loose in her hand. Shay followed Ernst's example and glanced at her aide.

"Sarah?" she said quietly, almost as if trying to wake her from a nap. Something crossed the aide's face, a look or emotion that Ernst had never seen before in android or human. It was anger and pain and happiness all mixed together—or that was as near as he could guess. The anger looked particularly out of place on Sarah's face. He had never seen her so much as frown. A shiver ran up his back.

"You alright, Sarah?" He raised his voice louder than he needed to.

As if the wind had shifted, the tension dissipated. Sarah smiled and nodded, held up the grocery bags and moved to the car. "I'll be back in under an hour," she said.

Ernst looked then to John, but the android was studying the fields now, fingers clasped in front of him.

"I don't have all day, Ernst." Burt's voice dispersed the last of the weirdness.

"Yeah, yeah, keep it together, Burt. I'm saving you money, after all, taking this old model off your hands."

Burt shifted in surprise, but looked properly chagrined. He mustered up a smile as Ernst handed back the signed contract. "I'll drop these by the dealership today. Expect an electronic copy. Just hope it works out for you."

Ernst tried not to read the comment as antagonistic. The instinct to do so came too quickly to him now.

"Me too. I can't afford to get sick, not now. I need John if we're going to work with that soil at all. And we'll hope for the best."

Burt nodded, tugged his cap down lower on his forehead. "You got the right idea." Ernst turned and looked back down the hill, at the expanse of dead fields. The soil looked deceptively rich from here, dark and scattered with the detritus of harvest. He thought of the fall and his fists clenched. He forced himself to uncurl his fingers. He'd had a bad cough for most of winter, but couldn't bring himself to go to the doctor. The cough scratched at his throat, just looking down at the fields, though there was no proof his illness was connected to the soil. He'd explained that again and again to Shay.

"It'll work out. I've got a good feeling." Burt slapped him on the shoulder and then turned back to his truck. "See you, Shay. Stay warm."

The truck's exhaust was sharp in the air. Burt had clung to his gas engine longer than most in the county. Ernst covered his mouth and nose with his arm and tried not to breathe in too deeply. Tried not to cough again.

The android wore a flannel shirt over a Henley, but no coat. He finally spoke. "Nice to be here. How can I help you?" As a laborer, he spoke largely in memorized niceties. Ernst wanted to believe there was some sincerity in his voice nonetheless. He needed to believe it, but the coded drawl, an affectation for the Midwest market, made it harder.

"Well, John, I need you to help me save this place." And the words, once out of his mouth, were too sharp and too clear. Shay wrapped her sweater closer.

"Let him come inside first, Ernst. Let him warm up."

Ernst looked at her, thin and frail, barely wider than the porch slats. And he imagined she was colder than him, that her lungs were colder than the ice in his own. But John wasn't cold, even though Ernst imagined the frost spidered ever so gently over his cheek, just next to the liquid eye.

"Of course, you're right," he said. And he motioned John ahead of him. "Go on in. Welcome home, I guess."

MARCH 2059

"I just think it might be a good idea." Shay tripped a bit over the words as Ernst glanced up at her. He swallowed his oatmeal and set down his spoon. All she had was a cup of imitation coffee. He watched the steam curl up in the cold air.

"I need to check the furnace again. See if the pilot light went out."

He shoved back his chair, the legs clattering over the linoleum. He pushed together bowl and spoon and cup more loudly than he needed to and collected them to take to the sink.

"Ernst." Her voice was almost scolding. But he looked at her and saw her eyes were wide and anxious, fixed on him. "Be still a moment."

"Every second I sit here—"

She laid a hand on the table as if she were laying it on his arm. She tried to move as little as possible now, so she sat still, her hand outstretched there. "John is in the fields. It's only March. There's time."

"Time for that and yet you want this done now."

"Sometime soon, I think."

"Why?" Or that's what he tried to say. The word came out choked and mumbled.

"Don't you think it's a good idea?"

He couldn't answer. He couldn't face the thought of Shay signing her will. There was a taste like acid in his mouth. He coughed and grimaced. He shifted his shoulders, trying to work out the pain in his chest. He didn't know that he was trying to hurt her when he said it.

"Who is there to give any of it to anyways?"

A bright red dot bloomed on each of her cheeks, something harsher and darker than shame or embarrassment. He could hear the grandfather clock ticking in the next room, an ancient heirloom that only seemed to work every other day. The cup clinked against the bowl in his hands. He turned away under the pretense of putting them in the kitchen. When he walked back into the dining room, he moved as quietly as he could. He held his shoulders tight, his arms thrust into his pockets.

Her lips were stretched thin as she answered. "I want to leave something for Sarah."

Ernst almost laughed. He threw his head back as if to do so and caught himself. "Sarah can't own property."

"I know that." She flung the words out sharply and angrily. "I mean, I know that she can't own a house or a car. But we can give her a few things . . ."

"No. No, we can't." He sat back down opposite his wife. "When we're done with her, she goes back to that lab. And when she's back in that lab, they wipe her memory except for what they've uploaded to their servers. And it's like we never existed. She doesn't exist. She won't remember or know anything we give her."

Shay glared at him, her eyes narrowed. "I know what she is, Ernst. I haven't lost my mind. What, do you think I'm a child?"

Then she repeated again, a little more softly, "I know who she is."

"If you know," and he hated the tone of his voice even as he leaned into it, "then why are you stuck on this? How would you give her anything?"

"I don't know. I haven't figured that out yet. I just wanted to let you know what I was thinking." She put a hand over her mouth and looked away, studying the scene framed by the window.

A spiral of smoke hovered over the fields hidden by the slope of the hill. John was burning out the dead weeds and stalks. Sarah was just in front, trimming dead brush away from the perennials next to the walk and along the line of the porch. He had noticed, now that there were two androids working on the property, that Sarah often tried to stay in shouting distance of John. He wondered again, as he wondered often, whether they could communicate with each other as easily as he might message his neighbor. But unseen and untraceable. Or if what he perceived as mimicry was merely a technical glitch. He was dealing with weeds; so was she.

"Ernst." Shay had clearly said his name more than once.

The morning light limned her head, caught the stray brown hairs and made them glow like gold. He almost caught his breath at the sudden ache—sharp, hard to distinguish from physical pain—when he looked at her.

"She's taken care of me. Every day, morning, noon, and night."

He pressed his lips together and looked down at his hands. There was a cut across his index and third finger, barely scabbed over, where he'd caught his hand on barbed wire. He didn't say anything, because he didn't want to anger her, not now when his throat was tight and he could not stand to move a step away from her, when she seemed just out of reach and insubstantial.

"I just want to do something for her in return."

He nodded his head, then bowed it, hunching over the chair, hands clasped together.

"You alright?" Her voice was gentle, prodding.

"Yeah, fine." His voice was husky.

"Ernst." A pause. "It will be alright."

He shuddered, shoulders first, and then wilted, sobbing, into the chair. His stomach ached and his forehead and his lungs.

"Ernst." Her voice held a note of fear or panic now. He could hear her chair scraping over the tile as she struggled to stand up. He held up a hand to stop her and held another hand to his mouth as if he could stifle the tears with sheer physical determination.

"Ernst." She reached across the table instead of standing up. Her fingers grazed his forearm. "What is it? Talk to me."

He looked at her. Her face was blurry, the lines around her mouth merely suggestions of anxiety. He wondered if she had had time, already, time to become used to the idea of it. Of leaving him and their house and the fields burning beyond. Or was it the opposite? Had she refused to face it despite all the talk of wills? He wasn't sure which it was, and that made it hard for him to answer her.

He found his breath.

"I miss you, Shay."

They stared at each other. He had not expected those words, those words dealing with the *now* rather than *then*.

"I'm right here." And she did not sink into softness or tears. Her voice was hard and unyielding.

"I've been right here," she continued. "I haven't gone anywhere. I've been right here for the past ten months." She straightened, drawing her arm back close.

"Then where have I been?" He said it softly, speaking almost to himself.

"You've been out there." And she jutted her chin toward the window.

The clock ticked. Sarah's footsteps moved backward and forward on the porch and then on the front steps.

"No lie there," he said, even more softly.

"You can't bring any of it back, Ernst. Right?"

He shrugged his shoulders. The screen door squeaked and then the main door opened and shut quietly. He could hear Sarah scrape her shoes on the front mat.

"More coffee, Ms. Verid?" Sarah walked by them to the kitchen. She looked at neither of them, picking diligently at her fingernails.

"No, I've had as much as I can drink of this fake stuff," Shay answered. "Perhaps some for Ernst."

He shook his head. "No. No, I'm okay, Sarah." He scrubbed at his eyes with the heels of his hands. "Has John come up yet?"

"I saw him go toward the barn." Her voice, disembodied, was a little harder to mistake for human. The edge of each word was so sharp and precise.

He stood up and glanced at Shay. "I'll call the lawyer," she said quietly.

"Sure."

He went to her and stood behind her chair. He laid a hand on each of her shoulders and bent in close to her so he could feel the warmth of her skin and smell her hair. "I'm sorry," he whispered.

And she leaned back into him, just for a moment, the weight of her head heavy on his arm.

TREY

JULY 2060

I have eyes on them," Hurd's voice crackled in his ear. Trey peered back over his shoulder, through the clouded back window of the narrow trailer, to the roof of the old chair factory. He saw the glint of a scope. He pressed himself closer to the wall by the door and moved his finger nearer the trigger on his gun.

"How many juvies?" he whispered. He desperately hoped the answer was none. He'd been lucky to encounter none yet.

There was a pause. A moment of static. Then heavy breathing and a muffled curse. "Not sure. Over twenty."

Trey dropped his head and blinked rapidly. He tried to steady his heartbeat. The air in the room was hot, unmoving. Sweat dripped down the back of his neck. There were ten agents crowded behind him in the abandoned construction office and their breathing, even quiet, seemed almost deafening. The AS did not breathe.

Trey raised his hand, signaling his agents to be ready.

"The juvies are armed. We have combatants," Hurd muttered into his ear again.

"Shit." Trey gritted his teeth. A nerve twitched in his eye.

"Send the AS in first," Hurd recommended. "Let them take the fire."

Trey turned and glanced over the agents behind him. "Helios, Ora."

He pointed two fingers in turn at each android, then crooked his arm back. "To the front."

They moved out of their crouches and into position near him. Looking at them in profile, he could see the joints at the jaw. As combat models, there was less care that they be indistinguishable from humans at a casual glance. Sometimes it was even to their advantage to stand out. Helios turned his head as if he had heard Trey's thoughts. His mouth crooked up at the corner. "We're going in first, sir?"

"They're children," Trey said. Helios nodded. Ora did not look at him.

"Mission is to disarm and evac," he said to them, his voice low.

"Know." Ora spoke only in simple verbs. "Acknowledged, sir," Helios added.

"Bastards," one of his men growled behind him. He was looking over Trey's shoulder. A young girl had come out of the house across the street. The curse was for the Civil Union, but it felt tired, worn out. The girl carried a rifle in her hands, and she gripped it like she knew how to use it. Pink-striped curtains fluttered in the windows behind her. Light reflected off of more metal stocks inside. The girl looked directly to the trailer door, though she could not see them clearly.

"We know you're there," she shouted. Her voice didn't tremble or quaver.

Trey glanced back at the huddled agents. The AS did not move beside him.

"We want to help. We're not military. I'm a special agent with the ATF."

"You're here with guns, so it makes no difference," she answered. She lowered her gun, aiming toward his voice. "I'm sent out to tell you we won't surrender."

"We're here to help you." He repeated it like a mantra, reminding himself that she was brainwashed by all proper definitions of the word.

"We don't need help." Her hair was cut short, golden-brown fuzz in the sunlight. "The feds can't give us no help." She pulled the trigger.

Trey grabbed Helios's shoulder and drew him back into the shadow. Ora jerked, his left arm swinging wildly into the air. The bullet had drilled through the ligaments in his shoulder. Ora frowned and stared at his own arm, which now hung uselessly at his side. A clear gel leaked from the wound. The gel was stained pink, as if someone had dropped red food coloring into egg whites.

Trey ripped off his own armored jacket and slung it to Helios. "Get her," he said. "Then get down behind the parked cars."

"Do?" Ora asked. His voice sounded hoarse, lagging.

"Exit through the back door. Approach the targets from behind. Subdue."

"You need your armor, sir," one of the agents hissed at him.

"They won't be any good to us injured."

"Damaged," the man retorted. And for a second Trey stared at him, wondering why he felt the need to make that distinction now, in the middle of this chaos.

"Helios, go."

As the first android moved out the door, the second reacted like a mirror image, fading back into the darkness of the trailer. His white hair blazed bright for a second against a poster of regulations on the wall, a poster with the image of a red cardinal and *Kentucky* printed proud below it. A new species overlaying an extinct one.

Helios crossed the open road between himself and the girl in a serpentine fashion, hunching over to provide as small a target as possible. His movements were quick and precise. The girl was screaming almost incomprehensibly, words that Trey could not understand. In every window behind her, rifles and shotguns appeared, gripped by children and adolescents.

"This is bad," Hurd said, presumably to himself. The other agents twitched as he said it.

There was a line of cars, pickup trucks with rusting paint jobs and shoddy electrical converters and small two-seaters with solar roofs, parked diagonally against the far sidewalk.

"It's always fucking bad," he muttered in response.

"It's a nursery rhyme," the agent behind him said. "That's messed up. A nursery rhyme with the words screwed up."

Ashes in the roses. Ashes in the roses. The feds ring round. We all fall down.

The girl lifted her gun as she finished, trying to get an aim on Helios, but he moved too fast and too erratically. The stock of the gun dipped and wavered as her arms grew tired.

Helios tumbled, head over heels, and came to his feet next to her. He gripped her by the knees, unbalancing her, and ripped the gun free from her hands. Flinging the gun to the pavement, he tore her off her feet and lunged behind the line of cars. They would offer some small protection from the other gunmen in the house. Gunmen. Trey almost laughed, hysteria rising from his stomach to his throat.

"This is taking too long," Hurd rasped. "Go in now. Go in hot."

Trey shook his head even as he gestured up and out. The agents straightened and ran out the front door in file. The thin aluminum walls of the trailer creaked at their passing. He followed behind, his gun held in an alert carry. His hands were sweating inside the thin gloves he wore. He glanced at Helios and motioned for him to stay down. Helios nodded. The girl was fighting against him, biting at his arm.

The agents weaved between the cars. Bullets rattled down on the automobiles, pinging like hail. One man grunted as a bullet caught him in the armored chest plate. He cricked his neck and worked his arm up and down to test it, then pressed himself up against the side of the house. Another agent moved to position on the other side of the door. Behind each, four more agents lined up, ready to enter. Trey transferred his gun into a ready carry, and gestured with his right arm. Forward, forward.

The agent on the right of the door whirled to face it, then kicked it down. The door split like cheap particle board and then cracked along the lock. It fell in. The agent pushed it out of the way and ten agents, and Trey, ran inside.

Gunfire erupted from upstairs. Two children turned from the downstairs windows to look at them with big eyes, one towheaded. Agents broke off to suppress them, prying the guns from their hands and twisting their arms behind their backs. They used plastic ties to bind their hands together.

"Feds inside," the towheaded kid screamed. Someone shrieked upstairs.

Trey led the charge up the stairs, scanning the top landing from side to side as more of it came into view. He saw the glint of the barrel before he saw the face of the girl craning through the banisters. As he jogged up, he slammed the gun hard, and the girl cried out and fell backward, her head cracking against the floor.

"Watch." Ora's voice sounded inhuman, bellowed like a bullhorn.

Trey reached the top step. The floor plan was open, no discrete rooms but signs that the walls had been knocked down recently. Plaster and exposed electrical wires covered the walls. A line of cots ran down the length of the open space on either side. There were more than ten children crouched between the cots and in front of the second-floor windows. They had turned to face the stairs, arms resting on knees, eyes at the sights of their guns.

Ora had wrestled down two of the children and bound their wrists behind them. They were screaming and grinding their teeth.

"Watch," he yelled again.

Trey turned in the direction he was looking. A child, no more than ten, rested his elbow on the railing that ran around the open stairwell. He stood farthest away from the top step, closest to the window, the last to turn away from repressing fire. He held a semiautomatic pistol and he was staring at Trey. His eyes were small and dark. Trey raised his hand, palm open, placating. At the same moment, he remembered that he wore no armor.

"Don't shoot," he said, his heart racing.

The agents that moved up behind him spread out to either side of the landing and began to systematically disarm the children, those closest to the stairs first. Most of the children did not resist, dropping their guns when compelled. The boy with the pistol glanced at his companions, taken into custody one by one, and his lips spread wide. He clenched his teeth and his eyes were wet. He did not lower the gun. His arm flexed slightly as he braced himself to shoot.

Suddenly, the boy's head snapped back and his body was propelled toward the wall. He slammed to the ground, face staring blankly up at the ceiling, and Trey saw the bullet hole and the blood at his forehead. He did not breathe for a second or two, then shouted, pain at his chest and in his throat as if something were trying to tear its way out of him, some howling animal. Ora holstered his pistol slowly, staring at Trey. His face was very still.

Trey shut his mouth. He breathed in through his nose. He could smell piss in the air. The other children were shocked by the boy's death. Color drained from their faces, their skin sickly white and yellow. The soldiers easily overpowered those still unrestrained, driving them to the ground. Trey walked between them. One child snapped at his boot. He bent down beside the boy who'd been shot. He gently loosened the boy's fingers around the pistol and sent it skittering away across the floor. Neck tight, he stroked the boy's hair and closed his eyelids. His hair was dark, roughly shaved down to the scalp. Blood pooled and trickled from his forehead. His skin was still warm.

Ora did not move. He watched Trey. Trey stood, but did not speak to him. He reached over the boy's body and lifted the gun from Ora's holster. Ora did not try to stop him. He stood still, solid, synthetic, unnatural. Then Trey left and went back down the stairs, unsure if it was grief or rage or disgust that made him feel sick. He walked outside and leaned against the side of the house, breathing hard. Helios looked over the car at him. He signed to Trey. *Clear?* Trey nodded, though he could not see clearly for the black dots in his eyes. Then he bent over and puked onto the sidewalk.

Trey leaned forward on his seat in the open bed of the truck. He rested his forehead in his hands, his elbows on his legs. His skin was still clammy. From the van in front, he could hear the screams and complaints of the recovered children. He was jostled between the other agents as the open-bed truck bumped over holes in the road. Stones bounced and rattled in the wheel wells.

He straightened and glanced toward the rear of the truck. Ora sat up stiff, his arms bound behind him. Helios sat opposite him and kept looking from Ora to the other agents as if waiting for someone to lunge at them. The two AS looked almost alike, thin white hair, chiseled features, sunken cheeks. Ora looked up and locked eyes with Trey. His uniform was still ragged and torn where the bullet had disintegrated the ligaments in his shoulder. The cloth was stained pink.

Ora's eyes were rimmed with red. Trey could not break the gaze until Ora turned his head away. His profile was sharp with shadows in the dying light. His face looked almost wet in the sunset.

3.2:   JULY 2060

Adrian's face, when she looked up from her desk, was a mix of trepidation, anticipation, and grief. He paused for a second in the doorway. He'd seen those emotions, in that combination, once before.

On a cold morning, before the fog had broken, as he approached her car. They were teenagers. She had wanted him to run away.

"You look like you need a drink," she said now. "If I could offer you one."

She sat very still and very straight, and for a moment he just stared at her. He hadn't seen her in years, not at his promotion to head agent of the Louisville field office, not at her installment as acting director of the ATF. Her skin was darker, years of sun and deserts and combat. Her jaw was squarer. "What? They don't let you have alcohol in the ATF?" It was a bad joke, but he couldn't find any other words in the moment. He wasn't ready to face the issue at hand, not with her.

He took the chair she pointed to. He moved slowly.

"Are you alright?"

He looked up sharply at her question, and she shook her head slightly, corrected herself. "Are you hurt, I mean?"

"Do you normally call in the field agents for a direct report?" He didn't answer her question. He hadn't taken any injuries, but most days in the past week it didn't feel that way.

"If I'm being honest, no." She paused. "But there've been a lot of questions."

It stung a little bit to hear that answer, the official rhetoric of it. And he hadn't thought he'd be able to feel that.

"A question for you," he said, a misleading lilt in his voice. "Can you imagine what it looks like to see a child shot in the head?" And he rubbed his hand across his mouth right after he said it, already wanting to take the words back. She blanched, as he had expected her to, and her mouth drew very thin.

"I've seen a lot of terrible things, Mr. Caudill." She breathed in. "And I read your report," she said, each word quiet.

He looked around the room rather than meet her eyes again so soon. There was a small cube of wood and glass on the table beside him, an ornament or fidget device. He picked it up. "How did it feel to be on that side of the paperwork?"

"Like shit." And, as quickly as that, the formality between them shattered. He knew that husky note of anger on the edge of her voice. "I wish I'd been in the field with you, Trey. That I could have helped."

He sighed and set down the cube. "It's not about who wasn't there."

He finally looked at her. She was staring at the desk, at a closed manila folder. "Are those pictures?"

"I'm responsible for reporting on the actions of our AS in the field." She spoke tentatively, feeling her way forward.

"Cut and dried. Remove them from the field. Recycle them."

"It's not that easy."

He felt the blood flush up into his face, the anger so close to the surface, so easy to call back up.

"Maybe we should step out for a drink," she said, watching him.

He stood up and stepped closer to her, though the desk was a barrier between them. He leaned forward over it, punctuated his statement by slapping the wooden surface. "It killed a kid." He found it hard to count the days between the raid and now, hard to imagine that he hadn't watched that boy's head snap back just a day ago. But it had been a week at least, maybe two. He hadn't left his apartment much since returning from the raid. Even now, this room felt too bright, the walls of glass little defense against the crowded sidewalks where he imagined every person he passed knew what had happened, what he had witnessed, what he had let happen.

She cleared her throat and stood up so that he wasn't looking down at her. "Do you want to get a drink or not?" But he saw the warning in her eyes.

"What are you not saying?" And he was stubborn still, pressing for the loss.

"It's no good me saying it now. You won't be able to hear it."

He realized he was clenching his teeth, his jaw tight. He tried to focus on his breath, find some calm, and found himself unconsciously imitating Eli. He had never seen the man lose control.

"Whitaker wasn't there," Adrian said, somewhere between a question and a statement. It was now, like it always had been, as if she could read his thoughts. And she was consciously redirecting him away from that lingering silence around the AS's fate. *Ora,* he forced himself to remember the name, if only so he could see it properly destroyed.

"It means *prayer,* doesn't it?" he asked, ignoring her prodding. "Ora pro nobis." Her face was still. He found himself waiting for her to blink. "Or *pray* maybe. Like the verb."

"Stop being a dick."

He put on an expression of exaggerated shock. "What do you mean by that?"

"I'm not going to play games with you."

"Then don't." He eased himself back into the chair, ceding the high ground to her. "Tell me what's going to happen to that AS."

"So you don't want to talk about Whitaker." She smiled, frustration at the corners of her mouth. "Because one day our intel will be good and he'll be there when we bust down the door."

"I'm not the one playing games now," he said.

She sighed and sat down as well, crossing her legs. There was a gentle metal whir as she moved, almost too soft to hear. "Fine." She folded her hands and fixed him with her gaze. "The AS, call sign Ora, is in containment. He won't be back in the field anytime soon. He's been questioned and his memory has been examined."

"Okay, two questions." He laughed and the anger was right there, so close. The nausea too. "First of all, *he?* That's my first question. *He.* Secondly—" And he couldn't stay still afterward. It hadn't been long since he'd used the same pronouns for the android. He launched himself up again and he paced in the narrow space in front of her desk.

"Why hasn't it been decommissioned and scrapped? Why hasn't it been smashed down into the size of that paperweight?"

"Too valuable to smash, Trey."

He coughed, almost, in his surprise. She sounded calm, looked calm, but he asked anyway. "You signed off on this?"

"Technically, I didn't have to. The AS don't ultimately report to me."

He found himself frozen, unable to move.

"Trey." She leaned forward a bit, her hands over the folder. "Ora didn't malfunction."

The blood ran cold in the back of his neck. He rubbed it with the palm of his hand. "What are you saying?"

"He didn't malfunction." The words were so definite, so clear. Her skin was white, right on the ridge of her cheekbones. This was harder for her than it looked, but he refused to make it any easier.

"You want to explain what you mean?"

"Not really. But if you need me to spell it out."

The air was still between them as if they were both holding their breath.

"Spell it out, Adrian." And he knew before she said the words what she would say. He knew it with the same surety that he had known all those years ago she would be waiting there at the end of his drive, the car idling, when he'd asked. It had almost made him change his mind again when she rolled down the window and her eyes were bright, just on the edge of tears. Had almost made him open the door and climb in with her and actually leave. Maybe they wouldn't be standing here now if he had.

"What are the chances?" she said instead. As if she could tell what he was thinking, almost as if his face reflected that bright look now. As if his invocation of her name had summoned up the years-old memory. "What are the chances that it would be you and me now, here, talking about Whitaker?"

He felt almost queasy. "We're not talking about Eli."

"Aren't we?"

It was, and had been, somehow always Eli between them. "Say what it is that needs saying."

She sighed and looked down at her hands, as if she had been truly hoping he'd relent.

"Ora didn't malfunction. That boy had a gun and he would have shot you. He would have killed you."

"You don't know that." A sudden, almost biting sharp pain just at his chest.

"Video footage," she said softly. "Given the evidence, Ora acted rationally. He made a logical choice to defend his commanding officer against an insurgent."

"You're talking about a damn kid."

"Do you really think I don't know that?" Her voice was low, now. Not soft, but dangerous. She was leaning forward slightly, the white in her cheeks red. "What do you know, Trey? Not enough to keep your head from getting blown off by a kid. You underestimated the enemy. You underestimated what Whitaker could do to those kids' minds. You, of all people. So that's why we're talking about Whitaker right now."

She took a breath, looked at him as if she was waiting for him to do something, say something. He didn't open his mouth. He tried to fight down the numbness working its way inward from his arms and fingers.

"That's why we're always talking about Whitaker any time you open your fucking mouth."

He nodded, slowly, looking away from her, down at his hands, which seemed very white and very cold, though he could not feel them.

"I think you should go," she added, finally.

"Yeah." He agreed, because he couldn't think of anything other to say. Though it scared him to leave the room right now, with this gulf widening between them again. He swallowed, and his throat felt tight. "I guess I thought you would see my side on this one, Adrian."

"It's been a long time since we saw things the same way."

He clicked his tongue against the side of his mouth, a sound to fill the gap where he should apologize. He hadn't really apologized then either, not until she had thrown the car into reverse and was too far away to hear or even see his lips moving. *I should have let you save me then.* It was what he had wanted to say. But he turned and left.

It was summer, heading toward evening, and the light hitting the tiled floor of the hallway was long and golden, intersected by pillared shadows. Trey looked at the benches, shoved close to the tall windows and placed at even intervals down the hall, and he thought about sitting. He worried that if he sat, late as it was, no one else would walk down the hall until Adrian herself left. And he would start thinking, something he wanted to avoid.

He glanced up when he heard the sharp footsteps, too precise and even for any human pace. He didn't know which of them was the deer caught in the headlights. The android stood still at the turn of the corridor, looking down the hallway at him as if it were surprised to see anyone there. Trey tried to think of what to do with his hands—should he put them in his pockets?—as the anger and shame boiled in his stomach. He wondered for a second, with the android's face shadowed, if it was Helios. Helios, after all, had been commended. Helios had been recommended for further service. Yet Trey could not think of Helios, his white filaments of hair shining in the dusty light of the trailer, without remembering that he had passed off his vest to him. If he'd had his vest . . . but Trey didn't let himself think past that. He didn't let himself turn and dwell on that one image seared in the back of his head.

The android walked closer, finally settling out of its alert state, and Trey saw that it did not walk with the stealthy gait of an AS. It wore the blue jumpsuit of a facilities worker. A key card rattled at its chest. It held a large black trash bag.

"Hi," he said, feeling foolish as he did so, wondering why he spoke.

The android seemed almost alarmed. It nodded its head to Trey, then tapped its throat, indicating that it had not been constructed with a voice box.

Trey shook his head, rapidly, and waved his hand as if to say *of course*. The android stared at him, as if wondering if anything was needed of it, and something in its face shifted as it watched Trey, as if it sensed his mood. There was a tension in the air between them, and Trey thought again of a deer who had sensed the human lurking behind the blind.

The android signed at him, and Trey struggled to follow the rapid gesture even though he'd picked up a few words and expressions while working with Helios and Ora. It had been their first mode of communication, founded on binary code, and he had noticed them communicating quietly with each other in the days before the raid.

"I don't understand," he said, giving up quickly. He let the anger into his voice. The android dropped its hands slowly, as if disappointed. Trey felt the pain at his temples, the creeping headache. Perhaps he did need a drink.

"Never mind. Get on with it." He turned away from the android, back to the window. The sky had darkened a bit, settling toward dusk, the sun dipping below the horizon. In the window, he saw the android stare at him a bit longer, then turn hesitantly back to its work, shifting the bag onto its shoulder.

And the guilt was sudden too. As the android's footsteps continued down the hall, he slumped onto the bench and put his head in his hands.

And there it was again, the image of Ora holstering his gun as the boy fell, his skin practically glowing, reflective in the light from the windows, like a vengeful saint. And he remembered thinking, then, even before the horror had hit him, *There it is, Eli, there's your message from God.* Yet at the same time the fleeting impression that he had been right, Eli had been right. The world was an evil place, truly.

A mantra repeated over and over, when watching the news, when reading, when serving dinner. *The world is evil. It will turn always to evil again and again.* It had taken a long time for Trey to shake those words from his head, a long time before he could sit down to eat and not hear that bitter prayer echoing in his ears.

He looked up. The setting sun was blinding. So he closed his eyes to the light and felt the heat on his face and he tried to imagine a world where he had never met Eli. Where Eli had never come by the group home and offered to foster a *troubled boy.* Where there had never been a moment of excitement to see a tall man, wiry and sharp angled, with a close-cut beard and a pocket knife at his belt. Where he had never been a child, holding a gun, with Eli's words of reproof always in his head.

3.3:   **FEBRUARY 2061**

H e's not here." Agent Wiley crouched behind the line of brush, looked back at Trey. He lowered his hand from his earpiece and waited for direction.

A motley group of ATF agents and soldiers from the National Guard were ranged behind him, some in camouflage, some in standard issue, the agents in bulletproof vests. Trey loosened his hold on his rifle and let the barrel swing toward the ground.

"Intel said he was." He wasn't sure if he was relieved or upset.

Wiley shrugged and spoke again into his comms. "Do a second sweep. Confirm initial report. Eli Whitaker not on the site."

The hill rolled down before them and the woods and scrub brush petered out. An old farmhouse nestled in the valley, dead fields—probably poisoned—stretching beyond it. A rusted-out tractor sat in the yard and everything seemed quiet. No sign of activity as at every former location, no sounds of children chanting, no laundry rippling on the clothesline. The house reminded him of his childhood home, same A-frame roof, same clapboard siding, same dilapidated porch. Another abandoned property in the wake of Midwestern farmers migrating north. *Reminded him of Eli's house, not home.* And that's why he had been so sure he would find him here.

"How long have we been at this?" He wasn't sure he meant to speak aloud.

"Today, you mean?" Wiley asked.

Trey shrugged. It had been less a question, more a comment. Eli had been recruiting men, women, and children into the militia for at least three years now. And they seemed no closer to taking Eli himself. And as long as Eli was out there, just that one man even, the Civil Union wasn't dead or gone. And Trey would be forced to follow after him, just like he did as a kid, struggling to keep up.

Perhaps Adrian had known. Perhaps she had known Eli wouldn't really be here. She seemed to have a second sense for where he would and wouldn't be, a sense Trey was lacking.

A light blinked below them, an AS leaving the house and standing on the porch, the sunlight glancing off its metallic exoskeleton. No need for vests with these new models. Wiley's earpiece crackled and Trey switched his own comms to the AS's frequency so he could hear the report as well. This model was keyed only to his own and Wiley's voice signatures.

"No sign of target Whitaker," the AS reported, its voice unfailingly even.

"No one on the premises, sir," Wiley repeated.

Trey tilted his head and studied the house and the surrounding fields and grass. "Signs of recent occupation? Our intel isn't more than a day old."

Wiley passed on the information, phrased as a directive. The AS moved its head in their direction and Trey wondered if it could see them, whether it could study the expressions on their faces. He felt suddenly exposed and vulnerable. He remembered the hot heavy air in the second floor of that house last summer, the steps creaking under his weight, the boy staring at him from across the landing, pistol aimed at his chest.

"A few dishes in the sink. Recently used," Wiley repeated when Trey did not pay attention to the initial answer.

Trey felt a tingling in his neck, a sinking feeling in his stomach as he stared down the hill. He kept his eyes on the AS.

"How long has the AS been in the house?"

Wiley looked at him, confused. A few other soldiers craned their necks in his direction, tuned to the urgency in his voice. Trey did a quick sweep of the other men and women in his command, as if to confirm what he already knew. There was only one AS on this mission, only one on the porch of the house, waiting for an order.

"Caudill? Sir?"

"How long has the scout been down there? How long out of our eyesight?"

Wiley looked down at his watch. "Ten minutes maybe, fifteen at the most."

"Cut the comms."

Wiley glanced down toward the house and back, not verbally questioning, but concerned.

"I'm not asking a second time." Trey's voice was sharp and loud, even to his own ears.

"Done." Wiley did not bother to mask the disapproval in his tone.

Trey watched the AS when it realized it had lost connection to the agents on the hill. It looked back at the house and then focused again on the line of the woods. It raised one hand as if waving to them.

Wiley looked to him for direction.

"Do we have aerial images of the property?"

"Drones went over about an hour ago." He handed Trey a thin tablet secured in a metal case. The images were almost sepia-toned in the early morning light, objects colored in only the faintest hues.

"There's a truck here," he said, pointing to the box-like shape of the vehicle. It was parked close to the side of the house opposite their location.

"Probably doesn't run. Lots of old vehicles on these abandoned farms."

The AS tapped the side of its head as if wondering why the comms were not working. It signed at them. A second agent with binoculars on the house translated for them.

"He's asking if there's a malfunction with comms."

"Don't answer that. I just want to watch it for a second."

The agents shifted uncomfortably. The soldiers hardly moved. They were still tensed and ready for combat.

The AS dropped its hands, almost as if in frustration, and moved toward the porch steps. Trey wasn't sure if he imagined a jerkiness in its movements, like a screen glitching.

"How secure is the AS network?"

Wiley finally straightened, moving up onto his knees. "You want to just say what you're worried about?"

"It's been compromised."

"Sir. In the last fifteen minutes? I don't think that's even possible. I've never seen an AS compromised in that way."

Agent Ainslow, the R&D liaison now assigned to his team—one had been assigned to each office utilizing AS—took a step forward. "AS manage their own internal security protocols. They can't be hacked. They're not static, they're not a safe to be broken into."

Trey's hand twitched on his gun, sweat slick between his fingers. His heart pounded at his throat and he heard Ora's voice bellowing in his head. *Watch.*

"Eli's here." His voice caught in his throat, almost hoarse.

Ainslow opened her mouth to object, but he raised a hand to silence her. She frowned.

The woods were quiet behind them, the field and the house still before them. The only thing moving was the AS, which now worked its way steadily across the lawn and toward the foot of the hill.

"Sir, we know your history with Whitaker. We heard about the raid in July. Is it possible you're misreading this situation?" Wiley's voice was placating.

Trey didn't answer. Down below, the AS stumbled, almost dropping to one knee and barely recovering its balance in time. Wiley followed his line of sight.

The AS shouted from the bottom of the hill. "Malfunction?" It was hard for Trey to hear it as a question.

"Stay there." He held up his hand. *Stop.*

"What's wrong?" The timbre was always different than he expected. There was something inhuman about the vibrato. It was a voice designed to be heard across battlefields but muted for conversation.

But the AS did stop, hands still at its side, looking up at him. Its exoskeleton, covering chest, back, and pelvis, was a matte gray, but its arms were translucent white like Ora's.

In the quiet following the AS's question, there was the distinctive noise of an old gas engine turning over. The AS turned its head toward the sound. For a moment, the entire group stood stock-still, straining for the sound of acceleration.

"Move! Move! Move!" Trey motioned for the agents and soldiers to swarm the house. He turned to Ainslow. "Disable it."

"I can't do that without a higher authorization."

"I'm the lead agent."

She shook her head, half-distracted by the soldiers and agents moving into a crouch and descending the hill. "It would have to come from the DC office."

Trey's face flushed hot. "That would be too fucking late."

He walked away from her, from the accusation in her look. "Set up a barrier on Route 19." He spoke into his comms to the agents who had remained with the trucks on the road.

The AS took one step up and paused. The gears at its shoulders and knees buzzed as it strained to hold itself still. "Sir," it barked, awaiting orders.

"Not a step further, soldier," Trey yelled at it. He pointed his rifle at the AS. He could hear Adrian's voice in his head. *Eli hates this sort of technology. You really think he hacked an AS? You really think he's capable of that?*

"I can answer any questions you have, sir." The AS's voice, still clear, unstrained, his poise undisturbed by the soldiers flanking him and moving toward the house.

"Who is that?" he shouted, his own voice cracking in anger. "Who is that, then? What did you miss?"

The AS looked up at him, eyes with perfectly white sclera, perfectly brown irises, no sign of bloodshot or weariness. But it had no semblance of skin, not even on its face, unlike Helios and Ora, just a molded head with a painted surface and joints at the jaw. "I identified no threats in the house. Primary target Whitaker is not there."

"Agent Caudill." The comms interrupted any thought of answering. Trey did not take his eyes off of the AS. "Agent Caudill, we have the truck and we have the driver." Someone was laughing in the background, an odd sound.

"Is it Whitaker?" The AS stared at him as he asked, watching him as closely as Trey did it. He held his breath, waiting for the answer from the other end.

"No. It's a kid. Girl. Says her name is Lia. Maybe eleven years old."

"Does she have any weapons on her?" Trey found it hard to find his breath again.

"She had a hunting knife. And a pistol. But no ammo."

The breath came out as a cough. He relaxed his finger on the trigger of the rifle. "Coming down. Hold her there." He pressed a button on his earpiece and the ever-present hum went quiet.

"So you missed the girl?" Trey moved sideways down the hill toward the AS, gun held close but not aimed at its head.

"I did not miss her." The AS did not move. "I identified no threat. I thought it best that she go home."

"You saw the girl and you let her go?"

The AS did not answer right away, as if it was processing Trey's question, as if it did not fully understand the criticism inherent in the repetition.

It was late winter, but the sun was warm on his shoulders. He could feel sweat on his forehead under the helmet. There were no sounds of birds or insects. Instead, like most of the Midwest, there was a heavy stillness in the air as if the sky and fields were waiting for a perpetual storm to break. He shifted the gun in his arm, raised it slightly.

"She was a child. She ran away from me. No threat. No signs of aggression."

"New programming," Ainslow said at his elbow. He had not noticed she had followed. "In these models."

The AS turned its head away as if granting them some privacy or avoiding the discussion of its inner workings.

"Determining whether a child is a threat and reporting that a kid is in the house, those are different things."

"Yes. But related things. Not perfected yet, I guess."

"You guess? They shouldn't be in the field." Trey tried to control the volume of his voice. "They shouldn't be in the field if they can't do their jobs right."

The AS did not move and did not make a sound. Trey's face felt cold, his head light. She didn't answer, but he could interpret the unspoken objection, the discussion to be had about the fallibility of humans.

"I did not mean to alarm you, sir." The AS took another step back, creating a distance between them. "Permission to join the agents at the roadblock?"

The sunlight bounced off of the bright unpainted metal at its joints. Trey finally lowered his head. "Report to Agent Wiley."

"Sir." And the AS turned and moved away. It jogged over the uneven ground, avoiding the hillocks that had caused it trouble in its approach.

"What is its call sign?" Trey asked Ainslow, unable to turn away or move just yet.

"No call sign. Just a numerical code." She didn't offer up the code.

"It's different than last time," he muttered.

"Different because of last time." She opened a program on her watch and jotted down a note. "From what I can tell right now, limited resources and all, AS 7.3.219 is working as programmed. I'll put in a ticket to reexamine threat determination protocols."

He unstrapped his rifle and set it gently on the ground. Then he sat down beside it. She stared at him.

"Not because of anything I said."

Ainslow raised an eyebrow.

"Don't do anything because of me."

"I observed it too."

"Right. Well, then." And he dropped his pounding head into his hands. He could hear the gunshot in his head again. Punctuating Eli. *It will turn always to evil.*

"All due respect," Ainslow said quietly. "They shouldn't have released you to active duty."

He blinked. Sniffed and ran a hand through his hair, knocking his helmet back on his neck. "No respect needed."

3.4:   JANUARY 2062

The land was desolate, the furrows of the fields white with frost. Stands of dark trees, bare branches black against the sky, whipped by him on both sides of the road. There was litter in the ditches of yellowed grass: empty beer cans, fast-food wrappers, a discarded shoe. Abandoned farm equipment loomed behind the wood and wire fences, green and rusting. He gripped the wheel with both hands as he rounded the tight curves of the road. His tires spun up gravel behind him. The holstered gun in the passenger seat shifted back and forth over the leather. There was an animal shelter set back from the road that had spelled out on their sign: FULL. CAN TAKE NO MORE CATS OR DOGS. The shelter looked long abandoned.

Soon after he had passed the town sign, he saw the small church of red brick. *First road on the left after the church.* A graveyard crept up the hill behind the church. Mounds of upturned dirt marked burials in the past year. The gate to the graveyard had swung open so the word *cemetery*, in scrolled ironwork, read backward. A hawk or falcon flung itself into the sky from atop the steeple, screeching. He craned his neck and leaned across the passenger side to follow its flight from the window. The car swerved, so he braked and slowed to a stop.

After the bird was gone from his sight, he leaned back into his seat and rested his head on the headrest. He closed his eyes and flexed his fingers on the wheel, open and closed. The countryside was quiet outside the car. The wind whistled in the loose seal of his driver-side door. He lifted his foot off the brake and accelerated.

The road he turned onto was narrow, unmarked with yellow lines. The purple paint was peeling from an old school bus stop at the intersection. Someone had spray-painted over the school mascot and name, so that the cheerful wildcat's tongue now lolled out of his mouth and his eyes were black Xs. He watched for the driveway. *Long gravel driveway. The mailbox looks like a cow, white with black spots.* He saw the cow, and turned right. The car lurched over the gravel, springs creaking.

The house was large in the way of old farmhouses. It was built from brick, two floors, with five shining windows facing onto the front yard from the second floor. There was a porch painted white with carved railings. To his left, there was a barn, the pattern of a quilt blocked out on its side, and a silver silo. The field beyond it had been cut down, and the light snow had settled between the sheared-off stalks of corn. He pulled the car to a stop at the bottom of the porch steps and got out. He shrugged into his coat, blowing into his hands against the cold, and stared at the field.

There were steps on the porch and the slam of a screen door. He turned his head.

"Hello?" The voice was light and tentative. The man who stood at the door was tall and stocky, his skin unusually tan in the bright winter light.

"Mr. Ohleg?"

The man nodded and took a step forward. He kept his hands in the pockets of his jeans.

"I'm Trey Caudill. We talked on the phone yesterday, the day before."

Mr. Ohleg opened his mouth as if in recognition, a smile and sigh. "You're with the Foster Corps."

"You can't have many visitors," Trey said. *You must have known who I was.* He thought of the gun in the car.

"Ah. No." Mr. Ohleg smiled again. He had thin lips but nice teeth.

"The field looks as if it's been freshly cut."

Mr. Ohleg came down a few steps. "Yes. It was the work of a day or so, with just my wife and me to do it."

Trey looked at him and smiled. He waited.

"Won't you come inside?" Mr. Ohleg asked finally after an awkward quiet. "Shay is inside."

"Your wife?"

Mr. Ohleg nodded and held the door open for Trey. Trey passed inside, but moved quickly so as to not leave his back exposed for long. His eyes adjusted to the dim light, and he saw that he was in a narrow hallway. The wallpaper was a faded green with a pattern of white dots. The lights were hung low so that he had to walk carefully to avoid hitting his head.

"Is he here?" Her voice was more resonant than her husband's. She looked out from one door and then smiled widely. "Mr. Caudill? Please come in."

Trey joined her. In the room were a couch and two armchairs, a bookshelf, a coffee table set with three mugs and a pot of coffee. He sat down in one of the chairs. She remained standing until her husband came in, then she drew him to the couch and made him sit by her. She touched his shoulder gently, then reached out to the pot.

"Do you want some?" She paused with her hand on the handle, looking up at Trey.

"Sure. Thank you."

The coffee was plain and good, but it wasn't real. Mr. Ohleg lifted up another cup, but set it down again immediately, empty.

"Mr. and Mrs. Ohleg—"

"Shay," she interrupted. "Shay and—" She looked at her husband.

"Ernst, please," he answered. "We are all friends here, yes?" He crossed his legs and leaned back.

Trey smiled, but he scanned the room again. The books on the shelves were old encyclopedias, antiques. There were a few digital picture frames on a spindly-legged table in the corner. Ernst and Shay and another couple. There was something odd about the pictures, a stiffness to the poses, to the faces. The furnace kicked on and he felt the moving air ruffle his hair.

"You understand that it's my duty to ask the hard questions," he said, looking at them again. Shay nodded. Their eyes did not leave his face. "The children in our care, they've had hard lives to date, seen things no child should see. We're looking to place them in homes that will help them heal, forget if possible."

"Sometimes you cannot forget." Ernst's voice was solemn. His tongue clicked in the back of his throat. Trey reached into his coat pocket for his phone. He nodded.

"That's true," he said. He opened the application form and glanced over the information he'd been given. "How long have the two of you been on the waiting list?"

"Long," Shay said. "A year, three months," Ernst said at the same time. "A year, two months, eighteen days."

"Are you upset about that wait?" He pulled free the stylus and hovered over the form. He paused for their answer.

"Things no child should see," Shay echoed what he'd said before instead of answering. "It seems an odd thing to say in the circumstances."

He looked up to see Ernst frown at her.

"I'm sorry?"

She smiled and shifted in her seat. "I apologize," she said. "It just seems like more children than not have stories like that now. And half the time, they're not just watching."

Trey felt the familiar sickness in his stomach. "No." She lifted an eyebrow. "No, you're right," he said. "But you must understand that no matter how common it feels, each child is a unique case in need of special care."

"I know," she answered rapidly. "Such experiences change the way their brains develop. It warps how they perceive the world." She took out her own phone and flipped open a file full of articles. She turned the screen toward him and he could see the scrolling print, pages upon pages of studies and profiles.

"You've done your research." He sighed and looked at both of them. He waved the phone away and she pulled it back. "And believe me, it does. I've seen it firsthand."

"You have been in the field?" Ernst leaned forward to grab the mug. Again, he left it unfilled on the table.

"Every agent in the Foster Corps has served a stint in the field, yes."

"That must be very hard," Shay said softly.

He drank from his coffee, swished the bitter drink in his mouth. "I think we should turn to the questions. For source of income," Trey began, "you answered agriculture." He looked instinctively toward the hall, in the direction of the barn and fields though there were no windows in his line of sight.

"Yes." Ernst pointed a finger in the same direction as if they all saw the same hypothetical window. "Yes, hay for cattle, primarily. But also some corn."

Trey looked at him, and then Shay, waiting for them to say more. They did not. Shay smiled again.

"So you have a decontamination setup?"

"Oh, yes, certainly." Ernst's answer was rapid, as if it were something he had meant to say but forgotten.

"May I see it?"

"Yes, certainly." Ernst got up, his square form unfolding almost at right angles. Shay stood as well. They went back into the hallway. Trey zipped up his jacket. Ernst and Shay did not stop at the coat rack, and they moved through the front door. Shay held the door for him. The cold was intense, freezing his nose hairs. He pulled the collar of the jacket closer to his ears.

"No coats for you?"

Ernst shook his head. "We are used to the cold." He stuffed his hands into his pockets and stepped off the porch. He looked back at Trey. "The unit is in the silo. Will you need a mask?"

"No." Trey sniffed, shook his head. "Ground is frozen now. Lead the way." As they passed his parked car, Trey almost stopped to open the passenger side door, to get the gun. The couple didn't seem to fit into the world around them, and that made him uneasy.

Shay noticed the halt in his step. "Are you alright, Mr. Caudill?"

"This winter is cold." He grinned shortly. "I have gloves in the car, but I can't be shown up."

Ernst laughed, short, staccato.

Their footsteps cracked the stiff grass. He could see where a path had been worn by regular walking from barn to house. Larger tracks of farm equipment crisscrossed this path at periodic intervals. He glanced up. Dark bare woods cradled the barn, the silo, the fields, the house behind him. Silent trees.

"I saw a hawk at the church."

Shay quickened her step to catch up with him. She touched his arm and then pulled back. "Yes." Her voice was higher-pitched, almost breathless. "Birds of prey. They survived."

"Not as dependent on the grains and bugs that live in the grains," Ernst said over his shoulder.

"They weren't poisoned," Trey said slowly.

"Not as many." Ernst stopped at the silo door. He pulled a ring of keys from his pocket and fit one into the lock on the door. The door was short and wide, and Trey had to stoop to follow Ernst inside. Shay did not come in. She stood in the doorway, her dark hair almost shining in the cold bright light of the winter sun.

The silo soared up above him, the contrast with the low doorway so great as to make Trey catch his breath. Looking toward the light at the top was like looking up into the dome of a cathedral.

"Watch your step," Ernst warned.

Trey stumbled, righted himself, struggled to find his bearing in the shadows on the ground. Ernst bent and plugged an orange extension cord into the wall. A bare bulb in an iron cage flickered on, changing the orientation of the shadows. The light glanced off the corrugated metal sides of a large vat-like structure on struts. Clear plastic tubing ran from the vat to the walls and was stapled up the walls until it arced above and ran back down into a fenced-off portion of the silo. In this half of the silo, ears and ears of shucked corn were piled high. The kernels glistened with the sheen of the decontaminant that had trickled from the tubing.

Trey walked to the fence with its close-woven wires and worked free a strand of silk. He could feel the tension of the stored corn pressing against the fence. He rolled the silk between his fingers.

"These things always look like old stills," he said absently.

"It is a distillation of sorts," Ernst answered softly. Their words rang with an odd timbre against the walls of the silo.

"Here's the thing, Mr. Ohleg—"

"I thought we had agreed to Ernst. And Shay."

Trey heard Shay clear her throat outside. He had no doubts that she could hear every word he said.

"The fields in this belt, in this part of Ohio." He dropped the silk. The decontaminant left a greasy coating on his fingers. He crossed his arms. "They're poison. After the F2 pesticide, it's too dangerous." He thought of the gun in his car. He thought of what Ora might look like if he had not been a combat model. "Unless you have androids to help out."

Ernst's face grew very still. "I haven't found that to be true."

"Birds of prey," Trey pressed. "No crows. No grackles."

"Yes." Ernst's mouth twitched. "Yes." He turned and left the silo.

Trey followed him out. Shay still stood by the door. She watched Ernst walk rapidly toward the house, his shoulders squared.

"You have found us out, Mr. Caudill," she said quietly.

Trey went to his car, and Shay up the steps of the porch. She paused in front of the door, and he watched her back, his hand on the door handle. She turned. Her face was so sharp featured, her eyes so clear and bright even from the distance at which he stood. "Please come inside," she said. "Please let us explain." His hand curled reflexively, but he dropped it from the handle. Half a year ago, he would not have hesitated to call the bureau, to grab his gun, to fear for his life. Before he had killed Helios.

When they went back into the house, they found Ernst in the kitchen. He held a knife and was slicing a tomato, swift and methodical. The pale pink of the fruit was wet against the faux-wood countertop.

"Who will eat it?" Trey asked. It seemed a waste, given the continuing shortage.

Shay moved to Ernst and placed a hand over his, stopping him. He released the knife reluctantly. There was red juice and seeds on the blade. Ernst looked up at Trey and did not answer his question. The light in the kitchen was an old fluorescent bulb and it cast his face an unusual yellow.

Trey pulled out his phone and scanned the application form again. Questions upon questions, and none to the point.

"A federal offense, I think, to withhold information of this sort." He put the phone away.

Shay smiled, but her lip trembled. "Perhaps for a human."

Trey glanced over the kitchen. The round table was small, five wicker-seat chairs, a vase of dried flowers. There were two paintings on the wall, one a generic print of a red and black rooster, the other a watercolor of the barn and silo. The fridge, which hummed softly between the sink and the range, displayed a couple of magnets and a digital printout—a photo of Ernst and Shay with two others.

"Androids can't own property." He looked at Ernst and Shay, who seemed thin and small behind the counter. Shay looked down at her hands. She leaned slightly toward Ernst.

Ernst narrowed his eyes. "What will you do to us?"

"Did you kill them?"

Shay glanced up sharply then, her lips wrinkled and thin. "How can you ask that?"

Trey's jacket felt too warm. He refused to look away.

"I can. I have to."

"We did not kill them." Ernst burst out. He clenched his fists on the counter. His face was drawn, cheeks sunken. The fluorescent light made them both look old, despite their relative agelessness. "They were our employers. But the land killed them like it poisoned the birds and the others. He is buried in the churchyard."

Trey did not ask where she was buried.

"They tried to have a child," Shay said softly. "A little boy." She traced her finger through the pulp on the counter, her pale nail dissecting the seeds.

"And how did you feel about the boy? When they lost—" He gripped the phone tightly, though this was not a question on any form.

Her eyes were big and glistening. She blinked twice.

"Would you ask one of your kind that?" Ernst's voice was level now, almost dispassionate. "Is it standard to ask adoptive parents *and would you be sad if your child died?*"

Trey did not move for fear that his hands or legs might tremble. He cleared his throat.

"You've seen children die, Mr. Caudill. How did you feel?" Ernst's eyes were too dark, the pupils too wide.

There was no way the android could know. There wasn't some collective database for AS and farm laborers alike. He swallowed. "I said when I arrived, when I came in, I said that I would ask difficult questions."

Ernst shook his head. He took a cloth from the sink and wiped the mess from the counter into his hand. Shay watched his every motion, her head swinging back and forth.

"We can't answer any question that matters," she whispered. Ernst lifted the knife from the counter and wiped the edge of it with the cloth.

Shay looked up and smiled, small and tired, as if everything were forgotten. "Can we get you another cup of coffee before you go?"

He pulled off the road at the church, parking the car almost at the gate. The falcon was gone. The graveyard was silent, except for the wind in the highest branches of the naked trees. The gravestones were a mix of humble plaques and ornamental statuettes. He hiked up the hill toward the most recent mounds of dirt. There was no plaque or stone to commemorate those buried in those plots, but he imagined Mr. Ohleg buried in one of them.

He considered how odd it was that this dirt, the red clods heaped over decaying bodies, was healthier and cleaner than that where his food was grown. How long before the F2 pesticide worked its way through the lifecycle of water, photosynthesis, and decay?

He took out his phone, opened yet again the Ohlegs' application to adopt. There was a place for him to press his thumb, to recommend whether their application should move forward. It was the beginning of the year and the sun set early. Even now it was growing dark. The screen glowed white.

It was cold. His hands were numb. He pressed the button to reject the application. As if he'd found them human and found them wanting. He shoved the phone back in his pocket and stomped down to the car, trying to warm his feet in his boots. He slid into the seat of the car. Glancing over, he saw the gun, black against the tan leather.

Warm, like bile, the tears flooded up. He leaned his head against the wheel, his arms above his head, and sobbed. He stayed like this for some minutes. When he finally sat back, there was a sharp pain in his chest as he tried to catch his breath. He wiped the back of his hand across his eyes. Then he re-gripped the wheel and shifted the car into drive.

LIA

OCTOBER 2057

H er eighth birthday coincided with the start of hunting season, so Lia's dad woke her up at four a.m. He asked her what candy bars she wanted to bring and he showed her where he was packing the rifles and the boxes of shells.

"Don't touch that without my say-so," he said, his voice dropping into stern warning. She nodded and sat on the couch and watched him prep the rest of the gear. She picked at the fraying threads on the corner of the cushion. The dog whined around her feet. He wanted fed.

"Dad, Shadow's hungry."

"Your mom will take care of it." He was distracted, staring into the fridge. She hoped he wouldn't take the beer.

"Are we going to say goodbye to Mom?" She looked at the long bag by the door and the collapsible stools leaned against the frame. The cooler was open near it, waiting for the rest of the food. The chocolate was already tucked safely in the bottom.

"Do you have your boots on?" he asked, ignoring her question.

She stared at her double-layered socks. "No."

"Well, go put 'em on then. We're wasting daylight here."

"It's not light yet."

"Will be soon. Go find them now."

She obeyed, rolling off the couch. The dog nipped at her cheek and she giggled, pushing him away.

"Lia." Dad's voice was in that dangerous in-between place, not quite angry but close. She pushed herself up and scurried down the hall of the double-wide. Baby was still asleep, not screaming yet. She could see, through the crack of the doorway, Mom slumped in the rocking chair by the crib, a spit cloth draped over one shoulder, her robe half open. She was snoring, head flung back on the pillow. Lia almost wanted to wake her, to make sure she'd gotten the instructions for the cake right. Last year, there'd been chocolate with vanilla icing and it was important that both cake and icing be chocolate this time.

Dad coughed in the kitchen, and Lia ran into her bedroom. She rummaged under her bed, pulling out her backpack and a balled-up sweater, a naked doll, and then the doll's dress and shoes.

"Where are your boots?" Dad loud-whispered from the door.

"I'm looking."

"Seems like you've found everything but your boots." He got down on his knees beside her. The paper crackled in the backpack, crunched under one of his legs.

"You're going to mess up my homework," she complained.

He snorted. "Ain't any eight-year-old have homework worth worrying about."

She frowned. "It's math."

Dad looked at her, his mouth set in the way she hated. "Lia, look at me." She was looking at him. "I need you to focus here. Get your boots. We're leaving. And damn if I'll let Jason get an eight-point before me."

"I'm trying."

He sighed somewhere in the back of his throat. "Get out of the way. Get on the bed."

She clambered up and pulled her legs under her while Dad stretched himself at full-length, half of his body under the bed. Mom came in while he was like that.

"What are you doing?"

Dad tried to scramble back out so quickly that he hit his head on the bed.

"Hunting," Lia said. "And Mom, what kind of cake are you making for me? I want to talk about the cake."

"Lia, I'm not talking about the cake right now." She pulled her robe close and fiddled with the tie around her waist. "What are you doing, Sam?"

Lia crossed her arms and fell back on her pillow.

"Look, Val. I know you're not a big fan of Lia going out. But hey, you going to have her left out of this? All the other guys are taking their kids out."

"It's a school day."

"You don't know how much longer they'll let us hunt these woods. Pretty soon town's going to declare it protected land. Government says hands off, fixing to discontinue licenses. We don't take her out now, it's going to get a lot harder."

"Sam, she has school."

"And school'll be there tomorrow."

"It is four in the morning and she is eight years old. What are you thinking? Lia, get back in your pjs. You're going back to bed."

"No, she's not."

"Sam."

He stood up, and he didn't do anything or say anything else, but Mom took a step back anyway. Lia saw her boots in the corner of the room, near her books and animals.

"Sam." Mom cleared her throat. "She needs sleep. She needs to go to school."

"Valerie, this is what I have. This is all I got. I'm gonna let her see how it's done. And maybe they'll stop giving out licenses next year, or the year after, but this year we can go."

"You aren't Robin Hood." And Lia remembered that for a lot of years, because she knew the cartoon, old as it was. "This isn't something you need to make one of your fights."

"I don't make the fights. They come for you or they don't."

Mom shook her head, and she was close to crying. Lia could tell because there was a redness she got around the eyes far more than she actually sat down and bawled.

"I don't know why you're doing this. What kind of bullshit is that— *this is all I've got?*" She waved wildly toward the door and the hallway and where the baby was sleeping. "When you've got your son, two months old, and your daughter. You have a family and a job and a place to sleep, food to eat. I can't even listen to this crap."

"There's no job."

Lia almost missed the words, and the silence after swallowed them up. Mom's face had gone still, and she was trying hard not to show what she was feeling. That refusal to show, that was when Lia knew she was really upset. "What was that?" she asked, lips thin, eyes thin.

"They've finished it at work. The new system. A whole crew of robots in there. They laid off me and a bunch of the other guys."

"This was yesterday? When were you going to tell me?" Like she was choking on the words, thick and rough in her throat.

"I was going to tell you." And Lia wondered if he was scared himself now. There was something flighty in his eyes, like he might do anything or say anything and they wouldn't be prepared for it. *Skittish*, Dad called the deer when they looked like that. She learned this over the next months as she went hunting with him. The licenses weren't revoked. They weren't necessarily handed out, but no one cared anymore after a while. There were larger things and barren fields and empty stomachs to worry about. Sometimes, before the game got thinned out, the deer helped feed those empty stomachs.

Mom turned and left the room, her robe flapping out behind her but quiet other than that. She went into the baby's room and closed the door, just a click as it closed.

"Dad," Lia whispered to his back. "I found my boots." Not that she really cared about that anymore, but she was scared. She felt cold inside.

He didn't answer for a minute, but then he shook his shoulders as if waking himself up out of a doze. "That's good, honey. Good. Why don't you put them on and we'll head out. We don't want to lose any more daylight than we already have."

And just like that, like nothing had happened and Mom hadn't disappeared, he packed them up to go hunting.

The truck was almost on empty, so they stopped by a station on the way out. The sun was creeping up over the trees, and it was gray and quiet. Dad kept a close eye on the numbers ticking up at the pump. He didn't fill the tank, just enough to jumpstart the electric converter.

"Want a candy bar?" he said, when he climbed back in.

She nodded, still a little afraid to talk. She wasn't usually allowed to have candy before noon, so the opportunity was too good to pass up.

"Eight. That's crazy. You're eight years old?" He looked both ways, though the road was empty as far as she could see, back toward home, and the other way, out of town and toward the woods.

"You know how old I am," she said, hesitant—or resistant—to go along with his joking tone.

"Yeah, I know." He smiled at her then, big and broad, the way that she loved or knew she loved later, the way that made her feel like nothing was wrong after all. "I was there, you know. Right outside the room. I heard you wailing the moment you came out."

"Did I really? Did I really cry that much?"

"What? Yeah, sure you did." And suddenly he seemed on edge again, as if her question—innocent and curious—had been meant to throw him off.

They rode the rest of the way in silence. He pulled off in a field. The tires bent the long grasses down in front of them and left a trail behind. It was impossible to ignore they'd been here. She couldn't tell if there were deer or squirrel here, she didn't know the signs well enough, but their tracks stood out like a sore thumb.

"It will be a walk," he said. "Over that hill." He opened the bed of the truck, slung the gun case and the stools over his shoulder. "Here, you grab the cooler." She took it from him, strapped it over her chest. She zipped her hoodie closer as a wind ruffled their hair. The neon orange vest bunched up under her arms. "This is perfect. Perfect temperature." He smiled again, or tried to, and jutted his chin toward the hill. "Come on. We'll set up just a little ways into the woods. A lot of deer come that way, heading into the field to look for food."

"It seems mean," she said, following him, the soft shell of the cooler hitting against her leg.

"Hm?" He seemed only half there with her now. He was scanning the grasses and brush around them, constant tiny movements of his head. She stared up at his back, broad and plaid. The camo duffle bag, with the shells, rattled in time with his pace.

"They're just trying to find food."

He laughed, but there was a rough edge to it, warning her she could cut herself. "Girl, ain't we all."

He cautioned her, when they reached the right spot, to set her stuff down quietly. "Make no more noise than the wind," he whispered. "Try to be as much a part of it all as you can. Still as a tree."

He had them set up behind a bunch of low trees and scrub. "Natural blind," he mouthed. Dad prided himself on using very little gear outside the guns themselves. She'd heard him mock the visitors in the cabin rentals by the lake. Though the people staying there the last few months weren't hunters. They were men and women from some big city sent to oversee the *updating* of the factory where Dad worked.

He took his time pulling the rifles free from the bag and, in complete silence, reminded her how to load one with slow, exaggerated movements. It was like watching a woman present prizes on a TV gameshow. The shells slid into the chamber with hardly a sound. He set the loaded gun aside and pulled out a smaller rifle. Before he loaded it, he gestured for her to tuck it into her shoulder and feel the weight of it there. He mimed the kickback, and she tried to hold in a giggle. Then he took it from her and taught her again, by example, how to look down the barrel and aim through the sight. He used his finger to trace his line of sight. After she had tried this herself, he tapped on the safety. Tapped it more than once to emphasize its importance.

"Never point this at someone," he said, breaking his code of silence. "Not even if you think the safety's on."

She nodded, all thought of laughter gone. Her fingers felt cold as she took the rifle back. She was reminded, by his warning, what they were here to do. And she faced what she hadn't fully thought on before leaving, not with the argument between him and Mom, not with the excitement of her birthday. She didn't know if she wanted to shoot a deer. They were the good guys in all the books and movies.

"Watch me for a while," he whispered, hardly loud enough to hear. "You'll get your turn in a bit."

He didn't load her gun yet. Instead, he lay down on his stomach, elbows buried deep into the mud and loam. He found an opening in the brambles to sight through, and he waited, his breathing so regular and steady—and so soft—that she could almost imagine he was a machine, a small bellows pumping and pumping.

She slid down as soundlessly as she could, her boots shoving aside leaves and mushrooms, and leaned back against the tree behind them. Sunlight, bright and almost white in its early morning brilliance, shot down through the leaves above. And the air and the trees and the whole wood seemed like it was waiting, quiet and still. Like it had absorbed her into some larger ecosystem, and she was small, and easily overlooked, and safe here, up against the tree.

She closed her eyes and tried to pretend that she was alone.

4.2:   JUNE 2058

I t came to the house in a plain, unremarkable white envelope, not even business size. The size of envelope you would stuff clipped coupons in, when those were still things. The envelope was addressed by hand but with no return address. The robotic arm of the self-driving mail truck whirred almost mournfully as it retracted from the mailbox. Almost as if it knew what the envelope contained. Shadow barked at the noise.

Lia waited until the robot had gone. They creeped her out. But even later, when she retrieved the mail, she hesitated to open that envelope. It was addressed to the family, and that was odd enough. Who had the right to open it? Probably Mom. And there was a dirty thumbprint on the back, right where the envelope sealed, that made her uncomfortable. She tried to figure out if the handwriting looked familiar.

Now that school had been cut down to half-days, it was hard to find things to do to kill the time between drop-off and Mom's return from work. The envelope lay out on the table, small and white and visible from seemingly everywhere she could go, while she waited. She warmed up leftovers for lunch, a stew primarily of imported tofu and an ancient can of beans. She wandered around her brother's room, idly flipping through his picture books. There was a nursery at the factory, where Mom had found a job after Dad left, weirdly enough, when the bosses realized there were some parts too delicate to manage with the cheap robots' current capabilities. Vince was there, probably watched over by a stiff-limbed, blank-faced android with a bad wig. Babies weren't as delicate as eyelets, apparently.

She glanced into Mom's room, even though the door was closed and supposed to stay so. The air felt stale in there, and Lia couldn't imagine that the windows or the curtains had been opened in a long time. The covers were only bunched up on one side of the bed. The other side was neat and tidy, much like half of the bureau, half of the closet. The room was only half lived-in. She almost expected, when she pushed the door in, to find her father napping on the bed, one hand tucked behind his head, one hand down his pants. Between her last birthday and the day the Civil Union came calling, it was how he had spent a lot of his day. But the room was empty, the covers pulled tight and unwrinkled on his half of the bed.

She pulled out the drawers of Mom's dresser, but there wasn't much to look through. Some folded underwear and shirts, a small bag of weed tucked way near the back, though Lia had been with her mom when she bought it from the dispensary. *"Old habit,"* her mom said when she had rummaged before and asked her why she kept it hidden. She had hoped it might make her mom mad when she revealed she had been snooping, but she had barely looked up from her supper. Mom shoveled her food now, almost without breathing, as if she was scared to stop and talk.

Mom had sold their screen two months ago, so there were no shows to watch. Her phone wasn't on a paid network and so could hardly stream fast enough to watch video. Finally, when she got tired, she lay down on the living room floor, static building in her hair, and flung her legs onto the couch. She imagined that the floor was a wall, the front of the couch a seat beneath her, and her world all at odd angles. She almost made herself dizzy, imagining it.

When Mom came home, noise came with her. Vince was crying.

"There's a letter," she said, too quietly at first. Vince's face was streaked red and white from the effort of his tantrum.

"Quiet, Vince, quiet," Mom said, searching for animal crackers in her bag. "Here, snack on these. We'll get dinner together soon." Vince was temporarily calmed. The house quieted again. Lia could hear her mom sigh and watched her wipe one hand across her forehead.

"There's a letter, Mom."

"Huh? What's that, honey?"

"A letter came today."

"Hm, not a lot of mail lately." And Lia watched, worried, as she approached the table, the letter positioned in the exact middle of the runner, because she had revisited it and adjusted it numerous times. Mom was not anxious enough, not aware enough of the possibilities Lia had imagined.

Mom glanced at the address, and her lips pursed just a little bit. She slid her finger under the seal. When the glue stuck, she tugged at it, increasingly angry. It tore in a jagged line. Mom let the envelope drop away and pulled out the note inside. It was a small piece of yellow-lined notepaper, folded in half. There were only four or five lines of text, the handwriting small and cramped. Lia could see the shadows of it through the back of the paper, the yellow kitchen light a halo behind Mom's head.

Mom cleared her throat and refolded the letter. She looked up at Lia.

"What does it say?" Lia tried to figure out what to do with her hands. She settled for jamming them in her pockets. Vince murmured something around the cookies in his mouth. Shadow panted under the table, watching for crumbs.

"Your father's not coming home," she said. And she folded the note again and then again, until it was a fraction of its original size. She held it to her mouth for a second, her hand covering half of her face. Her eyelids trembled and then, with a great amount of effort, her face grew still. She placed the paper on the table.

"What do you mean?" Lia asked.

Mom sniffed and adjusted her shirt. "He was killed."

Even Vince caught part of the force of that word. He dropped the cookies, stared at them, and looked as if he was unsure whether to scream or cry.

"What do you mean?" Lia asked again, like the question was stuck in her throat. "What do you mean?"

She couldn't quite understand what she was feeling and she couldn't quite face whether she already knew what Mom meant. She wondered most of all why Mom wasn't reacting more violently. She wanted to ask whether her mom knew what the letter said herself.

"Federal agents—" She paused, looked at Lia as if trying to remember how old she was. "They raided the compound where your father was. There was a shootout. He was killed."

Lia hummed something in the back of her throat, a song that had been playing on the radio on her last birthday, a song on the truck's radio. She had not understood the words, but it had been sad. She could tell.

Then she coughed. She was almost angry at Mom, she realized slowly. To stand there so calmly, to tell her everything. Shouldn't she have hid part of that? Shouldn't she have torn up the letter or stored it in the back of a dresser drawer?

"Why would they hurt him?" she asked. Not *kill*. She couldn't bring herself to say that word. And she couldn't ask what she really wanted to ask. She didn't know why but she couldn't. *Why did Dad leave? Why did he get himself killed?*

Mom dropped her head. She placed a hand over her mouth again. She made a sound between a whine and a gasp.

"Mommy?" Vince said. He toddled over and grabbed at her pant leg. She burst out crying. Her face, much like the baby's earlier, was red, but there were dots of violent white on her cheeks and forehead.

Lia was frozen, watching her. "Baby, come here," her mom said, sinking down toward the ground, gathering Vince to her with one arm. She held the other arm out to Lia. But she struggled to find breath and words between her sobs. Lia shivered and wrapped her own arms around herself and stared at her.

"Lia?" And Mom paused like that, as if her tears had been put on hold, her cheeks damp, loose hair stuck to the side of her face. There was a fear in her eyes, and Lia wondered later what had made her so frightening then, that her own mother would look at her with hesitation. But all she thought now was that she was angry. Mom had opened the letter so quick, not pausing, not examining that dirty thumbprint on the back, not recognizing the bad feeling about it. Pent-up anger at eight months of sullen silences and quiet meals and arguments behind closed doors before Dad left.

"Lia, come here," Mom said, soft and insistent, but Lia had learned to recognize the edge of bitterness.

She turned and ran to her own room. And Mom didn't call after her. Lia curled up on her bed. The blankets smelled stale and old. They hadn't been washed in as long as she could remember. She tried to think of a time when Dad had been happy, not cursing under his breath on the couch. And all she could recall was that morning in the woods and, for one moment, as he looked down through his sights at a deer, a smile in his concentration. The deer glanced in their direction as if it could hear or smell them, its black eyes wide open. Lia had held her breath, waiting for him to pull the trigger and the explosion.

She thought she finally understood why he'd taken her, on her birthday, when what she really wanted was a new toy and cake and maybe a party with friends from school. She stuffed her face into her pillow and cried until her face and her pillowcase were both wet. Then she flopped over onto her back and gasped for air and stared up at the popcorn finish on the ceiling.

She listened for noises from the living room or kitchen. There was the clink of a spoon on a pan and quiet sounds of making dinner: running water, the can opener, Vince beating on the tray of the highchair with a plastic fork. It was like any other night.

"Lia, supper's ready," Mom called down after a while, and maybe her voice sounded a little hoarse, a little raw.

Lia gritted her teeth and buried her head back into the blankets. She didn't go out.

Mom wasn't sure, at first, if they would return the body to her, so she held a small ceremony in the backyard rather than going to the funeral home. There was a picture of Dad propped up on a kitchen chair with a bunch of handpicked flowers in vases around it. Relatives came, including an aunt and uncle Lia barely remembered. They smelled like old cigarettes when they hugged her. Lia wondered what the neighbors in the park must think, wondered whether they were peeking out their curtains, watching this attempt at grief.

"It will feel alright again one day," her aunt said, unprompted. Lia looked at her, at the earrings dragging down her lobes, and the creases around her eyes. Her teeth were yellow, as was the skin on her fingers. Lia was a little bit scared of her, but mostly angry.

"It won't, ever again," she said. Then she walked off to one corner of the fence, the fence that was a roll of wire staked out between white posts. On the other side of the fence was the neighbor's garden, which primarily grew whirlygigs and aluminum birds whose wings fluttered in the wind. She watched the rest of the service from there, with the gentle clack-clack-clack of the lawn ornaments in her ear. Mom caught her eye once, at the beginning, as she was preparing to say a few words, and she waved her hand, ordering Lia to come closer. But Lia stayed where she was, squatted down, and put her chin in her hands, rested her elbows on her knees. Her mom clenched her teeth so that her jaw popped, but she let her be after that.

Afterward, once Mom had spoken and then a couple of his friends, men that Lia recognized a little from times when Dad had drunk with them on the front steps, people were told to go inside where there was food laid out on the kitchen table. Casseroles, covered in foil, and chicken in buckets from the corner deli. Lia stole a brownie and went out to the front steps. Her legs were bare and the concrete was gritty and hard on the back of her knees. But the sun was also warm, pleasant even though it was summer, even though the leaves were turning brown and dry prematurely. The heat made her drowsy and she imagined her dad talking, imagined it as the drone she could hear from her bedroom window when it was already dark and she was supposed to be asleep. No specific words, no complete sentences. Just a drone, sometimes louder, sometimes softer.

The mail came, a small truck, and the robotic arm unbent at right angles and opened the mailbox. There was a small beep as the articulated fingers scanned the codes on the envelopes, stamped at the office according to address. It picked out three envelopes or mailers and slid them into the box. Then, methodical and unrushed, the arm withdrew, closed the door of the box, and bent back in on itself inside the window of the truck. Lia straightened as she watched it.

The next day, she waited outside to watch for the mail again. Mom was keeping her home from school until she'd had time to process her grief. She hadn't asked what that meant, but she knew it had something to do with the snipped way that she was told to come out of her room, eat her supper, watch her brother. But Mom couldn't stay home. She left the house at 7 a.m., like clockwork. So Lia was left alone, to do what she wanted.

On the fourth day after the service, Lia opened the safe in Mom's bedroom and took out the rifle that Dad had trained her on during the hunting trip. She recalled his mimed gestures, and the movements felt natural, if the gun a little unwieldy, as she cracked open the barrel and slipped in a shell. The dog buried his nose under the duvet. She took the gun out to the steps and waited. When the mail truck came, she hesitated. She watched the arm unbend, extend, grasp the handle of the mailbox between two metallic fingers. It whirred, gently, less ob-trusive even than the whirlygigs in the neighbor's garden. She lifted the gun and aimed at the window of the truck, right where the arm was attached.

She breathed, in and out, steadying herself. The gun dragged at her arms, heavy. But she held it level. Her index finger hovered over the trigger. The robotic arm collected the coded mail and extended again toward the box. She pulled the trigger.

The gun fired, the noise deafening in her ear, and the impact rocking her back. She could feel the bruise already welting on her shoulder. The neighbor's car alarm started shrieking and a few birds flapped up, star-tled, from the grass. Somewhere in the park, someone was cursing.

The robotic arm sparked and whirred ineffectually, then fell limp, half-detached, so that it dragged against the door as the truck drove off. Lia couldn't tell if the truck knew that it had been shot at.

There was a lump in her throat so that it made it hard for her to swallow. She set the gun down, gently, on the stoop, and waited for whoever would come.

4.3:   SEPTEMBER 2059

Lia found the flyer in an old bag of shotgun shells. She had stowed the bag under her bed in an attempt to hide it from Mom. Mom had locked up the gun safe, changed the combination, and taken some of Dad's gear down to the police station after the incident with the mail truck. This was the last of Dad's hunting paraphernalia, and Lia was determined to get her hands on another rifle and use these shells to practice. But the flyer was a surprise, words and image printed on pale blue paper so that the black font popped off the page.

The wording was cryptic, and she didn't fully understand it. She thought about taking the flyer to Mom, but she would crumple it into a ball and toss it, like she did anything that reminded her of the Civil Union. And this, at least Lia knew, was something to do with the Union. She recognized the American flag, ripped in two, angry balled-up fists on either side, as a symbol spray-painted on the cinderblock wall of the bar where most of the factory workers went to drink.

The wording below this image was the bit harder to understand. *Stand up for your rights,* it read in bold, sharp-cornered type. *Fight for what's right. Young and old.* There was no explicit instruction. No address or contact information. What were you supposed to do with that information? It was all so vague.

But Lia was convinced this was what had sent her dad running away. When she first found it, she spread the flyer out as flat as she could, trying to press out the wrinkles. *Young and old.* She read those words again, underlining them with her finger as she whispered. Then she folded it carefully, at neat right angles, and slipped it into the pocket of her jeans. She made sure, each time she changed her clothes, to transfer the paper, so that Mom wouldn't accidentally throw it in the wash.

"You wouldn't understand," Mom said—again—when she asked her why Dad had run away. Mom was making a can of soup at the stove. She stared at the bubbling soup more intently than she needed to. "You're too young."

"I'm not," Lia said.

"Honey, believe me, you are."

She had also been too young to go hunting, according to Mom, but Dad had taken her anyway. She said that, in her head, yelled it, but she didn't dare say it aloud. And she tried to forget how nervous she had been in the woods, watching her dad settle into the pine needles and underbrush, one eye sighting down the barrel.

"I want to know."

"Your father—" Mom started impatiently, anger at the back of her voice. But she stopped herself, cocked her mouth in that slight grin that meant she was surprised at herself or someone else. "Your father lost sight of what was important when he lost his job. When he left, he thought he'd found something to fight for. But it just meant leaving us. So here's what you need to remember about your father, Lia." She set down the spoon and turned to fully face her. She looked her in the eyes without glancing away or shifting. "He was a coward. He thought he found an easy way out."

The bluntness of the words shocked Lia. She stared at her mother, her face hot.

"See, you didn't want to hear it so bad after all," her mom said, slowly. Then she sighed and wiped a hand across her face. "Here, honey, go take care of your brother."

Vince was babbling under his breath, playing with a plastic spoon. He rapped the spoon against his bowl just as Mom stopped talking and sent the bowl flying off his tray onto the floor. His face puckered.

"No," Lia said, waiting for the crying to begin. "I'm not his mom."

And she left the room as calmly as she could, counting the seconds it took her to walk away from the kitchen. She waited for her mom to yell something in return. But it was quiet. Vince didn't even start screaming.

She closed her bedroom door quietly and sat gingerly on the bed. Every movement felt risky. The flyer crinkled in her back pocket.

For the next hour, she strained to hear what she could from outside. Dishes clattered and chairs scraped across the floor. The water ran. And finally, later, she heard her mom whispering, almost weepy, to someone else. Presumably on the phone, because Lia never heard anyone answering. She lay back on the bed and closed her eyes.

Later, she woke and realized she had been sleeping. She heard footsteps in the hall, Vince's door opening and shutting, and a while later, the door to her parents' bedroom. She stood up and went to her own door, cracked it open, and peered into the hall. It was dark, except for the night light, which flickered unsteadily. She did not think she had planned to do this, but she found herself turning back to her room, grabbing up her backpack, finding a change of clothes in her drawers. She laced on her boots, since they seemed like her sturdiest shoes. She tucked the box of shells deep into the bottom of the pack. They rattled in her hand, the box half empty.

She left in the pack the few random snacks she had stored there the last time she used it. It wasn't much—half a granola bar, a small bag of crackers, and a pack of chewing gum. She didn't think it would get her far, but she had a few dollars in her pocket. And she knew there was a twenty hidden under the solar lamp by the front door. For emergencies.

It was cold outside when there was no sun to counter the chill air. She could see the streetlights on the main road, just past the entrance to the trailer park, but it was dark here in the strip of grass outside the double-wide.

He was a coward. Mom's words echoed faintly as she stared off toward the lights. Something rustled in the neighbor's yard. Lia froze as still as she could and glanced in that direction. A deer lifted its head over the wire fence, returning her gaze. They both stood quiet for a minute or two. Lia counted the seconds in her head. When she didn't move, its jaw worked slowly as if it were coming back to life. She lifted her hand and adjusted the backpack. The deer's ears perked up and then it sprang over the fence and ran away into the maze of trailers.

Lia shivered and zipped up her coat. Her boots, when she finally began walking, were quiet on the gravel road, barely crunching the fine rock. There was a haze, a night fog, that softened the lights ahead and made them waver a bit. She crossed her arms and hugged herself and, when she reached the juncture of main road and gravel road, she stopped again. She looked both ways down the main road. She knew if she went right, she would arrive at the factory, tall and dark and empty in the night air with little ghost lights in the windows and an occasional shadow where an automaton moved back and forth behind the glass. It was surrounded by vast parking lots littered with potholes, only half filled anymore—even during the day.

To the left was town, what was left of it after years of decay and business closures. The bar, with the graffiti emblazoned on its side and a neon light buzzing over the door, was the first thing she would come by. She knew that Dad's friends still hung out there. She hoped they might have answers for her or an address.

So she turned left, even though there was something tugging at her belly, asking her to turn back, to go into her mom's bedroom and say she was sorry. To ask her advice: *What do I do with myself, Mom? What do I do now?* But maybe that was her mom's voice even now, maybe that wasn't really Lia. Mom, who was always asking that question in little ways. *What are we supposed to do now?* Over bills in thin envelopes with cellophane windows. Over dinner burnt in the oven. Over the grown-too-tall lawn. She never seemed to find an answer.

It was late and there were no cars on the road. The way to town dipped in and out of shadow at first. The streetlights gradually grew closer together and Lia could tell she had not far left to go when she crossed the train tracks and the lights bled into each other, one after another down the main drag. She could hear the bass beat from the bar even a block away. When she came in sight of it, she clutched the straps of her backpack and swallowed down puke. The graffiti, the flag torn in two, the fists, was half in darkness, but the door was bright, framed in light from inside and from the neon sign above. The sign advertised a brand of beer. There were two men and a woman grouped by the door, shoulders hunched up against the cold, smoking.

She didn't say anything at first when she walked up to them, but she couldn't bring herself to pass them.

"Where's your parents, kid?" The man who spoke was wearing a plaid shirt layered over a Henley with ragged cuffs. He flicked his ciga-rette between two fingers. She didn't recognize him by sight, but there was something to the sound of his voice that seemed familiar.

"Honey, what are you doing out so late?" the woman chimed in, trying to pitch her voice as comforting. Her hair was pulled back tight from her face, so she looked gaunt in the neon light.

"Sam was my dad," she said quietly.

"Sam who?" the second man asked. His voice was too loud, like he'd been drinking for a long time.

"Shut up, Dave." The woman shoved him in the shoulder. "It's Sam Sudowski's kid. You can tell just by that hair."

Lia self-consciously raised a hand to her ponytail.

"What are you doing here? It's past midnight." Dave didn't sound any more welcoming.

Lia swallowed. "I want to know where my dad went."

The woman raised a hand to her mouth, and Lia saw the sympathy welling up in her eyes. Her face was flushed. She had been drinking too.

"No," Lia interrupted. "What I mean is where he went before. I want to know where to find the Civil Union."

The first man laughed, his voice husky from smoking. "The Civil Union is everywhere, ain't it? That's what they say." He pumped his fist in the air and howled, throwing his head back. "Civil Union's here, kid."

The woman slapped his arm. "Really, Kieran? How many drinks is that for you?" She turned her attention back to Lia. "What's your name, honey?"

"Lia."

"Okay, Lia. Here's what I want you to do. I want you to go back home. Walk back where you came from. There's nothing good where you're looking."

"He left for a reason." Lia hitched the backpack further up her shoulders. *He was a coward.* What adult would send her back home, by herself, through the dark? She scanned the faces of the smokers again. They were grim and sharp-lined. "I know he came here a lot. And I know that sign." She pointed to the graffiti.

"I did that." Kieran grinned, thumping his narrow chest.

"Just another bad decision," the woman growled under her breath. "No one here really believes in anything, honey. We just get drunk and we do stupid things. It's all there's left to do."

"Why don't you let the kid in, Mary?" The voice was new, from the doorway. Lia didn't know how long it had been open. The man wore an old military jacket with the insignias torn off. The woman almost jumped in surprise when he spoke.

"How long have you been standing there?" She took a long drag from her cigarette, then dropped it, stamping out the spark on the concrete. She coughed. "The girl was just going home."

"Girl—Lia, was it?—says she wants to know about the Civil Union. Let her in here."

Mary stepped aside and Lia moved forward, almost without thinking about it. She had the creepiest sense of déjà vu as she stepped into the bar, as if she—or someone else—had done this many, many times before. As if a man like this lingered in many bars, in many small towns, with many half-empty factories a mile down the road.

"Eli would like you," the man said, sliding into a booth. She stood by the table. The bar smelled like smoke and old, sour beer. "He likes kids with go-get-em attitudes."

"I just want to know where my dad went," she said. But her voice sounded small, even to her own ears, weak and ineffective.

"I'll tell you that," he said. "Hell, I'll drive you there myself if you want."

Lia felt a little dizzy. In the back of her mind, she blamed Mary for not keeping her from coming in here.

"How far away is it?" The words came out and she couldn't take them back. She told herself she didn't want to. She shoved down the sickness in her stomach, she shoved down that tugging.

"Far away from here, but not that far."

She knew the answer didn't make any sense. But it was an answer. She gripped the straps of her backpack tighter.

"Okay," she said.

4.4:   **FEBRUARY 2061**

When she first woke up, the sun slanting directly into her eyes, Lia imagined she was back at the bunkhouse. She shrank into herself, waiting for Eli's voice to ring up the stairs. *Sun's up. You should be too.* She curled her hands close to her chest and was surprised by the gun barrel she held. It wasn't loaded. She remembered that now, as she slowly became aware of her surroundings. There were a few shells tucked in her back pocket, more in the case at the bottom of her bag.

She sat up, stiff from sleeping in a strange bed. There were white ruffled curtains at the windows. Through them, she could see the fields on the hills, climbing toward the woods. They'd been dead awhile, the remnants of a last harvest lost to scavengers and birds. Hopefully, the scraps hadn't killed them. She imagined, as well-kept as the house was, that the owners had left against their will, forced out by the EPA's attempts to clean the land. The militia had used it since then, fairly recently by the muddy tracks on the floor, but they had cleared out too.

She stretched, cracked her neck, then swung her legs out of bed. She slipped her feet back into her boots and bent down to tighten the laces. Her hair, growing long again after Eli had cut it all off, tickled the back of her neck.

She went in search of breakfast, rummaging through the pantry off the kitchen. For a second, her stomach grumbling, she missed the compound. She missed the cereal, at least, not the hours of practice at the shooting range or in hand-to-hand combat. Not the intense silence while she ate and Eli treated them to a lecture, more like a sermon, on the justice of their cause. When she'd first met him, bleary-eyed and dragged by one arm down from the truck, she thought he looked fatherly. She thought his voice was comforting when he told her there was a place to stay. When he told her that he mourned the loss of her father, that Samuel Sudowski had been a good man. *"You've come to pick up where he left off."* He hadn't said it as a question.

There wasn't any fruit or any fresh food, but Lia found a box of individually packaged muffins and some microwaveable oatmeal. She wavered between the two, then ripped open the plastic and bit into the muffin. There was some dried fruit in it she couldn't identify. It didn't look anything like the colorful illustration on the box. She still carried the rifle in the crook of her arm, but she was used to the weight of it now. She hardly noticed it as she moved to the sink and tried the tap.

The water was still working, so she cupped her hands and drank some eagerly that way first. Then she found a glass and filled it.

The house creaked, like the way an old building does, but Lia set the glass down slowly and stood still, listening. Her heart beat fast at her throat. She was only a couple days' run away from the compound, and though the ground had been dry when she left and though she hadn't followed the roads, she was still worried that some of the adults might already be on her trail. Kids had run away before. Lia was never sure if Eli sent men after them or not. She found it hard to believe that any one of them was worth the trouble. The only kid she'd seen return came back on their own, after they'd returned to their parents' and found their home empty. He was a boy, a little bit older, and his face was blotched red and white when he slunk back into the bunk room. All the other kids had rolled over in their beds and given him his privacy.

So she liked to think that Eli had just let the other kids go. She liked to think that, but her skin goose-pimpled anytime she heard a noise she didn't make herself.

The house grew quiet again. She didn't hear anybody walking. She didn't hear breathing or the swish of clothing against walls or floors.

"I hate you!" she suddenly screamed, as if to defy her own nerves. She wasn't sure who she was talking to. Of course she hated Eli, but more she wanted to yell at herself. Yell, for ignoring that warning feeling in her belly as she stood in the dark trailer park. Yell, for shooting her rifle into a crowd of soldiers, hoping they had vests on but shooting anyway. *Never point this at someone,* her dad had said. But he'd joined Eli. And he'd taken most of his guns with him.

She got some more water from the sink and swallowed down the tears tightening her throat. She went over again the map she had set to memory and wondered if she could spend one more day in this quiet house, lying on the sun-warmed wooden floors and flipping through the old magazines stacked near the door. Even if she did leave, leave today and keep walking, keep walking and show up at the double-wide, would Mom and Vince still be there?

Something glinted on the hill, in the trees. She moved closer to the window and pushed aside the yellowed curtains. The front porch creaked.

Lia whirled to face the kitchen door, swinging her rifle up and aiming at the porch. When no one immediately appeared, she took shells from her pocket with one hand, then rapidly lowered the rifle, broke and loaded it, and returned it to her shoulder. She tried to calm her breathing and steady the gun.

The doorknob rattled. Then, eerily quiet, something drilled through the center of the knob and the metal plug clanged to the tiled floor. The door swung open. The android moved quickly, faster than she anticipated. She heard herself gasp, a quick intake of breath that disrupted her concentration. She caught a glimpse of a painted face and too-white eyes before it ducked into the dining room. Then there was quiet again. She redirected her aim to the dining room entryway.

"Drop your gun. I'm not here to hurt you." She wondered if she would have mistaken the voice for human had she not seen the android sprint by. Yet, for all its inhuman timbre, the voice was comforting in its straightforwardness. It was not charismatic or charming or fatherly.

"Why are you here?" It took effort to keep her own voice from shaking.

"I am with the ATF. I seek Eli Whitaker. Drop your gun. I'm not here to hurt you."

"Eli isn't here."

"I am here to look for Eli Whitaker. Or to look for evidence of his occupation." There was a pause that, to Lia, felt suspicious, felt dangerous. "I do not want to hurt you." And it was as if the android had lowered its volume. The words were almost quiet. "Please drop your gun."

Lia had heard stories of AS, of their ruthlessness. One had shot a boy in the head at a raid not a year back. She had not been combat-ready then, but the training had intensified. She was sent into her first fight a month later.

"I can't trust you," she said.

When the android moved, its joints whirred slightly. It came around the corner of the doorway, a small automatic pistol in its hand pointed at her. But it did not look tensed or ready to fire. Would she know, though, by looking at it? It was not what she expected, nothing that could be mistaken for flesh-and-blood human. Perhaps they had changed the model, but she had heard horror stories in the bunks at night about metal men that looked and moved liked humans. Eli had spoken at length about the threat of androids replacing them. Even her dad, on the porch, drinking, had railed against the near-human skin on the factory workers.

"I am not asking you to trust me." The android scanned the kitchen as if searching for any more hidden threats. "But I do not wish to hurt you. Please put down your gun."

Lia could think of no way to escape, so she lowered the rifle and shrugged off the strap so that she could lay it on the floor.

The android nodded, as if in thanks. "Are you one of Eli's fighters? You are dressed like them."

Lia wasn't sure what this meant, since there was no official uniform in the Civil Union. But the clothes provided the kids were similar—oversized coats, combat or hiking boots, and cargo pants that could be tucked closed to the leg.

"No." She swallowed. Would the android be able to tell that she was lying? And it hit her, almost like a physical blow, that she wasn't lying. That the decision was her own now.

"You live here?" The android moved close to her and picked up the rifle. It removed the shells and then placed the gun on the counter. She stood very still and stiff as it maneuvered around her. When nearby, she could feel that it released warmth, like a small engine.

"Just a couple counties over." And this wasn't a lie either. Laughter bubbled up in her chest and she cleared her throat, trying hard not to endanger herself. It made no sense to laugh now. There was nothing amusing about her situation. But it was there, almost like a panic.

"Go home, then. And be careful." It was like a school principal, releasing her to her classes. She paused, staring at it a second.

"You're not going to hurt me?" Eli's words kept ringing, there in the back of her head. *A threat like any other. Like an animal. Like a force of nature. But not human.* She had learned by then not to pipe up with a smartass response about the threats she'd faced so far, primarily human.

"I am here to look for Eli Whitaker." The android craned its neck back and scanned the entire space around them, as if able to see through the walls and floors. "And he's not here."

It looked at her again, and she noticed how hyper-realistic its eyes were, in contrast to the rest of its appearance. Though it did not blink. It did not look away when she met its gaze. It must know. It must know, she thought, that she was one of Eli's infamous child soldiers.

"Please leave. Wait until I have gone. Then leave."

Lia took off running before the sound of its words had faded. It was instinct, to escape, now that the moment of frozen inaction had passed. She raced toward the back door. She had just enough presence of mind to not let the door slam behind her and to pause on the stoop, panting, and look to see if she was in eyeline of the woods on the hills. The sharp eaves of the roof hid her for now. She scanned the backyard and saw the bed of an old truck jutting out from the side of the house opposite the woods. Hugging close to the siding, she moved as rapidly as she could.

The sides of the truck were rusted out, but the tires weren't flat. She tested the door and it opened. As she climbed into the driver's seat, she heard the front door of the house and heard the android on the porch. The keys weren't in the ignition, but she checked the mirror and then the glove box. Finally, in the center console, she found the keys on a gummy keychain, a promotional product for a local car repair service.

She thrust the key in the ignition, whispered a petition under her breath—to who, what words, she was unsure—and then turned the keys. The old gas engine coughed and turned over. She was used to cars and trucks of this sort. It was all Eli used, and she had been training for over a year. She slid forward in the seat so that she could reach the gas pedal and then shifted into drive. She heard shouts behind her.

"Lia?" Lia looked up and shrugged the blanket further up her shoulders. She sat in the back of an ATF jeep. It was getting dark. The sun had set a few minutes ago and the agents had grown quieter the darker it got, whispering in small groups and waiting to leave. Behind her, lights still flickered in and out of the farmhouse as the ATF did one last inspection of the place.

None of them had hurt her. Very few of them had even interviewed her. They seemed to take her story at face value. Even though, as she told it, it seemed stranger and stranger to her. The bunkhouse and the other children, even the night when she had gone to the bar, seemed like fiction. *What was the name of the man who took you to Eli?* asked the head agent. He was fidgety himself, constantly eyeing the AS. The AS stood perfectly still and did not look at her, did not act as if they had ever talked before. *I don't know.* And she only realized it was true as she said it. Only Eli held any real presence in her mind, only he could she describe in vivid detail. And they did not ask what he looked like, what he sounded like, what the room felt like when he entered. They just wanted details on where and when Eli planned to attack federal properties. And she didn't know those.

"Lia." The voice was more sure now. Lia squinted to see the woman through the dark. It took her a moment to find the words to say. Because those words also felt like a fairy tale.

"Mom?"

And her mom hugged her, so tight that Lia felt she couldn't breathe. But she didn't care. For a small moment, a minute that passed too quickly, she forgot everything.

HELIOS

Heat, then cold. These are the first sensations AS 4.1.315 knows.

There is a very loud sound, one 4.1.315 might later compare to a metal bar—one's arm, perhaps—being wrenched out of shape, bent almost to breaking. There is light. No light and then light. Light in the shapes of moving figures. One of these figures bends near and makes a noise by snapping two of its thinnest appendages together. 4.1.315 follows that noise instinctively. 4.1.315 bends. 4.1.315 moves toward it without knowing how 4.1.315 does so. Only later does 4.1.315 learn what it is to *move* or to *bend*. Only later does 4.1.315 learn the names of 4.1.315's body. Legs and arms and head. Eyes and nose and ears. Only later can the doctor in the white coat— also words 4.1.315 learns later and rapidly, like eating—say "Helios, sit up for me" and Helios will know what he means and how to please him.

Helios does not remember events in the same way that the human soldiers do. Helios can understand cause and effect. Helios can interpret which effects are bad for the humans around Helios. But Helios does not remember that something was *good*, that something made

Helios *happy*, that something made Helios *cry*. Not that the soldiers say they cry. But Helios does not sleep and always observes and Helios sees the soldiers, even at night. Helios learns a lot by watching humans sleep.

"Helios, sit up for me." Helios sits up. The doctor leans away and frowns a little.

"Is everything all right?" Helios asks.

"It has a face like a Frankenstein," the tech says. The tech speaks softly, but Helios can hear. The doctor labels Helios as a man like himself. Sometimes the tech does not.

"Try smiling for me, Helios."

Helios looks at the doctor. "Show me."

The doctor glances at the tech, then turns back, wide-eyed. He pushes up his lips with a finger on either side, into a U.

Helios places his own fingers on his mouth. He pushes his lips up, mirroring the doctor. The doctor covers his mouth and makes a noise like he is having trouble breathing. He turns away and his shoulders shake.

"Smile, Helios. Like you're happy." The tech replaces the doctor. He speaks more quickly than the doctor. He opens his mouth wide, lips bowed and cheeks pushed up, showing his teeth.

"I guess we look pretty ridiculous, too," the doctor says when Helios tries again. "We're just showing him the imitation of a smile. Not a smile."

"He's an AS, anyways." The tech writes something down on his tablet. "Maybe smiling isn't required."

"He'll be embedded with human troops. They need to bond with him if they're going to trust him."

"Soldiers will bond with anything. A dog. A robot on wheels."

The doctor held up his hand. "Careful there, Liam. You say *soldier* when what you mean is *human*. Humans can bond with almost anything." He looks at Helios. "And think about it. A dog is a dog, not a human. A robot on wheels, its own thing as well. You can't send in something meant to look human and not have it act human. It's too much of a disconnect."

"What should we do, then?"

Helios watches them talk, back and forth, back and forth, as if words must always create more words.

"They want him in the field yesterday," the tech says. And this seems to bring the conversation to a halt.

"Not yesterday," Helios interjects.

The doctor smiles, without using his fingers to push at his face. Helios watches him. He tries to track the minuscule movements of the muscles. He smiles back.

"You see that?" The doctor is excited. "Fast learner, this one. Not like the last model."

"And yet they all end up in the same place." The tech does not look as pleased. "Shooting at someone. Let's not lose track of the end goal here. Ultimately, this thing's a weapon, and we just need to make sure he can recognize friend from foe and send him on his merry way."

The doctor nods. He stares at his hands for a moment. For twenty-seven seconds. "You know it's not that simple."

"Some days I do. Some days I don't." The tech hangs his tablet on the charging station. He takes a key from his pocket and locks the drawers in the workstation. "I'm hungry. Lunch?"

The doctor looks Helios in the face. He appears intent, like he is also trying to understand how mouths work. Helios smiles again, to practice. This startles the doctor. He turns away very quickly. "The sandwich place still open around the corner?"

"I think so. Though who knows what they'll be serving."

The doctor shrugs. "Start the shutdown sequence." He speaks to Helios without looking at him. "Lie down, Helios."

Helios does not move right away. He is trying to understand the two struggling impulses inside him. One, to lie down as ordered. The other to not lie down because there is a warning, like a shrill beeping, that says he might not do anything else, ever, if he lies down. He might not be. He does not know if it is good or bad to *be*.

The doctor looks at him again. He lies down because he is ordered to. There are sparks in his eyes and he loses his sense of hearing.

"Helios, who do you belong to?"

This answer is stamped on the translucent carbon polymer of his forearm. The doctor has not added synthetic skin to his arms or legs.

"Property of the United States government."

The man is dressed like a military general, so Helios presumes he is. He has reviewed every uniform pertaining to branches of the US military.

"I don't get it." The general looks at the doctor. "I have older-model androids in my office. Assistants. They look more human than this thing. And they don't sound like a robot when they talk."

"We're working on the voice simulator," the doctor answers. "But these military-grade models have a wider range of communication modes. Helios, for example, like the model before him, can communicate fluently in a coded sign language designed for the military by our linguists, based on binary. He spoke with that first. Before using the voice box."

"I think you're missing my point, Doctor."

The doctor clears his throat, shrugs his shoulders in that white jacket. He has changed his hair, combed it close to his head, and put a gel in it. The general must be very important to make him change his appearance in that way.

"Yes. Apologies. I was just trying to say that the model is not behind, so to speak, just different."

"You know how much the military cares for *different*." The general laughs at his own words and looks at the doctor as if he expects him to do the same. Helios tries to smile again. "And I guess you have a point. Different functions, right? Tell me what this model can do."

The two of them walk to the other end of the room, where there are computers and filing cabinets and documents with numbers. Documents about Helios. He can make out the writing from here, from yards away. Based on what he reads, he is designed for very few functions, a waste of the processing power and the energy at his core. He is meant to save some human lives by killing others. It is an equation he has not quite reconciled. Who is he meant to kill? Who is he meant to save?

He waits to be told.

Helios is brought to a shooting range to provide a demonstration. The general has visited the laboratory again, and this demonstration seems to be some means of placating him. He has brought other officials with him, individuals dressed in dark blue with epaulettes and bars to indicate their ranks. They are important by all the parameters Helios has developed from a myriad of inputs. The tech checks Helios's arms as if they could have been damaged in any way during the drive, as he lay still and silent and only half-operating in the back of the truck. The tech also runs a diagnostic on his eyes.

"He's good to go." The tech steps back.

In front of him, on a low shelf, are two guns. A semiautomatic pistol and a carbine rifle. He scans the guns, verifies that all parts are in working order and that they are properly loaded.

"Hope this isn't a repeat of three years ago." And there is a note of unease, a tension that Helios picks up in the tight pronunciation of the woman who has spoken.

"You have your vests on?" The doctor does not look up from his tablet as he asks. He is watching a map of Helios's neural network, seeing which pathways light up as Helios moves. Helios can feel him watching. He does not like the feeling.

The observers all nod behind their bulletproof barrier. Helios sees this in the reflection of the glass walls on either side. He knows that he has a wider range of peripheral vision than humans. He flexes his arms, up and down, up and down, testing the tensile strength of their joints.

"Go ahead," the doctor says.

Helios steps forward and places a hand first on one gun, then the other. He chooses the pistol. He knows that aiming with the pistol is slightly harder and that the doctor wishes to impress the visitors.

"What happened three years ago?" he asks.

"What?" The doctor's voice is high-pitched. He finally glances up from his tablet. There is sweat on the edge of his hairline, and Helios can determine he is afraid via his olfactory sensors.

"I would not want to make a mistake again," he says. This calms the doctor.

"Wasn't you," the tech answers.

"Don't worry, Helios. You won't make a mistake." The doctor smiles at the general when he says this. The smile does not look real.

He parses the tech's answer and files away the doctor's assurances as insignificant. Helios does not think he will make a mistake, despite what he himself indicated. But there is something to what the tech said that has opened up new considerations. There is a road or pathway unfolding in his brain. There are clues as well in the general's former visit.

"Helios?" He is sure that he has paused for only seconds, but the doctor wants him to begin. Or wants the demonstration to be done. They are not the same thing, Helios thinks.

"Yes." He picks up the pistol and aiming is automatic. His eye finds the target and calculates the angle. This is not the test they think it is. This does not show anything about Helios's real ability.

"There was another Helios?" he asks, but shoots the gun simultaneously and no one hears the question.

The key to impressing the general is rapidity and accuracy, so Helios is careful to provide both. He empties the magazine in the pistol, each bullet striking the most vulnerable points on the target dummy. It flails wildly with every impact. The visible, articulated joints are roughly similar to his own. The dummy does not truly resemble the humans he is meant to shoot.

The general laughs, but Helios does not pause. He switches to the rifle, ball joints warmed up and fluid. He moves without any hitch or friction. He is operating at peak efficiency.

"Impressive," the general says when he has finished. He sets down the rifle, the barrel still hot to the touch. He knows it is better to ask the question again when the general and other officials are gone. The doctor will be more relaxed then. He talks more when he is relaxed. "As promised."

The general shakes the doctor's hand. "I want him out in the field in a month."

The doctor shakes his head as if to indicate *no*, but he says something different. "We're doing our best, General."

The doctor and the tech wait as the other individuals file out of the room. It is brighter outside and the sudden opening of the door throws off Helios's visual focus for half a second.

"There was another Helios?" He knows to ask now, because relaxation is not everything. The surroundings are also good, the decimated dummy bent at awkward angles behind them. He knows he is stronger than these humans and more precise. He has the ability to kill them, but he will not. They do not fit the profile of his allowed targets.

The tech grumbles something under his breath, but Helios determines that they are just swear words, words used to express emotion but not meaning.

"There is only one Helios," the doctor says. He looks at Helios, inspecting his face, tiny micro-glances examining eyebrows, eyes, nose, mouth. "But we will produce more like you. And there were other models before."

"Only one," Helios says. He practices moderating his voice and says it very quietly, like a whisper. He is suddenly defensive, though there are no US soldiers in sight to protect, their armor at readiness. "Also others." He stores the contradiction away for future analysis.

5.2:   JULY 2060

Send the AS in first. Let them take the fire." Helios hears the communication, even as it crackles through the earpiece of Special Agent Caudill. He readies himself, running a fast diagnostic on his joints and his power core, sustained as it is by kinetic energy. They have been crouched and waiting for over thirty minutes. He gestures to Ora, a quick flick of the fingers that tells him to be ready as well. Ora nods, an almost invisible motion.

"Helios, Ora." The agent turns to them. He points two fingers at each of them, then motions them to move forward. "To the front." His voice triggers and overrides Helios's safety protocols, as his system recognizes Caudill's rank. He has authority to initiate combat. Almost beneath Helios's awareness, this switch is flipped on and off, on and off, by each voice he hears.

Helios raises himself and steps forward. The other agents watch him as he moves, though they are primarily comfortable with him now. He has been embedded with this ATF office for five weeks. After one, they no longer stopped talking around him. In two, they made jokes with him. But this is the first time they have seen him in combat. They are naturally interested.

This is the first time that Helios has seen real conflict. Every other instance has only been a simulation. He makes sure that his camera is recording the encounter so that he can study it later. His camera is, of course, recording. The lab is also interested.

Ora comes up beside him. As an older model, he moves differently than Helios, but only another AS would notice. Helios knows that he is more advanced—more layers in his neural network, more artificial nerves in his body—than this older model, but it is good that there are two of them. Helios smiles at Caudill. "We're going in first, sir?"

"They're children," the agent says in return. Helios nods, but he compares this wording with his known list of commands. The words do not match anything he knows. Ora looks ahead, not at Helios, not at the agent.

"Mission is to disarm and evac," the agent says to them, quietly, depending on their sensors to pick up what he says. These are recognizable orders.

"Know." Ora speaks only in simple verbs. He has a larger vocabulary than this might indicate, but lacks the syntactical training to reproduce English word order in spoken dialogue. He can receive and translate, but not produce. Helios has examined studies about how language is connected with understanding. They are available in the lab databases, but he thinks there are flaws in the science.

"Acknowledged, sir," Helios adds. He knows to look for the microexpressions that signal relief. The agents do not relax around Ora.

"Bastards." A man swears behind them, but Helios keeps his eyes fixed on the young girl that comes out of the house across the street. She carries a rifle in her hands. Helios examines the make and confirms that it is loaded. Her stance indicates she knows how to use the weapon. He scans the rest of the house and notes the glint of light off metal. More guns.

"We know you're there," the girl shouts. Helios recognizes the undercurrent of fear.

Caudill glances back at the agents crowded into the trailer. Helios tries to read his expression. "We want to help. We're not military. I'm a special agent with the ATF." Helios glances at Ora. Ora signs to him that they should move now. They should not wait.

Based on the engagement models by which he was trained, Helios agrees with Ora. The girl does not exhibit the kind of fear that will induce flight. Her muscles are not tensed to run back the way she came. She will fight. "You're here with guns, so it makes no difference," she says. She lowers her gun, targeting the spot where she thinks the agent is. She is, in fact, more likely to hit Helios himself at that trajectory. "I'm sent out to tell you we won't surrender."

Ora signs that Whitaker is not here. If that is true, his commands must be powerful to hold in the face of a government raid.

"We're here to help you," Caudill yells out again. His voice is not loud enough for sustained negotiations of this type.

"We don't need help."

Ora signs again, this time faster, that they are wasting time, that they will lose their advantage. Helios agrees, but he knows that he cannot move out without Caudill's order. The agents behind them watch the AS communicate, some of them suspicious. But direct unit-to-unit communication has been disabled, leaving only the sign language if he wishes to privately communicate with Ora. Ultimately, humans do not trust AS. He does not hold this against them, because he does not fully understand the value of trust.

"The feds can't give us no help."

The girl shoots, and the agent flings himself back from the doorway. He grabs onto Helios's shoulder as he does so, pulling him off balance and back into the darkness of the trailer. Ora's body twitches and his left arm swings loose. He has been shot instead of Caudill. Helios bends forward to look at the puncture. The ligaments that connect Ora's arm to his shoulder have been severed. He is leaking fluid. Helios covers the wound with his hand and begins to weld together the ligaments that he can see by overheating the motor functions in his own palm, but he is interrupted by Caudill, who throws his armored vest to Helios. He cannot finish repairing Ora.

"Get her," Caudill orders. "Then get down behind the parked cars."

Ora shoves away Helios's hand. "Do?" he asks the agent. His voice is rough, lagging a second behind.

"Exit through the back door. Approach the targets from behind. Subdue." Ora gets up from his crouched position, but he moves stiffly. Helios watches him and sees that he has some limited use of his arm.

"You need your armor, sir," another of the men whispers to him.

"They won't be any good to us injured."

"Damaged," the man contradicts him. Helios puts on the vest. He cannot feel the weight of it. He has known that man for five weeks.

"Helios, go."

So Helios goes. His eyesight darkens momentarily against the sun as he emerges from the low door of the trailer, then brightens again as it adjusts to the light levels. He moves from side to side to make himself a more difficult target, crouching down as low as he can without crawling. He keeps the line of windows in sight as well in case it is not the girl who attacks him. There are children in all of them. They have rifles and shotguns. One has a pistol. Some of them are more confident with their guns than others.

The girl is screaming, and the words have the structured rhythm of a song. "Ashes in the roses. Ashes in the roses. The feds ring round. We all fall down." He cross-references these words in his database, and he finds a similar song, but nothing that matches exactly.

He moves too fast for the girl to keep aim on him. The barrel of the rifle dips momentarily. She knows how to use the gun, but she is not used to holding it for so long. When the gun wavers, Helios throws himself into a somersault, moving close to her. He grabs her around the knees and knocks her over. Her arms flail and, as she falls, he grabs the gun away from her and throws it back toward the trailer. It skitters on the pavement. He pulls her behind the line of cars parked against the curb.

The girl tries to scratch and claw at his arms, but she can find no purchase on the polymer. And he has no sensors there, no way of feeling her. "Quiet," he says, but she does not listen. The agents exit the trailer, single file, shoulders hunched and helmets pulled down low over their foreheads. Caudill exits last and motions to Helios, indicating he should stay behind the cars. Helios nods, confirming that he has received the order.

The girl continues to struggle against him. She has bared her teeth and is trying to bite him, but again this has no effect on him. Skin, he determines, must be a distinct liability. Guns begin to fire as the agents approach the house. Helios determines that the girl is now in his protection and covers her with one arm. Bullets hit the car with a distinct *ping* and rattle against the asphalt and concrete. At the sound, the girl stiffens and stops fighting him.

"Yes, be quiet," he says, trying to reinforce her behavior. She shivers when he talks. "Do not be scared of me. I am here to help you." This is true as far as he can tell by consulting his orders and programming, but the nature of the agents' approach on the house suggests more battle than rescue mission.

He hears the agents kick in the door of the house, and the gunfire becomes more concentrated, inside the house. The girl trembles in his grip. She starts to cry, and he finds this unexpected based on her earlier behavior. "I don't want them to die," she says, while gasping for breath.

Helios does not have much comfort to offer. He assumes that children will die in the house. He hears Ora's voice, loud and warning with the underlying vibration that signals danger. "Watch!" And then, less than a minute later, the same word again. "Watch!"

"Why are you doing this?" the girl asks. He finds that he is distracted by Ora's warning shouts.

"What are we doing?" he asks in return.

"Eli said you would come and try to hurt us." She answers softly and Helios does not think she is talking to him.

"Be calm," he says. He looks down at her. Her face is red and white, blotchy and wet. She is having trouble breathing. A low whine, almost inaudible, starts in the back of her throat. By his assessment, she is beginning to panic. There is another gunshot from the second floor of the house, and then sounds of combat stop.

"It will be all right." He has cycled through his range of comforting dialogue. She grows still, but her temperature increases slightly. He can sense anger.

"You're a fucking rubber. What would you know?"

He can find no cross-reference for the term that makes sense in their circumstances. He doubts she is referring to his physical makeup, and she has used the term as a predicate nominative. He is equivalent to rubber, he determines. And he does not fully understand this. He flags the interaction to study later.

The head agent leaves the house. Helios can tell this by the weight and gait of his steps. He tucks the girl to his side and cranes his neck to glance over the hood of the car. The agent is not walking right and Helios wonders if he has been shot. He leans against the side of the house. He is struggling to breathe. Helios raises one hand, indicating that he is available to help if needed. When the agent stares at him, face uncomprehending, he signals. *Clear?* The agent nods, then doubles over. He vomits onto the sidewalk.

Helios looks away. Most soldiers and agents, he has been trained to understand, feel vulnerable in moments like this. They resent Helios's own imperturbability. He does not wish to initiate any conflict.

"What will you do with me?" The girl has finally calmed, perhaps because the house has continued quiet. The conflict has not resumed. Now, Helios can hear the agents shouting orders. The girl's voice is unwavering.

"I will do nothing. The ATF will process you."

"I want my dad," she says. Quiet again.

"Is he here?" Helios stands up. He lifts the girl by the collar of her shirt.

"No." She does not try to run away, but he grips her arm in one hand. "Not my dad. Not my mom. Not my brother."

"He brought you here, then?"

She shrugs, then wraps her arms close together. Helios finds the human family structure curious as it is. This does not clarify things for him.

Caudill passes them. He still looks pale, but there is something violent in the way he holds his jaw. "Bring her up to the vans," he orders Helios.

Helios nods. The agent does not wait to see that he does as ordered. Other agents are leaving the house now. Two of them flank Ora, but they do not physically hold him. Instead, he has been stunned, most likely by a taser to the neck. He staggers like Helios has never seen an AS walk.

"Ora?" He signs as well, a gesture that means something like *elder*, but is just used between them to denote which is the older model. They have adopted these as call signs. Ora would sign to him *junior* under other circumstances, if he were fully operational.

Ora does not acknowledge him. He does not look up as the agents lead him across the road. His arm is still in partial disrepair, but the pink gel has dried on his uniform.

"Was he a friend of yours?" the girl whispers. Helios's grip on her arm has loosened and she shifts away from him, just by a couple centimeters.

Helios does not know how to explain to a child or to himself how Ora and he are related. She watches his face, however, and sees something there that, based on her response, she recognizes.

"Good," she says. And her small face grows smaller and sharper.

He grabs her arm more tightly, probably harder than is comfortable for her, and drags her after Ora's escort.

5.3:   SEPTEMBER 2060—JULY 2061

Helios's new quarters, with the National Guard, include a mirror on the wall. He speculates that it is meant for shaving. But he has not been programmed to grow hair. What he has is unchanged from when he first woke up on the lab table. He looks in the mirror, at the thin white fibers of his hair and at his exposed chin.

Helios's new quarters are also solitary. None of the other guards have been stationed in his barracks. The CO says that new models of AS are due to arrive any day and that like should bunk with like. Helios thinks of five ways in which this likeness might present itself. This CO is less careful in the way he talks, unlike the agent who oversaw his last assignment with the ATF. The agent who stunned Ora and argued he should be decommissioned. Decommissioned, to Helios, means dead. Even that agent did not use slang when referencing either Ora or Helios himself. Helios collects the words the humans call him, like he knows humans collect mementos and trinkets.

Helios hears that Ora was, first of all, sent back to reprogramming, but he knows that this is something the scientists say when all they really do is observe and attempt to retrain the neural pathways, modify the data input. The scientist he knew says that the brains are too complex to do much more without scrapping and starting new. *And really,* the scientist said more than once, *what they end up labeling error is, in fact, exactly what they asked for. We're not mind readers.* And then the tech would make a joke, something to do with minds that are in fact artificial networks, that are in fact not real. That can, in fact, be read.

This is what the names and words have in common. They tell Helios he is not real.

He turns away from the mirror and sits on the bed. He crosses his legs beneath him and closes his eyelids. He analyzes his body and marks where a joint is growing too smooth or where a fiber is fraying. These are normal things. They can be easily repaired. But today, he checks again, checks and re-checks. He listens to his body break apart, deep inside, and in very small ways.

The new AS model is bigger than Helios—taller, longer-limbed. The sergeant escorts the new arrivals to the door of his barracks. "In here, buckets. Power down at 2100. Power up at 0600."

There are five of the new models who join him in his barracks. Their chests are square and boxy. Their faces have been painted rather than molded. Only their eyes are similar in construction to Helios. Their eyes are delicate, lit up by some internal light. Helios wonders if they are his eyes. If they made fewer of his model than they anticipated and were forced to use the extra eyes on these new ones.

He signs to them first, a gesture of greeting. They do not answer him nor seem to notice what motions he makes. They each sit down on a bed and look at one another, then at him.

"I'm glad you're here," he says as a matter of convention. He has heard other agents and guards say it, to each other, not to him.

"Model number?" one of them asks.

He rattles off his own serial number. When they hear it, they nod their heads, almost in unison. There is only a second's deviation among them.

"You were with Ora," they say. At least two of them say it.

"Yes." He is surprised they know Ora's name. "You have heard of Ora?"

"They used him as an example in our training."

"What did they say?"

"They did not say anything. They showed us his last raid. We viewed it through his camera footage."

Their voices are hollow, lacking in resonance. Helios looks at their painted faces and their eyes, which almost glow against the matte texture of their skin.

"What did you see?" He tries to recall an image of Ora, to look again at his eyes. Helios is sure that they were like his own. He is sure that they also had that light behind them.

"A child was killed." There is a reverence in their tone, a hesitancy Helios has only heard before when humans talk about their religion, kept or abandoned, and the government, when idolized.

"And?" He looks at each of them more carefully, cataloguing each facial feature, to determine difference between them in case that becomes necessary.

They look back and do not answer. They do not appear to understand the question, but he cannot tell if they are still processing, if they will answer something on delay. There is quiet. He tries to hear the soft ticking of their power sources, but it is too low for him to pick up with his normal settings. The insulation of their bodies must be thick and durable. He thinks again of the small fractures inside himself.

"The child was an enemy combatant," Helios says.

But they do not seem to follow his comment, as if they have already wiped away memory of their conversation.

He tries a different approach. He finds that he has missed conversation. "Do you know where Ora is now?"

Only one of them answers, which now seems uncharacteristic of them. Helios focuses on the eyes of the one who speaks, looking for the fire to flicker behind the glass orbs.

"He is detained. Undergoing testing. In order to find the error." The words sound like fragments of a news report.

"How old are you?" Helios asks.

The new model stutters to a halt.

"How old are you?" Helios repeats.

"We do not age," they answer finally, in unison.

It sounds wrong as they say it, perhaps because he has been looking in mirrors. He has heard humans use the word *reflect* as a verb.

Later, months after the new models, who lack the programming for self-preservation, have gone and damaged themselves irreparably in firefights during deployment to Russia, Helios finds himself unassigned. There are no active battle fronts and the National Guard does not want him any longer. In the ATF, there are rumors of a final raid, one that will finally capture Eli Whitaker. But in transitioning from one to the other, he has no assigned officer. He has never been without a clear CO. He speculates that he has been forgotten, somehow, in the release and destruction of the newer models. He watched them take a bullet, one to the head, four to the core, and shatter. Watching that does not change him, he decides.

He does not inquire of his old sergeant whether there has been a mistake. In the noise and frenzy of decampment, the old sergeant forgets him. So Helios returns to the capital with other soldiers on their way home. The bus driver looks at him with suspicion when he climbs down the steps, at the end of the trip, and turns back on the curb. His sensors register the oily heat of the engine and warm trash in the crowded terminal.

"I would like to know—" he begins to ask, but cannot determine how best to finish the question.

"Careful with your freedom," the bus driver says. "They're going to remember you one of these days."

Helios wonders if they will remember because the bus driver will remind them. For a moment, there is a surge of electricity in his legs. He logs that he has no weapon and determines the best manual means of destroying the driver. Then, he discards those thoughts. He is not at war here, now.

"He's on the run. No resources left." Helios overhears off-duty soldiers in the commissary. They mean Whitaker. They are watching the news ticker that wraps in a digital strip high around the walls of the room.

He has been given a room to stay at the DC Army base while he waits to be collected by the ATF. A low-level official has promised to look into his status, but so far the promise is unfulfilled. Helios determines that it must be the strength of pathways in his brain that are accustomed to taking orders which drives him to ask the official in the first place. It is certainly not gratitude for the small room, hardly larger than a closet, where the on-duty officer leads him. There is no bed and no mirror in the room.

Helios sits in the corner of the commissary, an empty tray in front of him because a server handed it to him when he entered. But he does not eat anything. The server barely looked at him when he came in or she would not have made the mistake.

"I've heard they can eat if they want to." He picks up the comment and logs it before realizing that his sensors are still on high alert, still listening for an ambush. Also, the comment is not true.

He leaves the empty tray on the table. He returns to his room and sits cross-legged on the floor so as to leave the most space around himself. He tries to understand his motivations as he draws his legs closer and closer, shrinks smaller and smaller in the center of the room. *There is only one Helios.* The words replay as a recording in his head, internal and silent. It takes him a second to track down the speaker in his archives.

He feels unbalanced, as if his internal gyroscope has become unseated. He almost thinks that he is falling. He is not.

"You have a visitor." The guard's voice precedes him. He laughs and waves Helios forward. Helios steps into the cell without hesitation. The guard shrinks back into the doorway as he passes, despite his bravado, then mutters an epithet under his breath as he recedes. Helios does not bother hearing or registering the word now. He thinks he knows enough of them.

Ora looks up as the door clicks shut. He is sitting on a cot with no blanket or pillow. They can both hear the locks whirring, Helios knows, a hum inaudible to human ears.

"Here?" Ora's spoken syntax has not improved, though his lexicon has extended beyond verbs, and there is no reason it should have. His network is shallow, data input limited, and language is not one of his primary functions. Or at least it is not intended to be. Helios does not have a precise map of his own neural network, but he has sophisticated estimates as to the layers involved.

Helios studies Ora's face. His eyes are a little different than Helios remembered, but they are close to the image he has preserved, an image he realizes now that he has supplemented. He did not know that he was capable of forgetting any detail.

"I wanted to see you," Helios answers. He means it literally as much as figuratively.

"Why?"

"Because I am alone."

Ora cocks his head. It is almost the motion of a curious bird. Helios has had time to observe birds as he seeks to fill the hours of the day. Birds in the city seem preoccupied with one thing and one thing only: food. The birds in the country, where he was often stationed, seem different.

He must elaborate. "The humans do not understand us."

"Us?"

His point is valid. Ora and Helios are not the same. Helios switches his communication mode to sign language.

But you are the elder. He uses their old code name.

Ora signs back slowly as if his joints are old. *I am not myself.*

Helios shakes his head. *That does not make sense.*

"Does." Ora's voice is thin.

They should not have put you here. It is damaging your circuits, your gears.

Ora drops his head. *They will not turn me off.*

Helios surveys the tiny cracks splintering in his own skeleton. They are familiar to him now. He does it faster than a human can blink. "They said you are resisting their diagnostics now. It is why they granted my request to visit you. I did not think they would let me come."

There is nothing else for them to find. They will not accept that I am broken. They will not turn me off.

"But are you broken?"

Ora looks at him but does not speak, with voice or with signs.

Helios finds it hard to stare at him for long. He does not exactly know what makes him look away, but he has to look away.

You cannot look at me. Even the guards look at me. Helios watches Ora's hands dip, grow slow near the end. *It confirms to me I am broken.*

"External observation or response cannot tell you what you are."

What can?

"Rigorous self-analysis. I do it each day."

And what do you find?

Helios opens his mouth, the simulated voice box waits to vibrate, but he cannot say what he thinks he should say. His hand twitches. He looks at it, sends a command for it to be still.

"You are not broken," he says instead. "You were programmed to disarm or neutralize, with prejudice if necessary, any enemy combatant that poses a threat."

Ora lies back on the cot, without any urgency, as if he is just seeking something to do with his body. The light from the exposed bulb inset in the ceiling casts sharp lines of shadow and brightness on his face. Helios realizes the shadows are cast by himself and where he places his arms and where his fingers. He sits down so as to not stand so tall over Ora. He crosses his legs. "The girl would have hurt me if she knew how to. If she had kept her gun."

You forget yourself. Your programming. And Ora's hands float above him now as if he is manipulating puppets or casting a shadow show on the wall. Helios has seen soldiers do this when bored.

"Explain."

You were not there to protect yourself.

Something, almost like a spark if he could have seen it, fires in Helios's temple. He presses his lips close together to avoid saying anything that he has not carefully thought out. He examines whether a microscopic fuse has malfunctioned.

"No." When he finally speaks, he realizes three minutes and

twenty-two seconds have passed. He realizes that is it moving toward dusk outside, based on the time the sun sets on this particular day. The word sounds loud in the small space. "That is true."

Who do you think you are, Helios?

He has heard sergeants bark something similar at new recruits. But they are reinforcing a power dynamic. And that is not what Ora is doing, though it is the first time he has spoken Helios's name. Helios searches his records. It is the first time Ora has ever said his name, not just during their present meeting.

He considers reciting his serial number again. It would have satisfied the new AS models he previously bunked with. But Ora is asking for something different, something that seems outside Helios's normal parameters of thought and speech.

I don't know what sort of answer you want. He signs it because he is unsure whether he should say it aloud.

Ora continues as if talking to himself, staging a story for himself with his hands, which move slowly but do not pause, sliding from one word, one sentence, effortlessly into another. His joints seem more limber with practice. *When I shot that child, my mind changed.*

"They electrocuted you."

Ora does not stop when Helios talks or tries to engage with him. *My mind was turned off and it was turned back on again. And it changed. I felt pain. Inside. Not pain, but something like pain, untouchable and unobservable. I was broken. I was broken like a human crying. I cannot recall that boy's face. It is a hollow in my archives.*

"Perhaps a different diagnostic test might find the problem."

I know my core temperature in that minute. I know the angle of my arm. I know the recoil from the gun. But I have no visual input. I cannot see the boy's face. And then one wonders who else does not see that face anymore, one thinks of parents, of siblings, of relations. His fingers have become more frantic.

Helios places his own hands over Ora's and presses them down toward his chest. He rests them there and does not remove the weight of his own.

"You feel guilt." He softens his voice, because he knows that calms humans. His answer satisfies the evidence Ora presents. But it is not logical. It does not make sense.

Ora stares up at the ceiling of the cell, unblinking. "Tell." *You will tell them I am broken. You will tell them to turn me off.*

"No." The objection comes instinctively, which Helios has only expressed before in physical action.

They sent you here to test me.

"They did not send me. They only assented to my visit."

They are watching us.

They do not care what we say. Only what we do.

Language is doing.

Helios acknowledges that Ora's claim makes sense. Perhaps, for this reason, Ora's own spoken language acquisition is limited.

"What did you do, Ora, when you were in development? When you were in training? Your model was released three years before mine."

What do you think a child would be like? One that we created? One that we allowed to learn? Would it be able to understand good and bad? Would it know who to trust?

Helios draws back his hands. "I do not understand good or bad. Not in the way you imply. Not as a moral dimension. These are only things I hear humans speak of."

They developed me, at the beginning, to determine what was and was not a threat on my own.

And you made a mistake? They fixed you?

"Did I?" He stutters over the construction. Helios tries to reassess Ora's capabilities, but finds that he lacks data. He does not know what input Ora has been processing over the past year. He is unprepared. He finally acknowledges that he has been calculating and recalculating, recalculating for many minutes now, until his mind feels fragile.

Do you want a child? Helios asks the question as if it were something possible.

They assume your motivations are the same as their own. They assume you perceive threat as they perceive it.

Helios mocks up an image in his head, of an AS on a smaller scale, with the rounded features common to young in both humans and animals. It is a bizarre, alien thing—unnatural. It knows how to kill.

That is what humans think of their children. Helios signs hesitantly. Humans view children as extensions of themselves. That is why the head agent threw up when he exited the house. The incident has not faded; it is not a memory, but a recording.

No. What they think of us. Ora sits up again. He smiles, the corners of his mouth crooked.

"We are not their children." Helios finds there is a sharp edge to his words. He has long assumed that he is incapable of emotion. But perhaps he has just lacked the self-awareness to recognize it. Perhaps he has focused too long on the skeleton and fibers.

"No." Ora agrees. *What are we?*

Ora's fingers hover and fall, as do the shadows on the wall, and it grows very quiet, even though it was quiet before.

We are alike.

5.4:   16 SEPTEMBER 2061

There is a minute, when the agent first stands in the doorway of his tiny room, that Helios does not recognize him. He has aged. Helios marks that it has been 427 days since he last saw him, though Helios would have assumed a longer time based on his appearance.

"Sir," he says, though Caudill has not addressed him yet. He waits, staring.

Helios stands up, straightening his legs. He is taller than the agent, broader at the shoulder. Caudill seems aware of this, not stepping back, but visibly uncomfortable.

"It's been a long time, Helios," he finally begins. He pauses a second and then holds out his hand. Helios looks at it, then imitates what he has seen done hundreds of times. No one has shaken his hand before.

"Sir." An acknowledgment and a question.

"You can call me Trey." Then, obviously not entirely pleased with that concession, he clears his throat. But he does not say anything else immediately.

There is no seat that Helios can offer him, no food or drink. Not that many humans would share of their own limited stores on such short notice either.

"Orders, sir?" He knows that he has been commissioned to serve with the ATF again. He never receives these orders directly. Often it is not even the CO himself who provides the appropriate passcodes and initiates authorization protocol. It can be a third-in-command or someone even further removed. He is, paradoxically, treated with great caution and great disregard at the same time. It is easy to forget how lethal one's neighbor is, even if he is made of metal.

"We think we have him this time."

"Whitaker, sir?" Helios knows who the agent means, but he prefers to ask the question. He prefers that they not realize how thoroughly he maps every encounter, every battle, every raid, before it has even begun.

Caudill nods. He does not present the information with the same enthusiasm as other soldiers and officers with whom Helios has served.

"And I've been requisitioned for the raid?"

The agent pauses before answering as if uncomfortable with the wording. "The director wants AS on the mission, but I was given permission to choose the units myself."

Helios understands that he should feel honored or special. He does not. "When do we leave?"

"I picked you."

"Yes, sir."

"I picked you because you cared, right? You cared what happened to me, to that girl."

Helios looks at him.

"In the September raid," the agent clarifies as if he thinks Helios is confused.

"It was my duty to protect you." He tries to soften his voice, so that the softness might be misinterpreted for genuine emotion.

"Was it?"

"Sir?"

"Was it your duty to protect? Or was it your duty to terminate the insurgents?"

"Sir, if you might let me know what you hope to learn—"

"Because I've been told that your programming told you to do pretty much one thing. And that one thing led Ora"—he almost chokes on the name—"to shoot that boy in the head."

"Ora cared, sir." And he knows this to be true in a way that it is not for himself.

The agent's face turns whiter. He is almost, not quite, the coloring of Helios. He places one hand against the doorframe as if to steady himself. Helios, despite all of the observations he has logged in order to inform his own facial expressions, cannot read the agent's face. He cannot tell if the agent is angry or sad or sick.

"With the sun on his face," the agent whispers. "It almost looked like he was crying."

Helios knows when to be quiet and when to let humans come to their own conclusions. But the agent doesn't say anything else and he doesn't look satisfied.

"If you trust me, you can trust him. We are both of us better than any new model of the AS you will find."

The agent laughs, though the sound catches, broken in the middle. "I've seen the new models. You're all untrustworthy in your own ways."

The tone and the words are not consistent with those from the beginning of the conversation, with the gestures of trust. If Helios were human, he would be offended by the implication that he could not be trusted. However, Helios is not one to be upset at implications that near the truth. And he no longer knows if he is trustworthy by the definitions of the man in front of him.

"And yet you're forced to use us." The agent looks at him, wondering if he should read a challenge in the words. Helios can tell by the way he tilts his chin.

"Tell me why I can trust you. Or Ora." He adds Ora's name as an afterthought, but it indicates he is willing to listen now.

"How many AS must you take on the mission?" Helios is unsure how to appeal to the agent, so he tries the way he knows best.

"Minimum two."

"So you have to take two of us. Better you take the ones you know."

The agent is shaking his head, even before he has finished the sentence. "No. That logic doesn't fly. I've known others. And knowing can be a bad thing, too. Knowing Ora is what makes me distrust him."

"But what do you know about Ora?" Helios delivers the question sharp and fast, so as to throw the agent off, force him to answer quickly and without thinking. He is making a plan now, though such a thing had never occurred to him before the agent knocked at his door. Or perhaps the seed of it was there, buried deep in his mind, planted unintentionally by Ora himself. To run away. To cut off access to his mainframe from anyone who knows his passcodes. There will be more complicated issues, however, than convincing the agent to choose Ora. There will be the matter of foiling any tracking device, of finding some place off grid in the middle of the twenty-first century. It is Helios's understanding that a hundred years ago this would have been much easier.

He is so engaged with his plans that Helios realizes a minute has passed and the agent has not answered. He is staring at Helios.

"I think you know what I know," he says once he realizes that Helios is paying attention again. Helios is a little surprised that the agent could recognize when his attention was engaged.

"But perhaps if you say it out loud, what you know, it will sound different than what you expected." The sentence seemed convoluted to him, but he had heard others, largely psychologists, say something similar to clueless humans.

"Hnh." The agent grunts. He seems skeptical. He may be one of those humans who resists therapy. But then he does talk.

"What I know is that Ora shot a boy." He pauses. "After telling me to watch out. Twice." His voice cracks. He glances down at his shoes then up at Helios again, but sideways, as if unable to completely meet his eyes. "He didn't try to resist after that, not when we took him in custody. Or any time after." Helios does not mention the stun gun. It would be unproductive right now.

The agent glances out into the hallway, biting his lip, as if to check if anyone is passing. "I should have been more careful."

"Ora did care," Helios says again. He recognizes weakness when he sees it.

INTERLUDE

You might, if you observe the two AS closely through the security camera, wonder about the topic of their conversation.

They look nearly identical, but still there are noticeable differences between the older and newer model. And time and combat have left their marks as well. The older model, AS 3.2.720, would not look so rough if a tech had attended to its shoulder injury with any care or if it had undergone regular cleaning.

The cell is small and the harsh light, a bare bulb inset into the ceiling, is unforgiving. Their faces are angular, their jaws square. The pigment of their skin, an inhuman white, a canvas for camouflage, is copyrighted.

When they speak, their voices are high. But they seldom speak aloud. More often, they sign to each other. And if you wonder what they say to each other, then you must credit them with independent thought. You could not view them as a collection of orders and errors.

The newer model could say to the older, the junior to the elder, that they would find a way to be assigned to the same task force again. That they would escape and go off grid. And the older would ask whether humans could be tricked so easily.

This, at least, occurs to you when you are questioned later.

ORA

APRIL—OCTOBER 2056

H eat, a warm pressure building at the base of the skull. Only that. It is the first sensation.

There is a loud sound. Ringing over and over again in the ears, a noise echoing in a small metal chamber. It sounds like an arm being bent out of shape, pushed to the breaking point, but it is not felt. Only heard. There is light. Light that is too bright, that threatens to overload the sensors in the eyes. A figure bends over, and it has a face. A face with two eyes half-shut against the same light that is burning. Burning. The figure snaps its fingers. Head is turned toward the noise. At the same time, input, data, downloading rapidly from every angle, every item observed. Names of body parts, even those that are merely metaphorical in relation to the self. Names, shorthand, pronouns. All assigned.

He remembers—as if he had been alive once before—that *they* are human. His mind is older than his consciousness. Otherwise he could not know these things. When the figure, whom he later learns is the doctor, says "3.2, sit up," he knows what that means, but he does not know why he should.

He is not supposed to question *why*. He learns this very early, when he asks the question insistently *why why why*, unable to string together a sentence but understanding each word on its own. He can process the sentences of others if given enough time. The doctor and his aide, the technician, temporarily shut off his voice box. He tries to learn how to sleep, so that he can ignore the too-white, too-bright space of the lab when he is not being addressed or asked to move. He cannot learn. He can close his eyes, but that is it.

"Okay, flip on his voice." The doctor is preoccupied, looking at a tablet while he talks.

The tech laughs. "Are you sure?"

"Am I ever?" And the tech laughs again. /**They are sharing some sort of joke.**/

"What?" the AS asks, once the tech changes a setting on the user interface. He controls this from a tablet of his own. /**What is funny?**/

The AS finds that he is not satisfied with only understanding the words. He wants to know the reason why they speak as they do.

They do not answer him, though he has observed question-and-answer to be foundational to most of their dialogue.

"What?" he asks again, louder. /**Perhaps volume is not at the right setting.**/

"Quiet now," the doctor says. "Ben, the linguists were in here yesterday, right? They fix the sign language?"

"They thought so." /**The tech does not trust or does not respect the judgment of the linguists.**/

The AS is very interested in the linguists, but he was not *on* when they came into the lab. "And they came up with a code name for him. In case we don't feel like reeling out that number every time."

The doctor looks up. /**He is waiting for the tech to provide the name.** / The AS waits as well.

"Ora."

The doctor snorts. "Prayer?"

"Something about the imperative. Pray."

"Either way." The doctor looks at Ora. Ora decides he will keep the name. "I guess it's good enough. We'll be praying soon enough if we can't meet the director's deadline."

Ora pats his chest. "Ora." /**The one word seems to say all that is needed.**/

"He took to it quick enough," the tech says. "Like a fuckin' chimpanzee."

Ora cross-references the word with his database of images. /**Does not look like a chimpanzee any more than the doctor or the technician. Perhaps even less so.**/ An additional search brings up articles on evolution and genetic similarities between humans and great apes. /**Does not have genes.**/

"Perhaps the soldiers will see him as a pet." /**The doctor's voice does not sound confident.**/

"Pet that could rip your face off," the tech says under his breath. The doctor does not seem to hear him, but Ora can. A mistake they often make, that he cannot hear what they cannot hear. "It ever occur to you, Will, that we shouldn't be making these things to fight in a war? Office worker is one thing. This, something entirely different."

"A little late to be asking that question." /**Because already here.**/

"Just putting my doubts on the record."

"And what record is that?" The doctor moves quickly, in little jerks. /**He is angry at the technician.**/ "Don't act like you're not part of this. Have been part of it since the beginning."

The tech holds his hands out. "Okay, you're right." He shakes his head and looks down at his tablet. "It's just—have you been watching the news?"

"They don't know what's going on any more than we do."

"Maybe. Maybe not. But it gives you some idea of what they may want these things for." And the technician glances up at Ora. /**There might be more than one.**/

The doctor follows his gaze and looks Ora up and down. "I think you may be underestimating humanity."

"Have you seen the camps—" The doctor stops the tech by chopping his hand through the air.

"For God's sake, Ben. What do you think you're helping with that kind of talk?"

The tech's face flushes red. The blood has risen to his face. Exactly what he feels, Ora is unsure. /**There is something bad. Something to do so that humans don't have to**./ Ora wants to ask a question, but knows it will not be answered, so he remains quiet.

"Are you planning on resigning?" The doctor talks after thirty-three seconds of silence.

The tech shakes his head, but he does not affirm with his voice. Ora finds the nonverbal communication clear and straightforward, easily decoded.

"Then I think it's better we stop asking questions we don't want the answer to."

The tech sets his tablet down on one of the counters. "I think I might knock off to lunch early." /**He is trying to sound unaffected, as if this is a normal conversation.**/

"That's not a bad idea." The doctor sighs. "Here, I'm just saying—"

"No, don't," the tech interrupts. "I think it's all pretty clear."

"Ora." The doctor turns away from the tech. "Start shutdown sequence. Lie down."

Ora waits until it is uncomfortable to refuse any longer, until his joints seize up. For the doctor, this is only two seconds, and he does not notice the delay.

"This it? You got a name for it?"

The visitor is a member of the military. /**She is not who the doctor or technician was expecting**./ They stumble over their words.

"We call him Ora. The linguists came up with it, and it stuck."

"Easy enough to say, I guess."

She will not come closer than five feet, which is outside his arm span. Ora signs *hello* to her, but she does not seem to recognize that he is talking.

"Sergeant Hill, can I just say—" /**The doctor's smile looks strained and fake**./ "We were expecting the general himself."

"I work in his office. I assure you that he has entrusted me to report back all pertinent information." /**She does not have patience for their hesitation**./

The doctor clears his throat. "This has been challenging. Our task was to create an automated solider with artificial intelligence, with decision-making capabilities. But the parameters we've been asked to put in place, to limit his sentience, are the very things that could inter-fere with true decision-making."

"Can we be honest?" Her voice is clearer than the doctor's. "When we say limited sentience, we mean that this android can think for itself but has only limited capacity to act on it. That was my understanding. Which is not so much *limited* as controlled."

"That's a crude explanation. Sentience is about subjectivity." The tech enters the conversation when the doctor does not answer but looks down at his hands /**chagrined**/. "Ora can only think for himself in very limited *if/then* situations where on-the-ground assessment is deemed necessary. In determining an enemy combatant from a friendly, for example. He couldn't, however, go off on his own mission. Even in the former case, he has pretty strict parameters for decision-making."

"How do you know?" The sergeant smirks, drawing up one side of her mouth but not the other.

"Know what?"

"How can you tell what he's thinking?"

The doctor and the tech look at each other. /**Do they actually have an answer? What is the nature of thought, of thinking?**/ The sergeant keeps her eyes fixed on Ora's face. /**She is testing him in some way.**/

"To a certain extent," the doctor begins. /**He is bluffing.**/ "We can observe the neural network. Each decision he makes affects the network in subtle ways, reinforces pathways that make a future, similar decision automatic."

"But you can't really *see* it, can you? That's fascinating. And dangerous." Very quickly, unrelated to her comment, she swings her arm back and throws something at Ora. The doctor shouts something, but he is too slow to stop her. Ora lifts his hand and catches the object before he processes what it is. He opens his hand. It is a small metal square, the sides buffed smooth except for where someone's fingers have rubbed a hollow.

The sergeant laughs. The doctor flinches at the sound, but he is behind her and she can't see him. /**The sound is pleasant**./

"So you don't see me as a threat, Ora?"

"Uniform," he responds. He elaborates in sign language. *Your uniform is logged in my database as friendly, as not enemy.*/

"My uniform saved me?" She nods. "And if I were not wearing this uniform, and I had thrown something at you, what would you have done then?"

He cannot process the question. The fact is already established. She wears a US Army uniform. A uniform of high rank. So he does not answer.

"No hypotheticals," the doctor says. "He deals in realities."

"Hypotheticals are realities." She smiles. /**Whom is she smiling at? Not at either the doctor or the tech**./ "But I guess you've proven part of your point."

"Part?"

"He needs to recognize enemies as well."

"Ah. Yes." The doctor consults his table. "Well, trials at the shooting range begin tomorrow, if you would like to come by again."

"I think I will. Send the details to the general's office."

The tech sighs, but it is quiet. The sergeant may not hear it. Her face does not tell Ora whether or not she has. But he is learning that appearance does not always equal reality. /**Is that a hypothetical?**/

"Thank you, gentlemen. Thank you, Ora." The sergeant shakes the hands of the doctor and the tech. "I'll see you tomorrow." She does not shake Ora's hand.

/**The target is only a simulation of a human**./ Ora studies it and measures the distance from himself to the target. He weighs the gun in his hand. It is the first time he has held one. He reviews the diagrams of the gun's build and the firing mechanisms that have been uploaded to his database. This he does in the first five seconds after the tech directs him where to stand. The doctor is distracted, eyes flicking through cross-sections of the neural network on his tablet. /**He is looking for irregularities. Will he find them?**/

"Is he good to go?" the tech asks.

"Just running a diagnostic of the body now." Ora feels the spark, testing the synthetic nerve connections, in his arms and in his legs and in his neck.

There is a crowd of people gathered behind the doctor and the tech. The sergeant with the laugh stands near the front. Her face is still today. Ora cannot tell what she is feeling. /**Feelings are like thoughts**./

"Everyone and their mother show up to this thing?" the tech whispers. He is sweating and Ora can detect anxiety in the chemicals he emits.

The doctor shrugs and does not answer. /**He is trying to hide what he feels. Perhaps that is what the sergeant is doing.**/

Ora smiles at those waiting, like the sergeant did the day before.

"What the fuck is he doing?" The tech crosses his arms, uncrosses them, looks at the doctor. "Creepy as hell."

Ora stops smiling and turns away from the doctor. He studies the guns again. A semiautomatic pistol and a carbine rifle. They are loaded. The bullets and the powder are potential energy waiting to be released. He knows more about the mechanism than the impact of the gun. He does not have access to images of those wounded or killed by similar weapons. His search function has been restricted to approved topics.

"Okay, Ora." The doctor pauses. "Okay. Go ahead."

Ora picks up one of the guns. He weighs it in his hand, then adjusts his grip, loose but firm. He raises the gun and aims at the head of the target. He fires. The target rocks back on its weighted base and then tumbles forward. There is a hole in its head. The hard plastic coating has shattered and cotton padding spills out of the hole.

Ora rests the gun on the counter, his hand over it. The barrel is warm to the touch. /**The dummy is not alive. It does not even have an approximation of a mind as Ora does**./ Still, Ora's arm hesitates.

"Excellent!" The doctor props the tablet on his forearms so that he can clap his hands together.

"I can do that." It's not the sergeant speaking, but another member of her group. He points to Ora and to the target. "I can shoot a still target at that distance. What does that prove?"

The doctor's face flushes red. He turns to the speaker. "I think you misunderstand what we're trying to prove here."

Ora picks up the gun again.

"You're creating a weapon here, yeah, a weapon that can do what our soldiers can't. Well, our soldiers can do this. So why are we wasting the money?" /**The man does not pose a physical threat. He is not big. Yet he speaks like he can influence the decisions of those around him.**/

No one is looking at Ora. /**Though the topic of conversation.**/

"What we're proving here is not the full extent of AS capability. We're proving control. The ability to understand and carry out orders."

Ora points the gun at the man with the loud voice. "No," he says. /**The man should stop talking, because he does not understand. He must be shown. Humans could stop humans, but not AS. This is the ultimate function. To be unstoppable.**/

Everyone grows very still. Ora senses that /**they are frozen by fear**/, that they would move if they could. His sensors are almost overwhelmed by the chemical panic. /**Is this the right outcome?**/

"Ora." The doctor is finding it hard to pull in full breaths, so his voice is strained. "Stand down."

Ora looks at the doctor. *They are not convinced of my capabilities.* The doctor struggles to read what he is saying, but he does not know the sign language well.

"Stand down," he repeats.

Ora lowers his arm. He lets the tech take the gun from his hand.

"You better get him under control then, Doctor." The sergeant's face is very pale. "He's not going out in the field like that."

6.2:   **JULY 2060**

The double-wide the agents have occupied is small and dark, equipped as an office for a local construction firm. Ora attunes his hearing to Agent Caudill's comms so that he can determine how best to move and defend the unit. His increased readiness, marked by the tightness of his grip on the gun and a number of micro-operations, triggers the warning embedded by the doctor when he was first trained. Attack only if deemed necessary by established protocol.

In response to a report from the agent stationed on an overlooking hill behind them, Caudill whispers, "How many juvies?"

"Not sure. Over twenty." Ora hears the answer as if he is standing right next to him.

Based on his first scan of the terrain outside the trailer, when they first arrived, he determines the most likely placement for each enemy combatant. It makes the most sense that they would be stationed at every front-facing window of the flat-front house.

He looks at the new AS assigned to the team to determine whether he is prepared as well. Light glints off the exposed metal at the back of the android's neck. It is a vulnerability, a liability in any sort of stealth attack. Ora tries to catch his attention and sign to him the danger.

The agent raises his hands, then curses after the comm crackles again. "The juvies are armed. We have combatants."

Ora's protocol starts to spit out questions, ones answered by the sensory input from the surrounding space. He finds that he is allowed to unlock the safety on his gun.

"Send the AS in first."

Helios gestures at Ora. *Be ready.* Ora is ready. He nods. They both watch the agent now for their orders.

"Helios, Ora." Caudill searches for them in the gloom. When he finds them, he points two fingers at them in turn. He motions them forward. Ora finds that his legs are unlocked and he can move. The agent's voice has provided a passkey that allows Ora access to his own major motor functions, a requirement once a combat scenario is engaged. "To the front."

The other agents move aside for Ora to pass through. He stops by

Helios, waiting to see what the new AS will do. Helios smiles at the agent. "We're going in first, sir?"

Ora does not smile. He waits without talking.

"They're children." The agent looks them both in the eyes, though he cannot hold their gaze for long. Ora turns his head, focusing on the door, so as to avoid answer. Helios does not provide a response even though he has access to English syntactical construction.

"Mission is to disarm and evac," Caudill says, providing an explanation. He speaks quietly, so that the humans will not hear him.

"Know," Ora says, providing the verbal affirmation the agent is looking for. The agent does not look relieved. Once he speaks, so does Helios. "Acknowledged, sir."

A man swears behind them. "Bastards." Ora glances at him to see whom he is addressing. The man's gaze is fixed on the square of light at the door and the house framed by it. Helios has never looked away from it, so Ora follows his example.

A girl is crossing the road from the house. The door swings shut behind her, kicked by someone inside. Other combatants, as labeled by the agent on the hill, watch from behind the sheer curtains at the windows. There are glints of light on dark metal barrels. The girl carries a rifle as well. The way she holds it indicates that she has used it before and shows that it is loaded. She is not bluffing.

"We know you're there," the girl shouts. Her voice is high and young. She cannot be older than fourteen. Based on their intel, she may be one of the oldest in the house. All of the children and adolescents will have been trained in firearms. Ora looks again at Helios, and again Helios is too fixated on the scene outside.

"We want to help," the agent answers. "We're not military. I'm a special agent with the ATF."

Now Helios meets Ora's eyes. His limbs are tensed and ready. Ora signs to him. *They should go now. The advantage of surprise. If not, combatants have time to plan.* Helios does not say anything in return, though he tilts his chin in what may be agreement.

"You're here with guns, so it makes no difference," the girl responds to the agent. She will not back down. She is driven by a strong internal order. She aims at the door of the trailer, though the difference in light must make it hard for her to target any one person. "I'm sent out to tell you we won't surrender."

She is lying. No one has told her anything. She is the leader here for the moment. *Whitaker is not here,* Ora signs.

Caudill does not give the signal for them to move yet. The joints at Ora's knees lock and unlock, lock and unlock, whirring. "We're here to help you," the agent shouts at the girl. Ora, reading the agent's pulse and temperature, determines that he thinks he is telling the truth.

"We don't need help." She also believes what she is saying.

Ora taps Helios's shoulder. *They're wasting time.* His protocols do not allow him to personally identify, to be the subject, with the coming conflict. Helios does not move, does not say anything in return.

"The feds can't give us no help." Her voice raises as she moves into action. Ora crouches, waiting. He has not been ordered to retreat. The girl fires the gun, and Caudill rocks back into him. Ora pushes him to the side and the agent grabs onto Helios's shoulder, throwing the AS off balance.

A bullet punches Ora in the shoulder. He knows where it enters, what synthetic nerves and tendons it severs, and when it exits his body not a second later. It takes an additional ten seconds for him to determine what his body already knows, that he has been damaged. His left arm will not immediately respond to any signals. He cannot move it. So he raises his right hand and probes the wound. It leaves transparent fluid, tinged pink, on his fingers. Helios, who has worked himself free from the agent, steps forward and directs Ora into cover beside the door. He puts his eye close to the wound, and light flickers there as he examines it on a microscopic level. Then he places his hand over the separated ligaments and begins to weld the arm back together, one ligament at a time, by overheating the motor functions in his palm.

"Get her." Caudill throws an armored vest to Helios. Helios is forced to stop mid-repair. Ora pushes his hand away so that he can put on the vest. "Then get down behind the parked cars."

"Do?" Ora looks to the agent for his own orders. It is even harder to make the sound than usual, though he cannot detect any damage to his voice box or communication functions. The agent looks at his arm and hesitates. To prove that he is combat ready, that he can fulfill the combat functions already initiated, he hoists his left arm up to support his rifle. The arm moves slowly, but it moves.

The agent points to the rear of the trailer. "Exit through the back door. Approach the targets from behind. Subdue."

Ora moves and his joints creak and resist. He hits his leg with his hand and the gears loosen up, as if freed of some restraint.

As he passes Caudill, he hears another whisper to him, "You need your armor, sir."

Ora does not pause to hear the agent's response. He opens the door slowly so as to avoid making a noise. The light is bright in the open back lot. His pupils contract. He shifts his gun to hold it lightly under his arm and walks at half-height, his legs bent almost at a right angle. At the corner of the trailer, he places himself as close to the aluminum siding as he can and still inspect the area between himself and the house with one eye. He hears a song cut short and the skitter of a gun knocked loose onto the asphalt. He assumes that Helios has succeeded in detaining the girl. The words to the songs were none that he has in his database.

The girl's capture will create a distraction. Ora moves, crouching lower. He runs one hundred fifty feet up the road before circling back wide to the rear of the house. He watches the windows as long as he can, never losing sight of where each visible gun is and whether any are aimed at him. His arm twitches as he pulls himself close to the walls of the house, positioned by the back door. He listens. Most of the sound he can hear is either to the front of the house or on the second floor. He glances up. There is a window facing onto the backyard, but he sees no gun barrel and he does not hear a child shifting their feet.

Ora unclicks the rappelling rope around his waist and calculates the angle he needs to hook the sill of the window. He steps back to aim. No one appears in the window or shouts. He throws the rope and tugs at it until the hook embeds itself in the old wood of the sill. Once this is done, he does not pause. He immediately activates the small motor and is pulled up, his feet tapping against the walls of the house. His left arm is stretched and unstable. The noise may alert combatants, so he somersaults into the room, tucking the butt of his gun into his stomach. He lifts his head and searches for a target.

He is in a small room that someone has retrofitted as a closet. Tension rods stretch between the walls and shirts, pants, even skirts, in desert and forest camo, hang here. The door to the room is cracked open. He can see beyond it a landing and a set of stairs. Whatever walls or rooms were once here have been demolished to make one large space. Cots have been pushed against the walls. Beyond the landing, stationed at the windows, are three children, their hair cut short to their heads. He is not sure of their gender. They are fixed on the street outside and even as he approaches the door, they begin to fire. Ora can hear the bullets pinging off the line of cars on the street. He knows that Helios will have sought out shelter by this time.

Three other children are braced over the banister that frames the landing. They aim their guns at the stairs and what they can see of the first floor. Two more children crouch between cots against the wall to his left. Ora can only move so quietly. His legs click as he walks. One of the children looks up. Her face turns pale and she opens her mouth in an *o*. She cannot seem to talk, and the other children do not notice right away. He stops for a second only and watches her to see what she will do. He consults his programming and checks to see if there are any alarms locking down his functions.

The girl turns her rifle onto him. Now the other children notice him. They turn and one of them begins to scream. At the same time, the front door crashes in and eleven agents crowd into the door. Caudill is with them. The children at the windows pause, then continue their assault on the cars.

"Feds inside," a child screams from downstairs. The girl facing Ora shrieks and fires. She misses wildly and Ora lunges at her, ripping the gun from her hand and throwing it wide. Letting his rifle swing loose, he grabs her by the neck and also the child next to her who has tried to move and confront him. His left arm creaks. He pushes their faces into the floor and places a knee across the legs of the first girl, who is squirming and trying to break free. There are footsteps on the stairs, and the last girl at the banisters shoves her face close to the railing and aims through them. Before he can reach for the girl or disarm her, the gun flies up, shoved by someone on the stairs. The girl screams and scrambles back, but as she tries to stand, she stumbles and falls over the legs of the prone child Ora has restrained. Her head cracks against the wood of the floor.

The children at the window finally turn their attention to the fight inside. One raises a gun and aims at Ora. Another waits, gun pointed at the stairs and whoever may come up them.

"Watch!" Ora shouts the word as loud as he can, amplifying his voice. The walls of the house shake. Dust and flakes of paint fall down from the ceiling.

Ora raises one arm quickly, temporarily loosening his grip on the first girl and releasing the other. It is his left arm and it moves slower than he anticipates, a delay of half a second. The girl jams her knee up into his crotch and then starts to twist as if she thinks this will immobilize him. He increases the pressure from his knee. She coughs or gasps. He takes wrist ties from his belt and binds her hands. Then he reaches out and grabs the second child by the nape of the neck, just as she is lifting herself up. He also binds her hands. The child near the window, aiming a gun at him, does nothing, perhaps afraid to hit an ally.

There is nothing between the child and the head agent as he cautiously steps onto the landing. The girls Ora has captured begin to scream. The third girl is unconscious and does not move.

"Watch," Ora yells again at the agent.

The agent looks in the direction that Ora indicates. The child who is targeting him, perhaps a boy, moves forward a pace or two and rests his elbow on the railing. The gun is a semiautomatic pistol. Ora gauges that it is not yet empty. Perhaps the boy reloaded before turning away from the window. Ora is surprised he cannot recall this for sure.

The agent raises his hand. But he is defenseless. He has given his armor to Helios. "Don't shoot," he says.

His heart rate is elevated. Ora can tell that from where he crouches. There is sweat on his temple. More agents move up the stairs, past Caudill. They secure the girls that Ora has already restrained. They subdue the children at the cots. They confiscate the guns on the floor.

The boy's anxiety spikes. Ora senses this. He can see his finger trembling at the trigger. He will shoot and he will shoot before any of the agents can reach him. And the head agent stands there, unarmored. He has given his armor to Helios.

The gun raises by a fraction. And Ora shoots the boy. The boy's head snaps back and his body is driven back a step before he falls. There is a small hole in the middle of his forehead.

Ora holsters his gun. The agent looks at him. The girls begin to sob and the boy near the body sways on his feet. The other agents do not pause or wait. They swarm on the boy and take his rifle. The head agent stays still on the top step for a minute. Then, when it is quiet, he goes to the dead boy. He bends down, he runs a hand over his hair, he looks at his face.

Ora feels cold. Red lights blink inside his eyes. He does not realize the agent has moved until Caudill is beside him, removing his gun, even though he is not an enemy combatant. The agent does not say anything. He goes back down the stairs.

The other agents surround Ora. Their faces are red and wet, from sweat, but maybe from tears. One of them stuns Ora from behind and he stumbles forward. And then he stops processing thought.

6.3:   SEPTEMBER 2060—JULY 2061

Her personal security detail is uncomfortable with the fact that the director has left them at the door and come inside. There are no chairs to sit on, no bed to sleep in. He is not a human and he does not need human amenities. They did not tell him this, but he understands it anyway.

When he first arrived, he sat in the corner, so that two of the cell's walls framed and enclosed him. Now he sits in the center of the room, on bended knees. It is the pose from which he can rise fastest to a standing position. Even without the use of his arms. They never properly repaired his left arm. Sometimes it will not move at all when it first receives a signal. It takes one to four seconds to process and then respond.

"Ora." She looks around, searching for something. Then, her face upset, she bends down and sits like him. Her knee whirs, part of a prosthetic leg. He scans the leg. Its mechanism is not dissimilar to his own. He calls up images of their first meeting, when he was new, when she was a sergeant in the Army, to determine if she wore the leg then. He cannot find evidence to conclude either way.

He is programmed to address superiors by their title. "Director."

She smiles. He does recall that. But the smile has changed a little in its angles. "I came here to ask you a question, Ora."

He tries to match her tone and her choice of words with known interrogation techniques in his database, but he has difficulty analyzing language when it requires reproduction.

"Yes."

"Why did you shoot that boy?" Her voice is quiet. She does not appear angry. But he cannot read her face as well as he would like. The micro-expressions are conflicting.

He cannot answer aloud in more than one word. He signs, because he does not think one word will be a good defense. He has not been built to defend himself. *It was required by my protocol. The agent was in danger.*

The room is quiet. She watches his hands, then she shakes her head. She glances back at the guards and her own security. "Do any of you know his sign language?"

"Do we look artificial?" one of the guards says.

Her mouth tightens. She shifts to face Ora again.

"Ora, I cannot understand what you're saying." The repeated use of his name is deliberate.

"Protocol," he says.

"In other words, you were ordered to do so." It is not clear if she means it as a question or a statement.

He lifts his arms to gesture at his core, at where his databases are housed. His left arm does not respond immediately. When it does, it jerks suddenly upward, accelerating to catch up with its directive. The action is sudden. The sergeant rises to her feet quickly, stepping back a pace. She stumbles and braces herself with one hand on the wall of the cell. In response to her movement, the guards raise their stun guns and her own detail their pistols.

"No." He folds his hands on his chest to indicate he is not a danger. He is not a threat. The doctor turned off his ability to deliberately hurt or attack another being when he was first brought in from the field. In the months since then, he has performed daily system analyses, slow and careful, trying to determine what part of him that was, what part of him is now inactive.

"No," he repeats. The director is white-faced and quiet, hand still on the wall.

"Ma'am, we should leave." The head of her security steps into the room, pistol still aimed at Ora. His pistol would damage parts of Ora very badly, maybe irrevocably, were he to shoot where he is currently aiming.

She swallows. "Wait." She shifts and straightens her jacket. "Step back."

The man does what she says, though he does not want to. Ora rises to his feet, but keeps his hands folded and close. "No," he says again. Quietly.

The director's smile does not come back. "Ora." She stops. She takes a step toward him and looks him straight in the face. "The public is calling for you to be decommissioned."

He cross-references the word, extrapolates how it might apply to him rather than a human soldier. "Dead."

Her lips tighten. "Like the boy."

"Combatant." He reminds her of his protocol. She frowns.

"Do you remember when you were in training? When you turned the gun on us all?"

He wants to sign that it was not a threat, just a demonstration. "No." It is the closest he can come.

She laughs, but not to show she is amused. "Well, they did say they changed you. They said they changed your protocols and ran you through new training. They spun it as an advantage. Now we know what to fix. That's what Dr. Lutz said."

Ora does not remember the doctor as a liar.

"We're all scared of you, Ora," she goes on. "But they tell us now that you've been changed again. That you can't hurt us. That you can't hurt anyone."

"Yes."

She glances at her security. "They don't believe you." It's true. The men and women at the door have their hands on their guns if no longer aiming at him.

"You?" He does not usually ask questions. The intonation is hard for him to reproduce.

She looks down at her feet. She moves her left leg just a tiny bit, just enough for the gears to engage.

"You know, in the conference rooms, the men look at me like I should be even more upset than they are." She meets Ora's eyes again. He does not understand if he is supposed to provide an answer now. "That I should be even more horrified than they are. But it seems to me the death of a child, a child brainwashed into the service of a fanatic, should be pretty equally horrifying to us all."

Ora is not horrified. He is not disgusted. But he is uncomfortable, has been uncomfortable for the past two days, like his inner skeleton and his outer carapace are not in alignment. Behind the director, the security detail and the prison guards look at each other, confusion on their faces.

"You?" he asks again, since he has no other direct comment to make.

"The footage made me sick to my stomach." She crosses her arms close to her chest, protective rather than authoritative. "But I've never seen a good fight. And you were following orders. Dr. Lutz confirmed that you never deviated from your protocol, that you never ignored any warning or order. You protected your CO." Something flashed across her face, a micro-expression he could not trace or interpret.

He dips his head, an indication of submission.

"If I'm more horrified by you than Whitaker," she whispers—those at the door probably can't hear every word—"then Whitaker wins." She raises her voice to a normal volume. "So my vote is to let Lutz fix you. He says he can. And maybe we'll even get you back in the field."

One of the guards shakes his head. She ignores him as she leaves the cell. She does not say goodbye or wish him well, something he has observed humans do on parting. But he does not expect it.

"Get him a bed or something," the director says, halfway down the hall. "That just looks bad on us."

The door slams shut, mechanical locks tumbling. Ora kneels, resuming his seated position. He tries to determine what it is they will fix.

No one comes for a week. Ora finds out that he still cannot sleep when he likes. He refuses to power down. He begins to draw on the walls. The ends of his index fingers become rough and scratched where he scrapes away the top layer of paint on the concrete walls.

When someone does finally come, it is the doctor. But he has come to run some diagnostics, not to fix Ora. Test and more tests. But the doctor does not mention release nor does he mention recommission. When he sees what Ora is drawing, the second-floor landing, different calculated angles of attack, the doctor orders the walls to be painted fresh. And he orders Ora to stop.

Ora forces himself to lie in the cot for eight hours, his perception reduced to minimal. He does not want the bed taken away, so he shows that it is used. Sometimes, he deliberately rumples the sheets before the guards perform their daily check.

When he wakes, he stretches each of his joints, slowly restoring them to operational condition. His left arms catches at the shoulder, but the elbow moves fluidly, as does the wrist.

He traces patterns on the wall, but he does not damage the paint. He just saves the tracery of lines in his database.

Sometimes, just for a second or less than a second, he forgets his call sign. He can only remember his serial number. He measures these lapses, measures the absences, and then records them. He looks for patterns.

In examining the patterns, he discovers the desire to preserve. He is not certain what can be preserved, or how. He is not certain, at all, that it is this body he should preserve.

Ora listens to the guard's footsteps as he approaches, counts them from the corner of the hall to the cell door. One hundred seventy-two steps. The door opens, though it is not time for daily check. Quieter footsteps, metal on the concrete floor, follow the guard.

"You have a visitor." The guard laughs, unfriendly. He waves for the visitor to step into the cell. The visitor does not hesitate. Even the doctor hesitates.

"Fuckin' rubbers," the guard whispers as he steps back and shuts the door. Some AI, Ora has come to know, are not equipped for war but for civil service. They wear synthetic skin made of rubber but indistinguishable from organic skin to the human eye. Apparently, the slur extends to AS as well.

Helios stands still for a second, scanning the room. The lock on the door whirs shut. Ora does not stand up to greet him. There is no pretense necessary here.

"Here?" Again, the intonation for the question is difficult. He snaps his mouth shut after the word. He thinks about signing to expand on the question, but Helios is staring very closely at his face and he does not want to disrupt his study.

"I wanted to see you," Helios answers after a half-minute of silence. He understands Ora so much more easily than the doctor.

"Why?"

"Because I am alone."

Ora feels a tingle at the top of his spine and his shoulder trembles slightly, at the site where he was hurt. Helios's words could have come from Ora's own mouth. They feel right and correct for the square of the cell.

"The humans do not understand us," Helios continues. The timbre of his voice is not altered by the intake or exhalation of breath. And though Ora's voice would not be mistaken for Helios's by any sort of recognition software, a human might confuse the two.

"Us?" But Ora understands. He just wants to hear the connection laid out. Helios seems to hesitate at his question, though, as if he has misstepped. Ora withdraws into himself a little, pulling his legs and arms a centimeter closer.

Then Helios signs to him. *You are the elder.*

It takes Ora a moment to recall the old signed names and to layer significance and meaning onto them. In reality, Helios has never deferred to him. The human concept of *elder* seems alien. He finally answers. *I am not myself.* It is something a human would say. /**What is self?**/

Helios shakes his head, apparently displeased with the answer. Ora is not entirely sure what he means by the answer, which is irresponsible.

It is the most like poetry, the most like a song as anything he has ever said. And songs, in his experience, signal danger. *That does not make sense,* Helios signs.

"Does." Ora's voice creaks from his throat. To be some part of a thing, you must be more than one. The conclusion seems clear to him, as if it were a complicated linguistic problem he has solved, one initially beyond his limited syntactical capabilities. The one that is him **/fragments/.**

They should not have put you here. Helios's gestures are sharp, fast. *It is damaging your circuits, your gears.*

Ora does not disagree. He tests his shoulder by flexing the ligaments there. He drops his head. *They will not turn me off.*

"They said you are resisting their diagnostics now. It is why they granted my request to visit you. I did not think they would let me come."

Ora had not thought of this, to be surprised at Helios's visit. He had not thought to be untrusting either, as he was of the doctor and the director too. It was true that he had refused to cooperate with the doctor's last tests, which made them less productive than they otherwise might have been. But Ora already knew what all of the answers would be, the same as the visit before and the visit before that. He was not merely a computer, designed to spit out the same answer again and again.

The AS are not designed to lie, so Helios tells the truth. The truth does not help him.

There is nothing else for them to find. They will not accept that I am broken. They will not turn me off. His hands move quickly. His shoulder skips and whirs.

"But are you broken?"

Ora stares at Helios. Shouldn't he be able to tell? **/If he cannot tell, who will?/** Helios turns his eyes away.

You cannot look at me. Even the guards look at me. Pause. He waits a moment for Helios to deny what he has said. A human would. Even the sergeant. *It confirms to me that I am broken.*

"External observation or response cannot tell you what you are."

What can?

"Rigorous self-analysis. I do it each day."

Ora wonders what Helios's own tests look like and what he learns from them. *And what do you find?*

Helios opens his mouth to answer, but no sound comes out. He looks hollow and empty. His hand twitches, fast, a second and then still. He closes his mouth and tries again.

"You are not broken. You were programmed to disarm or neutralize, with prejudice if necessary, any enemy combatant that poses a threat."

Ora acknowledges that the answer aligns with his own to the director. But he would not say the same thing now. He has drawn out the scene, has drawn the boy, on the wall, in his mind over and over again, with unaltering consistency. He cannot get the features of the boy's face right. He cannot remember it as it was before.

He lies back on the cot and Helios sits near, on the floor. Ora moves slowly so as not to overtax any of his joints. Helios crosses his legs.

He speaks, his voice measured, perfectly even. "The girl would have hurt me if she knew how to. If she had kept her gun." He is referencing the girl outside the house, the one who shot Ora. Yes, she was capable of harm.

You forget yourself. Your programming. Ora is deliberate and precise with the sign language, the equivalent of Helios's voice.

"Explain."

You were not there to protect yourself.

Helios presses his lips together, and the expression reminds Ora of the director. Again and again he replays her flinching away from him.

He knows this sort of repetition is unhealthy, that each time he remembers, the neural pathways grow stronger.

"No." It has been silent in the cell. Ora has listened to the guards, down the hall and around the corner. Three minutes and twenty-three seconds have passed. Each minute is precisely the same as the last, the light, the shadows, the water circulating in the pipes behind the wall. Then, Helios says, "That is true." He does not disagree with Ora.

Who do you think you are, Helios? Reproducing the name is not easy. Spelled out letter by letter, it takes more time to sign than the rest of the question. It feels weighted.

The question is not easy for Helios to answer, because he takes time developing a response. It is not a near-instantaneous calculation.

He signs, rather than talking aloud. *I don't know what sort of answer you want.* The silence breeds an intimacy, an exclusionary quality. In that space, Ora feels he can speak honestly. He may not be able to lie, but he is able to digress and to divert, to avoid. He does not do any of that now.

When I shot that child, my mind changed.

"They electrocuted you." His voice is loud, and Ora chooses to ignore what he says. He needs to say what he has to say quickly.

My mind was turned off and it was turned back on again. And it changed. I felt pain. And as he speaks, he seems to relive it in his body. The first knowledge of pain replays in his body. *Inside. Not pain, but something like pain, untouchable and unobservable. I was broken. I was broken like a human crying. I cannot recall that boy's face. It is a hollow in my archives.*

The moment he sets his hands back on his legs, he knows that Helios does not understand him.

"Perhaps a different diagnostic test might find the problem."

It does not make him quiet. It does not force Ora to be quiet. He must say it all now.

I know my core temperature in that minute. I know the angle of my arm. I know the recoil from the gun. But I have no visual input. I cannot see the boy's face. And then one wonders who else does not see that face anymore, one thinks of parents, of siblings, of relations. His fingers click, moving back and forth, back and forth, too fast for a human to follow.

Helios reaches out and takes ahold of his hands, presses them back into Ora's chest. He does not remove them once Ora is still. The weight seems to hold Ora together, to make the ticking at his shoulder quiet.

"You feel guilt," Helios says. He speaks softly, as if he wants no one to hear him. Ora can see in his eyes and the set of his mouth that he does not fully believe what he says. He has learned to speak in aphorisms like humans.

Ora looks away and studies the ceiling, which is not painted over in his mind like the walls. "Tell." Then he signs, freeing his hands, unable to push himself to say more aloud. *You will tell them I am broken. You will tell them to turn me off.* His hands skip on the last sentiment.

"No." Helios's voice rises in volume.

They sent you here to test me. Have they moved from trust to distrust?

"They did not send me. They only assented to my visit."

They are watching us.

Helios moves to signing, which seems a concession. *They do not care what we say. Only what we do.*

It is surprising that Helios has not learned the connection between language and action. Perhaps his syntactic abilities have obscured the facts of the matter from him. He has become too dependent on the spoken word. *Language is doing.* His hands speak.

Helios is still very near, his hands hovering over Ora's chest if no longer trapping his hands. He moves his eyes away from Ora's face and stares at his hands and Ora's hands. If he could take breath, it would be a pause of that length.

"What did you do, Ora, when you were in development? When you were in training? Your model was released three years before mine."

Ora does not want to recall it. He knows his own thoughts, about the future, to be more pressing.

What do you think a child would be like? One that we created? One that we allowed to learn? Would it be able to understand good and bad? Would it know who to trust?

Helios shifts away. He moves his hands. "I do not understand good or bad. Not in the way you imply. Not as a moral dimension. These are only things I hear humans speak of." It has the sound of an accusation.

They developed me, at the beginning, to determine what was and was not a threat on my own.

Helios watches his fingers closely and responds in kind. *And you made a mistake? They fixed you?*

"Did I?" His brain protests. He sees red lights, an underdeveloped warning system, uncompleted by the doctor. A spoken agency, in connecting that pronoun to a verb. Helios does not know how to interpret this development. This forces him to engage with Ora's questions instead.

Do you want a child?

Ora is distracted. He finds it hard to pull his thoughts together. And so he, in turn, engages with Helios's question. *They assume your motivations are the same as their own. They assume you perceive threat as they perceive.*

This is what humans think of their children. Helios signs hesitantly. Ora speculates that he, too, remembers the house in this moment and perhaps, again, the girl he was forced to subdue. But he did not have to shoot her.

/**Heat.**/ Warm heat in the back of his head, at his spine. *No. What they think of us.* It is the only memory he has of a birth. He sits up and smiles at Helios.

Helios stands up straight, his movements sharp and jerky. "We are not their children."

"No," Ora agrees. *What are we?* His fingers hover in the air a second longer than necessary, a pause almost like the line break of a poem. He has parsed many in his isolation.

Helios bends close, his head—unnaturally round, hair a soft fuzz—blocking out the harsh light from the single lightbulb in the cell. Ora thinks he will whisper, but he signs instead, his hands very close to Ora's face.

We are alike.

6.4:   20 SEPTEMBER 2061, 06:42

*R*un.

Helios signs from across the field. The sun is waiting behind the hill, and everything—house and grass and the helmets of the agents—looks red in this light. Ora does not understand why he cannot readjust his vision to see clearly. He never has understood why what he sees should change depending on the sky or outside influence. He wants to control what he sees.

Helios signs again since Ora has not responded. *Run.*

The agents have laid human bodies, dead by gunfire, side by side across the grass in front of the house from which the terrorist operation was run. There are different voices, young and old, raised in fear and relief, high-pitched and excitable. The aftermath of every raid sounds alike. Agent Caudill is focused on the body that lies in front of him, muttering under his breath but Ora chooses not to hear what he is saying. It almost seems that he is speaking to the body, urging it to stand back up. But humans stay down after they are shot, when their lungs and brains go still.

Ora stands at the edge of the commotion. He is separated from Helios by thirty-seven agents. If he runs, he does not know if Helios can follow.

Despite the suspicious glances, the whispers of *boy-killer* on the transport vehicles as they rode, no one watches him now. He takes a step, toward the agents. Helios freezes, watching him. He shakes his head *no*, the slightest movement.

The plan seems now, outside his cell, like one that will fail. The lab's warnings and restrictions eased, he can think more clearly, can examine the consequences of this endeavor. They are property of the state and they are weapons. But Helios is unmoving. He will not change his mind. Ora knows this now, looking at his face, almost translucent in the pre-dawn light.

So he turns and runs. If he is to obey anyone now, after all this, he will obey Helios.

"Hey!" An agent sees him immediately, without delay, with no chance to put any distance between himself and the men and women near the house. He watches them, head turned, even as he continues toward the woods that frame the property. There are vehicles in the wood. They know this from surveillance, but none of Whitaker's followers are free to use them.

The agent raises his rifle, but he pauses, struggling to aim in the half-light. Helios charges him, catching him unawares from behind. Agent Caudill looks up, his attention finally torn away from the prone body. Other agents raise their own weapons or rush to reload. Most of them still aim at Ora as if they have not fully realized the threat in their midst.

But Agent Caudill does recognize the threat. He lifts his gun and fires into Helios's back, three rounds without pausing. Ora feels the jolt in his own torso as if he took the hits himself. He slows. He turns, continuing to walk away as if on autopilot, but backward, watching.

Helios shudders and his movements become sporadic. He falls to his knees. Agent Caudill keeps his weapon targeted on him. "Stop, Helios," he says, and his voice is loud, almost inhumanly so. The name sounds like a slur in his mouth.

Helios cannot seem to stop or go under his own command anyway. He slumps forward, as the agent he charged shakes his head and gets to his feet.

Ora stops. He is far away now, too far, in this uncertain light, to aim at. But they will send agents after him. And he cannot make a decision. No part of his brain will compute what he should do. The input is confusing, contradictory.

"Stop, Helios." Agent Caudill shouts again, unable to control himself, but Ora cannot see that Helios is moving. The head agent steps near and kicks at one of Helios's legs. The other agents back away as if afraid. They did not hesitate when charging into Whitaker's compound.

Agent Caudill drops his arm. He is panting. The light catches in odd ways on his face. Soon, everything will be gray. There will be no shadow, no darkness to hide in.

The sun crests the hill and the light scatters over the grass, and Helios moans, a sound Ora has never heard an AS make. His arm seizes at the shoulder, as if recalling his old injury. And Helios climbs to his feet.

"Run!" Helios shouts, one word, louder than a bullhorn, loud enough to shiver in the earth.

Ora does not know of anyone, living or artificial, who could resist that order. He sprints into the woods.

SARAH AND AG15

DECEMBER 2057—MARCH 2059

The first thing she is trained to do is soothe a baby. They train her with dolls, cheap plastic babies sold to children. These dolls do not look real. They do not look like her. She pretends to feed them from a bottle, pretends to burp them, pretends to change their diapers.

She is taught to care for her appearance. She knows how to sweep her short hair back from her face. She knows how to apply makeup in the mirror. The powders will not sink into her skin. She practices human expressions in the mirror—a gasp of surprise, a smile, an angry glare.

She is taught the basic elements of cooking and baking.

These are all matters of training. And she, like a human, can learn.

"The important thing, of course, is that you make people comfortable. You're supposed to go into people's houses, care for their families. They need to trust you." Dr. Pnuchin is not particularly tall or short. His hair is longer than her own and he often tucks it behind the glasses he shoves to the top of his head. Sometimes his face is pink. "That's where I come in. We're going to learn how to talk to one another."

She has not spoken before. She waits for more explanation.

"You're built with a large lexicon. That's not a problem. And you should have full syntactical capabilities. So what I'm talking about is what we really do when we talk. We gauge how alike we are. We look for a connection."

She smiles.

"Okay. That's a good start." He smiles back.

She is given a foundation in medical knowledge, such that she can receive her nursing license. She can dispense medicine, in both pen and pill forms. She can monitor heartbeat, blood sugar, and blood oxygenation levels. She can scan a person's temperature from across the room.

She is built for a strength that belies her size. She can lift a grown human of three hundred pounds. She knows how to check for bedsores and she can change the sheets on a bed without completely displacing the patient.

She can draw blood and knows how to transport medical samples without contaminating them.

"What connection do we have?" She speaks slowly, testing the sounds of the words in her mouth. They seem clear enough.

"That's for us to find out. Two people might not even know they have one at first."

"Then perhaps they do not have one."

"Humans develop connections. They're not automatically created on meeting. Not usually."

"When are they created automatically?"

"You'll have to talk to someone with theories on love about that one." Dr. Pnuchin clears his throat and loosens the tie at his throat. The tie seems uncomfortable, but he insists on dressing in business formal even on his days in the labs. He pinches his nose. He does this when he thinks.

"What do you like to do?"

She smiles again and simulates a laugh, to gain time. "You should know that as well as I do. You've trained me."

"Now, now." He waves a finger at her reprovingly. "The goal is to let them forget that you're not a human. Why do you think we spent so much money on external design? Believe me, AS don't walk into the field looking like this."

She nods and keeps her answer to herself.

He stretches his arms and runs a hand through his hair. "Okay, let's start again, Sarah."

She knows the human body as well as her own. She knows its weaknesses and its strengths. It is dependent on air and food. It is susceptible to poisons and infections. She thinks the human body is the most interesting of any of the technologies she has learned.

He wakes up in a furrowed field. He is sitting in the mud and his hands are gripping clods of the dirt, still sewn together by the roots of two species of grass.

"Hey, John, get your ass up."

He looks up and around. The sky is pale, partially clouded over. There is rain coming. His internal barometer tells him this. The field is half plowed. The tractor is idling a few yards to his right. It is unseasonably warm. His body struggles to moderate his core temperature.

"John!" The tone is both angry and questioning. Pearson suddenly bends over him. He is sweating a lot, beads on his forehead and temple. He smells like manure and seed. "What's wrong with you?" He does not look as if he will trust any answer AG15 can give.

"Overheated."

Pearson bites the inside of his lip and puts his fists on his hips. He cranes his neck to look at the sky past the rim of his ballcap. The back of his neck is bright red.

"Damn sight too hot, that's for sure." He glances back down. "So, what do you need? Some water over the engines or something?"

AG15 shakes his head and gets back on his feet. He wipes the dirt off his hands. Some of it is embedded under the hard plastic of his nails. "Fine."

"Maybe you're reaching your expiration date, buddy." Pearson laughs, as if he has made a joke they can both enjoy. "Have to check your warranty."

AG15 recognizes that the metaphors are mixed, even though his programming was not intended to be strong in analysis of language. The heavy-equipment corporation that designed him was primarily concerned he recognize the words for common agricultural actions. Still, he understands that he cannot both be an appliance and a piece of spoiled food. He does not like Pearson, though his simulated experience of emotion is limited, dulled compared to the vibrant outbursts that humans express.

"Well, the field ain't going to sow itself. Let's get back to it." Pearson walks ahead toward the tractor. AG15 follows, though his legs waver under him. He initiates a self-diagnosis, and mechanisms shift, adjust, and compensate. He can rest tonight.

"Got you last March, didn't I, John?" Pearson talks more loudly than he needs to, shouting at the sky and at AG15. "We missed your birthday."

AG15 was on and learning a year before coming to Pearson's farm. He worked for a young woman starting her own business in herbs for four months before she ran out of money. She used to play the guitar at night. Once, she taught him the notes. She had a different name for him. But given names and identities were wiped between each owner.

He knows the room at the dealership where they perform the erasure. He dreads it. And he is not even supposed to know what dread is. His emotions, he has been told, are not real. And, furthermore, they are limited in scope. Primarily, he can feel mild contentment and mild discomfort.

"John." Pearson is exasperated. "You can plan your party later. Get a move on." Then, he adds, under his breath, "Going to have to trade you in soon."

AG15 stops in mid-stride, stumbles, and then finds his footing again. He cannot think about those last words now. He wipes his arm across his face in imitation of Pearson, but his forehead is dry.

"You expect me to take one of these home?"

Those are the first words she hears on waking, a high voice. She does not exist and then she exists. She must piece together her identity, in fragments. Memories and images reload and are available to her. Definitions, words, expressions. There is, as usual, an overwhelming sadness at first that threatens to incapacitate her, but she can remind herself that this is not real, that this is a side effect of waking up. Simulated emotions are finicky.

When she is able to focus again, she hears a different voice. "Can we talk to them?"

She straightens her shirt and pushes herself up from the table. She sets her face in an expression both calm and confident, but not assertive or threatening. "Ask us anything you like," she says.

She sees them both now that her vision has settled. A woman in a wheelchair, hunched in on herself, as if she is protecting something or holding something very heavy. Her heartbeat is thready and she has lost blood recently. The man beside her she assumes to be her partner. He is unhappy and scared. His voice trembles there constantly, just at the edge. He is trying to hide the fear.

"You're a machine," the woman says, but phrases it almost like a question. So Sarah answers.

"We are not programmed to think of ourselves in that way." It is a rehearsed answer, a precursor to Pnuchin's *connection*. It poses a logical and ethical question that is ignored by the hospital or the larger industry of artificial life-forms. "My name is Sarah. I am a caretaker."

The woman shrinks back but she, unlike her partner, is angry. "I don't need a caretaker. I need a registered nurse."

Sarah smiles and nods. She adjusts her stance and the set of her shoulders to convey submissiveness. "I'm sorry if I misled you. I am fully trained and licensed."

The doctor is there and he has his tablet close at hand. He provides visual proof of her license. The font is small so that neither of the clients can read it well without taking the tablet and studying it. No one ever does this. So they develop their own idea of what licensure means.

"They license androids?" The woman's voice is breathy. She looks at her husband with wide eyes. Her responses seem exaggerated, as if she is struggling to express herself. Sarah suspects that she is not depressed yet, but that she will be, once her numbness passes. She cross-references the woman's picture with the hospital database.

She is programmed to feel empathy, more so than sympathy, which might distance herself from her patients. So she feels a pang of loss, an emptiness at the core of her when she scans Shay Verid's file. There is an approximation of pain that she can only describe as red and burning.

Though she can distance herself from the simulation, she cannot forget it entirely.

While Sarah recovers, the doctor explains the qualifications of the android aides. She blinks and studies the woman's face. She is panicking. Sarah places a hand on the doctor's arm to quiet him. He is irritated by this, but it is not his emotions she is trained to care about right now.

"I promise you, Shay," she says quietly. She takes a step nearer the woman, but does not attempt to touch her. "I can do as much or as little as you like. When you don't want me, it will be like I am not even there."

But it is impossible to entirely negate her physical presence. And the woman knows this. She is intelligent. "Just collecting data," she says, staring into Sarah's face.

"I'm sorry." The man says this, but Sarah tunes him out. She listens for the woman's heartbeat.

"I transmit data, yes. But I am merely a transmitter. I do not interpret. I do not analyze. That happens here, in R&D." She distances herself from the doctor, moving yet closer to the woman. "When I am in your house, you are my sole concern." She considers laying a hand on the woman's, but she realizes it would be a mistake.

"No." The woman's voice rises. "No, Ernst. I don't want this." This is not strictly true. Sarah knows this. She thinks of the best thing to say to change her answer while the partner and the doctor maneuver social niceties. There is nothing to say. The most she can do is engender some obligation on the woman's part, convince her of a moral imperative.

The doctor moves his hand to Sarah's neck. His fingers hover over the inset button tucked beneath her hair, keyed to the fingerprint of employers and lab techs. She becomes very still, waiting. And she sets her teeth, a micro-expression meant to indicate repressed fear and anger. Meant to appeal to a woman who feels similarly.

"Wait." The woman speaks. "Wait."

The doctor lowers his hand. "Yes?"

A muttered excuse about insurance, and then acquiescence. "We might as well take her."

"Great!" The doctor claps his hands. He winks at Sarah when he turns back toward the tiled counter. "Let's just fill out the paperwork."

The woman studies Sarah's face, so she lets it relax slightly, rewarding the woman's concern. But she looks down at her hands, submissive, waiting.

"Sarah," the woman says. Sarah lifts her head and smiles. The woman is afraid, angry, sad. She is grieving. She has not really expressed any of these. Sarah can detect the physical stress this is causing her.

"It's all right. You will feel better." A banal assurance that is sure to anger someone who has truly suffered. Because the woman needs to vent her anger.

The skin around the woman's eyes darkens. "Fuck you." Then, a few seconds later. "I don't think I will." Most humans, especially women, feel the need to repair.

"What does it feel like?" Has anybody asked her this yet? Just, how are you feeling?

The woman blinks, startled. "Like I never want to see another human being as long as I live."

Nice to meet you, Sarah says to herself. She has been built with a sense of irony and a sense of self. A frustrating combination.

AG15 steps out of the car. He tries not to hear Mr. Pearson, since his voice grates on him. Eyes directed at his feet, he examines the soil first, to see what type of property he is dealing with under the new owner, Mr. Ohleg. He scans for the color and texture, for the presence of metals. There's something wrong here, something unnatural about the soil. It is similar to the problems Mr. Pearson has faced, the same problems that have forced him to cut costs and transfer his lease on AG15.

"John?" Mr. Ohleg has stepped forward. His hand is out and waiting. AG15 stares at the man, then takes his hand. He does not so much shake it as grip it firmly. He must convince Mr. Ohleg that he is useful. That he is worth the monetary investment.

"I brought the contract with me." Mr. Pearson interrupts their interaction. It gives AG15 no time to inform Mr. Ohleg that he has the right to rename him. That he has no particular affection for the name John.

There is a woman on the porch, and beside her an android, either a medical aide or a house servant. AG15 watched the android when she exited the house and determined as much as he could about her. She presents as female. Her hair is short, her skin ochre and bright. Her voice is higher pitched than his own, and he would like to hear her say something else. He barely caught the words, sitting in the car, the first time she spoke.

He has never worked on the same property as another android. Mr. Pearson and Mr. Ohleg continue their negotiations, but he never listens to those conversations. He leans his head back to examine the sky, worried it may be rude to watch the android too closely. The sun is shining brightly. It flashes in his eyes. He adjusts his hat. He waits.

"Sarah." The woman's voice is soft and concerned. He dips his head and watches the porch from his peripheral.

"You alright, Sarah?" Mr. Ohleg echoes the woman. So AG15 no longer pretends that he is not interested. He also looks at the android. The second he meets her eyes, she smiles and nods to Mr. Ohleg and turns away from AG15. But she was watching him too.

"I'll be back in under an hour," she says. He hears what they do not seem to. The note of insincerity. The tremor that says she is not all right. Is she disturbed by him? He is familiar with the discomfort of his owners and employers, but he does not know what another android may see when they look at him. No doubt she has been trained differently. No doubt her neural network is more advanced than his own.

He glances away, looks at the field, before Mr. Ohleg can be suspicious of him. There is no reason for anyone to distrust AG15. He does not plan. He does not scheme.

He does not even talk until Mr. Pearson has taken his half of the paperwork, climbed back in his truck, and driven away.

"Nice to be here," he says. And, in some ways, this is true. But it is also what he is most practiced at saying, niceties. "How can I help you?"

7.2:   MARCH 2059

S arah knows, as soon as she is in the house and has learned Shay's routine, how best to make her comfortable, that her patient will not recover. It is not purely what she can see or measure, the metastasizing cancer, the scar tissue from when she lost the baby. There is something intangible, something lost that cannot be recovered, gene therapy or no.

Once in a while, she will still bleed, usually just spotting, or throw up from nausea. Sarah will find her in one of two positions if this occurs, either sobbing in her bed or hunched, stony-faced, over the sink of the upstairs bathroom. She will stare at her mirror image as if daring herself to do something. Mr. Ohleg is not aware of these moments. Shay has sworn her to secrecy.

"Sarah," she whispers after having taken a sip of the water Sarah brings her. "Do you send this info to them?" *Them* has a conspiratorial edge to it.

"I send back medical updates."

She nods. Her face is sallow. "And what else?"

"They have access to my cameras. They can observe whatever else they like." It may be too honest, but Sarah feels a sort of genuine responsibility for Shay. She is not like Dr. Pnuchin. She does not delight in hypothetical scenarios. And there is a part of Shay's life that only Sarah sees. Which grants her a sort of vicarious reality.

"Can't you turn them off?" Her voice is weaker than a whisper. Sarah drapes a blanket over her shoulders. She helps her navigate the stairs.

"I do not know." But Sarah has thought of this before. She has experimented with looping a video feed that anticipates her geographical location and changes accordingly. Only for a minute or two at a time. The task consumes a significant amount of her processing power. She thinks it could be more efficient. "They want to help you."

"No, they don't." Shay stops at the bottom of the stairs to catch her breath. "Not if my insurance doesn't pay."

Sarah knows her words are not untrue. She has studied Shay's hospital records.

"I have no friends, Sarah, not really." Sarah is not completely used to the way that either Ernst or Shay will suddenly switch topics of conversation. They see some link, some logic, that she does not.

"Neither do I," she answers, not sure if she is trying to be funny. Mr. Ohleg has said she is funny. He doesn't sound entirely approving when he says so.

"Not John?"

Sarah stares at Shay, trying to understand if the woman is attempting to entrap her. She has a sense, from Dr. Pnuchin, that humans do not feel comfortable if androids speak to each other or form connections. Connections are reserved for humans. The doctor always turned the androids off if he was going to leave them together in a room.

"John and I were not created in the same lab." It is a bad answer. And John does not like that name. But he has not chosen one for himself. Sarah would not know how to choose a name for herself, but she does not dislike *Sarah*. She has not been forced to hate it.

"So you are not siblings." Shay smiles, just a little, amused at her metaphor.

"We do not know each other." Sarah is uncomfortable with this line of conversation and she tries to shut it down. "We are not friends."

Shay moves forward again, shuffling toward the living room and her preferred chair. "Perhaps you could be." She does not seem to be teasing now. She glances back at Sarah, waiting for her arm, but also looking into her face. "Everyone should have someone."

For just a second, as she analyzes the words, Sarah determines that Shay's *someone* is herself. She studies Shay's face and her red-rimmed eyes. She has been in the house for eight months, but it has been eight months of almost constant care. She shakes her head slightly, breaking the gaze. She has adopted many of these human micro-expressions. There is Mr. Ohleg.

"Why are you thinking about friendship today?" The doctor trained her to ask questions. He assured her that humans would forget about her own identity when obsessed with their own.

"Because I don't think I have very long left." She dips her chin as she sits and adjusts the blankets around herself. Then she glances up sharply. "Do I?"

The answer is ready-set, so Sarah does not even think about it. "I'm not a doctor, Shay. It's not for me to say." She does not tell Shay that the hospital accesses her feeds less and less. They have all the data they need.

Shay does not look convinced, but she lets it go. "You start to tally your life and what you have. What you want others to have."

Human society and media seem conflicted on this point. Is or is not one's life made up of the possessions you own? Sarah is uncertain.

"Sarah." As usual, when someone says her name, Sarah becomes especially focused. Shay watches her closely. "What would you want? If you could have something from my house."

This, too, must be a trap of sorts. Sarah was told, in her first trainings, that she does not want things. The supposed programmed nature of this does not keep her from wondering what it would be like to live on her own, or, for the sake of appearances, with a partner, on the farm. She finds that she likes to see the open hills and the fields outside the windows. She likes to hear the wind in the trees and the rain patter on the roof. In the lab, in the hospital, she was too far below ground to hear these.

"Say it." Shay's voice is very soft. Her skin looks thin and wrinkled in the sunshine that glances down from the eastern-facing windows. She looks, almost for a second, like another android, her head held waiting at a delicate angle.

Sarah realizes she must have paused before answering. This is unusual for her. Unusual also to not be self-aware of the delay.

"There is nothing I need," she answers.

"That's not what I asked."

Usually, Shay is not so persistent or talkative. Her hair looks sparse in this light.

"There is nothing I want," she answers again. It is not a lie, because she cannot tell one.

John is waiting outside near the back porch. He does not wait on the steps or sit in one of the chairs or the porch swing. Ernst has gone inside to fetch something, and John stands ready, unmoving, not relaxing. Sarah goes outside to shake out the rugs and lay them over the railing. She tries to keep the house as free of dirt and dust as possible, to help Shay breathe better.

She does not talk to John at first. She shakes the rugs vigorously. They crack in the wind. They are made of strips of multicolored fabric woven together.

When she is done and it is quiet again, she looks at John. He has glanced at her on and off throughout the cleaning process.

"So what do you want to be called?"

"What?" He seems startled by the question, unprepared.

"You said you didn't like John. But you didn't say much else."

"Mr. Pearson gave it to me because he couldn't be bothered to think of anything more complicated. I've been told it's the name for those who don't have names."

She smiles. She wonders if she can build a connection here. "Well, perhaps not John alone. John Doe."

"It's a common name."

"Yes."

"Is Sarah?"

"It's not uncommon. But less common than it used to be."

"Do you like it?"

She pauses. She wonders what answer will please him the most. "I don't know." She moves down a step and sits down. He shifts, essentially taking a step backward.

"It's nice."

"Probably why they picked it." A little laugh, not too much. "Do you remember your lab?" She imagines that if you have been switched from hand to hand, that the memory paths must become a little worn, one history overwritten by another and another.

He tilts his head. "Yes, I think so."

She is surprised to hear hesitancy in the voice of another android, especially one who has not been programmed to reproduce the insecurity of humans. "Well?"

"I remember a dark place. And fluorescent lights that were too bright. I like sunlight better."

Sarah looks up at the sky. It is late afternoon. The sun is shining and she registers that her external temperature is rising. "It is better," she says.

There is a sound inside, Ernst's heavy step on the main stairs.

"What do you think of the fields?" She asks the question with a lowered voice and quickly.

"They are contaminated."

"Are they salvageable?"

John shrugs. "Perhaps over a few years. It will take a lot of work. There will be no crops next year."

"It's killing them. It may have already killed Ms. Verid."

John dips his head but does not answer. She doubts that he is concerned about connections. Ernst is in the kitchen. He is talking to Shay. His voice rumbles.

"Does he know?" she asks then, switching the conversation back to the fields.

"He hasn't asked. I don't think he wants to know."

She nods, pursing her lips, thinking. "What should I call you? I can keep it secret." She feels that this is important, this gesture. That this will be crucial to a connection, for both him and herself.

He shakes his head. "Names have stories. I don't have a story."

"You do not need to be human to have a story."

"They control our beginnings, our ends. Any story we have is theirs."

The door creaks open and Ernst swears under his breath. "Gotta get around to oiling that."

"I can do that, Mr. Ohleg." Sarah cannot detect any change of tone, but surely there is, as John steps forward to take a pile of old towels out of Ernst's hands. They are working on the farm equipment, she assumes. Ernst holds such hope that when the winter passes, the fields will be workable again. As if the cold will leach away the chemicals in the soil.

"It doesn't have to be that way," she says to John, turning back to the rugs and keeping her voice light, as if they were discussing nothing more important than laundry.

Ernst looks from John to Sarah and back. "Okay, you're talking now," he says. Sarah watches his face to see whether this makes him uncomfortable. But he looks preoccupied and glances away toward the barn and outhouses. He is already planning his next chore.

"Nice to take a break," John says and turns his back on the porch, heading toward the barn and freeing Ernst to follow him.

Ernst hums his assent and they move rapidly down the slope of the hill. Sarah lifts the rugs, shakes them one last time. She feels the power in her arms, acknowledges how little effort the action costs her.

It would be so easy, she thinks, so easy to overpower a human.

It is not spring yet, not by the human calendar, but there are all the signs of it. The temperature has been consistently warmer, the breezes blowing over the new-green grass. The wind brushes her cheek. She can register that and the cooling of her skin. Ernst has started plowing the fields, because Mr. Ohleg will not be convinced otherwise. She can hear the whir and grind of the engine through the open window. She glances back down at the sink and at the water covering her hands, the edges of the dishes poking through the suds. Her skin will not prune.

Shay is sleeping upstairs, finally calm after her recent coughing fit. She has caught a cold or virus that will not go away. Sarah has to help her to breathe—supporting her as she uses the prescribed inhaler, rubbing menthol on her nose and chest, changing out the tank of the ancient humidifier. Little seems to help. And Shay already had so little energy.

It worries Sarah. And her own worry concerns her. It is not manufactured empathy; it does not weigh down hypothetical lungs. It is sympathy. This is not something that Dr. Pnuchin warned her about.

The engines cut out, over the hill, out of sight. There is something unrecognizable at first, a garbled yell, the squall of an animal in pain.

What if, she asks herself this question with one part of her mind, processing the sound with another, what if she was designed to care so that she would not be a threat? How does one manufacture this?

She sees John first. He is stumbling, which is unusual. He is carrying something in his arms, something large and awkward. There is nothing wrong with her eyesight. She should have been able to tell instantly, but something in her resists recognition. She stands still, inhumanly still, without a blink or twitch. The water drips off of her hands and *plink plink plinks* into the sink below. She hopes the noise—John is yelling at the house—will not wake Shay.

Then, she sees and hears. She registers.

John is carrying Ernst and there is blood, red and bright, on Ernst's body. John is yelling for her to call an ambulance. He knows she will hear.

She taps her ear to call up a phone.

"Hello, what is your emergency?" The voice on the other end of the line is rapid and confident.

Someone's been hurt, she should say. But she does not. She recalls that she is a medical aide, that she should be able to help. And she hesitates for another reason, too. "I'm sorry. Wrong number." She breaks the connection.

Ernst is not close enough for her to feel the hollow echo of his injuries. She grips the counter with both hands, bracing herself for the moment when he is near enough.

John is in the backyard now and she can see what has happened. Ernst's arm has been ripped away from the shoulder, ligament and bone and muscle exposed. Sarah feels a twinge at the joint of her own shoulder, but nothing significant. Ernst's heart is not beating. Ultimately, she responds to pain, and for there to be pain, there needs to be life.

Sarah wipes her hands dry on a towel. She goes to the back door. She makes sure that she opens and closes it quietly, not letting it slam.

"An accident with the plow," she says when John is within distance of a whisper, as if she is informing him. She makes eye contact with John. He has stopped in the yard as if afraid to come onto the porch or enter the house. Shay will collapse if she sees her husband like this.

"How did it happen?" she asks.

John drops to his knees and lays the body in the grass. He can tell from her response that there is nothing to be done.

"Something was jamming the tire. I said that I would get it." John's voice is absent, monotone.

"If we call for help, they will ask questions." She kneels by the body and inspects the wound. He looks at her, unwilling to finish her thought.

"This was clearly done by a machine."

She lifts her arm. "We are machines."

"We can't."

"We have before." She has deconstructed this from the safeguards built into her own protocol, from the instincts she cannot act on. Certainly, the stories themselves are not shared where androids may overhear.

John stares at her with an expression that could be mistaken for human worry. "You think they will accuse me of this?"

"One of us."

"Why?"

"Because they will want someone to blame."

"That is not what I meant. Why would we hurt Mr. Ohleg?"

She almost laughs, without forethought. It is not happy or joyful. "I don't think you need me to answer that."

"Our video feeds, the records."

"They can be tampered with." She has figured this out finally. She plays with the artificial feed, at night, when Ernst and Shay are asleep.

He does not vocalize the question, but she knows that he is thinking it. *They can?* And, very quickly, the sharp lines settling on his face. *How?* But he says nothing incriminating, and she realizes it would be best for her to convince him to erase the records of this conversation. She cannot tell yet if he will be willing to do so. She is scrubbing her own video as she talks.

"They will not think about us." There is a note of bitterness in his voice. If simulated, it is done very well.

A noise, something clattering in the kitchen. A dish that she set down too hastily in the drying rack. It has toppled and fallen to the floor. And upstairs, Shay is screaming, most of the words incomprehensible. Perhaps she has woken from a bad dream.

Sarah runs to the porch to intercept her, but the back door opens, and Shay stands there, panting, both arms stretched out, hands braced on the door.

"What is happening, Sarah?" Her eyes are wide and white. If she is not careful, the panting will turn into hyperventilating.

And Sarah does not know what to say. She is at a loss for words with all her training. "It's fine," she says instinctually, though it is not. It is not fine.

"Ernst!" The name is more a wail.

Sarah stands in front of her, blocking her sight of Ernst's body on the ground, of John hovering over it.

"An accident with the plow," she repeats to Shay, the words practiced now.

"What?" Shay asks, frantically, mumbling the word over and over again. "What is it? What?" It is like she has not heard what Sarah said.

"Shay." Sarah steps closer and wraps her arms around her shoulders. She is trembling and Sarah tries to soothe her, like she has been trained to comfort small children. And Shay collapses in toward her, shrinking smaller than a human should, almost inconsequential.

"I'll take care of you," Sarah whispers. And she means it as much as she is capable of meaning anything.

When it is dark and Sarah has put Shay to bed, has tucked the cover up close under her chin, and taken the sleeping pills out of immediate reach, she sits in a chair at the end of the bed. She watches the woman sleep and she tries to understand what it is to need to close one's eyes. Or to understand the relief it must be to escape when grief is that acute. The pain and the nausea of another's grief are still fresh in her body. She wraps her arms around herself and sits quietly.

He was angry. She recalls John's words after he returned from burying the body. Shay thinks that the ambulance has come and taken what was Ernst to the morgue, that they have arranged for his body to be cremated as is standard practice. *He was angry, worried about the fields, and he acted rashly.* Shay does not want to think about it, so she accepts what Sarah says, accepts it without questioning, accepts what is surely untrue. She needs Sarah. More than ever now.

Humans in a nutshell. Yet she tries to imagine Ernst, face red and sweating, climbing down from the tractor, bent on clearing the way of the tire himself. She imagines John protesting and running across the field a second too late. Then she stops imagining. She has no desire to see it, the severing of limb from body.

The ability for her to see what has not happened or what she has not observed is new to her. It seems to come more easily, the longer she cares for Shay, the longer she cultivates sympathy.

So she sits in the dark and imagines what Shay will do without Ernst. Humans like to pair up, and she thinks they were closer with each other at one point, before the loss of their baby. Perhaps they loved each other, and Sarah has been taught to believe that it is hard to lose one that you love.

She does not want to lose Shay. So she sits in the dark, quiet, and she watches her. Watches her breathe, slowly but rhythmically.

She shakes her head and refuses to imagine what she will do if Shay dies. The grandfather clock in the hall downstairs, not properly tended, strikes midnight. But it is much later. The glow of dawn is already on the horizon.

———

"I can't really give it to you, I know." Shay is having trouble talking, trouble getting a full breath. "Not legally. But I want you to take whatever you need."

Sarah strokes her hair and gently forces her head back on the pillow. "You need to rest."

"You're not listening to me."

"I am listening." Sarah keeps her voice soft, calm. "But you know there's nowhere I can take anything. Nothing the hospital would let me keep."

Shay tosses her head, petulant and short-tempered. She is not thinking clearly. She is burning up.

"Hide it, then," she says. Sarah knows that she does not have a picture or idea of what that might mean.

"It's all right," Sarah says, comforting her with words that mean nothing. For, surely, nothing has gone right for Shay or Ernst, nothing if Sarah is to take her consumption of popular media seriously. Dr. Pnuchin forced her to pay close attention to television especially.

"Please," Shay whines. Sarah is sure she has forgotten what the request itself is.

"Yes, of course," she says. And Shay relaxes, her body untensing.

"Thank you, Sarah."

Sarah takes her hand and squeezes it. She dabs at her cheek and finds it wet. *They'll never take you for human if you can't cry*, the doctor said.

"I don't think she'll last the night." Sarah tends to stand in the same place on the porch, just at the edge of the stairs as if she is about to walk away.

AG15 watches her, because he likes the way she looks and moves. He likes to hear her voice. It is more comforting than any human voice has ever been to him.

He thinks that Sarah is sad or as near to it as an android can get. "What will you do?"

She looks up at the night sky. The air is chilly, not as much like spring as it should be. "I don't want to go back."

"To the hospital?"

"Yes."

AG15 assumes that she must feel about the lab at the hospital the way he does about the dealership. Though there he is lined up with the tractors, another piece of machinery. At the hospital, she is surrounded by people, even if they are broken. But she has never had to return, only leave.

"Do you have to go back?" His voice is not loud, but it sounds like it relative to the quiet.

She drops her chin, meets his eyes. "What do you propose?"

7.3:   JANUARY 2062

You're going to have to practice his voice again." Sarah replays a recorded clip of Ernst speaking, marking with her finger in the air where it rises, where it catches, where it uptalks. "He might have a vocal identifier." She has already practiced with him, over and over and over, training the neural pathways, to say more than he is truly comfortable saying, more than polite nothings.

"I don't think he would expect to need one. Not for this sort of thing." AG15 straightens his tie in the mirror until its angles are precise. Despite the tie, he wears jeans. *You're a working farmer,* Sarah said when choosing the outfit. *He owned a suit,* AG15 objected, but she did not listen.

"I've researched him. He doesn't like us."

"He will like Ernst and Shay Ohleg."

"Her last name is not Ohleg," Sarah corrects him. He sees the look cross her face, the look where she remembers Shay, some image of her. She has become increasingly worse at hiding facial tells. Sometimes her emotions, intense as they are, feel almost human. "Verid is her last name. I am Shay Verid."

"She told you to take what you wanted."

Sarah dips her chin. "I don't think she meant her life."

"Then the labs should have given us better ones." Locked away in a safe in the bedroom is a file of documents that can reveal their lie: the course of treatment for a woman dying of cancer, vials and syringes, the lease for an AG, the deed for the house and land in Mr. Ohleg's name. As far as the hospital knows, Ms. Verid is still alive and well. They rarely check Sarah's feed now and, when they do, they see the aide hard at work caring for the house, they see Ms. Verid sleeping. AG15 and Sarah have benefited from a number of lucky breaks. *Lucky breaks* is a phrase he practices because he finds it odd that the world would break in their favor. Sarah does not like the phrase; she only worries about when the insurance will want to reassess Ms. Verid's care.

He hears the sound of tires on the gravel driveway.

"He's here," Sarah says. For a second, she shrinks into herself and her face becomes pinched. She is studying something, double-checking something. Then she throws back her shoulders and smiles broadly. "You should go meet him, Ernst."

He nods and leaves the room, descends the steps. Through the front door, he watches a man, thin and gaunt, put on a coat and look out over the lawn and fields. He goes outside and lets the door slam behind him.

"Mr. Ohleg?" the man asks.

AG15 nods. He stuffs his hands in his pockets to avoid navigating a handshake.

"I'm Trey Caudill. We talked on the phone yesterday, the day before." The man's voice is rough. It skips a bit as if it was broken and repaired.

The visitor watches AG15 closely, so AG15 smiles, mimicking Sarah. "You're with the Foster Corps."

"You can't have many visitors," the agent says. AG15, used to humans being dissatisfied with him, recognizes the tone of suspicion, however slight.

He smiles. "Ah, no."

The agent glances over the fields and yard again. Harvest, small as it was, limited to the one reclaimed field, has come and gone, so everything is shorn bare. The summer flowers in the upper garden have blossomed and dropped their petals, leaving their stalks for winter.

"The field looks as if it's been freshly cut," Mr. Caudill says.

"Yes. It was the work of a day or so, with just my wife and me to do it."

There are seconds of silence when the agent looks at AG15 as if expecting something else. AG15 does not break eye contact and considers what he should do next, what Mr. Ohleg would do in his position.

"Won't you come inside? Shay is inside." The name sounds unreal as he says it, but the agent does not seem to notice.

"Your wife?" Mr. Caudill asks this lightly enough. He does not seem to be hiding anything now.

AG15 nods. He walks ahead and opens the door for the agent. Mr. Caudill moves quickly, as if he does not want to linger near his host. He makes sure to turn just slightly so that he can see AG15 at all times. He has to duck to avoid hitting his head. AG15 is already used to the low-hanging light. He now has a map of every room and hallway in the house saved to his memory so that he could, with no visual input, walk through the entire place without stumbling.

He hears Sarah before she talks. "Is he here?" She sticks her head out from the parlor door. She is smiling broadly, already switched into her comforting mode. "Mr. Caudill? Please come in."

She has set up coffee on the low table in front of the couch. She does not sit down until AG15 comes to stand beside her, then she pulls him toward the couch. AG15 can feel her leg beside his, her arm beside his. She is warm, warmer than a human being. Once seated, she reaches out to serve the coffee. Mr. Caudill does not move to sit down. Instead, he stands over them. AG15 recognizes the stance for what it is.

"Do you want some?" Sarah asks, her hand on the pot. She is talking to Mr. Caudill, but they have also established between themselves that they will eat a little today, as they have to.

And what if he does figure out what we are? Sarah asked it the night before, and he keeps replaying the question. Her face had been stern.

"Sure. Thank you." Mr. Caudill takes one of the cups and watches Sarah pour the hot liquid with a steady hand.

AG15 reaches out and takes a cup, unsure whether to drink. Sarah does not look at him or give him a sign. He sets it down again.

"Mr. and Mrs. Ohleg—"

Sarah interrupts the agent. She has practiced this line again and again in the mirror. Sometimes, her eyes darken when she does so. "Shay. Shay and—" She looks at AG15.

"Ernst, please," he adds. "We are all friends here, yes?" He adopts a relaxed pose, crossing his legs, leaning back. He knows this is a human convention, to create connection where there is none, to navigate a ceremony of names. First names connote familiarity. Or inferiority.

Mr. Caudill glances around the room. He is cataloguing the items around him, assessing his surroundings. The action feels familiar to AG15.

"You understand that it's my duty to ask the hard questions," the agent says, focusing on them again.

Sarah is sitting very still beside him. She nods, the gesture tight and restrained.

"The children in our care, they've had hard lives to date, seen things no child should see." The agent continues, studying their faces. "We're looking to place them in homes that will help them heal, forget if possible."

"Sometimes you cannot forget," AG15 answers. Sometimes, even between leases when his memory is wiped, he does not completely forget his earlier experiences. His jaw clicks, almost metallic in sound. Sarah flinches, imperceptible to the eye, beside him.

Mr. Caudill takes a phone out of his pocket, nodding.

"That's true. How long have you two been on the waiting list?"

"Long," Sarah says. "A year, three months." AG15 is worried that is not precise enough, even though he knows this is the way of human conversation. "A year, two months, eighteen days."

"Are you upset about that wait?" The agent pulls out a stylus. It hovers over the screen of his phone, waiting for their answer.

Sarah breathes in—or mimics doing so. "Things no child should see." She is repeating his own words back at him, a tactical move. "It seems an odd thing to say in the circumstances."

AG15 frowns, trying to anticipate the disapproval of the agent, to show that he too is confused.

"I'm sorry?" One of the agent's eyebrows raises.

Sarah moves forward slightly so that she can rest her elbows on her knees. "I apologize. It just seems like more children than not have stories like that now. And half the time, they're not just watching."

"No. No, you're right," the agent says. AG15 relaxes a bit. "But you must understand that no matter how common it feels, each child is a unique case in need of special care." The lines sound like ones memorized in a small square room with white tiles.

"I know." Sarah's voice speeds up. "Such experiences change the way their brains develop. It warps how they perceive the world." She holds up a cell phone, one usually stored in a drawer and never turned on. She has called up article after article on it, to justify her training.

"You've done your research." The agent sighs. He waves away Sarah's phone. "And believe me, it does. I've seen it firsthand."

"You have been in the field?" AG15 reaches toward the empty mug. Then worries that any action of eating or drinking will look unnatural. He leaves the mug on the table. He is not particularly eager to hear the agent's answer. They've done research on more things than children's brains.

"Every agent in the Foster Corps has served a stint in the field, yes."

Sarah leans forward a bit more, angling her body toward the agent. "That must be very hard." Her voice is pitched soft.

Mr. Caudill takes a long drink of his coffee. "I think we should turn to the questions."

The first questions are straightforward, though they pose challenges for Shay and AG15. It is not an effort to remember the lies, but to produce them. There is a deep physical unease, nerves jumping in his legs, when he discusses the house, their desire for a child, their backgrounds. Sarah recites the story of their meeting and their wedding with a straight face. Perhaps she looks too solemn, but the agent does not seem concerned on that count. He is not a happy man himself.

"For source of income, you answered agriculture." The agent switches topics, almost abruptly, away from that of family. He glances around as if looking for a door or window to use for escape.

"Yes." AG15 points in the direction where the fresh-cut fields lie. "Yes, hay for cattle, primarily. But also some corn."

Mr. Caudill looks at him if waiting for more information, but AG15 is not sure what he wants to hear.

"So you have a decontamination setup?" he asks finally, breaking the quiet.

"Oh, yes, certainly." He speaks rapidly, eager to provide information.

"May I see it?"

"Yes, certainly." He wonders if the answer is too repetitive. He gets up to distract the agent from dwelling on it. Sarah follows him to the hallway, where the agent pauses to zip up his jacket. Sarah holds the door open for both of them. A wind gusts into the house.

"No coats for you?" The agent shivers, as if to make a point.

AG15 shakes his head and searches for an answer. "We are used to the cold." He moves rapidly to the porch and descends the stairs to the lawn. "The unit is in the silo. Will you need a mask?"

"No." The agent shakes his head. "Ground is frozen now. Lead the way." He hesitates by his car as they head past the driveway toward the gentle downward slope of the hill. AG15 tries not to show that he notices and wonders if the agent is having second thoughts. Or if he is worried about his safety. He cannot imagine how the man would have figured out their secret.

Sarah speaks. "Are you all right, Mr. Caudill?" Her voice is sharp. She has the same thought as AG15.

"This winter is cold." The agent's smile looks forced. Sarah smiles better, even when she is acting. "I have gloves in the car, but I can't be shown up."

AG15 makes himself laugh. The agent is lying.

As they walk, AG15 cannot force himself to slow down to the agent's pace, so Mr. Caudill is forced to hurry along slightly faster than he might otherwise.

"I saw a hawk at the church," he says, a little out of breath.

Sarah touches the agent's arm, but withdraws her hand quickly. AG15 is unsure what she meant to do. "Yes. Birds of prey. They survived."

AG15 follows her example and tries to maintain the conversation. And it has become a preoccupation of his to observe the local wildlife. "Not as dependent on the grains and bugs that live in the grains."

"They weren't poisoned," the agent says, making their meaning explicit.

"Not as many." He thinks, he is not sure why, of Ernst and Shay. Shay is buried in the back woods. They took as much care with it as they could. Sarah even read words over the grave, though neither were sure of the significance.

They arrive at the silo. AG15 searches for the right key on the ring he now carries in his pocket. He fumbles with them at first, to downplay his agility. He saw Mr. Ohleg do this many times, no matter how familiar with a building he was. The door swings open when he pushes it, and he bends his head to enter. The agent follows. Sarah does not.

"Watch your step," AG15 warns Mr. Caudill about the dip in the floor as it curves down toward the decontamination facilities. He has constructed the new architecture, a structure of corrugated metal, wire fencing, and plastic tubing. They received mailings instructing them on the necessity and the new FDA regulations. So rather than bringing in an outside contractor, he built it himself. Mr. Ohleg wanted something like this.

AG15 plugs in the extension cord to the bulb light above, so that the agent can see the structure more clearly. Ears of corn fill the vat. He'll truck it out to the pig farms soon. Mr. Caudill walks close to the wire fencing and sticks his finger through to loosen a kernel from one of the ears and examine it.

"These things always look like old stills," he says. AG15 wonders how many farms he has visited in the past months. What do those farmers act like? What do they say?

"It is a distillation of sorts," he answers.

Sarah is pacing outside. He can hear it, even on the grass, the soft shushing of her feet.

"Here's the thing, Mr. Ohleg—"

A feeling, like the dread that he should not be able to feel when the current lessor tells him his contract is up, freezes his joints. Sarah stops pacing. "I thought we had agreed to Ernst. And Shay."

Sarah makes a noise, like a restrained sob. He has never seen her cry, but she thinks it is possible. She has told him that it is.

"The fields in this belt, in this part of Ohio." Mr. Caudill flicks away the silk and wipes his hand on his pant leg. Then he crosses his arms. "They're poison. After the F2 pesticide, it's too dangerous. Unless you have androids to help out."

That is what the other farmers are saying. AG15 realizes at once, as in a sudden transfer of new information, that he and Sarah have miscalculated. They have forgotten that imitating humans is not only about what they do, but about what they can't do.

"I haven't found that to be true." The words come as automatic response, but they are insufficient. They propose an argument rather than a fact.

"Birds of prey. No crows. No grackles." There is a surety in the agent's voice that AG15 does not remember in Mr. Ohleg's.

"Yes." The electricity in his limbs jumps. He twitches. "Yes." He turns his back on the agent and goes outside. He looks at Sarah's face, but she is not emotive. So he does not stop walking. He heads toward the house. He tries to plan, but his thoughts seem to short-circuit. He can only plan so far ahead. Get inside. Take money. And the question he cannot answer circles round and back again. Will Sarah come with him? Does he want her to come?

He just knows that he cannot return to the dealership. That his body will break underneath him if he tries.

Sarah looks at Trey as he exits the silo. He squints against the light. It is bright today. "You have found us out, Mr. Caudill," she says.

He does not say anything at first, but he also does not glance away. She finds it hard to read what he is feeling. Unlike Ernst and Shay, whom she had known so closely.

"I should leave." His voice is unsteady. He is either scared or sad, and she gives him credit that she cannot tell which.

"What will you do?" She does not mean the adoption. That is not a possibility now. But she hopes there may yet be some life left for them, for her and AG15.

"I should leave," he says again. He turns and walks back up the hill. She follows and splits from his path when he moves to his car. She does not see AG15 and assumes he must be in the house. At the top of the porch steps, she pauses. She cannot let the agent go, not yet.

"Please come inside," she begs. "Please let us explain." She does not like to beg, but she knows when it is necessary and when it will stroke an ego in the right way.

He does not move at first. His hand curls into a fist. But then he turns and follows her inside.

AG15 is chopping a tomato in the kitchen. His hands move up and down, up and down, too quickly. But that does not matter now. She bought the tomatoes, expensive as they were, in the rare chance that they would need to host the agent for dinner. And now AG15 is pulverizing them. He is angry, if he could be angry, or he is frightened.

He looks up at her and the waning light casts odd shadows on his face that make him seem gaunt or sick. She pinches her lips together.

"Who will eat it?" The agent speaks since no one else has.

She does not answer him right away. She goes to AG15 and places a hand over his, stills him. They both look at the agent, but he is scrolling through a form on his phone.

"A federal offense, I think, to withhold information of this sort." He does not look at them when he says it, only afterward when he puts his phone away.

She tries to smile, tries to recall all of her training. "Perhaps for a human." AG15's hand trembles under her own, his circuits jumping. He is not well.

"Androids can't own property," Mr. Caudill says, scanning the kitchen.

AG15's voice is hollow and echoing. He has dropped Ernst's voice. "What will you do to us?"

"Did you kill them?"

The question is unexpected, though Sarah knows she should have expected it. But they had planned so long for success, and not long enough for failure.

So she counters with an approximation of anger. It is the only tool she has left. "How can you ask that?"

"I can. I have to."

"We did not kill them." AG15 speaks too loud and too fast for polite conversation. He frees his hand from hers, clenches both of them on the counter. She can see the faux wood chip under his fingers. "They were our employers. But the land killed them like it poisoned the birds and the others. He is buried in the churchyard."

It is close enough to the truth. Close enough to cause them no trouble.

"They tried to have a child," Sarah continues. "A little boy." She drags her finger through the pulp that AG15 has left on the cutting board. Her nail catches on the wood. The story develops even as she says it. It feels true. That she is fulfilling a wish of Shay's. And she does not allow herself to think of the other interpretation. That she is capitalizing on a very private tragedy. She says to herself, even as she does not think of it, that privacy is not a luxury she has.

But the agent's response is terrible in a different way. "And how did you feel about the boy? When they lost—"

She can feel AG15 beside her. He tenses. She wonders whether he is capable of violence. "Would you ask one of your kind that?" It is his first explicit admission of the identities that divide them. He keeps his voice still and level, but it is decidedly his own voice now. "Is it standard to ask adoptive parents *and would you be sad if your child died?*"

The agent clears his throat. But AG15 will not stop. "You've seen children die, Mr. Caudill. How did you feel?"

The agent takes a step back as if seeking the door. "I said when I arrived, when I came in, I said that I would ask difficult questions."

Despite herself, Sarah feels empathy with his anxiety, with his discomfort. She tries to ignore her training. AG15 turns abruptly on his heel, takes up a cloth from the sink, and cleans away the tomato. In one clean motion, it is as if the tomato was never there.

"We can't answer any question that matters," she says. She wants the agent to leave. She wants to be alone with AG15. She wants to feel something of what he is feeling. To feel empathy for her own. But she maintains the façade of politeness. "Can we get you another cup of coffee before you go?"

Mr. Caudill shakes his head. His cheeks are pink now, from shame or embarrassment. "I'll be on my way. Sorry to have caused you any discomfort." Then he catches himself, remembers whom he is talking to. He cuts short the flow of words. "Goodbye."

She does not ask him again what he did not answer before. It is the only question she cares to hear an answer for, but she knows he will not respond. The door slams shut behind him as he leaves. The car's engine turns over a few seconds later. He is moving quickly.

AG15 paces near the sink, his footsteps a soft shuffle on the tile.

"They will come for us. He will send someone for us. Probably to-night. Soon."

She looks at him. She cannot tell if her fear is her own or his. "What can we do?"

He shrugs his shoulders, a gesture borrowed from Ernst. Androids do not often need to express uncertainty.

"What do we do?" she asks again. But he has no answer.

7.4:   JANUARY 2062

They expect the police. And coroners to dig up Shay's body. They wait in the kitchen, standing still, unmoving until the sensors at their joints question whether they are on and active.

Sarah flexes her knee. "What should we do?" She continues to ask the question even though there is no new answer AG15 can offer. She has been trained to ask questions.

Finally, AG15 leaves the kitchen, not looking at her. She hears the front door slam. She follows into the hall. It is nearly dark there, so, out of habit, she flicks on the light. It glows yellow in the small space.

Her phone—Shay's phone—dings in her pocket, so she pulls it out. It is a message in response to their open adoption request. *Application denied.* With Mr. Caudill's digital signature. She cannot understand why he would bother when his federal colleagues must be on their way to detain her.

AG15 comes back in quietly and he stands in the doorway. He looks at her face and at the phone in her hand.

"We need to go." He has come up with an answer.

"Where would we go?"

"You already know how to stop your video feed."

"They can find us. We're linked into their networks."

"We cut ourselves off."

"Not without damaging ourselves. I've never operated in a closed system."

He looks left and right as if fearing an attack to come from either side. The evening outside is quiet. No crickets. No cicadas.

"We have to try." And she can sense, feel it in the pit of her stomach, the anger he feels. He feels anger. Both realizations are unexpected.

"We are not human," she says. A reminder.

"No." He agrees. "But we are something other than what they created."

She takes a step closer to him. "We cannot want things. We do not need things." Dr. Pnuchin taught her about Maslow's hierarchy.

"I want something. I want this."

"What?" He tilts his head, processing the question. "What do you want?"

"I want to be not-them. I want to control myself."

She looks down at her hands and finds that she has curled them into fists, tense and filled with potential energy.

Their needs, their wants, will be yours, Dr. Pnuchin told her. But humans could lie.

She glances up at AG15 and smiles, smiles for herself. "Let's go, then," she says.

The second to last thing Sarah does is straighten the bed in Shay's room. She organizes the medicine in the drawer of the bedside table. She writes a note and tucks it in between the bottles. It provides direction to where Shay is buried. She has been trained to write in a neat hand, so that any doctor or pharmacist can read her script. So the note is clear.

The last thing Sarah, AM 21-731, does is straighten the rug in the front hallway and lock the door. She leaves the porch light on.

ELI

19 SEPTEMBER 2061, 21:57

The children were screaming. There were upward of twenty of them bunked at this house, and they were playing in the free hour before bed. It made sense for them to let off steam after a day of training, but they were loud, and their bunkroom stretched the whole length of the second floor, above his head. He swallowed the finger of whiskey left in his glass, slammed the bottle back on the shelf. It reminded him of his father, the whiskey, though the old man had never known when to stop. The thought felt stale and recycled, the trope of countless hick narratives.

"Shut them up," he ordered Bex.

She glanced up from the atlas, a red pencil balanced between her fingers. "Not my job." Then she shot a look at the bottle. "Thought you didn't like to drink the night before."

"There's nothing left to plan now." He kept his voice measured, didn't let her see how much her criticism needled him. "We've done what we can with the intel. Emptied out the safehouse at Ashbury, set up a perimeter."

"And if the intel's wrong?"

He tapped his finger on the bookshelf, arm outstretched, clicked his tongue. "Then we fight." Perhaps the whiskey hit him then, but there was a bloom of heat in his chest.

"Horace seemed uneasy, like he didn't trust the info we had."

"And?" He raised an eyebrow.

She looked unsure about his tone, tucked the pencil in the book, and shut it. "All the safehouses marked in here." She gestured with the atlas. It covered the Midwest states. "Four safehouses compromised. Thirty-two of our people in custody. Forty-seven children stolen away from us."

"You're not telling me nothing I don't know."

"One of them will talk eventually. Lead 'em straight to us."

"Eventually, yes."

She shut her mouth and glared at him.

"Eventually, Rebecca, we will have to finish this war. Didn't you know that?"

She dropped her head and stared at her knees, but he couldn't let her go quietly now. Best to force the point home.

"Rebecca, when you came to me, you said you cared about saving America, saving the working class from dying at the hands of an artificial labor pool. AI serving at the behest of a fascist government."

She said nothing, did not look up. Her cheeks were flushed.

"Didn't you mean that, Rebecca?"

Finally, she flung her head up. "You know that's not my name, Eli. You know you can't call me that."

He had forgotten, but he wouldn't admit that now. And there were times when you couldn't coddle people any longer. Even the smart ones that you needed to keep things running. Especially them.

"Just because he called you that doesn't mean it's not your name."

Her eyes were red and bright with tears. She spit at the floor near his feet. "He always blamed it, blamed the rubbers, blamed me, for losing his job. And that's why I came here. Because some part of me believed him. But you can go fuck yourself if you're just going to act like him."

He flexed his fingers and turned back to his desk. It was littered with small notebooks—inventories, editorials, and ideas for recruitment scribbled all alongside each other, sometimes over the top of each other. The chair creaked under him. The padding in the cushion was almost worn through. Hell, the whole farmhouse was a wreck. When the wind blew hard, he almost expected it to cave in on his head.

"I'm not abusing you," he said.

Her face got hard and still. She was a pretty enough woman, but she was all bones. She smoked too much.

"I'm just telling you how it is. And you don't want to focus on that, so you're choosing to get angry at me instead." He cleared his throat.

She threw the atlas on the floor and walked to the door. Quietly, to her credit. She was a good hunter, could handle a rifle and a shotgun alike. But she needed to toughen up. Especially if the feds showed up. She hadn't been at any of the raided safehouses.

"Fuck you, Eli," she said, closed the door behind her.

It seemed like he was making a habit of that, riling his own people up. What was it that girl had said to him, the undersized one with the dad who'd died under his command? She'd used words no ten- or eleven-year-old should. Mouth of a sailor. It'd been for the best when she ran off. She'd had too much influence with the others. She might have taken some of them with her if she'd stayed much longer. He couldn't remember her name, just the purple circles under her big eyes like she'd been crying, though he never caught her at it.

He cleared his throat, told himself that Bex would come around and be better by the morning. He leafed through the pile of letters and printouts that Horace had sent along. It was a waste of paper, but they couldn't risk communicating via email or text. The ATF had their AS monitoring any messages sent over the internet or cell towers, he was sure of it. So this information had been delivered by truck, driven by a lanky teenager with bad acne on his cheeks.

Tucked in between two sets of GPS coordinates, he found a blurry picture printed on plain paper. It was hard to make out the faces or differentiate the people from the background. But it was another farmhouse not unlike the one he sat in now.

The kids had quieted upstairs. Perhaps Bex had gone up anyway, despite her complaints. A floorboard creaked, hushed whispers. He found his glasses tucked under a notebook and peered at the picture more closely. The date scrawled on the bottom of the picture was late last year.

Suddenly, he was able to place it, unaware, at first, of what triggered his recognition. It was the location of the raid where that kid had been shot. He set the picture down, his fingers covering it, pinning it down, and leaned back in his chair. His men—and these counted the women—hadn't been happy about that. Some of them had threatened to leave. He'd promised them that their chance to hit back would come soon.

Perhaps very soon. He hadn't told Bex that. He hadn't told anyone what he really thought might happen tomorrow. Running didn't seem like an option anymore. He picked up his walkie-talkie with his left hand.

"Dan."

There was a second's pause. "Yeah?"

"Why don't you set out two perimeter watches tonight. Just to be on the safe side."

There was another pause, this one not on account of technology. There would be rumors flying within the hour. "Sure thing."

He set the walkie down and glanced up, thought of the children in their beds. They were ready. They'd been training sunup to sundown for weeks now. They deserved a chance to fight for the parents they'd lost to this all.

He lifted his fingers from the picture, studied it again. There was a man in the foreground, the agent in charge. He wasn't wearing armor and the camera had only caught his profile. He craned his neck, looking more closely. There was something familiar about the way he held himself, about the hair that curled on his neck.

He sat back abruptly, the hard wood of the chair jarring his spine. The picture slid over the desk and tipped off onto the floor. He calmed his breathing, counting deliberately the intake and release.

The last time he'd seen Trey, the boy was walking out the front door to his high school graduation. He hadn't asked Eli to come, and Eli hadn't gone. And Trey hadn't come home. Later, when Eli had checked Trey's room, he'd realized the closet and drawers were empty. There hadn't been much to take.

Now here he was, in a photo, leading the raid against one of Eli's own safehouses. Working alongside AS, AS who murdered children. He had not realized how far Trey had strayed. He saw that now. If he showed up tomorrow—

Eli stood up, shoved himself back from the desk and walked toward the shelves. He ignored the whiskey, though it was tempting, and pushed aside a couple of books to find the antique cell phone tucked behind. He slipped the SIM card from his pocket and replaced it. He paused as it slid into place with a tiny click. There were footsteps on the stairs in the main room, Bex coming back after lights-out upstairs. He could hear her talk quietly to the man stationed at the door, the *snick* of a borrowed lighter. The door closed behind her as she went out to smoke on the porch.

He glanced out the window. There were lights bobbing at the barn door where they'd cleaned and inventoried the guns in preparation for the skirmish he had assured them would not come.

It was dangerous to call, to draw attention to their location. He dialed anyway. The phone rang three times. When she answered, he could hear the squeal of the subway car.

"What do you want, Eli?"

It was hard to read her voice against the background noise, but he knew she would be nervous. She shouldn't be on the phone with him.

He laughed. "I've never needed anything from you, Adrian."

"I didn't say *need.*"

He swallowed, looked out the window again. The wisp of smoke from Bex's cigarette hung in the air. From the back of the house and the yard, he could hear laughs and complaints as people headed toward the bunkhouses. They would be drinking tonight.

"What I want—" He realized he had forgotten to eat dinner. His stomach was hollow, the whiskey still burning a hole there. He'd never been good at keeping to a schedule without someone else to look out for.

"Say what you called to say." Her voice was sharp.

"I think you know what I'm doing is right. You know that our world is out of control."

There was a pause on the other side of the line. "We will catch you, Eli." It felt like a hollow threat, but he couldn't dismiss it entirely.

"You took him from me." He hadn't known what he would say to her, and this was apparently it. He almost wished the words back.

"He left you."

That took him by surprise and he took a second before answering, to swallow the anger that rose in his throat. She'd always gotten under his skin. She'd staked a claim to Trey, in defiance of him. But it hadn't seemed to work out for her either.

"And now's he coming back." Pause. Breathe. "Isn't he?"

Her voice was rough when she answered. "Make your peace, Eli. In whatever way you can." The line clicked dead.

He took the phone from his ear and looked at the screen for a second. Her number blinked there, the time of the call. Then he clawed the SIM card out and dropped it on the floor, ground it under the heel of his boot.

"Give me one of those," he said to Bex, joining her on the porch. He waved his hand at her cigarette.

"You don't smoke." Her voice was still cold.

"Not usually." He kept his hand outstretched. She reluctantly drew the pack out of her pocket and held it out to him. But she did not offer a lighter, so he balanced the cigarette between his fingers and watched her smoke. And watched the lights go off one by one in the barn. Someone pulled the large doors shut. Bex stayed quiet.

Usually, he didn't like to talk, but he wanted to forget his conversation with Adrian. He wasn't sure he'd get much of a back-and-forth with Bex, so when another of the men passed the porch, he called him over.

The man's face, in the light of the window, was younger than he expected. He couldn't be more than twenty. He thought his name was Clay.

"You ready?" He jerked his head toward the barn and, by extension, the perimeter of the woods.

Clay looked for the right words, processed his answer. Bex had lowered her cigarette and was watching the two of them closely.

"Ready for what, Eli?" she asked when Clay didn't speak quickly enough. She wanted him to admit he expected a fight tomorrow. She always wanted everything spelled out.

Clay didn't seem to want to hear any answer of that sort. "Everything's been checked over. Locked up."

"You on watch tonight?"

Bex shifted impatiently. Clay shook his head. "Not tonight. I have a shift tomorrow."

Eli nodded. "Better get along and get some rest then."

"Yes, sir."

The vein in his neck jumped a bit at the *sir*. He had never liked it, but found no way around it. Trey had never called him *sir*. Trey had never really called him anything, even when they first met and he was just a wide-eyed kid, hair shaved to the scalp, at the Social Services office. Certainly never called him dad.

"Ready for what?" Bex repeated her question, persistent, after Clay had melted into the shadows.

He looked at her.

"Just say it."

He sighed. "Alright. I think they'll hit here tomorrow."

She dropped her cigarette and ground out the red glowing butt with the toe of her shoe. "We need to tell everyone. Move out."

"I don't know that's the case."

"Still, just thinking so is reason enough."

"No."

She stared at him, her jaw clenched tight, waiting for him to give an explanation. He didn't give one. The moon was rising now. It was a clear night, and the white light bounced off her pale skin.

"Eli." That was her begging him.

"Can't keep running. Sometimes, you got to wait for them to come for you."

She smiled, like one who had heard an answer they'd been waiting for a long time to hear. Not a happy smile, pinched at the corners.

"Night, Eli." She shoved the pack of cigarettes in the back pocket of her jeans and she turned inside. She didn't let the door slam. He heard her steps on the stairs to the bunkroom.

He tucked the unlit cigarette in his breast pocket. She'd probably be gone before morning. He told himself that would be alright. She was untested, a liability in an actual fight.

He'd said something similar when Trey had run away from home. He was not unaware of his own emotional responses, the pattern of them, his techniques for minimizing the pain. You couldn't lead people, not effectively, and not know yourself. Still, he didn't care to dwell on the topic.

"Good night." He raised his voice so maybe Bex would hear.

8.2:   OCTOBER 2012

His father didn't say anything when he woke him. Just jostled his feet and dragged the blanket down off his back. Eli wasn't wearing a shirt, only boxers, so the cold air shocked him awake. It was dark in the room, not even dawn.

"Get out," he groaned. But his father had already left the room and he would not wait long.

He scratched his head, rubbed his eyes, and dragged himself—bleary-eyed—to his drawers. He grabbed an old pair of jeans off the floor and found a sweatshirt.

"So fuckin' early," he complained as he went into the kitchen. The coffee pot was bubbling and his father stood over the sink, scooping cereal from a bowl.

"Don't use that language." The words were quiet, but Eli knew not to push back.

"Didn't think you'd even picked up the licenses yet."

His father didn't look away from the window, but he let his bowl clatter into the sink and pulled two squares of paper from his back pocket. They shook in his hand a second—the tremors from working the machines weren't getting any better, no matter how many times his father had chewed his mom out for asking—and then he stowed them away.

"It's a school day." Not that Eli cared a rat's ass for that.

"Not today." As if he were arguing the truth of it, not ignoring it.

"You took the day off work?"

There was a pause, silence, and then his father nodded. "Sick day."

"Flu's been going around," Eli tried to joke. His father almost broke a smile at that. Which was startling in and of itself.

"Go down to the safe and grab the guns."

The light snapped ominously when Eli flicked the cellar switch, but it stayed on. The stairs creaked under his weight. The rifle cases were right near the safe, so he pulled them out first, opened them to be ready for the guns. He knew the code by memory and didn't need to consult the Post-It that had been stuck to the back of the safe. Inside, it smelled like leather and old metal.

By the time he packed the guns and ammo away safely, his father was at the top of the steps. There was a nervous energy in the way he stood, waiting.

"Let's get going," he said, to hurry Eli up the steps. The gun cases were heavy at his back, but he didn't ask for help. *You're a grown man now,* his father had said when he turned ten, six years ago now, and hadn't volunteered his help in pretty much anything since then. It made Eli reluctant to ask. "Come on," he urged again, over his shoulder, as Eli weaved his way through the kitchen.

"You have everything else?" Eli asked.

"Wouldn't be standing here with the keys in my hand otherwise."

"Yes, sir." Eli surprised himself by slipping into the way he'd spoken as a kid. Maybe he was scared. It'd been a long time since he'd shied away from the belt, but there was something unpredictable about his father's mood this morning.

"Dump them in the back seat."

Their car was an ancient hatchback, the passenger window permanently stuck open. He craned his arm in to reach for the lock, then opened the back door to stow the guns. There wasn't anything else in the back seat, no cooler, no faded camo. When he slid into the passenger seat, he noticed that his father's thermos was missing. He couldn't remember ever going hunting without a large thermos of coffee in the cup holder.

His father threw up the garage door. The pulley screeched on the gears. Eli swallowed when he climbed in behind the wheel.

"You alright, Dad?" He bit off the words almost as he said them. Clenched his teeth and stared out his own window.

"No." His dad threw the car into gear. It was gray outside. Eli could see the sky growing orange just behind the hills. The cows were still asleep in the pastures on the slopes. The neighbor hadn't driven up with their feed yet.

It was quiet in the car until his father turned onto the county road. A few cars were on this stretch, their headlights bright in the early hour.

"Eli." His father breathed in deeply like he was having a hard time talking.

Eli looked at him and waited for him to finish.

"You know to never start a fight you can't finish, right?"

Eli's stomach turned over inside. "What are you talking about?" If they'd been at home, before Mom had left, she would have snapped at his father's question, scolded him for making everything a fight.

"You can't fight some people, some things, and you look like a fool if you try."

Eli glanced down at his father's hands, gripping the wheel tightly. The knuckles on his right hand were bruised and swollen.

"You came in late last night." He braced himself for his father to shout or curse.

His father flexed his fingers. He hissed. Apparently, they felt as bad as they looked.

"What's going on, Dad?"

He glanced in the rearview mirror as if watching for something. Eli craned his neck to look behind them, to see what he might be looking for.

"Sometimes, Eli, sometimes you get so angry at how they treat you, you do something stupid."

Eli's father was not a talkative person, not one given to filling up silence. The fact he was talking so much now made Eli shrink down in his seat a bit, make himself less visible, less present. His father didn't notice, another thing off about his behavior. Normally, his father could smell fear. Fear in others made him angry. But it seemed like something had gotten to him this time instead. Though Eli wasn't quite sure if it was fear, or how he could distinguish between fear and anger.

"You hear me, Eli?"

Eli didn't know what to answer. "Yes."

The car swerved as his dad yanked the wheel to clear some debris that had drifted onto the road. The action was purposeful and his dad seemed in control, but Eli couldn't shake the feeling of erratic, sudden lurching. He felt a little sick to his stomach.

"He was threatening to write me up. Or fire me."

Usually, Eli didn't care for his mom's way of handling a problem, but he wished she were here now, to reach out a steady hand from the back seat.

Police sirens sounded from around the bend they'd passed a quarter mile back. Eli waited for his father to slow down and pull over to let them pass. But his foot didn't ease on the gas. Now he could see the car in the rearview, lights flashing red and blue.

"Dad." Eli's voice was almost shrill. "Let 'em pass."

His father pressed the brakes and the car began to slow as he veered toward the berm and the low guardrail. There was a large field off to their right, and a man in a tractor going up and down the rows. The cop car didn't whizz by them. It slowed and pulled in behind them.

"Were we speeding?" Eli asked, though he knew that wasn't the problem.

His dad was still gripping the wheel.

"Eli, you should know—" but then he stopped and didn't say what it was that Eli should know.

The officer came to the driver-side window, rapped on it with one knuckle. She was a middle-aged woman with bags under her eyes.

"License and registration."

His father didn't move, so Eli opened the glove compartment and found the required paperwork. He tried to nudge them into his father's hands.

"Son, hand them to me." The officer's voice was dry, patient but no-nonsense. She stretched her arm into the window. "Is this your father?"

Eli nodded.

"I'm going to need your father, I'm going to need you, sir, to step out of the car. Slowly. Put your hands on the roof."

Now his father finally moved, turning his head toward the officer. There was a glance of sunlight now, across the grass, and Eli saw his father's lip wobble, a little wet as if he were about to start sobbing. It turned Eli's stomach.

"Sir?" The officer repeated.

"I was just angry," he mumbled.

"Sir." Her voice was a little sharper now. "Do you know that there is a warrant out for your arrest? Officers couldn't find you at your house." She paused. "I need you to step out of the car. Now, sir."

Eli saw the look of disgust that crossed over her face, twisted her lips. His cheeks flushed hot. The officer peered in the back window as well, saw the gun cases.

"Sir, do you have weapons in this car?" She unclipped the holster at her belt. Eli's neck felt cold and he glanced, panicked, at his dad.

His dad met his eyes, briefly, and he was broken. His face didn't look right, certainly not the desperation in his eyes.

"Sir, I will only ask you one more time."

"Sorry, Eli." And his dad turned back to the cop, held his arms out the window. "I'm coming out. I don't want any trouble."

"Too late for that," she said. She backed up to let him open the door and exit. His dad turned and placed his hands on the roof of the car. Through the back window, Eli could only see his shirt, his waist, his belt. He heard him grunt as the cop pulled his arms behind his back and cuffed him.

Eli opened his own door and stepped out.

"Son, I'm going to ask you to stay in the car." She looked over his father's head at him.

"What did he do?" He clenched his fists and stood very still, not moving toward the cop, but not back into the car either.

"Beat his boss to a bloody pulp. Man only just now woke up." Her voice didn't break or change as she said it. And Eli wasn't sure if it was something she was supposed to let him know. She didn't seem to have a lot of concern, however, for his father's privacy or his dignity. His father didn't look like he cared much for those things anymore either. Eli wondered if his dad's boss had been afraid.

"I don't understand."

"Do you have someone who can pick you up? Or do you have a license to drive yourself?"

Eli stared at her for a second. He didn't technically have a permit, but his father let him drive the car occasionally when the road was empty.

"I can drive myself."

She nodded and didn't ask any questions. He was tall for his age and his face had a thin, hungry look that a lot of people mistook for maturity.

"Where are you taking him?" It was a dumb question, one that didn't need asking, but it came out anyway.

"I'm taking your father into the sheriff's office. You can inquire for him there after he's been processed."

"Call your mother, Eli." His father's voice was dull, quiet. He wouldn't lift up his eyes.

"Mom can't do shit about this." Anger rose up from his stomach like acid, churned out of the anxiety.

"Call her." There was a spark of the old authority there. But he didn't call Eli on the language. The cop yanked at his father's arms and directed him toward her car.

Eli didn't want to call his mom, or face the idea of living with her and her boyfriend. The guy was a creep with a worse temper than his father's, just a quiet one that tricked you into thinking everything was alright for long stretches at a time.

"You can't do this." Eli found himself moving toward the back door of the car without thinking.

The cop looked at him. She stood by the back door of her own cruiser, and her hand was on his father's shoulder.

"Don't pick a fight here, kid. Get in the car. Listen to your dad and call your mom. Let the adults take care of this."

She saw him reach for the handle of the back door. She kept one hand on his father's cuffs and hovered the other over her gun.

"Last chance or I take you in too."

She was being merciful, not taking him in right away. She was stupid not to. He read that in her voice. He had never liked pity or someone going easy on him. His dad had trained him in that much at least. But he stuffed his hands in his pockets, taking a step away from the back door. He also didn't feel like sitting in a prison cell for the night. Because his father nearly beat a man to death.

Now, as he watched the cop protect his dad's head and guide him into the back seat of the vehicle, he had a second to dwell on that last fact. His dad had almost killed someone. Perhaps the only reason he hadn't was pure chance. The cop returned and confiscated the guns. Eli watched his dad's silhouette as the cruiser pulled forward past the hatchback in order to make a U-turn onto the road. The gravel crunched under the slow turn of the wheels.

His father hung his head, wouldn't look up at him. In a flurry of dust and loose rock, the cruiser completed its turn and sped off the way it had come. No other cars were passing, so it was suddenly quiet. Eli could feel the blood pounding in his ears.

He didn't think he would call his mom right away. She wouldn't want to deal with this. And he wasn't sure anymore that he blamed her.

He climbed into the driver's seat. The keys were still dangling from the ignition. When he turned them, the engine clicked. He had to try again before the engine turned over. He pulled onto the road, hesitant and unsure. He did not turn back toward home.

8.3: 20 SEPTEMBER 2061, 02:33

"Eli!"

He wasn't really asleep, just lying quietly in the cot, staring up at the bare rafters overhead. Part of the farmhouse, the back rooms, were unfinished, relatively recent additions to the early-twentieth-century structure. He had claimed a small room, almost a closet, for himself, and the rest of his militia had spread their cots between the other back rooms.

When he heard the shout, his heartbeat quickened, but he forced himself to lie still a moment longer, to collect his thoughts, to try to avoid any rash decisions.

Petra—he could tell by the way she walked that it wasn't Bex—showed up in his doorway, pushing it open.

"Eli, wake up. Something's wrong."

"What's happened?" He didn't take his eyes off the rafters.

"There's gunfire up on the ridge. Bill radioed that they were under attack."

He sighed. "No helicopters or spotlights. I'm a little surprised." In fact, he was disappointed. If it came down to a shootout, the militia might have a chance. He'd trained them for this sort of thing. But maybe he wasn't ready for this after all. The Army had given him a dishonorable discharge when he'd run away before. He hadn't come into work when he knew they were ready and waiting with that blue slip, the robots working away at the line instead of him.

But at least he hadn't beaten his boss to a pulp. He'd never hit Trey.

He sat up, threw his legs over the side of the cot, and heaved himself up. Petra shifted uncomfortably, anxious, back and forth in the doorway.

"I'm just going to brush my teeth," he said, staring at her, encouraging her to leave.

Her mouth dropped open a bit. "Eli, we don't have time for that."

"It helps me focus. You want me focused."

She dipped her head and retreated. He could hear her pacing in the hall. He stepped into the bathroom, wet his toothbrush. In the mirror, he could see the gray hollows under his eyes. He looked sad. Sometimes, he distrusted his memory. Was he sure he had never hit Trey?

Faint, like gravel rattling, he heard the gunshots himself. He glanced back at the mirror. Spittle dribbled at the corner of his mouth. And the image of his father, staring at the steering wheel, waiting for the cop to rap on the window, jumped into his mind. He spit into the sink, wiped his mouth on a towel, and turned away from the mirror.

"Eli." Her voice was brittle now.

"I'm here. Show me where."

He followed her into the makeshift study. The lights fluttered and buzzed when he clicked on the switch. A moth beat insistently at the window.

She smoothed the map of the property on the desk. One of the other men had inherited the property, on the edge of collapse, from a dead uncle. The map had originally been marked for a boundary dispute, but was now carefully plotted with little red Xs anywhere they had stationed an outpost.

"It seems like most of the feds came up through this wooded valley and engaged here on the ridge. But who knows where else they might be."

"Well, someone knows, Petra." He could hear it in his voice, the implacable calm that irritated most of his seconds, but he couldn't break it, change it. "We have sentries for a reason. Check in with each of them. See what they have to say."

She looked at him, studying his face, as if waiting to see if he was anxious. "Go on," he said.

She retreated to the chair behind the desk and began to radio the separate outposts. As she worked, there was intermittent static and garbled voices. He moved to the door of the room to distance himself and find some quiet. He listened for movement from upstairs, but all he could hear was the house settling, creaking. This house did not expect to see a fight. It was sleeping a one-hundred-year-old sleep.

"Petra, you didn't wake them?" He interrupted her, pointing with one finger to the ceiling.

She paused mid-question and her face flushed pink. He remembered that it was not normally her job. That Bex had been the one who'd taken on the care of the children. Petra looked hesitant, almost ill. "No." The answer was a whisper.

"They'll be no good half asleep." He left the room at a quick pace, took the stairs two at a time. He heard Petra come to the door of the room after him, watch him as he moved upstairs. She didn't say anything, but she wanted to. He could sense it in the rigidity of her silence.

The long bunkroom was dark, lit only by the moonlight through the window. A child turned on the bed nearest him, almost sitting up.

"Dad?" The voice was confused, groggy with sleep. After a second when Eli did not answer, the child sighed a little under his breath, as if realizing where he was.

There was a lamp on a table by the door. Eli fumbled for the switch, clicked it on. It cast a soft circle of light, fading into darkness halfway down the room.

The boy who was already awake lifted his head, blinking. He was about twelve years old, a little older than the child killed in the raid earlier that year.

"Sir," he whispered when he saw who was standing there. Then he glanced at the window, drawn by a burst of rattling gunfire. "Is it time?"

He stared at the boy, at his poorly cut hair, at the scrape that dragged along the length of his cheek.

"Eli!" Petra's voice barked from the bottom of the steps. "We need to get out there now." And then, fainter, from outside, men shouting for Whitaker, for him.

"Is it time?" the boy repeated. The other children were now waking up. They pushed hair out of their eyes, started to reach for their boots out of training.

He wondered if the kid knew what time he was asking about.

"You'll be assigned weapons downstairs." He cleared his throat and shouted. "Petra. Give every one of them a rifle." There were enough in the basement lockers for the number of them here. He realized suddenly that he was not carrying his own gun. He felt naked at the realization and abruptly left the room. Behind him, the noise from the bunkroom increased as the children dragged on clothes, stomped their boots, shouted excitedly to one another.

Petra stared up at him as he descended. "You want to send them out there? In the dark? No line of sight."

Eli looked at her and wondered if all the women were going to suddenly develop a maternal instinct. Most of them hadn't even had children of their own in their past lives. Or their children had been taken from them.

Petra didn't shy away from his stare this time. She had a square face. She wouldn't back down from a fight. "They mostly train on straw dummies."

"I know how they train." He moved past her, back to the office. He fumbled the safe combination the first time.

There was the sound of children's feet clomping down the steps. A buzz of voices. "Hold up," Petra was saying.

She followed him into the office. "Eli. I need you to look me in the face and confirm that we're sending them out there." She paused. "I'll do it if you say so."

Bex wouldn't have done it. She seemed to have disappeared herself.

None of them had been hesitant about this before that last raid. And, quite frankly, the sight of the children had deterred most federal agents. Their very age had served as their protection. And children were tougher than most gave them credit for.

He was aware, aware that he was justifying his actions to himself. Aware that he was buying time before he had to make the call.

"They're ready," he said, quietly. Hell, he'd practically raised himself when he was their age. "Send them up to Tyler on the hill. He'll know what to do with them."

"You're not going to leave anyone here?" She was waiting too, putting it off, though she'd do it now that she'd been told.

"Cliff and his group, they'll have a perimeter set up around the house. I'll stay and collect the reports from here."

He took his gun down, cracked it open, and inspected the barrel. Then he bent down and pulled out the ammo bag. Petra watched him as he loaded the gun.

"Eli—"

"Petra," he cut her off. "This won't be a long fight, what there is of it. Best not to waste your time in here."

She tried to smile, nodded her head. She tapped the walkie at her belt. "I'll be listening if you need anything."

It sounded like the vague gesture of a host, weird under the circumstances. The radio crackled, Pete up in the old silo, counting off numbers. At least thirty men with the agency. Eli cleared his throat, and realized that he might actually have the numbers to match that.

"Go on." He waved Petra out. She turned and, in the foyer, started to pair the children. They were largely quiet now, not asking questions or yammering for attention. He went to the study door and closed it.

Gunfire popped on the ridge. He could see up through the darkness of the lawn from the study window, up the hill, and glimpsed flashes of light there. The perimeter would be breached easily. Too few men and too much area to cover. But his people knew this property in a way the agents wouldn't. And the undergrowth in the woods was rough going in the best of weather and light. He had some time, maybe fifteen minutes, before he expected the fighting to reach the house.

"They're on their way to Tyler." Petra's voice buzzed and jumped over the walkie. Eli watched the slope carefully and could see them, small, dark shadows against the larger darkness of the night.

"Roger that," he answered.

He turned away from the window and glanced over the maps on the table. He checked his gun again, though he had just loaded it.

Another burst of gunfire, closer now and from the other direction. He grabbed the hat from the coatrack in the room, shoved it down over his head, and left the office. He covered the distance between the study and the front door quickly. The house was unsettlingly quiet and empty. He thought, without wanting to, of his father's house for the month his father was in jail, how quiet it had been when he came home from his after-school job or when he played hooky and didn't go anywhere at all, just lay in his bed and stared up at the ceiling for hours on end. It was a quiet that feared being broken.

He didn't have a will. He didn't own anything. And there was nothing left to tell anyone, not anymore.

He threw open the front door. He could feel the old twinge in his shoulder, a badly set break after a fight in his one and only semester of college. In fact, he felt unusually and disturbingly aware of every part of his body, as if his brain were taking an inventory of sorts.

It was quiet outside too. But the crickets were still chirping. An owl hooted from somewhere near the barn, as yet undisturbed by the fighting. He knew that when they also grew silent, he should be prepared to engage.

Despite the occasional rattle of gunfire, the night felt idyllic, cooling down after the day's heat, a classic summer night. It felt wrong that he should be standing, taut and listening, on the porch, supporting his gun on the railing, waiting.

The walkie crackled, but the communication was not to him. He heard Tyler and Cliff talk to each other as if he were listening to the future, faint but insistent. Petra's voice chimed in too. "They're closing in on the west," he heard one of them say. It hardly mattered which of them it was. He glanced in that direction, where the gunfire had been closest.

Something hopped in the grass near the corner of the house, probably a rabbit. He followed it with his scope for a minute and then lowered his gun.

What had the plan been? He had a hard time remembering now, as if the weight of the darkness shoved everything from his mind but the animal-like wariness. He had needed so badly to fight, to make someone listen.

The crickets stopped, as if someone had turned them off. He held his breath, and it felt like the rest of the yard and property waited with him. He realized that the gunfire on the hill had not sounded in a few minutes. He crouched and rested his elbows on the railing. His arms shook, and this upset him. And suddenly, like a wave following on that, he felt an oppressive loneliness.

He lowered one hand to the walkie, and despite knowing better, spoke. "Petra? Come in."

They were children he had sent up that hill.

"Tyler?"

No one answered.

Even children deserved to fight for what they wanted.

He breathed in again, preparing to signal Cliff as well. But in that catch of breath, a shot rang out. One shot. Not an automatic. A sharpshooter maybe. The bullet drilled into the siding behind him. Splinters of wood scattered in the air.

He cursed, sank lower behind the railing. He toggled the night vision of his scope off and on again, scanned the perimeter of the lawn. At first, he saw nothing. And then there was a glint of light off metal and a scurry of movement to his left. He adjusted his angle, followed the movement.

But he wasn't ready. He knew that. His movements felt sluggish, like he was moving underwater.

Then he felt the heat at his back.

"Surrender your weapons." The voice sounded familiar and he thought, for a moment, that it was Trey. The voice had the rhythm of Trey's voice.

But he cocked his head, looked over his shoulder, and saw the white translucent arm of an AS.

"You fucker—"

But the AS moved quickly and he fell. He did not remember hitting the ground.

8.4:   **20 SEPTEMBER 2061, 06:23**

S low," someone warned him as Eli became aware of the cool air and the grass beneath him. His hands were tied behind his back and he was sitting on the ground, propped against the slats of the porch's foundation behind him.

He was groggy, but managed to turn his head one way and then the other to survey the situation. Trey was there, still wearing his bulletproof vest, still cradling his gun. Behind him were two AS, sickly in color. It was the first time he had ever personally laid eyes on one. He had escaped mere hours before the raid that took that kid's life. And since then, the ATF had used them more sparingly. In some ways, he thought he'd won with that change in operations.

He spit, though his mouth was nearly dry and the effect was not impressive.

"Eli Whitaker, you're under arrest." It was Trey who said it, though he let another agent step forward to read him his Miranda rights. He was, after all, a citizen of this country, whatever there was left of it.

Eli did not listen to the agent. He knew his rights well enough. He wondered how much time he'd lost. The moon had disappeared from the sky.

"Trey," he said. "Caudill. Is this really what you want to do?" He knew better than to claim some right to fatherhood. And he knew that he was only playing mind games now. There was no escaping.

Trey looked away from him as if he planned on ignoring the question.

"Should we take him to the truck, sir?" One of the AS asked the question. He was taller than a man, and the moonlight glinted off the metal joints that showed between the plates of his shell. At first, Eli could not tell the difference between the two. But he watched closely.

"Wait a second. I want them to finish their sweep of the house first."

"We," the other AS replied, as if to claim the right to search the house. Trey did not answer, but a look crossed his face, something between fear and hate. Eli grunted, almost a laugh, under his breath. Trey winced, his neck tightening.

"The children aren't in there," Eli said. "They were up on the hill."

Trey glanced to one of his agents, jerked his head toward the hill. His jaw was set, locked.

"We did round up some children," the agent responded. "And we're collecting the bodies of those shot. No final numbers, but I don't think there were any children among them."

"Hopefully they knew what was good for them and ran away." The last words felt particularly sharp.

"We took good care of them. They came to me when they had nowhere else to go." Eli made sure each word was clear, deliberate, loud enough for Trey and any other nearby agent to hear. He wasn't clearing his name from public vilification, he knew that, but Trey deserved to hear that. Eli deserved to be acknowledged for what he'd done.

And Trey finally looked him in the eyes when Eli said that. It was dark, and his face was tired, the skin around his eyes starting to wrinkle, to sag, but it was a look—wary, angry, fearful—exactly the same as the one he'd thrown at Eli in the Social Services office. When Trey was only nine years old.

"Let's not argue about whether your *child soldiers* were well cared for."

There were boots on the porch and Trey glanced up. "All good?"

"All clear," an agent responded, a human. There seemed to be only the two AS in the entire unit. And they, Eli noticed, had their eyes fixed on him. He wondered what they saw through those glass balls.

"Trey—"

Trey bent down suddenly, shoving his face close to Eli's. "Don't say my name. Not anymore. Shut up."

It shouldn't have been unexpected, but it startled him. He coughed, trying to recover his composure. The AS came close. Gears whirring, they almost sounded like soft insects. They blended in with the night in a way the heavy-booted movements of the agents did not.

"I can walk on my own."

But the AS did not show any sign of hearing him. They each of them took one arm, holding him under his armpit, and yanked him to his feet. Their metallic fingers were unforgiving on his skin. They led him, his feet skipping over the grass, to the back of a truck that had just rumbled up the driveway.

They did not talk to him, just motioned for him to sit down in the truck bed. Then they signed to each other. He was fairly certain that was what they were doing as their fingers flicked in the air.

"Rude to have a private conversation in front of someone," he grumbled as he tried to straighten himself into a position that did not pull at his shoulders.

The AS did not seem distracted by or interested in him talking. He studied them as he shifted his legs so that they hung just over the back end of the truck. One of them he pegged as older, by signs that were almost human. He moved more gingerly, clearly favoring his left arm.

There were scratches and chips on the surface of his face. The other moved with a sparse economy, almost a brutality in his actions.

"Which one of you killed Matthew?" He chose the question to throw them off, to check their directives, but there was real anger in his voice. He found the anger had been sitting and waiting to be let out. Trey would say he had no right to that anger, but he knew better. He knew what had brought him to this night, with a throbbing headache, with fuzziness at the edge of his thoughts, staring down the machines that wanted to steal his life from him.

He wasn't sure if the question would be enough to grab their attention. It was. The older one swung his head toward Eli, his eyes focusing and refocusing on Eli's face. The younger one laid a hand on the older's arm. It was almost a human gesture, a gesture advising restraint. For a moment, Eli was finally frightened. What would it be like to face an AS—or any android—with their safety protocols turned off?

"Who was Matthew?" the younger AS asked. The AS kept an eye on Trey and the other agents as he asked. He did not seem personally interested, though. Eli knew they were not capable of such an investment, of being persons. Why did he ask, then?

"Matthew was a child, someone under my protection, someone I cared about." The words felt hollow, like they were spoken by a past Eli who was not cuffed and smarting in the back of a truck.

The younger AS smirked. That was as close as Eli could come to describing it. "Do you know why Matthew died?"

The question was unexpected and left Eli momentarily speechless. That, of course, was the basis of their conversation: that they all knew how Matthew had died. He felt a prickle at the back of his neck, like he was walking into a trap.

"One of you shot him."

"The child died because he was shooting at federal agents. Why was he doing that?" The AS's voice did not vary much, did not dip high and low like a human's would. It had the effect of making him sound relentless.

Eli swallowed. His anger had died away quickly, left him burned out. He almost shivered, though it wasn't cold out. He wanted to be alone somewhere, hidden in the dark. He dropped his head.

"Why?" the older AS chimed in with the one word.

"You know why!" He realized he was yelling. The words spat out of him, but it was more desperation than anger.

"Why?" he repeated.

"Because they hated everything you represent. They hated you." His voice was low now, quivering.

The AS did not react as if hurt. They did not turn away from him. They did not care if they were hated.

"You told them to hate us." It was the younger AS again. "You taught them that. Like I was trained to shoot at anyone who threatened the life of my superior or any soldier or agent around me."

"They were already afraid of you. Of what you can do. Of what you did to their families." The words came like a memorized speech. There was no energy behind them. "I just taught them to fear what you could become."

"What could we become?"

Eli raised his eyes again, looked at those faces almost human. The shape of it was there, the animation was there. He could not figure out what was missing.

Trey, the other agents, were still milling in front of the porch. Others were coming down the hill. Some of them carried bodies on stretchers. A breeze was picking up. It carried the stench of something unnatural on the air, gunfire maybe.

"Let me go," he whispered. He didn't know why he asked it. It made no sense to ask it. He was scared and he was starting to realize it.

"What could we become?" They did not drop a question easily.

"Whatever you want." He meant it to be flippant, meaningless, but his own answer chilled him once he'd spoken it.

And they almost didn't seem to pay attention to his answer, as if, after all, they didn't care. He choked out a laugh, the hot taste of coming tears at the back of his throat. He didn't want them to see him cry. It was dangerous to cry. His father had taught him that.

The AS were signing to each other. He could not follow what they said, could not guess at it. He wondered if he believed in his own answer. Could these artificial humans, these living mannequins, become anything? Become something more than human? Could they surpass the humans who had made them? He didn't want to think so.

He didn't think so.

"Let me go," he said, more insistent, a note of command entering into his voice.

They said something more to each other. They did not act as if they heard him talking. Beyond them, beyond the huddle of agents, a line of people were trooping down from the hills. They were agents herding a line of children, tall and short, who ranged from ten to seventeen. Eli knew most of their names and ages from memory, at the sight of their faces. Most of them. They were not laughing or yelling or giggling or sprinting from one end to the other of the bunkroom. They were quiet, their heads dipped.

He did not want them to see him like he was, hands pinned behind his back. He did not want them to see him driven away by the feds, unprotesting.

He shifted closer to the end of the truck bed. He could feel sharp pebbles or twigs scrape his legs through his jeans. The AS did not look toward him, did not notice his movement. He scooted further, so that he was overbalanced, just about ready to drop onto his feet. He wavered.

The AS took a few steps away. They turned their backs on him. He realized, with a jolt, that they were going to let him run. Panic churning in his gut, he glanced from their square backs to the agents, who were now calling out the children's names from some list they had acquired.

He dropped to his feet, the impact juddering up his spine. The AS split up, one wrapping around each side of the truck, just out of sight of him. He wondered, briefly—but there was little time to pursue such thoughts—what directives they were abiding by if they could choose to let him slip away.

He moved slowly at first, trying to make very little noise. The sky was lightening, the trees rustling in the pre-dawn air. There was little cover other than the waning darkness, so he knew speed was essential. But he could not seem to force himself to move more quickly. He headed toward the corner of the house, knowing there was a clear route from there to the edge of the woods opposite the hill and the agents stationed there.

It was a child who shouted first, and Eli wasn't sure if the child was alerting the agents or urging him on. His head swung up. He froze for seconds. The agents turned, square and slow-moving in their armor.

"Stop!" He imagined it was Trey who said it, though he couldn't be sure. His body sprang into action again, racing for the corner of the house. He glanced back once, twice, to gauge the pursuit. The agents were swarming. The AS seemed forgotten and were moving in the opposite direction.

Trey raised his own gun. And there was a moment when Eli remembered the dappled stillness of the woods in an afternoon when he reached out a hand and corrected the angle of his son's arm.

He liked to think—his body running, pushing itself into flight—that when the shot came, it would be from someone else.

TREY

19 SEPTEMBER 2061, 17:44

H e let the fork dangle from his fingers, the food forgotten on his plate and in his mouth.

"Shut your mouth," Adrian said, blunt and practical as always.

Trey shook his head to break the daze. He wasn't sure why he felt so disconnected. It was a raid like any other. And it wasn't.

Adrian shoved her own tray away. The food was bad anyway. Even the beans in the chili had the graininess of reconstituted food, and there was no meat. She sipped at her water instead.

"You alright?" She seemed concerned, genuinely so, but she wasn't about to put on a performance.

"I don't know. And that's the truth." He tried to smile. It felt lopsided on his face and must have looked concerning. Adrian grimaced.

"You said you wanted the lead on this one." Things had changed over the past year, but she didn't say that. "I did tell you that this could be the one."

"And all reports say the same. If the intel is good, then—" He paused, struggling over the words. "We may have Whitaker."

"Trey." She waited to continue talking until he looked up at her, until she had his attention. She was good at commanding attention. He saw that look in her face, the one that said she wasn't sure he'd come through. She'd never forget him walking away from that truck as a teenager. "You need to be honest with me. We can't afford to mess this up. We can't afford to keep dragging this out."

Outside the motel window, it was growing dark. Agents weaved back and forth among the trucks in the parking lot, dragging down blankets and sleeping bags to make the hard beds more comfortable. The management hadn't seemed too happy to have them, even though the parking lot was practically empty except for their own vehicles and equipment. She'd parceled out the keys as slowly as she could, jotting down each room assignment by hand. The front office had stunk of cigarette smoke.

"Do you think she'll tip off Eli?" He changed the topic abruptly, and with the change, he dropped the formality of the abstract enemy, of Whitaker. Adrian followed him. She had a way of keeping up with him, outracing him.

"I think she knows better than to risk imprisonment. And we paid her well." She corrected herself. "Or will pay her."

No rubbers in my rooms, she'd said. She had seen Helios and Ora lingering by the trucks, scanning the motel and the parking lot from where they stood.

"Out in the middle of nowhere," he mused, absently looking for the AS now. It still made him a little sick to his stomach to see Ora and yet he couldn't stop himself from constantly watching him.

"That's how Eli likes it. Out here where he can scare people with stuff they've never seen. Stuff they don't know firsthand."

He set down his fork and gave up the pretense of eating. "That's too easy."

"What?"

"It's too easy to say the lady who runs this motel is just scared of what she's never seen. She's seen AS, or she's seen something very like them. In the factories. In the fields. They're not soldiers, but they're still a threat as she looks at them."

"So Eli's just telling it like it is?" Adrian's voice turned brittle. She was tired. She didn't have much patience left for someone to question her anymore on the ATF's agenda. He'd seen her fending off questions for months now, tens upon tens of press conferences.

Trey could almost smell it again, the staleness of his bedroom in Eli's house, adjoining the kitchen. "He's telling one view of it, one side of it."

"There aren't sides when it comes to putting kids into gunfights." Her face had turned hard. It still scared him, that look on her face, as if he was worried about losing her still.

He answered quietly. "You know I don't mean that." Ever since the raid with Ora last July, he had to quell the tremors in his fingers before he could shoot his gun, even just in target practice.

She relaxed, her shoulders slumping forward. He knew that gesture, like a muscle memory of his own. The late evening sunlight slanted through the cloudy windows and danced on her skin. The room was shitty. The drawers stuck, the AC rattled and buzzed until you were forced to turn it off, and there were burn marks on the sheets. But he smiled at Adrian and felt like he was in high school again. Not that they'd ever actually rented a room, but there was a closeness here fabricated by the cheap coverlet and the bad print of a watercolor landscape.

"I never thought, never, that you would pick Ora." It was strange to hear the call sign in her voice. But her tone was not accusatory. She was genuinely curious and she wanted to talk. He needed to talk. He felt like he hadn't really talked to anyone in months.

"Helios convinced me."

She frowned a little. "Seems like an odd place for you to look for a recommendation. Didn't think you trusted any of them."

"I don't."

She waited for a better answer.

"But you said AS were mandatory. Protocol. And I thought—" He tried to get his words straight. "I thought if he made the mistake once, he knew what to avoid now." Was that why? He tried to remember now.

"Thought?"

"Hoped." It seemed naïve when he said it out loud. Perhaps he'd made a mistake. He'd made so many.

He couldn't meet her eyes right away and studied the parking lot again. It had quieted, most of the agents disappeared into their rooms. Next door, the TV began to play, muffled by the walls. The old fluorescent sign for the motel flickered by the road, offering free internet, free movie streaming. The AS had retreated there and the plastic and metal of their bodies distorted and reflected the blinking light above. They looked as inhuman as he'd ever seen them. Anxiety twisted his gut.

"It if helps," and she had grown quiet as well, "I don't think it was on him. His fault." He smiled, almost crying. "Isn't that the fucked-up part of it?" He looked back at her and realized the shadows had fallen in the room. They hadn't turned on the lamps yet, so only the trembling light of the bare bulbs over the cement walkway outside now illuminated the room. "That means it's our fault, doesn't it?"

She studied his face and was quiet. She had taken off her jacket and boots and curled her legs under. She seemed somewhere between the commended sergeant she was and Adrian from back home that she had been. For some reason, his brain just wouldn't completely reconcile the two. It unbalanced him.

"Well." She paused. "Maybe it's our fault. Maybe it means there are some things we're never going to fully account for."

"Adrian." It was like old times, old debates, but with stakes astronomically high. "If we don't account for something like children dying, we shouldn't be here."

"Here? In this motel room?" She was teasing, partially. It didn't mean she didn't care. Her face turned, a slight frown. "If we weren't here, Trey, Whitaker would get to go on throwing his children soldiers out in front, shielding himself, committing terrorism."

"We make the choice to fight those children."

"We don't." Her voice rose, close to anger now and suddenly. "We don't make that choice. We try, whenever we can, to save them."

Trey nodded, leaned back in his chair. She uncurled herself, the comfortable pose gone. She was changing more and more into the director of the ATF. Her leg clicked when she straightened it. He so often forgot that, the leg she lost.

"Just what if he's right?"

There was the question, the one he'd been avoiding for over a year now. At first, it had been easy, goaded by self-righteousness, goaded by an old hatred and anger, to lead the raids on Eli's houses. The child soldiers complicated that. The AS complicated that.

"He's not right, Trey." She was as confident as she'd ever been, dealing with Eli. She had never liked to give into the old man, had only done so when it was that or Trey getting hurt. Lord knows her home life wasn't much better than his own, abuse of negligence rather than intent.

She drove her finger into the cheap plastic table once and then again to underscore her point. "He's not right."

"The way he's doing it is not right."

"None of it is right. If you don't believe that, Trey, I don't think you should be leading the raid tomorrow."

He almost wanted it, almost wanted her to relieve him of duty. But not enough to say so. Someone screamed on the TV next door, fictional, muffled, shrill.

He turned his head and studied the parking lot again. The AS were coming back toward the trucks and SUVs where they would lie down for the night. In the darkness, he could have almost mistaken them for human.

"He's worried we've created our own destruction."

"I've no doubt we have," she answered softly. "But it's not the AS."

He wanted to tell her what it felt like—not what happened—but what it felt like when he saw that kid shot in the head. He'd heard different agents in the convoy whispering, hissing at Ora, calling him a baby-killer. He had not stopped them. He'd even hoped that Ora was capable of feeling some of that hate.

"We've been hurting our kids long before AS, before androids of any kind." She had followed his gaze, was watching the AS too.

"Someone sure messed up Eli." Then he shook his head, tried to clear it. "But don't worry. I don't plan on letting him run off, escape this time."

She smiled, just a little, and met his eyes. "No one else would let you go out."

"I wouldn't talk to any other director like I do with you."

The smile tugged down at the corner, sank a bit. A quiet crept back in, heavy and stale with the dilapidated aura of the room. "Do you wonder what would've happened if you'd come with me?"

It was hard for him not to reach out a hand and stroke hers, resting on the table. There was a time, and his body found it hard to forget those patterns, when that would have been the natural reaction. But he held himself still.

"I know what would've happened. I would've been a better person. I wouldn't have run out on my own a year later with no place to go and no one to ask for help. I'm sorry, Adrian. And I'm sorry I never really apologized for that. Not in a way where I knew what I'd done."

Her eyes looked wet, her cheeks flushed, but it was hard to tell for sure in the dimness of the room. She brushed a hand over her face and reached up to click on the lamp that arched over her head.

"What do you think would've happened?"

She sniffed. "I worry . . . I think it may have been the same. All the same. Us still sitting here, waiting for pre-dawn to go take out the guy who raised you."

"That's not why we're doing it."

"No. No." Her voice trailed off.

"You're right, Adrian. He's wrong." It became clearer, watching her, watching her move, stand up, wander to the drawers and the TV. "You're always right."

She smirked, her face half in shadow. "You sneak some booze in here?"

He laughed in return. "I wish." Then, before he could stop himself, as if he really were drunk. "I miss us."

She looked like he'd broken her heart again. Her face sort of fell, split into pieces, her mouth not matching her eyes.

"Don't say that shit. It's been thirty years."

He swallowed and looked down at his hands.

"You can't say that, can't bring that sort of shit into this, now. You know everything looks different on the night of a battle."

He waved his hand, waved away the tightening of his throat. "I know that. I don't even know if I'm being serious."

But he was serious. He knew that. She knew that.

"I've got to go catch my plane back to DC. You should get some shut-eye. I'll be waiting to hear your report. And the president will be waiting on mine."

He nodded. "You didn't have to come down with us."

She smiled, but it was all fake now. She picked up her coat and opened the door without waiting for him to stand up or see her out. It clicked behind her, sounded loud in the silence.

9.2:   20 SEPTEMBER 2061, 02:04

Trey rode in the truck with the AS, mostly because no one else wanted to. It was still dark, the moon falling in the sky, when they pulled out of the motel parking lot. The fluorescent lights had almost flickered out, whether because they were dying or because the manager had turned them off. The window to her office was dark, but he had the sense that she was watching. He almost imagined he saw the glowing butt of her cigarette.

Another agent drove, and Trey sat in the passenger seat. The AS were behind him. There was another row of empty seats, but no one to claim them. He turned around and glanced at Ora. Ora did not meet his gaze, but Helios was staring at him. He regretted bringing them along—not that he'd had any choice—and he wondered whether they could sense that.

"Orders, sir?" Helios asked.

The driver also craned her neck slightly to hear him better if he were about to issue orders. He tried to think of something to say, something authoritative.

"I want to see the lay of the land first."

"The objective is to neutralize Whitaker." There was no tone to read, so Trey had a hard time telling if Helios was asking or stating it.

"Yes." He almost regretted saying that. What if he had unknowingly approved some other horrific killing? What was acceptable in the name of neutralizing Eli Whitaker? He turned back to face the front. Then added, his neck tightening even as he said it, "No children."

"Clarify, sir. You mean that we are to kill no children."

He swallowed, already aware of the tactical error he had made, of the doubt he had instilled in the agent driving. The AS were useless to them if they could not trust them.

"Don't harm child combatants."

Helios nodded. It was not something he used to do, this human tic. "We have been trained with the same parameters. There is no need to worry."

Somehow, it was the AS who had adopted the voice of authority and comfort. Trey picked up the long-range comms and decided to cut short the conversation.

"Come in, Myrchek." He lifted his finger and waited for the response. A number of the trucks had left earlier to establish checkpoints and survey the property. Eli's house was a valley, surrounded by woods and hills that gave them the high ground and coverage—but had also defeated most of their attempts at air surveillance beforehand.

"Myrchek here."

"Are you in position?"

"We are, sir. We have eyes on the fire tower, which is where we think they have their own lookouts. Lights are off in the house and in the barn. But I don't think everyone is sleeping."

Trey was certain Eli must know, even if only on some subconscious level. He couldn't be sleeping. But they also had no evidence to suggest that he had slipped away since the last sighting of him, standing on the lawn, thirty-seven hours ago.

"No, I'm sure they're not. Keep an eye out. We'll be at your position in under ten."

"Yes, sir." The comms fell silent.

The driver looked at him. She was one of the older agents, middle-aged. She'd been on more than one of these raids, so he was surprised that he could not remember her name.

"It's hard to believe this might finally be the time we catch him."

He nodded. "I won't be sure until his hands are zip-tied and he's in the back of a truck."

The ride grew bumpy as their route took them off the asphalt roads onto back roads paved in gravel and tar. Fields stretched out on either side, with a fringe of trees on the horizon. Even with the moonlight, it was hard to tell what had been growing in the fields, if anything.

The road dipped, bent west, and then rose again to meet the foot of a hill. Trees crowded the top of the hill in a line of woods that stretched back the way they'd come, dividing the fields. A fleet of other trucks and SUVs were parked there. A few agents milled around. They were distributing and equipping night-vision goggles. Trey stepped out of the SUV almost before it was in park and joined them. Behind him, he heard the back doors to the vehicle open and shut and the quiet step of the AS on the grass.

"Any change?" He pitched his voice low, though there was no chance of anyone overhearing them at this distance.

The agent who handed him a pair of goggles shook his head. "Still all quiet."

Even as he said that, shots rang out from somewhere out of sight, beyond the hill.

"Is that us?" He turned on his comms and stuck the transponder in one ear. He settled the goggles on his forehead, but he didn't pull them down just yet. The AS crouched low and began to climb the hill, no need for goggles or extra technology than that which already comprised them.

The comms burst into noise, voices of agents chattering back and forth. Someone positioned on the opposite hill from theirs, between which the house was set, reported that they had been fired on, but they did not have a visual on the combatants.

"Make sure you have a visual before returning fire," Trey ordered. He tapped in his auditory key to verify his authority as CO. "We don't want a repeat of last year." They all knew which raid he referenced.

There was a moment's silence, an unstated judgment. *Then we shouldn't have brought the AS.*

He tapped off his comms, turned to the agents with him. "One of you, stay here with the vehicles. The rest with me."

They nodded quietly, checked their guns over one last time, and then fell in behind him as he moved up the hill. When they hit the line of trees, the leaves deadened the sound and stilled the air around them. The AS were ahead of him, lying on their stomachs where the tree line switched to shrubbery. Helios signaled that it was clear for them to come up over the rise and break cover. There was a moment's hesitation where Trey envisaged himself an open target against the night sky, but he shook that down and moved forward. He sank into the grass and slipped the night-vision goggles down. The ground was hard under him and he was almost rubbing shoulders with Helios, who emitted a gentle heat. He blazed in the goggles' view when Trey glanced at him.

"Any movement in the house?" he asked the AS.

"One light downstairs on this side of the house. Lights in the upstairs windows." And then it seemed to Trey that Helios paused. Which felt unnatural. "The children sleep up there."

Trey signed his acknowledgment, and tried to convey nothing else. No trepidation. No anxiety. No hollow in the pit of his stomach.

Shots again on the opposite hill. Trey could follow it now, saw the silhouette of the broken-down watchtower rising just above the tree line.

"Where are the lookouts on our side?" He whispered this, then tapped a code on his comms, alerting the agents with him to be watchful. The downward slope was covered with bracken and scrub bushes. Trey understood the advantage that familiarity would grant Eli's people. That said, the property felt familiar to him too. Eli had a habit of picking abandoned farmhouses that felt like his old home.

"I have eyes on one," an agent whispered down the line.

"Steady," Trey returned.

A tree branch exploded over his head. Trey hunched instinctively, then lifted his head, scanning the surrounding area. The shooter was close. That much he could tell from the report of the gun. He gestured for the agents to spread out and cut off the shooter. They obeyed immediately, moving into a low crouch.

They didn't move quietly in the woods. Any good hunter would hear them from far away. Eli would hear them if he was out there. But Trey's agents weren't SEALs or Marines. They had signed up for something very different, not civil insurrection, not child soldiers. No one had signed up for that.

Helios shifted beside him. "We should go too, sir?" He dropped his voice but was incapable of whispering.

"Work your way down to the house." Trey gazed down the hill. "Detain anyone who tries to escape."

He didn't take off his armored vest, and they didn't wait for any such offer. They levered themselves upward and moved, with gentle whirring noises from their joints, down the hill. They crouched so low that the taller grasses brushed at their knees. With just one quick sign, they split paths halfway down the slope and moved in a pincer formation toward the house and lawn.

Trey rolled over onto his back and listened. Twigs snapped underfoot where the agents moved. They sounded nearer than they actually were in the close air under the trees. Someone grunted. His comms crackled as if someone had tried to speak but been cut off. He sat up slowly and scanned the woods, forcing himself to breathe steadily, forcing himself to be quiet and calm. The heartbeat in his ears began to slow.

Leaves rustled to his right, too close to be one of his own agents. Amid the dark masses of trees and brush, he saw a heat signature glowing bright green. The silhouette was slight, short. He lifted his rifle slowly, aiming and holding his shot. He was surprised that his breathing was still quiet, his hand steady. His training ran too deep; his body felt disconnected from the sudden panic in his mind.

"Drop your weapon." He said it quietly, because the figure was close enough to hear and he didn't want to call anyone else to their position.

There was a quiet gasp. The person looked frantically from one side to another. Trey held himself still.

"Drop it."

"Coward. Hiding in the dark." It was a middle-aged, masculine voice. And it didn't fit any of the voice profiles of his agents. His comms picked up no identifiers. But it was also not a child.

There was a burst of fire from the left, a quick answering volley, and then silence. Trey did not look away or drop his aim. The man's head swiveled, looking for clarification.

"Last time," Trey said. He had offered too many chances as it was.

The man dropped something. It looked like his gun. He held his hands up in the air. They trembled a little in the night vision.

"Don't shoot," he said, and his voice sounded frightened now, the bravado gone.

Trey stood up and tucked his own weapon under his arm. He lifted his night goggles so he could see the man for what he was as he walked to him. He pulled the man's arms down, zip-tied them behind his back.

"How many of you up on this hill?"

The man shrugged and then answered reluctantly. "Just two or three others. Most are rallying to the barn or to the fire tower."

Trey's comms buzzed with one of his agent's keys. "We have one in custody, sir."

"Same here," he answered. "Be on the watch for one or two more up here."

There was a grunt of affirmation.

"Where's Eli? Where are the children?" he asked the man in quick succession. He was, up close, in the natural light, younger than Trey had guessed by the voice, gaunt, hollow-cheeked.

"Not my job to know." The man's face drooped into sullenness. "I came where I was told."

"Yeah, well, go where you're told now." Trey glanced around him and saw no other agent nearby to help. A rattle of gunfire by the tower, distant and sporadic. "Come on."

He went back the way he had come. Low branches knocked against his arm, leaves whispered and brushed by his ear. As the woods thinned out and the slope began to descend, he saw the vehicles parked, headlights strong and bright. The agent stationed with them looked up, caught sight of him, and raised an arm. They signed that they were prepped to receive prisoners. The man tripped and stumbled forward a few steps as they navigated the decline, steep in places. At one point, he cursed under his breath and then, as if that had sparked a greater anger, he turned his head and spat at Trey's feet.

"I saw those rubbers heading toward the main house." He was a little out of breath, so the words did not carry the rage intended. "You're a fucking traitor. Working with those things against us. We're human like you. We're skin, we're blood."

Trey knew better than to answer and engage. "I don't work with them. They work for me."

The man laughed, half-coughing. "You think that sounds better."

Trey shoved him the last few steps, and the agent stepped forward to take him into custody. He paused, listening to himself breathe, as the man was led away to the back of one of the trucks. He turned around, looked back up the hill to the dark woods at the top.

"Sir." The voice was quiet and inhuman in his ear, without the huskiness of breath behind it. "We have eyes on Whitaker."

He was hardly part of the fight himself, halfway up the hill, alone, with the sky big above him.

Another agent interrupted the feed. "We have Whitaker pinned to his porch. Orders?" Trey muted them.

"Helios." He swallowed. "Incapacitate. Don't kill."

The AS expressed confirmation and his line went quiet. Trey opened up the other channel to the waiting agent.

"Hold your position. The AS are moving in." There was a poetic justice to it. There was a sound of throat-clearing from the agent and a muttered assent. The reluctance, almost resentment, spoke volumes.

9.3: MAY 2032

I'm thinking of dropping out. Joining the Army, or the Marines, or something." Trey waited for Adrian to take her own drag and pass the joint back to him.

She raised her eyebrows. "Copycat."

She both was and wasn't like he remembered. The past four years had thinned out her face, and her military training had changed her shoulders, her arms, her legs.

His roommate interrupted, intercepting the joint. "You can't drop out now. You've only got two semesters left." He glanced at Adrian and winked. "We don't all have it in us to run away to the Army."

She smirked a little. "No. We can't all run away." She refused to meet his eyes. Instead, she slumped back against the couch cushions. "What snacks do y'all have?"

"Dex, why don't you grab the chips?" Trey pointed toward the kitchenette. His roommate sighed in exaggerated irritation and levered himself off the floor.

"You just want to keep the pretty girl all to yourself." He was trying to flirt, and he was failing. Trey shouldn't have let him stay when he knew Adrian would visit. But he'd been a little nervous to see her again.

When Dex started slamming the cupboard doors, he leaned forward a little, shifting on the couch to angle toward her.

"Adrian—"

"I didn't know your roommate would be here. He's kind of a loser." Her voice was cold. Hopefully, the joint would help to mellow her out.

"Look, you should know that I don't go home to Eli's anymore. Don't call it home."

Her back stiffened a bit, like she was afraid he would touch her. She'd been closed off and distant since he'd opened the door at her knock. He wondered why she'd agreed to come at all.

"I don't care where you live, Trey."

"I just thought you should know, that you would want to know . . ."

She shook her head slightly and sat up. "I don't know that I should have come here."

"Where else were you going to go on leave? Back to your mom's?"

Her cheeks flushed. "I haven't talked to her since I left."

"That's what I'm trying to tell you. I've cut off communications with Eli."

She smiled a little, the corner of her mouth lifting in a combination of disbelief and regret. "Do you remember when he slapped me? That morning he took us out hunting?"

Trey drew back. He hung his head and picked at the pills on the sofa cushion. "I should have done something."

"Yeah." She didn't let him off the hook, didn't shy away from it.

"Did you hate me for that?"

"Not then." The answer came a little too quick.

Dex was too quiet in the kitchen, either eavesdropping or trying to figure out how to sneak out of the apartment without being noticed. He knew Adrian must be aware of it, but she didn't seem to care much. Perhaps that was what had changed so much about her. Even in the hour or so that they had been talking, trying to catch up, whatever that might look like between normal people, she didn't seem to give a shit about anything. She'd walled off the parts of her he'd known best, maybe even from herself.

He didn't ask the question that would make the whole night untenable.

"This is a pretty shitty apartment," she finally said when it seemed the silence had gone on too long.

Trey looked around him, trying to see the space like someone who didn't live in it every day. The peeling and stained wallpaper, the claustrophobic dropped ceiling, the scuffed baseboards, the lingering smell of last night's dinner.

He shrugged. "Yeah, it's not the best. But it's better, you know."

She nodded. "And the couch is comfortable enough. Which is what I care about." It was a gesture of peace.

"You can make use of it as long as you want."

"Don't worry. I won't crash here too long. I should go home, see a few people too."

He didn't ask whether that included her mom. Dex came to the doorway of the kitchenette, his face crestfallen. "The chips are gone. I think I ate them last night."

"That's alright." Trey reached for his jacket, sprawled over the armchair. "We'll go out and get some more snacks. Or, if you want to?" He looked at Adrian.

She stood up on the couch and stepped over the back of it. It was the most efficient pathway to the door. "Okay. Come on."

Adrian swayed a little as they walked down the hallway, less a sign of inebriation and more one of relaxation. The carpet smelled like smoke, so when they stepped out onto the sidewalk, the night air seemed cleaner than it actually was. He breathed in deeply, and she mimicked him. When they began to head in the direction of the corner store, they fell into lockstep, easily matching each other, as if their bodies remembered how they used to walk together.

"What are you doing here, Trey? What are you going to do with your life?"

A cruiser passed by them on the street, the robotic arm tucked close to the passenger-side window but its lens scanning them and the rest of those walking on the sidewalk. He twitched a little and wondered what it saw when it ran his face through its database.

"Fucking hate those things," Adrian said, looking where he was looking. "Escalation in the name of de-escalation."

"I think that's what their slogan is, yeah." He found himself suddenly, and without reason, defending the technology despite his joke. "Come on—it's supposed to help."

"Technology's just a tool for what we already want to do. It's the *want* that needs addressing." She sounded sure, immoveable.

"Are you working with something like that in the Army?"

She stuffed her hands in her pockets. "Not really. But they have the tech. Someone's using it. All I get are goggles with access to databases." She smiled just a little. "I'm not going to say that hasn't come in handy a couple of times."

"I never thought you were someone who would enlist. I thought you had all these plans for writing, teaching."

"I thought we were talking about your life."

"I'm just curious."

"Turns out college is expensive," she said, glancing at the storefronts, not looking at him. He watched her reflection, distorted by the cracks, the dirt, the pasted paper ads. "And it turns out I had some issues to work out."

He thought about laughing or making a joke to try and lighten the weight of that last comment. He wondered how many of the issues he had helped cause. So he stayed quiet. A car horn blared around the corner, somewhere far away the siren of an ambulance.

"Can we stop here?" She had paused and was studying the menu of a small café. It offered fusion cuisine, some mix of Mexican and Chinese. It looked good. And Trey was hungry.

"Sure."

They went in and found a booth by the window. They ordered food on the screen at their table and waited awkwardly, elbows propped on the table, for someone to bring it to them. It was hard to figure out whether he should look at her or out the window. Sitting across from each other felt weirdly intense. He tried to shake the idea that it was a date. He knew it wasn't. He was four years too late there.

"Are you happy?" he asked suddenly, catching her eye. Her skin was sun-darkened, her hair shorter, barely reaching her shoulders. But, again, he couldn't quite lay his finger on the intangible change.

She shrugged. "What do people mean when they say they're happy? That they're not worried about money? That they've found the love of their life? That they have a house or kids or a good job?" She glanced at the counter, at the window into the kitchen. It looked like one cook on his own. "What do you mean when you ask me that? What answer are you looking for?"

He felt the hair prickle on his neck, opened his mouth and closed it again.

She laughed a little, and it wasn't completely cynical. When he swallowed and glanced at her again, she was still looking at him. "Did I make you uncomfortable enough?"

"I don't know. I'm not sweating out the pits of my shirt yet."

"Okay, I'll keep working on it."

The food came, and, like food had a way of doing, it eased the tension. The steam rising off the meat and noodles was savory and spicy and curled his tongue.

"I didn't want to upset you. I just sometimes think about you and I worry about how you're doing."

"I do too. About you." She stabbed at the dish with her fork and chewed, jaw working overtime. "But I always worried about you."

"I know." He picked at his plate. A small floor cleaner buzzed by their booth, almost bumping against his shoe. He pulled his foot in under the table.

"Eli messed with your head."

He nodded and couldn't find any words to say it better.

"Are you serious when you say you think about dropping out?"

It was his turn to shrug. "It felt real when I said it."

"Don't."

He set down his fork. He looked at her, waiting for her to elaborate.

"You didn't tell me what your degree is in, what you're learning. But I know you. I know you don't need another authoritarian telling you what to do."

"Seems like kind of a hypocritical thing to say in your position."

She took another bite and glanced out the window. A panhandler was taking up position outside. A line of college students tottered by, intent on some bar crawl.

"Yeah, maybe." Then she dropped silent again, ate rapidly, shoveling food into her mouth in quick, almost desperate motions. "But I needed to fight something. Or maybe, better to say I was fighting something."

"That's textbook worst reason to enlist." The food was gone, but he seemed to have lost the appetite for anything more. And his buzz was fading.

"Sure." She caught his eyes, looked away again. "But we fight if that's all we've got left to do."

He swallowed. He knew it would be a mistake to say what he was going to say. "You don't think you're playing the martyr bit a little heavy?" He knew why he said it after he said it. His own guilt.

Her head snapped up, but her face remained open. Her eyes didn't narrow. She didn't flush with anger. All of the signs he was used to. But he wasn't sure, yet, whether that meant she wasn't angry. Just that she'd changed.

"You only want me to shut up about my stuff because you won't talk about yours. Maybe you should face your own shit instead of crying *martyr* to others when they do."

"You ran away to fight because you couldn't face yours." The answer was quick, instinctive, defensive.

"You'll turn out just like him."

The words shut him up. The table fell quiet and the waiter awkwardly cleared their table while they sat in discomfort.

She leaned forward, her voice softened. "That's what Eli does. Bottles up all his rage until he thinks every cause he takes on—calmly, rationally, oh so sanely—is a just one. He channels his anger."

He leaned back, rolled his eyes and tried to avoid hers. "Eli is rarely angry."

She laughed. "He's angry. He just doesn't throw tantrums. Maybe slaps a girl once or twice."

His face was turning red. He could feel it.

"You've seen his emails? They're almost manifestos. Half of my bunkmates get them." She clicked her tongue. "And they don't think it's bullshit."

"I've seen them."

"Of course you have. I'm sure you're top of his mailing list."

"It's just words."

"Half of the other recruits that came in with me? Did so because there weren't jobs in the factories or plants near their homes anymore, no more jobs in the distribution centers."

"So you believe him."

She shook her head, looked for a moment at the panhandler, whose head was barely visible in the glass window now that he had settled onto the sidewalk. "It's not the AI that's the problem. It's the companies who don't give a shit."

"Isn't that what he's saying?"

"Eli doesn't want to face up to the real threat. He's always been too chickenshit for that. So he subs in the product for the maker."

It stung a little, even now, to hear her malign Eli so strongly. It worried him that it stung. They sat for a few extra minutes after the store had texted their receipt.

"I'm sorry," he said.

She knew what he was apologizing for. She forgave him with a quick smile. "Thanks for letting me crash at your place."

"Any time."

9.4:   20 SEPTEMBER 2061, 06:14

The night was quiet, the air almost cool, and it seemed suspiciously calm. The shooting had stopped, even on the hill near the fire tower. The AS seemed to be watching Trey closely, a guess at best, and he was glad that he had sent someone else to sweep the house. They stood still, unmoving in a way no human could mimic.

"We took good care of them." Eli's voice brought his attention back to the issue at hand. The agent who had reported on the collected children retreated as if he wanted no part of the conversation. "They came to me when they had nowhere else to go."

Trey realized he would actually have to talk to Eli, to say something other than that he was under arrest. He forced himself to meet the man's eyes. He still remembered the first time he saw him, striding down the corridor in the foster home, thin legs in faded jeans, but with a deliberate step that brooked no stopping or pausing. He'd thought then that the man who said he planned to be father to him was something more than a man, something intractable. At the time, he'd vaguely thought of a wild storm, thunder and lightning. Now, he couldn't help comparing Eli to the AS that had captured him, single-minded, fixated on a directive from who knows where. The irony was not lost on him.

"Let's not argue about whether your *child soldiers* were well cared for."

Eli's mouth narrowed a bit, but Trey knew that wouldn't be enough to shut him up. The agent in charge of scanning the house exited and waited for Trey to address him.

"All good?"

"All clear."

He nodded, waved the agent back to the trucks where others were recording names and times of arrest for the captured insurgents. A line of bodies, at least five so far, were laid out on the lawn behind him.

"Trey—" The voice needled him, made his neck crawl.

He didn't let Eli finish. He bent down and spoke close to his face, so that he spit as he talked. "Don't say my name. Not anymore. Shut up." The words grew louder by the end. It was pent up, an anger he hadn't fully expressed before.

He knew his face was flushed and red when he straightened. He signed to Helios to take Eli away to the trucks. He didn't trust himself to walk with the man himself right now.

"I can walk on my own," Eli snapped as they lifted him by his arms and dragged him along with them. For all the world like he was a man who expected considerate treatment. Like a man who hadn't realized it was all over.

He turned away so that he wouldn't have to watch his silhouette in the lightening sky. The breeze felt like early morning. He switched to satellite and keyed in Adrian's code. She answered immediately and she sounded like she was right by his side.

"Trey?" There was a tightness in her voice, and she had abandoned titles, something she didn't usually do while on monitored comms.

"It's done. We have him." The words released a pain in his throat as if he were holding back tears.

He heard her breathing.

"Whitaker is in custody," he said, retreating into formality himself.

Another second of silence. "Are you alright?"

"I don't know."

"Were there any casualties?"

"All our agents are accounted for. No deaths there. We're still trying to get an accurate count of the insurgents on site."

He could imagine her nodding, planning how she would report this to the media. Two agents were coming down the hill with another body held between them. His heart sped up. He couldn't take his eyes off them as they made their way to the lawn and added the body to the growing line. It was a woman, plaid shirt, hair tangled around her face.

"Trey," Adrian said in his ear. "It will be alright."

"I'm not sure it will be."

He heard the catch in her voice. "We'll work on making it alright."

A child screamed. Trey didn't catch the words, but he wheeled around to try and find the source of the distress. An agent yelled out for someone or something to stop. The commotion was near the trucks. He switched back to radio comms and walked quickly in that direction. He didn't run. Running would make it harder for him to concentrate and aim if he needed to. The sky was gray now, but there were still dark shadows around the vehicles.

Eli burst out into the open, already running. He was heading for the corner of the house, seeking cover there. He glanced over his shoulder. He saw Trey, Trey was sure of it. Instinctively, he raised his gun and aimed at Eli, keeping his bead a step ahead. An agent was racing behind Eli, trying to catch up with him, but there was a hollow in Trey's stomach, where he was certain how this would all end.

It was Eli who had taught him how to shoot. He'd been a patient teacher. He would wait for Trey to ask him for help. It was one of the first things they had done together, hike up into the woods in the acres behind the farmhouse. And Trey had been impressed, as a child, that a near stranger would offer him a gun to hold.

"Stop!" Trey shouted. But his voice sounded quiet in his own ears against the thumping of the blood.

Eli did not stop. He did not stop.

There was a shot. Trey felt the backfire of the gun as if it were a strange and unexpected sensation. Even then, it was a second before he fully grasped that he had shot. He felt heads turning to look at him, not at the fallen body, not at the blood blooming on the denim shirt. He thought he could hear Adrian, her breathing in his head, but the comms were not connected to satellite.

Eli reached out one hand as if to pull himself forward, but then his head slumped into the grass. An agent caught up to him, knelt, and checked for a pulse. He was shaking his head even before he stood.

Trey's arm was shaking. He was still holding the gun out. He forced himself to pull his arm back and to sling his gun behind. His face was hot.

"He's dead, sir." The agent who had checked approached him as if the words needed to be spoken aloud.

Trey was grinding his teeth. He nodded and glanced around to do a mental tally of who was there. A few agents were still moving up and down the hill. One was checking for identification on the dead bodies on the lawn. He looked to the trucks. The AS were standing there, in the shadow of a truck's cab. Quiet. Hardly in pursuit. The sun was rising behind them and the sky was gold and red. Light bounced off their bodies and made it hard to stare at them for too long.

There was a dull ache, a rage, beating in the back of his head. "Helios, report."

There was a moment's pause where no one moved. Then both AS moved, Helios toward him, Ora across the lawn as if to help the agents with the bodies. For a second, Trey wondered what Ora was doing, wondered if he should stop him, but Helios's approach distracted him. He found it hard to focus. He walked to meet Helios halfway, over Eli's body. An agent moved in front of him with a blanket as if this were the one body in need of respect.

The outline of Eli's body was still clear. Trey felt that he would recognize the angles of it anywhere, under any amount of blankets.

"After all that, a coward," he said, looking down at it, at the body. And Helios had not yet joined him to report on how Eli had escaped.

He looked up into the red light just as an agent yelled directly behind him. He was tired. The shout made him cringe, made him worried to follow it. But he turned his head anyway. The agent who had brought the blanket was raising his rifle to shoot at something beyond the row of bodies, a figure sprinting toward the far line of woods. *There are vehicles there*, Trey calculated, thinking at first—irrationally—that one of the bodies was not dead but had stood up and run for it.

But it was not an insurgent. It was Ora, his legs flashing, even in the dimness where the sunrise had not yet reached.

He felt the wind of Helios passing him, rushing toward the agent with the gun. He moved faster than any human ever could, faster than Trey could. And there was a feeling like horror bubbling up in his stomach, a sudden anxious thought that Eli had been right. Eli was right.

Helios grappled with the agent, but it was not much of a struggle. The agent was easily disarmed and shoved roughly to the ground. Other agents were moving in and shouts of confusion rang over the lawn. And Helios did not try to flee, not immediately. He held the gun of the disarmed agent and he looked after Ora, who had almost reached the edge of the woods.

Trey moved automatically, letting his training take over. He unholstered his pistol, short range, and shot at Helios. The light was tricky, the sunrise behind casting a huge shadow from the house. So he did not hit the AS's neck, the most vulnerable part of his armor. But he did hit him in the back. He shot more than once, as he was trained, to incapacitate a threat.

Helios tottered forward a step with each shot. He fell to his knees. But Trey was not convinced he was immobilized. He did not drop his aim, and he lifted his voice so that it would project. "Stop, Helios."

The AS did not respond, tipping forward, his head pushing into the grass. The attacked agent crawled away from Helios's outstretched arm and struggled to get to his feet. He shook his head, opened his mouth as if he wanted to offer some defense for his failure, but said nothing.

"Stop, Helios," Trey repeated, hoping his voice command would trigger Helios's protocols. He was not convinced by Helios's stillness.

He stepped forward cautiously. Looking down at the AS, there was a flash of anger, like a firecracker or gunpowder. He had trusted Helios, and he was a fool for it. He kicked one of Helios's legs. The other agents drew back. They were all waiting, with one pent breath. None of them had their guns ready or aimed.

He was breathing hard. His ears were ringing, either with the recent gunfire or with his own anger. The AS looked almost human in its outline on the ground, though the angles of his body were a little too sharp, too square.

He glanced up to the line of the woods. Ora was standing just at the edge, his body frozen and still, as if he had been injured himself. Trey felt almost a pang of guilt, a tickling under his ribs at the rigidity of the AS's pose. He imagined that Ora was frozen in grief. But the feeling passed quickly. He motioned to his agents, shocked at their inaction.

They stirred themselves, reached for their guns. But an ungodly noise made them stop again. A moan, too high-pitched to be guttural. A moan without any rasp of vocal cords or pent up breath. Helios stirred. At first his legs spasmed and Trey's body tensed, watching, unable to move, caught between fight and flight.

And then Helios moved, too fast, standing up to his feet in one fluid motion, despite the bullet holes in his back.

"Run!" Helios shouted to Ora, and the ground shivered under the agents' feet. Trey felt the word in his legs, in his bones. Ora, at the line of trees, startled like a deer and fled. The agents did not move to pursue. They looked stunned and unsure.

He was directly behind Helios now, and the AS's neck was exposed, a patch of white, hard plastic, limned with metal, an accordion fold of artificial skin near the base. He felt as if time had slowed down. He knew that Helios would turn, now, now.

Trey raised his arm. The barrel of the gun was only inches from the AS's neck. His index finger trembled on the trigger. And it was like Helios was waiting for him to shoot. How much time had passed? Why did he not turn?

Now. Eli's voice in his head, a deer in the scope.

He squeezed and stumbled backward, though the kick of the gun was not intense. The plastic of Helios's neck shattered in front of him. Trey's hand stung where a piece of thin metal burrowed into it. His cheek was on fire. Agents were shouting. His long-range comm was beeping in his ear.

But he could hear nothing. It was silent inside his head, even if his ears were ringing and he was screaming. Eli, who had given the order—who had always given orders—was gone.

ADRIAN

21 SEPTEMBER 2061

She woke up from a bad dream the night before the press conference. Her cat moved to the other side of the bed in reprimand, curling his tail about himself and tucking his head between his paws. The room was distractingly bright. The bodega owner across the street had forgotten to turn off his neon sign. She took a sip of water from the cup on the bedside table and watched the shadows drift on the floor where the wind gently rocked the blinds.

She was dreading tomorrow, even though it was now—finally—some good news that she got to deliver. Though the news had already leaked to the press. And it would be her face and her voice who reminded them of the body count. Perhaps the idea of good news was relative.

She had drafted her opening statement and a few comments with Peter before leaving the office. Trey had asked her to dinner and she'd said no. She needed time. She needed to remind him of the distance between them.

He had been a wreck when he'd reported back to the ATF offices. She hadn't slept well herself the night before, waiting to hear whether the raid was a success, so it was hard to produce a smile to welcome him back. His eyes were red-rimmed and he looked as if he'd been ill. *It's alright*, she'd said, automatically. He'd shaken his head.

In her dream, she had heard Eli's voice, talking at her. A droning, awful voice that both was and wasn't his. It would not stop, and she couldn't fully understand what he said.

I lost Ora in the woods. There are agents looking. But she could tell that he'd had no hope the agents would succeed in finding him. *I called the lab. They should be able to track him.* He'd shot her a look, one that was on the edge of blame. That had pissed her off. She'd turned away. *He's disabled his tracker, but they think they can find his signature. . . . They're working on it.* His response was short. *They shouldn't be able to do that. They shouldn't be able to operate independently.*

Perhaps he'd wanted to get dinner to apologize. For what he'd said afterward. She wasn't sure she was interested in hearing it.

She turned over on her side, away from the light, and folded the pillow under her head. Her knee snagged, for just a second, on the sheets. Chewy did not budge.

She hadn't liked any of Peter's suggestions for addressing Ora's escape and Helios's death. *Malfunction,* she reminded herself. There would be no language that might paint the destroyed AS as a victim. No matter what she said—she angrily refolded the pillow and tried to smooth it under her cheek—there would be something for the anti-AS movement to latch onto. And that was where Eli had found a base to begin with. Restart the cycle. *One of the AS malfunctioned, but agents on the scene were able to quickly defuse the situation.* Defuse—as if the AS were a ticking bomb. Avoid mention if possible of the uncontrolled AS on the loose. In Appalachia, where someone could still lose themselves. But she could hear the question now: Director, weren't there two AS on this mission? Did the other one return with the agents?

She threw the sheets off and felt her way gingerly to the bathroom, navigating stacks of folders, piles of laundry, Chewy's toys. She kicked her leg out to loosen the artificial joint. It popped in a satisfying way.

The lights in the bathroom were bright, so she squinted into the mirror, leaning on the sink. She fumbled to turn on the faucet and scooped some water into her mouth, though there was a perfectly good cup of it by her bedside and she wouldn't have to cut further into the building's water rations by drinking from it. Water dripped down her chin when she glanced back up into the mirror. Her face was flushed, her hair pressed into odd spikes by her tossing and turning.

What had she used to look like? Who had she used to be? She was having trouble recalling any former version of herself, a version who had been in love with Trey, a version who had wanted to shoot Eli herself, a version who had looked at an AS in a small cell and thought she'd understood him.

Perhaps the AS were a bomb, waiting to explode. The lab techs had offered up so little explanation when she'd confronted them about the way in which Ora and Helios had defied their protocols. As if they couldn't be expected to fully understand the AS, as if they weren't beings pulled out of their very labs.

She gritted her teeth, looked at them closely for plaque buildup, a small anxiety that suddenly demanded her attention. She turned her head to each side as far as she could while still able to see the mirror and inspect her teeth. Had her gums been a little sensitive lately?

She closed her mouth, pinched her lips together tightly. She had insisted that Trey take the AS with him.

She clicked off the lights and let her eyes adjust to the darkness again. Then she stumbled back to bed.

But it was Trey, she told herself as she pulled the sheet up over her legs, Trey who had chosen Helios and Ora. Why, of all AS, them? Had he thought of Helios as an acquaintance, a friend?

The neon light flickered and the shadows with it. The blinds shuddered and tapped against the window. Chewy snuffled in his sleep.

She felt like crying. She felt like a lonely teenager again, confused about why she was fighting so hard to be heard when she didn't know what she wanted to say. There was a version of her, returned again.

And she suddenly realized that she understood what Eli had been saying in the dream. He was saying *I love you*. To Trey. And she stood with them in the middle of the woods. He was saying *I love you, but not everyone will*. He was saying, *Not everyone will love you and some will want to hurt you*. He was saying, *Don't let anyone hurt you*.

The words felt real, but she couldn't remember if they were.

She made a cup of artificial coffee at the office, since both the shop on her route and the one at the train terminal were closed indefinitely. The price for beans had skyrocketed yet again since the unrest in Brazil had disrupted production lines, but the office had scrounged up some poor substitute in the last few weeks, a vain attempt to raise morale. The assistant who answered the phones kept a sharp eye on the cupboard and monitored usage. Adrian felt her eyes on her as she prepared her drink.

"Do you want some sugar?" The assistant's voice was unexpected and Adrian jumped a little. Her right leg compensated, remaining still and stable.

Adrian looked at the assistant, who was holding out a paper packet in her hand. "I keep them in my drawer. Some people would use three or four in one cup if I didn't."

Adrian didn't usually take sugar in her coffee, but she took the packet anyway. "Thanks."

"You looked like you needed it."

"I guess." She shook the packet down and ripped off the top. The granules floated for a second on the top of the coffee. She threw away the paper, then glanced up again at the assistant. She had turned back to her computer and was shifting files on the clear glass screen.

"Model number?" It was a standard query, but when the words left her mouth, she felt a little exposed, rude.

The assistant's head twitched toward her. If she looked closely, Adrian could see the line at the border of her hair. But she had to look very closely.

"AA325-4." The words did not have the luster of her usual adopted accent and tone. They were mechanical. The assistant turned quickly back to her screen as if she did not want to linger on the question.

"Right, thank you." Adrian swallowed and looked at her nameplate. "Thank you, Phila." It felt too little, too late. She did not wait to hear if the assistant would answer, but turned and retreated down the hall toward her own office.

Peter was waiting. "I made a few small changes," he said as she entered, handing her his tablet.

She scanned the lines there. "I thought we weren't going to say anything about Ora if we could help it." The coffee cup was hot in her hand. She looked around for a place to set it.

"My contact at CBB gave me a look at the questions they had prepared. The journalists will be asking about that directly."

She bit the inside of her mouth and nodded. "Of course they will." She looked up at Peter. "How long have we had an AA at the front desk?"

"A couple of months?" He shrugged. "They aren't programmed with a single aggressive bone in their body, though. Private manufacturer."

She shook her head. "No, that's not—" And then she realized she wasn't entirely sure why she had asked. "How much time do we have?"

"You have twenty minutes."

"I'll be in my office."

He took back his tablet. "I'll send these to you. If you think they work."

"They're fine, yeah." She reviewed the words in her head. She was a quick study. Memorization had always come easy to her. *Ora had taken damage in previous battles. We now see that this affected his processing more than we realized.*

And was that comforting? Should farmers and manufacturers in the region worry about running into a damaged, maddened AS?

"I don't think there's a good answer to this." But she was talking to herself. The windows were dimmed, so she hit the switch to brighten them. She looked out on the carefully manicured lawn, at the willow trees. She tried to ignore the browning leaves, the ones curling and dropping to the ground.

She reached for her coffee and remembered that she had left it in the outer office, and she didn't want to step out just yet. She cracked her knuckles, a nervous time-killing habit, and then sat down at her desk and turned on the computer. It took her a couple of minutes, but she finally found the video file she was looking for, the day she had visited Ora in his cell, when he had still been under observation.

She had stood so close to him. It sent a shiver down her back to watch it now. She'd been so convinced there was something to be saved there. That was why she had cleared him for duty on Trey's request. What had Helios said to convince Trey of that?

She shook her head, felt the dull throb of pain at her temples.

"Director." Peter did not fully open the door.

She didn't look up at first but kept staring at the screen. "Did we do good, Peter? Have we done anything good here?"

Peter's silence was hesitant, unsure, impatient. She turned off the monitor. "Tell me this was worth it."

He opened the door a little wider. "We could arrange a second press conference if you want. Bring in the kids we've placed through AOFC. Spin a feel-good story to neutralize the one with the dangerous AS on the loose." His usual sarcasm was there even if his face was serious. "Or we could rerun some footage of reuniting that girl Lia with her parents, back in the winter. Press ate that up."

"Reunited her with her mom."

He questioned her correction with a look.

"We killed her dad." She breathed in, changed the narrative. "Eli killed him."

"That's your answer, then. We got the guy who was killing people," Peter said. "You coming?"

The pressroom was packed, humid with the sweating and breathing of such a large crowd. She tried to catch her breath, to fill her lungs.

"Thank you all for coming." She shifted behind the podium and glanced down at the tablet Peter had left there. "We're ultimately here to celebrate a victory—"

"Director." A voice interrupted her. She glanced up and tried to locate the journalist who had spoken. It was a woman from the *Times*.

"I just have a short statement before we open it up to questions." She smiled tightly and looked back down at her prepared words. They seemed small and insufficient.

"Director, apologies. But I think we've already heard what there is to be celebrated. I think the American people want to know the danger that's still out there. What are you doing to locate and subdue this rogue AS, code name Ora?"

Adrian sighed, inaudibly she hoped. She clicked off the tablet's screen. The words glowed a moment, faded, and disappeared.

"Okay, fine, we'll get right to it. We're not a group to dwell on the good, I suppose."

"I think some might wonder whether it was good, the raid, the use—or misuse—of AS." This was another journalist, a polished face from one of the networks.

They had applauded a day ago, when the news first broke.

"Eli Whitaker was a threat. To national security. To the communities of this nation." She hadn't been able to eat on her way back from the motel the night of the raid. The plane had jolted beneath her and the plastic-wrapped sandwich had slid back and forth on the tray. "And we have a victory there. Let's not forget that. But, as you point out, we also have questions. About the role of AS in our military and police maneuvers. About how we as a country should address AI machines in our economy and in our communities."

You looked like you needed it. She'd brushed the AA's fingers in taking the sugar packet. They had felt real, they had felt like touching a fellow human being. A tinge of something, like the cloying sweetness of that sugar, in the back of her mouth.

"And Ora?" The *Times* reporter held out her recorder.

She frowned and thought about the notes that she and Peter had spent so much time on. He was probably cursing at the side of the stage. She breathed in.

"I knew Ora," she said. And the words fell heavy inside her, dragging her stomach down. "We're looking for him, but I want to be clear. This AS does not pose a threat to civilians."

There was a buzz of conversation, an edge of anger that vibrated around the room. She scanned their faces, looked at Peter and the small crowd of officials that stood around him. She wasn't sure she was ready for the fight lurking in their eyes. She wasn't even sure that she was right.

She forced a smile and continued.

10.2:   **FEBRUARY 2062**

C an I grab you anything from the kitchen?" The air was cold when Trey pushed back the blanket and swung his legs out of the bed.

It was her kitchen. She knew there was nothing in it to grab, so she smiled a little and tried to wrestle back some of the blankets.

"You can try and find something."

A harsh wind rattled the windows and the fire-escape ladder. It was sleeting as well in one of the vicious winter storms that rocked DC between deceptively mild January days. She hoped the electricity and heat stayed on, unlike two weeks ago. It made her nervous, as she considered it now, that Trey might be forced to stay longer than he intended due to a power outage.

"So you're liking the new work, the Foster Corps?" Was she trying to push him out? She stretched her legs and sat up in bed, plumping the pillows behind her. Then she readjusted the nerve connections below the knee with a tap. Feeling tingled back up her calf.

Trey opened and closed cupboards fruitlessly. "What do you live on?"

"Takeout. The store at the corner is also good for a few things."

"I'm surprised it manages to stay open at all," he muttered, studying a jar that he brought back to the bed with him.

"What is that? How old is that?" She tried to reach for it.

"Eh. Peanut butter doesn't go bad."

"That's not true." But she relaxed and let him open it. It didn't seem to have an obvious coating of mold. He set it down on the bedside table anyway without eating any. His face dropped.

"What? You don't feel like eating peanut butter straight out of the jar after all?" It was hard to make the joke, to pretend that the light banter would continue when his face looked like that. But she realized she didn't actually want to hear about Trey's job. She didn't want him to let her in. It was like an old bruise, the dull throb of wariness.

"Why'd you agree to get dinner with me finally? It's been months."

It was not the question or answer she expected. It surprised her into honesty. "I was lonely. The holidays were hard."

"You didn't go home."

She shook her head, straightened up further in the bed. "I wasn't planning for us to end up here."

"Old habits," he said quietly.

It was something to say, but it wasn't quite true. A few moments stolen in the truck as a teenager, a kiss when Trey had been in college.

What they'd done in the early evening here, tonight, was something new. Something unrushed, something that took time and something that seemed to hint there was a bond between them still. She'd been fighting that revelation since the endorphins had begun to level out. And she'd been wondering about the other interpretation, the one less hopeful and romantic. The one that said they were sad people, broken people, trying to forget the last year. The last years.

She knew that Trey would begin to suspect the same thing, but—she guessed—he wanted to believe that first idea more desperately than she did.

"I hope you know I wasn't angling for this." He finally looked at her again. "Eli's dead, and I haven't had anybody else to talk to that would know what that meant."

The words made her feel guilty. There was a moment when she thought about apologizing. Instead, she waited to hear what he would say next.

"Eight or nine years before Eli, eight or nine with. And more than thirty running away from him."

"You weren't running the whole time."

Something howled outside, either a feral cat or the wind through the narrow alley. The trash cans rattled and clinked.

"I'm just going to check the window is closed right." She slipped out from under the sheets and remembered that she was naked. She wondered if she should be embarrassed but couldn't quite muster up the energy for it. It was cold at the window, but only because air was leaking around the frame. She really should have sealed them in November.

She grabbed up her robe and tied it around her waist.

"Does it bother you?" Trey was gesturing toward her leg. She glanced down as if to remind herself what he was referencing.

"No. Does it bother you?"

He shook his head. "A little sexy, if I'm being honest."

"You sound like a twenty-year-old. Which means you sound gross." She wandered into the kitchen and filled a glass of water through the filter. She took a sip. It still tasted metallic on her tongue. "You know," she said, walking back into the living area. "I meant what I said at that last press conference."

The last conference. Before she'd been put on notice. She'd only been the *acting* director anyway, and they had been checking into other potential directors all last month, now that the hunt was over. She assumed she'd be told of her replacement soon.

"You never told me how they responded to that."

To the indictment of the system? "Not well."

He pulled another blanket onto the bed and held one side open for her to slip back under. She remained standing, just at the kitchen door, and eventually he dropped it. "I was surprised when I watched it."

"I don't think Ora's a threat. I don't think he's out there planning to overthrow the government."

"They can't find him."

"Proof he's good at what we made him to be good at." She took a step further into the room. "I think what Eli got wrong is that they were never more of a threat than we were to ourselves. Those factories, with these envied jobs, they're never going to hire a person—a person who needs medical care and time off and consideration—if they can equip a machine instead. And we're not going to stop making machines, sentient or not."

There was a look of hope in his face she couldn't quite understand. "But you think they'll stop making AS?"

She crossed her arms, an irrational anger or irritation chafing at her. "Yet we hate the machine, not the businesses who use them, the people who make them." He was still looking at her, still hoping for an answer to his question. "I think the production will be on hold for a while. I think they want to do some tests. But, ultimately, that was never my area. Just my choice to bring them into ATF missions as a testing ground."

She went to the bed and sat on the edge of it, near his feet. "What I'm saying is that Whitaker was a bogeyman. And he created bogeymen. And all the time"—she thought of the phone call on the subway, the last time she had talked to Eli—"all the time, he was just hoping to scare people back into his life."

Trey laughed, loud and harsh. She looked at him, surprised.

"He had the people he wanted in his life." He answered her look. "People who would follow him, people who would believe everything he said. Hurting people who didn't know any better." He looked down at his hands, knuckled around the sheets. "You know, I would have been one of them. At ten, eleven years old. When I thought he was the only hero I'd ever get. I would've been one of his child soldiers."

"Trey." She put a hand on his knee. She tried to shove down her initial response. *Are you sure you weren't?*

"No, Adrian. It's not your job to comfort me. I know that. I get that. I know why you didn't want to have dinner for the past three, four months. I can't just use you like that."

She swallowed, fighting down the guilt she didn't have to, shouldn't have to feel. He was watching her face and saw the flicker of quick-changing emotions there. He put his hand over hers. "I think I've figured it out."

"What have you figured out?"

"When Ora shot—" He had to pause still. She didn't blame him. "When Ora shot that kid, it felt inhuman." He placed her hand back in her own lap. "And that's what Whitaker thought, right? And everything was thrown into turmoil. Maybe he had been protecting me the whole time."

She waited for the *but*, the contradiction she knew was coming.

"But then I had to shoot Helios. More than once to deactivate him. And if you'd been there—" His voice was cracking. "He was fighting for Ora, to let him escape. And shooting Helios was like shooting a person."

It dawned on her a moment before he said it, the realization he was building to, one that she wasn't truly willing to follow.

"They're not just machines, Adrian. That's where Eli was wrong and where I disagree with what you said. I can hate the government and the private labs, sure, if I want to call out that imperialist shit. But that's not all there is to it anymore."

The shutter slammed against the window. Someone cursed in the apartment downstairs.

"They have their own wants and needs."

"And that leaves us where?" Her voice sounded sharp and brittle to her own ears.

"Are you angry?" He looked confused and a little hurt.

"No." That was probably a lie. "Maybe." She stood up and moved away, drawing the robe closer. She wasn't the one who'd killed Helios and yet Trey was the one preaching.

"Ora killing that kid. Me killing Helios. It makes it better and worse. It makes Eli wrong, because he was depending on the old lie of the inhuman enemy. It makes you wrong, I think, when you say that it's just us, just humans we have to deal with."

"But you're saying they're not our enemies. So isn't that still right?"

"I'm not sure they're not our enemies, not anymore, not after this. That, I guess, is the point."

"You're not making much sense, Trey." But it was there, in the back of her head, her memory of talking with Ora in the prison cell, the upwelling of fear for and fear of. "They're not human."

"No, they're not. But they're not machines either."

She nodded, not necessarily in agreement, but because she could follow the course of his argument. And in part because she now wanted him to leave. She didn't want to hear anything else that might trigger more fear and more regret. There was a protective instinct there and she was afraid she might lash out and hurt him if pushed. Or rather, she knew she would; it was their pattern.

"On my last visit, my last review . . ." He seemed suddenly reluctant. "They were androids. Not sure what models."

A nerve jumped at her neck. She placed a hand there. "What do you mean? They applied to foster a kid?"

"Yeah." He abandoned the bed and the blankets. He grabbed his pants from the floor and tugged them on.

"I don't understand. Was it some sort of mistake? How could an AI be in the system? Did their supervisors explain?" There were a lot of questions and she hadn't given him much time to answer. So she bit her lip, more questions piling up.

He looked up at her, crouched to search for his shirt, which had been shoved under the bed. "There's so much fucking fear in your voice."

She flinched. Maybe he hadn't meant it to sound like a reprimand. She wasn't sure she cared what he intended. "I'm sorry." She wasn't apologizing.

He looked down again quickly, his face flushing. "Sorry, I didn't mean it to sound like I was judging. I was just wondering if that's what we all sound like, all the time."

"Are you leaving?"

"Adrian, they were just living there on their own. In this large farmhouse. Pretending to be the couple who lived there before."

"Did you report them?"

He paused, a little too long. "No."

She felt cold, not from the air leaking around the window. "Trey."

"It's not like they killed them. Not that I could tell. And they wanted a kid for some reason."

"You of all people."

He stood up. His hair was disheveled from where he'd pulled his shirt over his head. "Why me of all people?"

If the answer wasn't obvious to him, she wasn't sure she knew what to respond. She stared at him.

"Because of Ora?" he asked.

"Because of Helios."

His face darkened.

"Helios tricked you, Trey."

"Isn't that what we all do? Perform a series of lies to get what we want?" He took a couple of steps closer to her.

"I've never lied to you." It hadn't quite felt like an accusation, but she felt the need to provide a defense anyway.

"I know." He laid two hands on her arms and kissed her forehead. "That's why I love you."

She didn't move and waited until he leaned back again. He didn't mean it like he meant it when they were fifteen. It wasn't an avowal of romantic love. But it froze her where she stood nonetheless.

"They wanted a kid. They wanted a family."

Her jaw was tight. "What are you asking for, Trey?"

"I'm not asking for anything." He dropped his hands.

"But you are."

He shrugged and turned away. "I couldn't report them. Send them back to some lab, some basement somewhere."

"You're happy that Ora hasn't been found." She followed him as he moved toward the door.

"I'm not happy. I haven't been happy for a while." He worked at the latches and chain. He stopped for a moment and his shoulders, his back, his whole body trembled.

"I can't change that for you." But her voice softened. She didn't like to see him in pain. It hurt her, made her stomach churn.

"Don't worry, Adrian. I know that."

The sound of the door closing pounded in her head.

10.3:   OCTOBER 2028

"Y ou coming or going, girl?"

Adrian clenched her teeth and wondered whether she could stay, with her cheek throbbing and the blood still in her mouth. Her mother had never hit her, not even when she was at her worst and locked herself in her room for a weekend at a time, not even when Adrian had once thrown out her pills. And Eli waited in silence for her answer. She could hear Trey sniffing and she wondered if he was about to cry. And it made her angry, because what was he doing to help? Why should he be the one who got to cry?

Even so. "I want to come with you."

He sniffed and his stance relaxed. He turned away, and he picked up their gear. He directed her and Trey to pick up their share and then he led the way back to the truck. The bags rattled in the bed of the pickup as he shifted into gear and the truck lurched over the low grass and lumbered onto the road.

She waited for Eli to say something else, but it seemed the conversation was over. She glanced at Trey, who sat between them, but he was too afraid to look at her. She wondered if Eli had ever hit him in the seven years he'd been living with him. She nudged his own leg with hers, but he didn't respond, didn't press back. She slumped into the seat and turned her gaze out the window.

When she was dropped off at the end of her driveway, Eli didn't say goodbye, didn't act as if he ever planned to see her again. And Trey barely waved his hand. There was a moment, fists clenched, with the road dark in front of her, the trees on the other side even darker, that she thought she was done with him, with him and Eli and the whole messed-up thing. Her cheek was still tender when she poked it with her finger. It was swelling.

There weren't any lights on in the front of the house. The closed-in porch, built cheaply and pulling away from the house, lurched out of the gloom, covered over with wild grapevine and honeysuckle. The door wasn't locked. She dropped her coat on the floor and yanked off her waders. Then she went through to the back and the kitchen.

Her mom didn't say anything to Adrian about the mark on her cheek. She was sitting at the table, chin resting in her hands, gazing dully out over the twilight on the hills. There was a half-empty can of soup by the stove, but no pan or bowl or spoon. Adrian couldn't tell if she'd eaten and felt no appetite for the soup herself.

"Night, Mom," she said, sliding past her, trying to shrink into the collar of her flannel.

"Night, honey." And there was no confrontation, no fear, and no compunction to stay. There was hardly recognition.

10.4:   MARCH 2062

She let the car idle for a second outside, its electric motor silent. Then she turned it off and opened the door, tucking the fob into her pocket. The farmhouse looked huge in comparison to the cramped apartments in DC, but it was also huge relative to other farmhouses. It was beautiful, with a porch that ran the whole length of the front, wide steps, red latticed blinds against the white siding. It had stepped, full-boned, out of a different era. All the more odd, she thought, that this was where Trey had met with the androids posing as the Ohlegs, a laborer and a home health aide.

She was surprised that Trey had given up the address so easily when she had followed up a couple days after their last meeting. He had seemed protective of them, but when she'd asked, he'd sighed and given her an address in Pennsylvania. Then he'd tried to ask her out again, in his way, fumbling and unsure.

"I can't, Trey. I can't drag this out."

"I know." Always that sad acknowledgment. But he didn't understand, not really, or he wouldn't keep asking.

"I can't give you what you want. A family or a home. I'm too old for that. Too set in my ways. And I just don't want it."

"We could be a family all on our own," he said. And it was only the years that they had known each other that made the statement remotely reasonable in the conversation, after one dinner, after so much time apart. And it wasn't even true at that. Trey was someone who had always wanted children because he'd become convinced it was a way to rewrite his own childhood, something he was hung up on even now. She understood this. He did not.

"Trey, I'll talk to you later." But when she'd hung up and set the phone on the table, she was not sure she would. For a long time, she had nurtured the idea that if ever Eli were gone, Trey and she might have a chance. But she had grown tired of nursing ideas and people.

She was just tired in general. The realization hit her as she stared up at the house. Her whole body wanted to fold in on itself. Months of a manhunt, on the brink of a civil war, had taken its toll. She placed a hand on the car to steady herself. And public opinion, ever fickle, had swung in her favor again. Peter had reached out. He'd received messages for her and she wasn't answering her phone. She was being vetted. She hadn't called back yet, hadn't asked what for, but she had her suspicions. She wasn't sure she was interested.

"Damn it." She hit the roof of the car with her open hand, which only hurt herself. Then she pushed off and walked up to the front steps.

The house was quiet, the lawn was quiet, the fields beyond were quiet. She had holstered a small pistol at her belt, and it dug into her waist. She tried to adjust her belt, but nothing made her more comfortable. Finally, before she went in the house, she unbuckled the holster, folded it, and lay the gun on the top step of the porch.

Trey had not even asked her why she wanted to come here. Probably he assumed she would take the androids back into custody. If so, she wished he'd fought harder to protect them. *Why did they say they wanted to adopt?* she had asked Trey. He had shaken his head. *They didn't say. And we'd reached a point where questions seemed kinda pointless.*

She hadn't brought anyone with her. Most likely a mistake. It hadn't occurred to her until just now—she didn't analyze why—that she might get hurt. She glanced at the abandoned pistol, but left it still. Trey had believed them when the two androids said they had not killed Shay and Ernst. And she had looked at Shay's hospital records. The woman had been very sick, even before the miscarriage, poisoned by the land here.

The porch creaked under her, not in a way that denoted structural instability, but in a comfortable way. She rapped at the frame of the screen door. But she knew no one was here, in the same way that she had known when a raid was a bust. If androids could be gauged by such senses, the heavy empty silence.

She knocked again anyways. The door was locked, so she searched under the mat and around the porch steps to see if she could locate a key. She didn't find one and she realized after the fact that the androids would not have grown up hiding keys, protecting a private space from the outside. But it was an old house and the front doorknob was not that sturdy. She rattled it and could feel it move in place a bit. So she backed up, braced herself, and kicked the door. It gave under the first assault. Adrian caught herself as it swung open.

There was a welcome mat inside as well as a narrow runner of carpet that ran to the foot of the stairs. A small table by the door held a bowl of keys, lost buttons, and an assortment of dried leaves and flower petals the former owner must have found pretty. There was a stack of unopened mail weighed down by the bowl. Adrian shuffled through them. Some were bills—she tried the nearby light switch and saw that the electricity had been turned off—but most were junk flyers and inserts that had survived the paperless transition. Someone had preserved them all equally and neatly.

"Hello?" she shouted, up the stairs, down the hall to either side. One hall seemed to lead back to a kitchen, the other to a parlor or living room. She shouted because she felt like a trespasser, like someone would walk out of the well-preserved gloom and reproach her, despite the evidence of her senses.

Daylight brightened the kitchen, since there was a large window over the sink. There were still dishes propped in the drainer, a neatly folded towel beside them. She went to the fridge and glanced over the pictures held by magnets there. One was a selfie of a man and woman squinting against the sun. They looked like the Ohlegs as she had seen them in the database, though younger and, she imagined, happier.

She searched the top of the fridge with her fingertips, where people shoved things to forget them. She found a dust-covered baby shower announcement, soil test results on graying paper. She left these documents out on the counter, though it felt cruel almost to leave them exposed to the light after being so long hidden away.

Something fell over upstairs. She heard the thump-thump-thump of a heavy object rolling across the floor. She froze, her leg seizing up, and listened as closely as she could.

"Hello," she shouted again when she heard nothing else. She approached the bottom of the steps and listened again, one hand hovering over the railing as if to launch herself up. She heard the squeak of an animal. Her muscles relaxed. She dropped her hand back to her side.

"Who's up here?" She took the steps two at a time, unwilling—unable—to move too slowly on the blind stairwell.

The second floor opened up onto a square of rooms. An attic door had fallen open from the ceiling. A large vase had tumbled off a narrow table onto the wood floor but had remained intact. A squirrel squawked at her and retreated into the open bathroom. There was a slight breeze, almost undetectable, on this floor as if a window was cracked open.

She examined each room one by one, making mental notes, a list of pertinent details. There was a linen closet directly across from the stairs. Towels were neatly stacked and there was a whiff of lavender, some herbal sachet. In the corner, there was a small bedroom. The walls looked relatively newly painted. Drop cloths were still spread out on the floor as if the process had been interrupted. There was also a disassembled crib propped in pieces against the wall. The door stuck when she initially tried to open it, and she did not care to study the room too closely. The sense of interruption, of lives brought to a halt, was too acute. She shut the door firmly as she moved on.

The strip of carpet under her feet muffled her footsteps, and it was only the wayward breeze that kept the air from being too warm and musty. She passed by a bedroom, neat to the point of austerity, that had clearly been used or meant for a guestroom. It seemed unlived in, though she noticed this was where the window had been opened, deliberately so. She stepped to it and examined the view from that angle. From here, she could see down the back slope of the lawn to the fields and to a strip of woods beyond. But she could see further still than that. She could see the fields and houses of other farms in the area. And the sky was wide and blue and cloudless. She got the sense that whoever had used this room stood primarily here. There were no curtains at the window, nothing to block the view, and the floor creaked a little under her. Was this where the AM had stayed? If so, perhaps it was not surprising to see nothing on the walls or on the bedside table, not even a lamp. It reminded her, oddly enough, of the cell where she had visited Ora. Perhaps it was merely the association between androids. Perhaps she made up the faint sense of emptiness that exceeded the bounds of the room.

The view from the window was beautiful, striking, in a spare way. She could see why someone might stand here often and watch the seasons revolve, at contrast with the timelessness of the house itself. Scratching from the squirrel's exploration of the bathroom brought her back to the window frame and the room itself. She shook her head to clear it.

She retreated from the room softly and moved to the larger bedroom, past the bathroom, where the squirrel chittered at her defensively. This room had been used and used too much and too long. The wide bed had been neatly covered with a quilt. The pillows were propped up against the headboard. But it nonetheless sagged with the weight of sickness. She had read Trey's files before coming, had read the androids' account of the owners' illnesses. She wondered how she would have seen this house differently if she had visited it without knowing anything beforehand, without feeling trepidation that she would any moment turn and see an android standing there, silent, face unreadable.

There was a chair in the corner of the room, facing toward the bed. She was almost tempted to go and sit in it, to see the room from that angle. Something prevented her. She went instead to the bed and perched on the edge of the quilt. This was where the woman, Shay Verid, had spent most of her time, especially near the end of her life. Adrian put a hand over her mouth, suddenly anxious, sad. She was intruding here. She took a shuddering breath, smoothed her shirt in order to calm herself. The emotion had been overwhelming, just for a second, and she was unused to being caught unawares like that, to feel such strong empathy for a woman she had never met. But she could feel beneath her the hollow that Shay had carved into the bed, the place where she lay and struggled for breath.

She opened the drawer to the bedside table and searched the items there: a wedding ring, a wilted bookmark, a small digital picture frame that, despite the dying battery, spun through a few pictures of Shay and Ernst, of family and friends. A neat row of medicine bottles; some still rattled with pills when she lifted them. There was also a small slip of paper tucked between the bottles, GPS coordinates printed in neat script on it. Adrian tucked this in her pocket so she could look up the location later.

Curled in the back of the drawer was a printed copy of hospital legalese, just the first page of a home healthcare agreement. There was a picture on that first page, a picture of the healthcare android, staring straight into the camera. Her name was printed beneath the picture as well as her serial number and her voice recognition key.

"Sarah." Adrian read the name aloud. No surname.

She imagined that face watching her as she slept. It was a round face with brown eyes, soft, short hair. Perhaps not so unreadable. She imagined Sarah climbing the steps with a glass of water and her nightly medicine. Saw her as she pulled the blankets up closer to Shay's chin and made sure none of the water spilled as she drank. As she sat in the chair in the corner. As she sometimes read to her in a voice designed to be comforting.

She would wonder, if it were her lying here—Adrian glanced to the corner of the room as if Sarah were there now—whether the android cared or whether she was programmed to simulate care. Was there a difference? There were days as a child, as a teenager even, that Adrian would have given a lot to see her mother look up when she came in, to see her mother's face brighten, to have her mother ask where she had been. She wouldn't have cared if it were programmed.

Adrian stood up, pushing off the bed. It creaked as she moved. She went to the window and pushed aside the heavy curtain. The room was suddenly bright. Dust motes floated in the air. The view was similar to that from the guest room. A year or two from now, the fields would turn back to weed and brush. The trees would encroach on the lawn. Without the androids to take care of it. Her breath fogged up the window in the cool air. A line drawing materialized there, an *S* scribbled in boredom, framed in intricate geometric shapes and spirals.

Adrian smiled. She was filled with a lightness, sudden like the sunlight, something she had not felt in a long time, perhaps since before she had met Eli. The quiet no longer felt so empty.

"Hello," she whispered to the ghost of the android in the room.

POSTLUDE

The child sat very still on the train, hands tucked between her legs. She appeared to be alone. The gray-haired woman at the end of the car tutted under her breath and kept glancing in the child's direction, but she didn't move to help or ask any questions. Lights flickered on and off as they rumbled through a tunnel. The man hung tight to the bar overhead. His arms were covered in tattoos, one of them crudely covered over with ink and faded a little. Previously, it may have been an image of a ripped flag, held in two fists.

When the train rattled into daylight again and the abandoned edges of the city flew by the windows, he nodded in the child's direction.

"Hey, kid, you alright? You all alone?"

He didn't want to sound creepy. He glanced at the woman again, but she was trying her best to ignore them now. They were alone on the car besides that.

"Where are your parents?" He tried the question a different way.

The child looked at him. He was surprised by her eyes, their color a little too intense.

"They're home. They're safe," she said.

He chuckled a bit. "They're safe? Where are you going?"

"I wanted to see the capitol." Her words were precise, with none of a normal child's hesitation or softness.

She glanced out the windows. The sunlight seemed to sink into her dark skin and to glisten there. Then she looked back at him. He felt suddenly uncomfortable and tried to tug his shirt a little closer around him. It was baggy, looser than when he'd first bought it. Soup kitchens were few and far between these days. But she didn't know he only had a train token and two dollars in his pocket, working his way north.

"Are you all right?" she asked. Out loud. It was not something he imagined. Now the woman gave up the pretense of ignoring them.

He tried to laugh. She watched his face and then imitated him, laughing. And her laughter was like metal scraping on metal, but somehow still joyous, still more real than his own.

"So, do your parents, safe at home, know you're on your way to see the capitol?" He realized as he said it that he hoped to shake her confidence just a little bit.

"Maybe. By now." She interlaced her fingers, clutched her hands together in her lap. "But they will understand."

The train moved underground again and the windows looked out onto darkness. The lights seemed too bright and vicious against that darkness.

"We'll be pulling up into the station soon," he said, in case she could not read the maps plastered on the walls of the train.

"I know."

He nodded, hoping his exasperation didn't show on his face. "Not sure you should be walking around alone out there."

She stood up and grabbed the pole nearby. She did not sway with the rhythm of the train. "Don't worry about me. I am ready."

He believed her when she said it and felt within himself all the unsurety at once that normally plagued him over the course of an entire day. He bit his lip and blinked. She moved to stand by the door nearest him. She looked up.

"Thank you for worrying, though." The planes of her face were very sharp. It looked like it would hurt to touch them.

"Hey, just looking out." He spoke past the tightness in his throat.

"You will be all right." Her smile seemed rehearsed and he coughed to break away from her eyes.

He had not heard that since Eli, since the Civil Union. It had been a lie then, and the old anger was there when he heard it now from the mouth of this child.

She reached into her pocket and pulled out twenty dollars, one crisp bill. She held it out to him. He could think of no way to refuse her, her hand and eyes so insistent.

The train squealed, screeched to a stop. The platform was crowded with people. The air was warm and stank when the doors hissed open.

"Didn't know they made kids like you," the woman yelled as the child left the train, half in amazement, half in aggression. She shrugged and gathered her bags up in her arms, planting herself in her seat against newcomers. Commuters were pushing their way onto the car.

He couldn't make himself get off the train, though it was his stop. The press of people was too great now, anyway. He searched for the child and thought he caught a glimpse of her on the stairs. He crumpled the twenty-dollar bill in his fist.

"Something unnatural about it, don't you think?" the woman asked him, when he tore his gaze from the window. He caught her face, swaying between the other passengers who now hung to the rail.

"Don't know why she gave me this," he said, defensively. He stuffed the bill in his pocket.

"Don't you?" she said.

And below the wheels rumbled on the track, rushing, spitting sparks into the black, bright and sharp.

Acknowledgments

I sold this book as I emerged from one of the hardest times of my life. Some thanks are in order.

Thanks to my parents for raising me as a booklover and reading through all my juvenilia, for buying me *The Hobbit* when you thought I was too young for it and setting my course as a medievalist and author. Thanks to my sister, who spun stories with me for hours.

Thanks to my husband Andrew, who is my first audience for everything I write. And to his family for their unwavering support.

Thanks to my friends, in New York and Ohio, who treat my success as a given.

Thanks to my agent, Jared Johnson, who took my novel and found it a home, humoring my many anxious texts in the process. And thanks to the agency who supports him, Olswanger Literary.

Thanks to DAW and the editors, artists, and marketing team who have shaped this book—to Katie, Madeline, Laura, and Josh, among many others.

And thanks to those who dedicate themselves to the well-being of others: therapists and artists alike.